For all of us who find comfort in the chaos,
it's okay to let the silence in.
*I did.*

A NOVEL

# THE BREATH BETWEEN US

## BIANCA MILLER

## Chapter One

Merriam-Webster defined a *best friend* as both "a person's closest and dearest friend" and "a person's most desirable or valuable possession or resource."

I bet when you read the word *best friend*, someone instantly came to mind. Someone in your world who fit that definition perfectly. A person you simply couldn't do without.

And if you got lucky enough, and I mean really lucky, that person wasn't just your friend. They were a soulmate in every sense of the word. Another human being that you'd swear was a part of you in another life. The one who could finish your sentence as soon as you opened your mouth. The one who could say nothing at all and still say everything you needed to hear.

The one you felt safe with.

The one who thought like you, acted like you, and said all the same things you did. Almost as if they were an extension of yourself. The one you could tell anything to, the one who would never judge you, no matter how ridiculous you sounded. The first one you called and the last one you wanted to leave. The one you fought with, argued with, and said hurtful things to, but somehow, always came back.

The one who cradled you at your worst and celebrated you at your best. The one who wiped away more tears than you could count because of stupid boyfriends, mean girls, and hard life moments. But most importantly, the person who made your world a better place.

And without them, you'd quite simply be lost.

If you were lucky, you had that one friend. For me, that friend was Olivia Mitchell. She was my other half, my soulmate, and my *best friend*.

*Then*
*September 2013*

"I'm not going," I said, dramatically stomping away from the mirror and tossing the sixth failed outfit onto my bed. The faded blue jeans landed directly on top of Olivia's legs.

"Miller, quit being dramatic. We're going to this damn party whether you like it or not," Olivia grumbled, maneuvering herself from the bed with a black T-shirt dress in tow.

"Wear this one. It really brings out your eyes." She smirked.

I huffed. "You're hilarious."

"But could you please hurry? I know I said I wanted to show up late, but I didn't mean *this* late." She held up her phone, pointing to the time. "It's not like it's almost my birthday or anything."

She snickered as she stepped in front of the mirror to take stock of her reflection. As she tousled her curls, her blonde hair bounced perfectly down her back while simultaneously shaping her face.

Olivia had always been a little loud with her outfit choices, but tonight's was especially so. She'd be eighteen at midnight, and she wanted to make sure everyone was aware. Her lilac dress was suctioned to her body, hitting her curves in all the right spots, and her black sandals wrapped up her ankles, tying neatly around her calves.

She swiveled on her toes, looking at her backside while she pressed her hands against her hips. "Does this look okay?"

"You look amazing, per usual."

"Promise?"

"Always."

Olivia Mitchell had been my best friend since before we were born. Her parents moved to Montauk in 1995 and bought the house next door to mine. When our moms found out they were both pregnant and due around the same time, their friendship quickly blossomed.

Liv was born on Labor Day in 1996, and I followed shortly after at the beginning of December. I'd been following after Liv ever since.

She was the fearless one, the one who acted without thinking and never apologized for who she was. She was always one step ahead of everyone else, and thankfully, I was never too far behind her. Leading had always been a strong suit of hers.

Mine? Not so much, which was why she and I worked so well as best friends. I was the calculated one. The one able to talk Liv off a cliff after she'd reacted too quickly. The one who studied the options before making a move. Some might even say I was the practical one.

Despite the fact that we were wildly different, it'd always been Olivia and Miller, Liv and MJ. Although, we were oddly similar too.

"Are you done checking yourself out?" I laughed.

"I'm about to make an entrance at one of the biggest parties of the year on the eve of my eighteenth birthday, do you expect anything else?"

"Touché."

"Okay, but really… how long until you're ready?" She looked in my direction as I stood in only a bra and underwear, a casual black dress draped over my arm.

"Ugh, give me five minutes." Shimmying into the dress, I said, "And honestly, it doesn't matter what I look like because I can promise you, no one is going to be looking at me. Not to mention, we've been to Caleb's Labor Day Eve party every summer since I can remember, and it's always a letdown."

Liv smirked. "Not this year."

Liv had her eyes set on Caleb Davis—at least for the moment. Caleb was the varsity lacrosse star at Montauk High and had always been out of reach. That was, until his recent breakup. Now, all bets were off.

"Which ones?" I asked as I held up two pairs of shoes. "Sneakers or sandals?"

She put her hand on her hip. "You know I'm going to say the sandals and then you're going to tell me that you don't want to wear sandals. We'll go back and forth, and ultimately, you'll choose your beloved sneakers."

"Damn, you do know me." I smiled sarcastically.

I sat on my bed and pulled on the white-and-black scuffed shoes. My laces were tied and tucked into the sides, allowing me to slip them on quickly.

I stepped in front of the mirror, and my reflection stared back. My blonde hair was loosely curled and tousled just enough to make it look like it wasn't dirty. My big blue eyes were engulfed with dark lashes that were coated with a thin layer of black mascara. A little lipstick decorated my plump lips in the softest shade of pink.

I dabbed at the corner of my mouth. "I'm ready," I told her.

"As hot as ever." She giggled, resting her weight against my desk.

"Ha. Let's go," I said, turning off the light as we left my room.

The smell of wine and smoked salmon filled the air as we walked downstairs to the sounds of chatting, presumably from both sets of our parents.

Friday night dinners were reserved for the Morgans and the Mitchells. It had been a tradition for as long as I could remember.

Mom, Dad, Jess, and John were just as close as Liv and me, which meant I didn't have just one mom and dad; I had two of each.

My mom's voice made its way to the bottom step. "Headed to Caleb's?"

That was the thing about growing up in a small town: everyone knew everyone. Caleb Davis had been throwing these parties since forever. Although, the activities that once consisted of hide-and-seek, popcorn, and late-night movies now looked more like loud music, underage drinking, and random hookups, but nonetheless, it was still a tradition.

And our parents weren't naïve—they knew what was happening. For the most part though, no one cared as long as we were safe.

John, Liv's dad, chimed in. "Be careful and let us know if you need a ride home."

"And by us, he means Kelli or me," Jess added.

Mom clinked her wineglass with Jess's before piping in. "Because we all know your fathers will be too busy doing something ridiculous like reorganizing the garage or smoking cigars out back while they reminisce on their younger years."

"What they said." Dad chuckled, and everyone else giggled.

"We will, love you!" Liv replied.

"Love you big," I said, blowing a kiss in their direction.

Liv and I swayed toward the front door, locking our arms together as we walked outside.

"My car or yours?" she asked.

"Yours. I need gas," I responded.

Making my way to the passenger side of her black VW Bug, I tugged at the door and slid in. The dead lilac hydrangeas caught my eye, perched lifeless against the plastic vase that sat directly next to her steering wheel. "Why is it that your flowers are always dead?"

"My flowers aren't always dead. However, just because they're dead doesn't mean they've lost their beauty or their purpose." She huffed. "In fact, it's quite the opposite. I prefer my flowers dead, because unless you're intentional with how you view them, you'll overlook their beauty, completely missing out on everything they are because you're looking for everything they once were."

"Oh, okay, Taylor Swift. Getting all poetic on me," I mocked. But her words somehow made sense. A sense of regret washed over me, making me sad for all the flowers I'd thrown in the trash after they'd lost their initial beauty. "Although, I guess you aren't wrong." I shrugged.

Slipping on my seat belt, I immediately reached for the aux cord to plug in my phone. "We Can't Stop" by Miley Cyrus gushed through the speakers, and I turned the volume up even higher as I rolled down my window, letting the late summer breeze take over my entire body. The warmth of the air sent shivers right through me.

I peered at Liv and then back at the road ahead of us. My life was pretty damn good. I was strolling into my senior year with my best friend in tow. We weren't exactly sure what our lives would look like after high school, but we didn't care. All we knew was that whatever lay ahead of us, we'd endure it together.

I traced the wind with my fingertips. "What's the plan tonight?"

Liv reached to turn down the music. "You mean, my plan?"

"Actually, let me guess—" I started.

"Caleb Davis!" we simultaneously shouted.

Our laughter filled the small space in the car.

"You little slut." I giggled, smacking my hand against her bare shoulder.

I was totally kidding. *Sort of.*

"Ouch! That hurt!" she said, grinning at me, her perfect white teeth exposing themselves from behind her glossy lips.

Liv liked her boys, and she liked to fuck with them too. She'd messed around with a good majority of our class and a few of the younger classmen, but that was just Liv. She toyed with them until they wanted her, and then she ditched them. All of them except Caleb.

Me, on the other hand, well, I envied her confidence. There had been a few random makeouts here and there, but nothing to write home about, and I had absolutely no plans that involved a boy, especially at tonight's party.

"He's the hottest guy in the entire school. He's had a girlfriend for the entirety of his high school career, and he's headed to Berkley after graduation. I've waited four years for this, and now is my only chance."

"I'm here for it. Especially because maybe then I won't have to hear about him anymore."

Ignoring my previous comment, Liv continued. "Did you see him yesterday, after lacrosse practice? Holy hell. He's simply a gift from the gods, I swear."

"That's a bit dramatic. But no, I didn't see him. Unlike you, I don't stand around after tennis practice pretending to"—I raised my hands to make air quotes—"*practice my serve* as I stalk Caleb Davis."

"I don't sta—"

"You do," I cut her off.

She released a loud breath and turned up the music again. The beat drifted through the speakers and the warm salty summer air whipped my hair across my face. Normally I'd be trying to tame it, but not tonight. Tonight, I'd let it run wild, taking in the sights around me.

We might've always talked about how ready we were to leave this town, but deep down, we both knew how special this place was to us. There was nowhere quite like it. The place we met, the place we grew up, and the place that would always be home.

"Taking the long way?" I asked.

"Always."

Montauk wasn't very big by any means, but any chance we got, Liv and I took the scenic route. It was our favorite, especially during the summer months when the town buzzed with an extra burst of energy from all the out-of-towners who flocked here for the summer.

Neither of us could pass up the opportunity to gawk at the parts of town that were inhabited with mostly empty mansions, massive boats, and the type of eye candy every girl wanted a taste of.

"Can you believe this is our last summer here?" she shouted over the music before cranking the volume down yet again.

A perk of our friendship was that we were always in the other's head. It happened so often it didn't even surprise me anymore.

"Honestly? No. It feels like just yesterday we were thirteen, lying on the beach, staring at the stars, and wondering what high school would be like. The boys we'd kiss. The sports we'd play, the dances we'd go to." My voice trailed off as I reminisced on a time that seemed so far away but somehow still like it was just yesterday.

"It's wild, you know? The feeling of eagerly wanting high school to come to an end so we can graduate and finally move to New York together, but on other hand, simply wanting this year to last forever so that we never have to grow up and leave this place." Liv's voice wavered slightly at the end, only enough that I would pick up on it.

Liv and I both applied to NYU, along with a few other backup schools, in hopes we'd get to go to college together. It'd always been our dream to graduate high school and take on the big city. Liv planned to study architecture, and I wanted to study creative writing.

We hadn't heard anything yet though. We never talked about it, but I knew the unknown hung over both of our heads.

"Olivia Mitchell…"

"What?"

"Are you getting sentimental on me?"

"No," she breathed. "Okay, maybe. But it's just that—"

"Liv, I'm messing with you. I get it. We're sort of in that limbo phase. While these are some of the best years of our lives and we have a friendship that most people won't ever experience, we also have a whole hell of a lot of unknowns in front of us. It's okay to feel a little unsure about everything."

"What if one of us doesn't get into NYU?"

I knew that was where she was headed. Anytime she got emotional, it was because of this.

We'd never been apart for longer than two weeks in our entire lives, and the thought of one of us not being accepted made us both extremely anxious.

"Don't go there, not tonight. We've got time. Tonight, let's focus on the task at hand: Caleb Davis." I smiled at her, hoping she'd let it go for now.

Just as quickly as she got sentimental, she snapped out of it.

"Damn, MJ, when did you become the level-headed one between the two of us?"

"Ha-ha, you're kidding, right? I'm one hundred percent always the level-headed one in this relationship," I replied.

"Uh huh, whatever makes you sleep better at night."

Looking through the open sunroof at the stars illuminating the night sky, I let my mind wander.

When the car stopped we weren't at Caleb's house, we were parked at the beach.

I looked over at Liv.

"I'm not parking at his house. If his party gets busted like it did last year, we need to have an out."

"Are you not planning on drinking?" I asked.

"Oh, *we* are planning on drinking, but I'll just leave my car here overnight. Caleb's house is only a few blocks away."

"My girl. Always thinking ahead." I grinned in her direction as I unbuckled my seat belt.

We stepped out of the car, shut our doors, and rearranged ourselves in the windows.

"Ready?"

"As I'll ever be," she replied.

"Let's go get Caleb Davis."

## Chapter Two

I knew we were getting close; the noise in the distance confirmed it. Not to mention the faint smell of beer that wafted through the air.

"Less than an hour until you're officially an adult," I said.

Liv latched her arm with mine and smirked as she said, "As much of an adult as a reckless teenager can be."

We turned down Manatee Drive, spotting Caleb's house immediately.

"Wow, he's really going all out this year, huh?" I commented.

"Doses and Mimosas" blared from a bunch of massive speakers that lined the wraparound porch of the light blue cottage, perched perfectly between two pastel yellow houses.

Even though most of our streets looked the same, the view never got old.

All the soft-colored houses with their creaky wooden steps, porch swings, and coastal décor made sure this place would always feel like home.

We strutted closer and the beat began to echo through my chest. My body unconsciously started swaying with the rhythm.

"So it's going to be one of those nights?" Liv asked, gesturing to my gyrating body.

I smirked. "I'm only having a few drinks. I have to get up early tomorrow to help Mom and Dad at the restaurant, but you know I can't turn down a good bop."

Her lips curled into a smile. "Come on. Just have a little fun."

Liv knew how to encourage me, but I really couldn't have too much fun. I'd promised to be at The Wharf by nine in the morning to help prepare for the Labor Day crowd. My parents bought The Wharf when I was in middle school, and it was second in line as their pride and joy.

Me being first, of course.

The Wharf was a tiny hole in the wall that was loved by locals and visitors all the same. The restaurant turned into more of a bar starting at nine each night. It was the epitome of the east coast, perched on a rickety wooden dock within the marina. The structured shack was quaint, full of both character and good memories. Not to mention it'd maintained the title of "the best damn bar in town" for years.

"Smells like a good time," Liv said, opening the door as a gust of sweat, beer, and teenage hormones smacked us right in the face.

"The best." I scrunched up my nose, laughing.

Grabbing my hand, she led us inside.

We weaved in and out of people talking loudly over the music, dodged a couple that was sucking face, and somehow ended up on the makeshift dance floor located in the living room. The furniture had been removed and one huge disco ball was placed strategically on the fireplace, allowing the light to ricochet off of it and cast the whole room in sparkles.

"Are you not going to go find Caleb?" I asked as Liv and I started dancing together.

"I already found him," she responded as she effortlessly swayed her body, signaling behind her.

Without being too obvious, I looked over her shoulder. Sure as shit, there he was, standing confidently but casually against the bottom of the stairs. He was everything you imagined in a tall, dark, handsome lacrosse player. There was a reason Liv had been pining for him since freshman year. There wasn't a part of him that you didn't want to look at.

As I gave him a once-over, I noticed his eyes were glued to Liv.

She'd gotten exactly what she'd wanted. She'd made herself known without giving herself up too easily. That was her M.O.

"You're good," I said loudly, trying to drown out the music.

"I know." She winked.

Shortly after that, Caleb approached us. "Can I get you girls a drink?" he asked, never taking his eyes off Liv.

"I'll take a shot of whatever you've got."

"Make that two," I chimed in.

He turned, leaving the scent of Abercrombie and Fitch's Fierce lingering.

"He's going to make this too easy, isn't he?" I giggled as we continued to dance.

"Just how I like it."

Liv grabbed my hand and spun me around as loud music played through the speakers, filling the room and leaving me floating through the air. I threw my head back, basking in the moment.

Until the moment was abruptly interrupted with, "Cops! Cops! Run!"

The frantic voices ripped me from the moment I was having with myself, while Liv ripped me from the living room dance floor. We were out of the house and on the run before I could comprehend what was happening.

We took off in the direction of the beach while everyone else shot down the street. This wasn't our first time running from the cops. When you lived in a town this small, it was almost a rite of passage for all of the best parties to get busted.

"Holy shit, I'm dying," I breathed, trying to get all my words out.

"Yeah, this outfit was absolutely not made for running, especially in these shoes."

Before too long, the sirens sounded closer, and I saw the lights reflecting off the street sign around the corner. Stealthily, we ducked behind the closest house.

"What the hell, they're relentless tonight."

"Well, yes, they are cops, Liv. That's their job."

"I know, I know. But they usually give up after they scare a few underclassmen and then leave the rest of us alone."

"Hey! Who's over there?" a cop's voice bellowed from the other side of the street.

"Not tonight," I said, grabbing her hand and making a dash for the beach.

Out of breath and out of sight of the police, we collapsed on the beach. The cold sand awakening the tiny hairs on my arms, sending chills across my entire body.

"MJ?"

"Yes?"

"Why were we running?"

Seeing the confusion written all over her face, I asked, "What do you mean?"

"We haven't had anything to drink!"

We both started laughing uncontrollably. A minute of belly laughs passed before we finally composed ourselves.

I gazed at the stars twinkling here and there while the waves crashed against the shore, giving us our own personal soundtrack.

We basked in each other's silence, taking it all in. Until you had a friend like Liv, you couldn't understand what it was like to have someone you could simply sit in complete and utter quietness with and still feel like you were having a full-blown conversation.

"We're always going to be best friends, right?"

"What? Of course we are. Where the hell did that come from?" I propped myself up on my elbows and looked in her direction, and her face explained it all. "Liv, I already told you. We'll figure it out. I promise. We always do."

"Are you sure?"

"Remember in eighth grade when your parents decided to move and we weren't going to be next-door neighbors anymore?"

"Yeah, we were convinced our friendship wouldn't last the move," she responded.

"And did we stop being best friends?"

"Obviously not."

"Exactly. Even though it felt like the most dire situation of our entire lives in that moment, it was fine in the end. Just like this is going to be."

"That's because we ended up only moving a few blocks away. But you're right. It's just that my anxiety creeps in and takes over without my consent," she admitted.

"That, I get," I said.

"Maybe that's what your book should be about."

"Our anxiety?" I joked.

"No," she snickered. "I meant our friendship. The story of us and all the crazy shit we've done."

"Intriguing. But no one needs to know that much about me—or us." I laughed.

"Ha. You're probably right."

Words had always been my thing, and I dreamed of writing a book someday, but I wasn't sure if a story about our friendship was what I had in mind.

We went back to admiring the perfect summer night around us. The breeze was warm as the cool waves barely grazed our toes. The sound of sirens no longer took up space around us, and we soaked up the sound of the splashing water mixed with the sea grass blowing in the wind.

"Happy Birthday, Liv."

She pulled out her phone and tapped the screen, seeing it was 12:01 a.m.

"Shit, I guess it is my birthday."

I giggled.

"What's so funny?" she asked.

"I'm just glad you exist."

"I'm glad you exist too."

"We should probably head home," Liv said as she stood.

Extending her hand in my direction, I used her to pull myself to my feet. "I'm right behind you."

Staring off into the dark abyss, I found myself in awe. I couldn't help but acknowledge the happiness that floated around me. Liv might have been the sentimental one tonight, but right here, in this moment, I knew that regardless of what happened in the next few months, we'd figure it out. Because we always did.

Walking up to the car, Liv looked up from her phone. "You good?"

"Just taking it all in, you know?"

She smiled.

Hopping into the car, I grabbed the aux cord again. It was an automatic response at this point. "Wake Me Up" by Avicii started playing.

"Damn, this song never gets old," Liv muttered.

Her car rumbled awake and then we were off, taking another long way around as we headed home.

We were only a few moments into the drive when she synced her voice to the lyrics. I jumped in, playing the air drums and belting the words as loud as I could.

Liv took a curve in the road and gravity pulled my body closer to her side, clinging to the "oh shit" handle with my right hand. We glanced at each other and couldn't help but laugh. We were ridiculous and so embarrassing, but I wouldn't change it for the world.

My song choice was good, but it was losing momentum, and I was ready for something different. That was a weakness of mine, never being able to listen to a song all the way through.

I looked down to peruse my phone for a split second before looking back up, but when I did, I wasn't greeted by the darkness of the once abandoned beach roads.

"Liv!" I shouted as two blinding headlights pierced my eyes. They crossed over into our lane and were coming fast.

I saw her hands drastically turn the wheel in the opposite direction, doing her best to overcompensate for the other driver, and then I didn't remember what happened next. I just registered the impact. Of what? I wasn't sure. But it was loud, it was abrasive, and it was something out of my worst nightmare.

Everything went black.

# Chapter Three

I blinked a few times before a sudden slice of pain shot through my entire body.

"Liv…" I muttered.

I cringed as her name left my mouth. The pain was worse than I initially thought, immediately firing up again and shooting through both my legs. I instinctively reached for them but was met with the feeling of cold plastic against my hands. I blinked a couple of times, trying to get my bearings, but ultimately failed.

"Liv!" I cried out.

Again, no response.

I did my best to turn my head in her direction, but the rest of my body wasn't responding to my cues.

Panic began to fill my lungs and my breaths quickened while I searched for more air, gasping for anything that resembled another breath. I slammed my eyes shut and inhaled, hoping to bring myself a second of calmness.

Opening them again, I looked around, reorientating myself. I was able to put together that we were upside down. The weight of my body hovering above the seat was unbearable, freeing a new set of intrusive thoughts.

*What happened? Is Liv okay? How bad is it? Is the other driver hurt?*

Peering over, all I could see was crushed metal. Pieces of what appeared to be the sunroof had fallen in between us, making it almost impossible to make out where she was. I took my left hand and began to feel around, desperate to land on anything that resembled Liv's body.

"MJ…" The faintest voice rippled through the air.

"Liv, I'm right here." My voice quivered even as I did my best to sound confident. "Everything's going to be okay."

There was blood.

*Everywhere.*

I didn't know if it was hers or mine, but from the lack of communication coming from her side of the car, part of me knew.

Everything was moving in slow motion. Thinking was hard. Hell, breathing was hard. The weight of being suspended upside down didn't help, and my vision was slowly edging toward blurry.

I blinked repeatedly, attempting to clear my eyes as my hand anxiously searched for anything that resembled Liv. I finally landed on what I thought was her arm, trailing my fingers around until they landed on her hand. I grabbed it tightly and squeezed. "We're going to be okay."

Silence echoed through the space between us, but relief flooded me when a faint squeeze sent tingles up my arm.

"I... I love you... deeper..." Her voice was soft, barely loud enough that I could make out what she was trying to say.

"I love you too, deeper than the ocean."

"Wake Me Up" was still pumping through the speakers and all I could think was I hoped we were lucky enough to wake up from this nightmare.

Because it *had* to be a nightmare.

I made one last-ditch effort to use what was left of my energy to draw attention to us.

"Help! We're stuck! Please, someone help us," I cried out as my voice weakened with each breath. The tears broke through the barrier of my eyelashes and swam up my forehead.

I began to fade in out of consciousness, everything slowly washing away from the forefront of my brain. Then, faintly, I heard sirens in the distance.

A bellowing voice came from outside the car. "Can anyone hear me?"

"I can," I mumbled.

"I'm Chief Williams with the Montauk Fire Department and we're going to get you out of there."

Tears plunged across my face and into my hair. "Please help us!" I cried out.

"What's your name?"

"Miller Morgan," I responded frantically.

"Miller, who's driving the car?"

"Liv..." I said, scrambling for more. "Olivia Mitchell."

"Okay, good. I'm going to walk you through what I'm doing as I make my way to you, but first—"

"No!" I shouted, "Please, help Liv first. I think she's hurt badly. I'll be fine. Please," I begged, gasping on each word.

"Don't worry, Miller. One of my other firefighters is on his way to your friend," he said, his voice calmer than it should be.

"You don't understand, she needs help. I just know it; I can feel it. Please, sir. Please help her," I said, desperate for him to believe me.

"I hear you. I need you to take a few deep breaths. I'm walking over to the driver's side of the car to check on your friend. Can you keep talking to me? What was the last thing you remember from before the accident?"

His footsteps echoed between the four windows as both the sound of his feet and the air were able to flow easily through the car. What I assumed was glass crunched underneath his boots with every step he took.

Sirens, voices, and movement filled the space around me. The air became heavy as it pressed against my body. I wanted to close my eyes to calm my breath, but I was afraid if I did, I would black out again.

"Olivia, I'm Chief Williams. I'm here to get you and your friend out of the car. Pretty good friend you got there, demanding that I help you first. Let's get you out of here so we can help her. How does that sound?"

A few seconds passed before I heard the softest mumble fall from her lips. It almost sounded as if Liv was trying to say something but the words were caught in her throat. Realizing our hands were still clasped together, I squeezed. I wanted her to know that I was here, and I wasn't going anywhere.

Gravity had taken advantage of me and my tears as they drained from my eyes and stained their way up my forehead.

"I love you deeper than the ocean, Liv," I whispered. I vaguely registered movement on my side of the car, but I couldn't turn my head away from Liv.

"Miller? I'm firefighter Goodwin and I'm going to get you out of here, okay?"

"Okay," I replied as my heavy eyes finally closed.

"Miller? Miller, can you hear me?" A deep voice bounced around my head before my eyes opened. I blinked a few times to adjust to the bright light that hung overhead. My body felt stabilized, but I could tell we were moving. It smelled clean, but in a sterile, harsh way. Looking around, all I could see were medical bags and equipment that jiggled as the vehicle moved.

I blurted out as many questions as I could think of. "Where's Liv? Is she okay? Have you called our parents?"

"We're on the way to the hospital. You and your friend were in an accident," a women's voice echoed next to me.

"I know. I need to know where Liv is," I demanded.

The paramedic started speaking to someone else who was bustling around the back of the ambulance. I could've screamed. I just wanted answers. I reached up to her, noticing the blood splashed across my hand and down my arm.

"Your friend is also on the way to the hospital. We've called your parents and they're going to meet us there."

"Is she okay? When can I see her?"

"Sweetie, I'm going to need you to calm down. You've banged yourself up pretty good and we need to keep you stable."

I wanted to say something back, beg her to tell me how Liv was, but I knew it was no use. My thoughts came barreling in and there was no energy left to stop them. I was nauseous, anxious, and completely terrified at what was going to be waiting for me once we reached the hospital.

I didn't know how long we'd been in the ambulance, but I was relieved when we finally came to a stop. Everyone around me was speaking in medical terms, and as much as I tried to piece together what they were saying, there was no such luck.

Somewhere between the transfer from the ambulance to the hospital room, everything blurred. The weight was heavy, almost unbearable. Like someone was holding me down and making me watch everything from outside of my body.

I blinked, trying to reorient myself and gain control of my limbs. The voices around me became muffled, and each time I opened my eyes, I was met with the glaring lights, forcing me to immediately shut them again. Slowly, the voices cleared.

"Miller, I'm Dr. Winterfield. Your parents are on their way, but in the meantime, I'm going to check a few things. If I press on something that hurts, just squeeze my hand. There is no need for you to waste your energy talking," he said.

His warm hand was comforting against my palm.

"Mmm," I muttered, ignoring his request. "I'm struggling to focus, and my eyes hurt every time I open them."

"That's okay. Your body is exhausted. You don't need to open them to communicate with me. Just squeeze my hand and let me do the rest of the work."

His free hand pressed and prodded against different areas of my body. He started with my stomach, mushing his hands into my lower abdomen.

"Anything?" he asked.

I shook my head while attempting to push out a few words.

"Ms. Morgan, what did I say about exerting your energy?" My eyes were glossy but clear enough that I caught the smile he was wearing.

I acknowledged his comment with a nod.

"Good. Now you're getting it."

Next, he slowly lifted my left leg and I winced. The pain was excruciating, shooting from the tips of my toes all the way to the top of my hip. My grip on his hand threatened his circulation.

"Okay, okay," he said apologetically. "We'll get you x-rayed for confirmation, but it looks like you've got a broken leg."

The rest of the examination was uneventful for the most part, *thankfully.*

He released his hand from mine. "You look all right, kid. Minus a few superficial cuts here and there, a broken leg, and a minor concussion that we'll want to monitor for a bit, I think you're going to be just fine. You're one of the lucky ones, Ms. Morgan.

Car accidents like that don't normally end up with minor breaks and bruises. I think someone's looking out for you," he said.

By now, my eyes had had a chance to focus, and the demeanor of the thirty-something doctor who stood before me appeared as kind as his voice had let on. His body shifted casually on my hospital bed as he made his way to his feet, gently placing his hand on my arm.

"I'll give you some time to rest and come back to check on you a bit later to see if you have any questions."

I let out a deep breath for what felt like the first time in forever, releasing some of the tension from my body.

"Can you tell me how my friend is? Olivia Mitchell. We came in together; we were both in the same accident. Where is she?" I pleaded, sucking in another big gulp of air as I shifted myself upright and managed to maneuver my legs to the side of the bed.

Dr. Winterfield was on his way out the door before quickly turning on his feet. "Woah, woah, woah! You're not going any-where! I'll try to get you some answers about your friend, but for right now, I need you to stay in bed." He stood in front of me, not allowing me to move any further.

His words angered me. What was he not understanding? The last time I saw my best friend, we were both suspended upside down in a wrecked car. Tears breached the surface as I begged, "Please let me go find her. I have to know that she's okay."

His voice was much sterner than before as he said, "Miller, I'm sorry, but if you don't calm down, I'm going to have to give you some meds that will do the work for you."

I wanted to listen to him, I really did, but my brain wasn't obeying. He'd moved toward the computer, and I took that as my sign to try to stand up. Awful idea on my part. The pain in my left leg immediately brought me to the floor, but not before a passing nurse caught me.

"Go ahead and get her a dose of Ativan to help her relax." The doctor walked toward me, acting as if I wasn't even in the room. "She needs some rest. I'll get her back in her bed if you can administer the meds through her IV." The doctor took the place of the nurse and gently lifted me to my feet, allowing me to bear all my weight on him, and slowly lowered me back into the bed.

Guilt washed over me. "I'm sorry. I'm just really worried about her."

"I understand. You've just experienced a very traumatic car accident, this is normal," he said, calmer now.

My eyelids suddenly drooped with heaviness. I found myself reaching for his hand in an attempt to give it a squeeze.

Everything cluttered together, my body tingled, and then everything went dark.

*Again.*

# Chapter Four

My eyes slowly fluttered open.

This time everything appeared a bit steadier. The haze that previously consumed me seemed to have lifted. Still, I looked around the room, trying to make sense of it all, taking in the hospital room as if this was my first time seeing it.

Hospitals had always been a strange place to me. On one floor, someone was watching their loved one take their last breath, while on the floor just above that, a baby was taking its first. It was all too raw for me, the emotions squeezed between the walls of one building. The quickness of both life and death. Hospitals were something I would never understand.

I focused on the four walls that surrounded me. To my right was a small window that gave a not-so-picturesque view of the building next door. Below that lay a familiar figure. Dad had passed out on the couch, if you could even call it that. It was a hideous shade of muted tan, and the cushions looked like they'd been there since before I was born—scraggly and missing their insides. I wasn't sure how one could even fall asleep here, but Dad looked rather peaceful, minus that fact that his body was far too long, leaving his legs dangling off the end.

Peering around, the rest of the room was unoccupied other than the ancient TV that hung on the wall and the beeping machines that were still connected to me. I tried to position myself upright only to notice the heavy weight on my left side.

I looked down to see my mom's body draped over my cold hospital bed. Her tall, slender frame looked so vulnerable, with half of her body sitting in a hard foldable chair and the other half as close to me as humanly possible. One hand interlocked with mine while the other rested up next to my face. She'd fallen asleep, and knowing her, she'd probably not done much of that since the accident. At this point, I wasn't sure how long ago that was.

"MJ?"

"Mom." My voice quivered. "I... I love you so much. I'm so sorry."

Emotion filled my body, leaving me feeling paralyzed. I didn't know if it was the realization that I was in fact okay or simply just seeing my parents, but either way, I was a mess. Tears hovered at the edge of my lids but only for a moment before I couldn't stop them from falling. The warm wetness trickled down my cheek and I gripped her arm.

As Mom peered up, our eyes locked, and I knew something wasn't right.

"Oh, MJ. My girl." Her voice was empty. She stood, leaning over to give me a proper hug. "I'm so glad you're okay. I... I don't know what I would've done had you…" Her words came in short spurts. "I love you big."

"I know, Mom. I'm so sorry. I didn't mean to scare you."

Her hands fumbled with mine.

The commotion must have woken Dad because he shifted into a sitting position.

"Oh, sweet girl, you scared us. Your mom and I thought we…" He trailed off.

"When can I go see Liv?" As glad as I was to see them, I needed to see her before I could really take a deep breath. I took their silence as an invitation to keep talking. "I begged the doctor to let me go see her, but he refused. I know I have a broken leg and all, but he could've at least wheeled me to see her, you know?"

This time, the silence surprised me.

"Mom… Dad?" I questioned.

"MJ, sweetheart. Liv, she…" she stuttered.

"Oh god." I shuffled on the bed. "How bad is it? I knew when I saw all that blood that she'd been hurt, badly. Can I please go see her?" I pleaded. The desperation in my voice spilled over into my bodily movements, making me antsy.

Mom opened her mouth to speak, but not before the door to my hospital room creaked open.

John and Jess, Olivia's parents, stepped inside.

"Jess." A faint smile crossed my face as a wave of relief crashed into me.

Seeing her parents was the closest thing I'd had to seeing Olivia since the accident. But my relief was quickly washed away as their faces moved into the light. Jess's mascara-stained cheeks and John's eyes, puffy behind his glasses, gave way to their emotional state.

As much as I wanted to say something, I couldn't. I was too afraid.

"MJ." Mom's voice caught me off guard, but I moved my attention to her.

"What it is? Whatever you have to tell me, I can handle it. I'll be by Olivia's side no matter what. Her recovery is my recovery. I just need to know, and I need to see her. Now." My voice was uneasy.

Jess walked over to the other side of my bed and grabbed my hand.

Her eyes never met mine. Instead, she stared at our joint hands. "Oh, my sweet girl." She went to speak again but was overcome with emotion, the words lodged in her throat.

John's tired voice chimed in from behind her. "Olivia didn't make it. Her injuries were too severe. We lost her on the way to the hospital."

I heard the first four words, but everything after was just noise.

The walls around me caved in with each breath I took. My breaths became shorter and more rapid. I reached for the hospital bed rails, grasping for anything that would anchor me.

The air in the room was scarce and I was terrified my next gasp would leave me breathless, but I spoke anyway. "No." Shaking my head, I continued. "No... She can't be gone. You're wrong. I made them take her out of the car first. She would've gotten help before me."

"They did everything they could," Dad said.

I wanted to scream or throw something, but the reality hung heavy around us and my tears turned audible.

John's head dropped like he didn't want to believe it either. Jess turned, collapsing into his embrace, as her sobs echoed through the room. Mom and Dad pretended to be brave for me, I knew, but I could see the devastation engulfing them with each second that passed.

It didn't matter who Olivia's biological parents were. In front of me stood two sets of parents that'd both lost a daughter in one way or another.

I swallowed, forcing the nausea down. "I don't understand. I don't know how to do life without her."

"None of us do," Mom replied.

I broke at her words. The unbearable truth of what lay in front of us was something I couldn't stomach.

A life without Olivia was a life I didn't think I could survive.

## Chapter Five

"MJ?" My dad's voice startled me from the daze that I'd found myself in for the past twelve hours. Darkness followed as I rolled over to face him.

Walking toward me, Dad took a seat on the hospital bed. "Honey, I'm not going to tell you that this won't be the hardest thing you'll ever do, but I will tell you that your mom and I will be right next to you the entire time, no matter what."

I sat up and rested my head on his shoulder. My eyelids were stiff and swollen from the constant flow of tears that'd made permanent paths down my cheeks. My feet dangled above the ground, one normal and one in a rather large cast. My toes grazed the cold linoleum floor, immediately sending a shiver down my spine.

"I want to go home," I said.

Without another word, he stood and reached out for my hand, helping me into the wheelchair that'd been placed next to the bed. Mom put the last of my things into a bag she must've brought from home and appeared at my side.

"Let's go home," she said.

Wheeling through the hospital, it was as if we were moving in slow motion while everything around us had been put in fast-forward. The nurses and doctors were blurry as they moved past us and down the hallway. We made our way to the front of the hospital only to see that it was a complete downpour.

*Figures.*

"Stay here, I'll go grab the car," Dad said.

Stationed in a rickety metal wheelchair, I found myself looking around and wondering what news each of these people would receive today. Would they be lucky and walk out of this place with their loved ones, or were they like me, leaving with a piece of themselves missing? The thought made me shudder. I gripped Mom's hand that was resting on my shoulder.

"You're going to be okay, MJ. I promise," she said. Her voice was far more confident than how I felt. "The hours will be brutal and the days will be dark, then slowly but surely, little slivers of light will sprinkle in, until one day you'll look in the mirror and see yourself again. It might take months or even years, and it won't ever fully go away, but it will become manageable. The darkness will no longer consume you. Instead, it will show up in song lyrics, or familiar scents, maybe even in a picture, but the light will eventually be brighter, and it will overcome all of this darkness," she said, and her words felt hopeful, even if only a little.

I squeezed her hand. "You promise?"

"I promise."

"Miller Morgan?" a man's voice called out from behind us.

Mom and I turned.

"I'm Chief Williams, I—"

"I remember you," I said softly.

He stood, towering over Mom and me in his navy firefighter uniform. His white hair was tight to his head and the wrinkles on his face depicted a much older man than the one I'd pictured the night of the accident.

"I was told you were getting released today and I just wanted to stop in and check on you." He smiled empathetically. "And whenever you're feeling up for it, I'd love to take you to lunch."

I nodded.

Words were too tough.

Mom chimed in: "Thank you, Chief Williams, we'll truly never be able to repay you."

"Don't mention it. It's why I do what I do," he said. "And Miller, I'm serious. When you're ready, lunch is on me."

Dad's black truck rumbled through the circle drive and Mom wheeled me closer toward the entrance. As we neared the doors, they slid open and a breeze of cooler than normal air rushed across my entire body. The smell of rain overtook my senses and flooded my nostrils.

I hadn't been outside since the accident, which at this point was only a little over seventy-two hours ago but felt like it had been years. The outside air didn't feel the same to me. Something was different, or rather, *I* was different.

An obnoxious lady in a white minivan laid on her horn and aggressively shook me back to reality. I slowly stood from the wheelchair and hobbled toward the truck on my crutches. With Mom's help, I made my way into the back seat.

The drive home from the hospital was every bit silent. It was obvious that Dad was going out of his way to bypass any street that was even remotely close to the scene of the accident, which I appreciated.

"MJ, are you hungry?" Mom asked as we pulled into our driveway. "I could make you a PB&H, if you'd like?"

Peanut butter and honey sandwiches had always been our favorite lunch choice.

*Had.*

That short little word brought such big, final feelings now.

"I'm all right, Mom. I think I'm going to go lay down for a bit, but thank you. I love you."

Dragging myself from the back seat, I forced my head down as the tears fought their way to the surface.

I took the stairs up to my room, one by one, each step bringing my body closer to crumbling. I barely made it to bed before my hobble faltered and I collapsed onto my back. A room that was once my safe haven now felt foreign. Nothing felt like mine anymore, and so far, nothing brought me comfort except the thought of closing my eyes.

The next few days were all the same. I spent the days sleeping and the nights trying to sleep. The only way to avoid the pain was to be unconscious. When I was awake, every little thing reminded me of her, and that was simply too much.

She was everywhere.

She was the glow-in-the-dark stars on my ceiling, she was the red lipstick kiss marks on the mirror in the corner of my room, she was the boy-band posters that still hung on the wall. Everywhere I looked, there she was.

Sleeping was the only valid option at this point.

Mom and Dad checked on me frequently, but they both knew that I needed my space.

Mornings turned into days, days into nights, and then started over again. I had no concept of time, everything blending together, but I didn't care. I wasn't sure how life seemed to be moving around me when everything within my line of sight seemed to stand still.

That is, until I was woken up by the sharpness of the sun beaming in from the window. I swore I'd shut those damn curtains last night.

It took me a second to wipe the sleep from my eyes, but once I did, I was able to make out my mom at the end of my bed. She held a black dress in one hand and a pair of black heels in the other.

"Honey, we need to leave in about thirty minutes." Her somber voice left me feeling sick. The black long-sleeved dress she wore seemed to drain the color from her face. She was barely wearing any makeup, and I was sure that was intentional. Tears always came fast for Mom, and I knew she wanted to prepare herself for the abundance of them that would fall today.

I rose from my bed and slowly hopped in her direction. Grabbing the dress from her hands, her arms embraced me as she whispered in my ear, "This is going to be one of the hardest moments of your entire life. I'm so sorry that you have to experience this at such a young age. If I could take your pain, I would do it in a heartbeat. Remember those slivers of light I talked about at the hospital. Look for those today. They'll be almost impossible to find, but when you do, the darkness won't seem as scary."

The softness of her voice almost masked the emotion that suffocated her words. I pulled from her embrace and stared into her eyes, and for a moment, a simple split second, I was okay.

"I love you big, Mom."

"I love you bigger, MJ." She nodded and gave me a small smile. "And, honey? Chief Williams dropped off a bag of stuff collected from Liv's car, said the police were done with it." She motioned toward my desk. "I don't know what's inside, but Jess told him she wanted you to have it. I just thought you'd want to know." Her voice was soft when she added, "We'll be downstairs when you're ready."

Part of me wanted to look in the bag, but I needed to get dressed first because I was afraid if I didn't, I never would.

Struggling into my black dress, I peered at the heels my mom picked out for me. Shaking my head, I made my way to the closet and opted for my favorite sneakers, or rather *one* of my favorite sneakers for my good leg. As I stood in front of the mirror, I couldn't help but think that the girl staring back at me wasn't someone I recognized.

Who was I without Liv?

"Liv, how the fuck am I supposed to do this?" The words left my mouth, and I couldn't help but gasp. I turned, sucking in a gust of air as the tears plummeted down my face. I shifted my weight to the other crutch and pushed my back against the mirror, slowly lowering my body to the ground. I was afraid if I moved too quickly, I might actually break.

Mentally, I knew I needed to at least attempt to pull it together. As I raised my head, the bag Mom had previously mentioned caught my eye across the room. Something purple peeked out from underneath the canvas bag.

I stood and made my way to the desk, but I already knew what it was.

Dead hydrangeas. *Liv's* dead hydrangeas.

The ones that had been in her car the night of the accident.

*Just because they're dead doesn't mean they've lost their beauty or their purpose.* Liv's words were as clear as if she were standing right behind me, speaking them.

Somehow, she was gone, and yet she was still giving me the strength I needed to keep going.

Grabbing the flowers, I made my way downstairs.

"Dad's already in the car, are you ready?" Mom asked.

"As ready as one can be to go bury their best friend."

Hobbling past Mom, I caught a whiff of her perfume, musty but feminine. With the rush of fragrance came the most vivid memory forcing me to slam my eyes shut. *Here comes that darkness.*

"Find the sliver," I muttered under my breath.

"Huh?" Mom asked.

"Nothing, just looking for a sliver."

"Keep looking."

And just like that, I was thirteen again, sneaking into my parents' room, Liv in tow, to borrow Mom's makeup and a little perfume before we made our way to our first boy-girl party. Liv had accidentally squirted one too many puffs of perfume and suddenly we were swimming in the scent. I couldn't get that smell out of my nose for weeks.

"—the flowers?" I missed the beginning of her question, but I assumed Mom was asking me why I had them.

"From her car. Hydrangeas. Her favorite," I said, each word choppier than the last as I did my best to keep my composure while sliding into the car.

The ride was nothing but deafening silence, although I didn't think I would've wanted it any other way. We were all still trying to work through the emotions and wrap our brains around the reality of our situation.

I hadn't been part of the funeral planning process, and thankfully so, but I didn't have to be involved to know that the funeral was going to be held at the beach. I guess I just didn't expect the beach to be the same one Olivia and I had run to after the cops busted Caleb's party.

Pulling into the parking lot, a sea of black nearly drowned out the sandy beach that lay in front of us. All of the darkness seemed to disguise the beauty that Liv and I had admired only a week ago. The car came to an abrupt halt as Dad pulled into the parking spot, and I lowered my head and gripped the stem of the dead flowers until the imperfections left indentions in my palms.

"I just want you both to know that I love you very much, and while I know this is going to be one of the hardest moments of our lives, you're doing this for Olivia. Remember that." The strength in Dad's voice was something I hadn't heard from him since everything happened, and I didn't realize how much I'd missed it.

I grasped onto his words, holding them tightly and committing them to memory so I could revisit them throughout the day, because I knew I'd need them more than just right now.

Lifting my head, my eyes met his in the rearview mirror. My muted "I love you" was met with a nod before he unlatched his door and stepped out. I took three big breaths, each one feeling a little deeper in my chest, and released them before pulling myself out of the car and walking toward my best friend's funeral.

# Chapter Six

The gravel wobbled beneath my crutches. I kept my head down, afraid that if I looked up, I'd lose all control of my emotions. The pit in my stomach was a mix of anger, sadness, devastation, and grief, making for a nice concoction of "ready to vomit at any moment."

Following closely behind Mom and Dad, I did everything possible to keep from turning around and heading straight back to the car as Dad's voice replayed over and over again. *You're doing this for Olivia. Remember that.*

I paused, but only for a second before Mom reached for my hand and gave me a squeeze. "We're right here," she whispered.

One tiny tear trickled out of my eye and down my cheek. I swiped it away as we moved to the front of the crowd. I spotted John and Jess, their somber figures leaning into one another for support.

I would be strong for them; I *had* to be strong for them.

Grinding my teeth to force the tears down, I balanced myself before wrapping my arms around Jess. A surge of strength pulsed through me, but then she released a breath and her body began heaving up and down within my embrace. Within seconds, my body mimicked hers.

"I love you," I breathed while trying to contain my sobs.

"I love you too."

My parents and I took our seats on the three chairs directly next to Liv's parents. My stomach sank as my eyes landed on the large black metal box that sat so prominently upon a raised platform directly in front of the ocean.

How could something so beautiful bear witness to something so fucking tragic?

The pastor started speaking as "Tears in Heaven" by Eric Clapton slowly faded. He spoke, but none of the words made sense. Everything was jumbled. I tried to focus while he went on about how beautiful Olivia was, how she lit up every room she entered, and how everyone who knew her loved her, and while everything he said was true, it didn't feel right. It didn't feel like he *really* knew her.

"And now, the family has asked for anyone who has something special they'd like to share to please do so at this time." The pastor's voice was soft and docile.

I wasn't sure at what point in time I decided that I was going to speak, but before I could talk myself out of it, I was staggering toward the microphone. I hadn't realized the number of people who'd shown up, but the sea of black extended far beyond the beach, flooding the entire parking lot. People were standing, sitting on top of their cars, and even parked on the side streets.

The sight alone could have brought me to my knees.

Breathing in a gulp of air, I closed my eyes and let my voice free. "Hi. I'm Miller Morgan. Olivia Mitchell was my best friend." I sucked in another deep breath, squeezing the stem of the hydrangeas that smooshed up against my palm and the crutches. "Liv was unlike any other person I've ever met. She was fierce and stubborn, but kind and loving too. She fought like hell for what she believed in, and she wasn't afraid to admit when she was wrong. She was beautiful, intelligent, and one of the most genuine human beings I've ever known." I paused and locked eyes with my mom.

The slightest nod of her head gave me what I needed to continue. "I still catch myself thanking the powers that be for somehow placing us on this earth at the same time, in the same place, and with the same undeniable love of trashy TV and gummy worms. Obviously forcing us to be best friends," I said, a small laugh piercing the audience as tears blurred my vision.

There it was. A tiny sliver.

But just as quickly as it appeared, it was gone, the somber faces of so many staring back at me. The childhood friends, the teachers, the parents, ultimately the entire town.

"I'm not sure how any of our lives will ever be the same now that something so bright has been ripped from us, but what I do know is that even though she's gone, her brightness will forever shine, through each and every one of us sitting here today." I sighed, collecting myself. "Whether it's the sparkly outfit that you swore you'd never wear or the party you said you wouldn't go to, one way or another, something will spark a memory, and Liv will come floating back, even if only for a second. When that happens, I want you to grasp onto the memory and never let it go. Not for you, but for her. We all need to remember the person she was and the person she would've been so we can carry a little piece of her everywhere we go."

I bowed my head as the tears became too forceful to fight, only finding the courage to continue when I imagined Dad's voice reminding me again: ...*for Olivia*.

I peered up and let the sound of the roaring waves behind me calm the roaring waves inside of me. "I'm not sure how to say goodbye to someone who has been with me for my whole life, but minute by minute, hour by hour, and day by day, I'll figure it out. We all will. I know some days are going to simply seem unbearable, but on those days, I'll look to the ocean. Liv always said she was jealous of the ocean because it had the ability to go anywhere and nowhere at the same time. So, I want you all to promise me that when you feel sad about losing Liv, you'll look to the ocean, because just as she once envied, Liv now has the ability to go anywhere and nowhere at the same time, within our hearts. She's here, she's there, and she's everywhere we need her to be. Never forget that, and never forget her."

Chills rushed down my spine and over my entire body, making the tiny hairs on my neck spike. I smiled because at that moment, I knew she was here. I turned toward the water and whispered, "I love you deeper than the ocean."

Bringing myself back to the crowd, I moved away from the microphone and made my way back to my seat. Shortly after I spoke, the funeral ended. Being so close to the Mitchells, the crowd treated us as though we were family too, coming up to offer their condolences.

At first, I thought I could handle it—I wanted to handle it—but it was too much.

Rain clouds rolled in and thunder boomed behind us, as did the heaviness in my chest. I gave one look to Mom and shook my head. I turned, crutching to the car as fast as I could, only for Dad to catch up to me in a few strides.

"Here, let me." He moved toward the passenger side, wrapping me in a hug. His strong embrace cradled my fragile frame as I let my weight fall.

"You're not driving with that leg of yours. I'll run you home and be back before Mom even knows I'm gone."

Dad pulled the car door open, and I responded with a nod because words felt impossible. I slipped into the front seat of the truck, my grip still tight on the dead hydrangeas I'd been holding since this morning.

The drive home was a blur. As our house came into view, I let out the deep breath that had been stuck in the pit of my stomach all morning. I barely made it inside and upstairs before I collapsed onto my bed, still in my black dress and single sneaker.

# Chapter Seven



*Now May 2024*

*Beep, beep, beep!*

"Shit," I murmured, rolling over to smack my phone.

Setting my alarm for six sounded like a good idea last night. Now, after listening to it scream at me for fifteen minutes, not so much.

"Ugh," I grumbled, peeling myself from my bed and stumbling to the bathroom.

I grabbed my toothbrush and layered a glob of toothpaste on it before looking into the mirror.

A disheveled mess stared back at me.

My wavy blonde hair was sticking out in every direction and persistent, residual mascara was smeared under my eyes. That was what I got for going to bed with wet hair and skipping my skincare regime. Trudging toward my closet, my mind wandered as I snagged my sports bra and shorts.

Running had been my form of free therapy ever since—

The wandering abruptly stopped as I approached the place I preferred to keep to myself. The place that constantly lingered in the darkest corners of my mind.

Running had been my escape for a while now. There was something about the quietness of our sleepy little town during those few hours when everyone except nature was still sleeping. The sound of the waves rushing against the shore, drowning out the thumping of my feet sinking into the sand underneath me. The rhythm of my heavy breaths as they filled the space in front of me. But mostly, my morning runs gave me time to talk out loud, just in case Liv was able to hear me.

I pulled open my apartment door and a gush of salty air whipped across my face. The best part of being this close to the water was the cool summer breeze that came just before the blazing heat invaded the day.

"Good morning, MJ."

My body jolted from the sound of Ms. Wilson's voice.

"Oh! Hi," I responded.

"Headed out for your morning run?"

"You know I can't pass up a good crisp jog before the rest of the town wakes up," I said, smiling.

She chuckled. "Why do you think I work nights?"

Ms. Wilson's dusty gray hair and wrinkles that decorated her face gave way to her older age. I didn't know how old that was exactly, but I knew it was somewhere in the early sixties. She was still in her scrubs from her twelve-hour shift that must've ended early. She'd worked nights since I'd known her, and considering she was one of the nurses who delivered me, it was safe to say I'd known her my whole life.

"Fair enough," I said.

"Any big plans for Memorial Day weekend?" Her voice was laced with interest.

Memorial Day weekend was a rite of passage around here. It signified the start of the summer season and was the first weekend when the town sprung to life. The shops were bombarded with red, white, and blue, and the energy that hummed through the streets was inescapable.

Just thinking about the hustle and bustle made me excited, but I wasn't sure why. I didn't have any big plans, or rather I didn't have any plans at all. Same as most weekends.

"Just the usual. The bar will be busy with the visiting city crowd, so along with my usual shifts, I'm sure I'll stick around and make sure Mom and Dad have everything covered."

"They're lucky to have you, sweet girl." She paused as if she had something else to say, but then landed on, "Have a good run, and say hello to the waves for me."

"You know I will." I grinned as I bounded down the concrete stairs that sat right outside our apartment doors.

The old brick building sat caddy corner from The Wharf—conveniently so—and was only a dash across Reef Road to the beach.

I placed my headphones over my ears, allowing silence to quickly engulf me before hitting shuffle on my running playlist. No matter what song started playing, it always got my blood pumping, and today was no different.

The rhythm was so intense I could feel it pulsing through the tips of my toes. I took one deep breath and let my feet do the rest as they forced me off the curb.

# Chapter Eight

My head swiveled as something in the usually deserted morning streets caught my eye. I froze as a sleek, black Range Rover came barreling toward me. The noise-cancelling headphones had worked right up until the screeching brakes broke through them.

Despite my circumstances, I couldn't seem to move. Cars and I had a rough history. Every time I found myself near one, I simply lost all ability to act like a normal human being. Eleven years might've passed since the accident, but I still only climbed into one when it was absolutely necessary.

Perks of living in a small beach town.

The shiny, clearly new Range Rover came to an abrupt stop a mere foot away from me. I took a step back, pulling my headphones from my ears and throwing my hands in the air.

*What the hell*, I mouthed.

My heart pulsed in my throat while my eyes moved toward the man behind the dash. His striking appearance didn't help the racing in my chest, but it did hinder the rage a tiny bit. His dark brown hair, shaggy and perfectly styled, stayed in place as he ripped off his classic-style Ray Bans. A look of panic flooded his dark eyes as they frantically scanned up and down my frame.

Still a little annoyed and now a bit anxious, adrenaline pumped through me. I turned away from him, expecting to return to my run and hopefully a normal heart rate.

"Hey!" he shouted, his voice wavering.

I wanted to keep moving, but as I heard him open his door and crunch toward me, my body had other plans. Spinning around with a little extra sass, I found myself gazing into his eyes. From this vantage point, I noticed they were actually more copper-colored than brown.

With broad shoulders and a large chest that seemed surprisingly steady, this man stood roughly six feet tall and appeared to have been plucked straight from a Ralph Lauren ad. He wore a tailored navy suit that was made to fit every inch of his body, further signaling that he clearly didn't belong in this town—at least not permanently. His trousers hit his ankles just so, and a pair of cognac loafers complemented the entire outfit. His chiseled jawline seemed to become even more defined by the second.

I stood, mesmerized, and watched the hand-crafted silver watch that fit snug on his left wrist shine as he swiped his fingers impatiently through his hair.

"I'm so sorry. Are you okay?"

"I'm fine."

"Holy shit. Thank god. You scared me," he said, canvasing my entire frame while he rubbed his chest back and forth.

"Maybe you could slow down next time," I said. "This town isn't big enough to be driving that fast."

I was criticizing him all while trying not to gawk at him.

He furrowed his bushy brows but not before letting a tiny smirk slip through his perfectly straight teeth. "Got it. Too fast. Slow down. Small town."

"Great. You're a quick learner. Now that we're done here, I can get back to my run."

As I turned, my foot got tripped up on the curb behind me, and in an instant, I was plummeting toward a complete face plant.

Until I wasn't.

Two strong hands wrapped around my lower half and twisted me upward. Within seconds, I was standing upright, my chest pressed against his. For a moment, the world paused, and all I could feel was the constant rhythm of his unwavering heartbeat.

Neither of us spoke a word, but we didn't need to. His expression mimicked mine. A blend of confusion and fascination drifted between us. I couldn't put my finger on it, but something about him felt familiar as my hand rested on his firm chest.

"Thanks," I muttered, briskly stepping out of his reach.

"Of course. It's the least I could do after nearly running you over."

"Did you just admit that you did in fact almost run me over?" I asked, a little less angsty and a little more playful.

"I'll always admit when I'm in the wrong, but..." His voice drug out the last word.

"But what?"

His right eyebrow rose up while the rest of his face displayed a to-die-for smile. "But... I do remember the light being green."

Quickly defending myself, I countered, "It *was* green, but that doesn't mean you shouldn't be aware of your surroundings and watch out for other people," I huffed. "You're clearly not from around here, so I'll let you in on a little secret. We look out for each other in this town, that's what makes this place so special."

"This place is special, there is no doubt in my mind about that." His comment caught my attention, but not for long. "Didn't your parents teach you to look both ways before crossing the street?" he teased.

Clearly, he wasn't done trying to make a point, but neither was I.

"Didn't your parents teach you to follow the speed limit?"

"Okay, okay. Touché. Can we agree that we're both in the wrong here?" He held out his hand, almost as if he wanted to confirm a truce between us.

Our hands grasped and I swore I felt tingles of energy shooting up my arm, but I wasn't about to make it obvious.

"Let's just say we can agree to disagree." I shot him a wink before shifting my body toward the water and away from him. Just as I was walking away and putting my headphones back in place, I heard his voice.

"Can I at least get your name?"

"My parents taught me to never give my name to strangers," I yelled.

I quickly pressed play, shoving my phone into the spandex pocket of my black biker shorts before I could see the song. The familiar beat of "Follow Me" by Uncle Kracker spilled into my ears, and I smirked as the wind ran across my face.

A *sliver.*

Picking up my pace, I started into jog. This had always been our song, Liv's and mine. It had been years since the accident, but not a day passed that she wasn't with me. She made sure of it.

I was fairly confident this was her way of telling me that she was proud of how I just handled that situation. Normally, I would've stumbled over my words in the presence of a man who looked like that. But not today. Today I'd been quicker and sassier than ever. My responses came straight from Liv's playbook.

"Proud of me, aren't ya, Liv?" The words quietly exited my mouth as a small smile crept across my face.

I was proud of myself too.

Lately, I'd been stuck. Set in my ways. Ways that weren't how I imagined my life turning out. Ways that seemed predictable, routine, almost automatic. Sometimes I caught myself remembering how I used to be. Before the accident. But that was when I had Liv. She was the lighthearted one, the wild one, the one whose spirit was so free no one was going to stop her. With her by my side, there was no choice but to embrace the chaos.

Sometimes, I wished I could go back to that place. That girl.

The salty air tickled my lips as I ran through town, and I used my tongue to wet them. I found myself daydreaming about Range Rover man and the automatic response my body had toward him.

Based on his attire and the car he drove, I could safely assume that he didn't live here, at least not full time. And while he looked the part of a summer regular, I'd never seen him before.

Because trust me when I say, I wouldn't forget someone like him.

He had an air about him. One that smelled intoxicating and carried a trace of arrogance, but not the annoying, in-your-face kind. More of the *damn, that's hot* kind. I half expected him to get out of the car, throw his hand in the air, and be a complete asshole. To be fair, I was in the wrong, so I wouldn't have been *that* shocked.

But instead, he'd stepped out of his car to make sure I was okay. He even appeared shaken up, and dare I say worried? My stomach danced, but only a little before I yanked myself back to reality.

I'd been mindlessly running around town for over an hour, and the coolness that'd floated through the air this morning had swiftly been replaced by sweltering heat.

That was my cue to go home.

My day was booked and busy. First on the list was a shower, because holy hell I was hot, and I wasn't convinced the sun was the only contributing factor.

Running up my apartment steps, I unlocked my door and bee-lined to the bathroom.

Sliding the white ruffle curtain to the side, I stepped in. The water sent a wave of shock up my spine as it washed my sweat down the drain. Under the spray, I ran through my to-do list for the day—grocery store, lunch with Chief Williams, and then home to get a few words in before my shift.

I'd been working on writing my first novel since... well, since forever. At this point, it was just a bunch of words in a Word document, but everyone had to start somewhere, right? It had always been my dream to move to New York City and become an author—something I'd only ever shared with Liv. After the accident, I stopped talking about it, but I'd be lying if I said it wasn't still my dream.

Wiping the mirror clean of steam, I stared at my reflection.

My damp hair looked almost brown, clinging to my wet body and hitting just below my boobs. Wavy in nature, the water only brought out the curls. I found myself questioning if I'd ever be the type of girl who could end up with someone like Range Rover man. Although, the thought made me chuckle. I was sure he'd prefer a woman with more of an *it* factor.

That notion sent a wave of disappointment flooding the base of my stomach.

I shrugged off the residual letdown and threw on a pair of ripped jeans and a loose linen button-up shirt.

As I grabbed my purse, my phone stopped me.

"Hey, Dad," I answered.

"Hey, MJ. Can you do me a favor?"

"Always. What's up?"

"The ice machine at the restaurant is on the fritz and I don't have time to run to the store before we open for the day. Can you grab some and run it by?"

"Yeah, of course. How many bags do you think you need?"

"Just a couple to get us through the afternoon. I talked to Charlie earlier. He's going to load up his truck with ice from the marina to fill our back freezer until I can get someone out here to fix it."

"Sounds good. I'm actually running to the grocery store right now, so I'll grab a few bags and drop them off on my way home."

I hadn't planned on getting that many things, but now that bags of ice were on the list, I grabbed my foldable wagon from the front closet and headed. out.

"Love you big."

"Love you bigger! See you soon!"

# Chapter Nine

"Dad!" I screeched, embarrassment filling my voice.

"What! Is everything okay?" He sprinted from behind the bar until he saw me, hands full of two large bags of ice, one in each arm.

"What in the hell is this doormat?" I chuckled as I leaned my butt on the wooden door, resting the ice against the frame.

Looking up, I was met by Dad and the biggest shit grin you've ever seen. "Funny, huh?" He started toward me, motioning for me to hand the ice over.

"It's ridiculous." I laughed, gladly giving him the two dumbbell-sized bags.

The tacky brown doormat lay under my feet, right at the front entrance of the restaurant. *Whalecum* was printed in large black letter, and a smiling whale sat just below it.

"I love you so much, but do we really think this is necessary?"

Dad was a sucker for a good cheesy pun, and over the years, he'd made a game out of buying the most random, usually inappropriate shit and somehow always finding a spot for it in the bar.

"Is any of the décor in this place necessary?" Clearly that was a rhetorical question because he kept talking. "*No*, but damn does it look good."

The smirk on his face gave way to how proud he was of this place, and who was I to take that away from him.

The Wharf had been around for decades and under my parents' ownership for almost sixteen years. From the outside, it was picturesque—the white shiplap and openness allowed for the most perfect view of the ocean. The old building sat upon stilts that had been built before I was born. The stilts permitted the building to reside just above the water, giving everyone a free soundtrack of waves with their meal. The string lights that Mom and I had weaved throughout the balcony reflected off the water and made for the most magical lighting.

Inside, it was everything you would imagine from the most perfect little dive bar. As soon as you walked in, you were greeted by a large rustic-looking bar that expanded across the entire back wall. The barstools were wooden and worn, having seen their fair share of late nights. Behind the bar, shelves of liquor lined the wall. Each shelf was underlit with a row of lights that illuminated the bottles. In the spaces between the bottles, there were knick-knacks and mementos, each one with a story just waiting to be told. The rest of the walls throughout were painted deep blue and were decorated with picture frames filled with trophy fish, family traditions, and memories that people never wanted to forget.

At this point, there was barely any blank space left, but it's what made this place so unique. It wasn't the fanciest place in town, but it didn't need to be. Everywhere you looked you were transported to a different celebration, a different sentimental moment that made you stop and experience it as if it were yours.

It wasn't just a local restaurant; it was a way of life. *My life.*

"Maybe one day the surprise will wear off, but until then, I'll continue to be astounded by the amount of random shit you come across," I said.

"Don't worry, I'll always surprise you." He winked. "We're expecting a busy lunch, so"—he held up the two bags of ice—"thanks for saving us."

"You know I've always got you covered."

"That's why you're the best!"

I walked toward Dad, grinning as I said, "Don't forget it." I pulled him in for a hug. "I'll be back around eight for my shift. Call me if you need me to come in earlier. I love you big."

"I love you bigger."

Snagging my wagon from out front, I bounded across the street and was home in less than two minutes. During my jaunt home, Chief Williams sent me a text asking for a raincheck, having forgotten about a different lunch he had. Although I did love our time together, I was quick to respond and let him know that I'd see him next Thursday.

I really could use the extra time to write.

He and I had maintained a relationship ever since he showed up at the hospital the day I was discharged. Although, I must admit I felt very lackluster about our relationship in the beginning, but he'd stayed persistent. Never pushy, but always persistent.

He'd dropped the bag off from the police station a few days after the accident and then proceeded to pop in on a weekly basis. More times than not, he came with gifts, usually a coffee or a sweet treat. Then, before I knew it, he was at my door every Thursday, like clockwork. When it was clear I'd warmed up to him, he began bringing lunch.

Sometimes I'd ask him questions about the accident, sometimes we'd talk about nothing in particular, and other times we'd just sit in silence and eat our lunches.

After a month or so, I returned to school and our lunches turned into late afternoons at the firehouse. Slowly, Thursdays became my favorite day of the week, and we rarely missed them. For those few hours that I got to spend with Chief Williams, everything felt like it was going to be okay. He'd been a safehouse for me. He'd been there during the most vulnerable and gut-wrenching moment of my entire life.

Most importantly, he'd saved me.

There was something that the two of us shared. We never spoke about it, but we both knew it was there.

Over the years, I realized I cherished his friendship more than I ever anticipated. He was kind and funny, and I found myself intrigued by all of his stories and knowledge. And if we're being honest, he'd always pushed me to continue writing, constantly reminding me that "some words are better than no words, darlin'." I could hear his voice as clearly as if he were standing right next to me.

So I knew he'd be proud to know that I would be spending the afternoon writing.

It was one o'clock by the time my microwave beeped, signaling my cheese and crackers were finished. Snagging my plate, I strolled to my bedroom to throw on some scrum clothes, because absolutely no writing was going to happen while I was still in jeans.

My tiny 900-square-foot apartment limited my ability to create the ultimate writing space, but I made do. My desk sat in the corner of my room, pushed up alongside the large window that overlooked Reef Road. An oversized green velvet chair that allowed me to sit cross-legged, and comfortably so, was pushed underneath it. The desk had been a gift from my parents, made from driftwood that Dad collected from the shores of our little town.

On the desk sat a vase with a familiar bouquet of dead lilac hydrangeas, a gold lamp, and a black-and-gold picture frame that held my favorite picture of Liv and me, both of us grinning from ear to ear as we held up our gray New York sweatshirts that we'd gotten for Christmas. She was my why and always would be. It didn't matter that I'd promised myself I'd finish this book; it mattered that I'd promised *her.*

We may not have made our way out of this small town, but that wasn't going to stop me from writing my story. Liv had always encouraged me to chase my dream of becoming a writer; she knew I needed a push, and she'd always done the pushing.

Slugging on my headphones, I did my best to drown out the noise within and get to work, but before I did, I pressed my fingers to that familiar picture frame. "For you, Liv. I love you deeper than the ocean."

# Chapter Ten

Five hours later and I'd actually accomplished something. I couldn't quite put it into words, but every time my fingers hit that keyboard, I felt a little less lost and a little closer to Liv.

The clock on my computer signaled it was time for me to get ready for work. I stood and trudged my way to my bed, the light-wash ripped jeans from this morning sprawled across it. Pulling up the denim, I wiggled the material over my ass and buttoned them before stepping toward my closet.

Usually, Dad preferred the staff to wear a Wharf-branded T-shirt, but all bets were off during the holiday weekends. It was practically a crime not to show up in patriotic attire, so I pulled a shirt off the hanger and slid into it. The white peplum top had puffy sleeves and tied together in the front with three dainty bows. I took in my put-together reflection in the mirror and watched a grin tug at my lips.

It wasn't that I had any expectations of impressing anyone—I basically saw the same faces every shift—but a tiny part of me was daydreaming about the mysterious man I'd seen earlier.

Our town kept the same company throughout the year, except during the summertime. Because for those few months, we were honored to share the same air as all the rich boys and girls who spent their days floating on big boats and their nights drinking at lavish parties that most of us townies were invited to. Despite the inconvenience of them overrunning our quaint little town, I never minded the eye candy that came with it.

As my curling iron heated up, "Heat Waves" by Glass Animals serenaded me. I was going to be early, but I was sure Dad wouldn't mind. I curled my hair, dabbed on some red lipstick, slipped into my white Converse, and glanced in the mirror one last time before feeling satisfied enough to switch off the lights.

Wallet, check. Keys, check. Phone, check.

I was out the door and down the stairs before I realized the copious amount of noise coming from the street. Twinkling lights were strung across the buildings, casting a sparkle across the road, and a wave of excitement danced through me as the sounds of laughter echoed around me.

Even though I knew I would regret saying this, because it didn't take long for the transplants to become a nuisance, I loved this time of year so much. And maybe, just maybe, this summer was going to be different.

As I strode across the sidewalk, my hair blew in the ocean breeze. I could already tell The Wharf was busier than usual. The gravel parking lot was busting at the seams, and the music was more than a couple notches louder than normal. As I swung the door open, I was shocked at the number of bodies that lined the bar. I immediately made eye contact with Sam, the other resident bartender and my friend, and the desperation splashed on her face signaled she needed help.

Dashing behind the bar, I shouted, "Holy shit, how long has it been this busy?"

"Not too long. The fireworks at the marina just ended and I think everyone made their way over here to continue the party!" she yelled, throwing a towel over her shoulder.

Samantha Murry was a few years older than me in school and, like me, had lived here her whole life. She was your typical badass bartender. Her fiery red hair fell down her back and she almost always opted for black outfits, specifically black outfits with leather. Both of her arms were covered in tattoos, all of which she designed herself.

Sam was one of the first people I let in after the accident. It had taken a lot of time, a lot of therapy, and some serious persistence on her end, but with each shift we worked side by side, I found myself slowly letting her in. The irrational fear of losing her lingered in the back of my mind, but before her, it was just me, and that got really lonely.

"It's buzzing in here. Dad has to be thrilled," I said. "Speaking of, where is he?"

"I'm not sure. Your parents have been running around like crazy since lunch. I've never seen a crowd like this." She grabbed a bottle of vodka from behind me. "All I have to say is thank god you're here."

"You should have called me! I would've come earlier. I told Dad I was free all afternoon and happy to help."

"Yes..." Her words hung in the air. "But you also told him you were writing, and that man would let this place go up in flames before he interrupted your writing time. And honestly, I feel the same," she said, her sarcasm giving way to a big smile.

"One day all that generosity will pay off," I joked.

"It better. And when it does, don't forget about lil' ol' me."

"I would never."

"Also, just so we're on the same page, there was nothing here I couldn't handle." She winked.

"Of course not. I never doubted you for a second," I said, playfully slapping her arm. "All right, now tell me where you need me!"

"End of the bar," she said, motioning to a group of guys in sport jackets. Clearly not regulars. "Those guys have been waiting for a while, and they've been surprisingly patient."

"On it." I strode over, snatching a few napkins and placing them in front of the group. "Hey, what can I get you all?" I looked up and almost choked on my words.

Those eyes.

The iridescent honey color reflected off the low lighting in the bar and made it almost impossible to take my next breath. I blinked, attempting to refocus.

He cocked his head to the side as he lifted his left hand, grazing his top lip with his pointer finger. "You again." His voice was deep and smooth as velvet.

"Me again."

"At least this time you can't run away." He grinned.

"At least this time you can't run me over," I said, tapping my finger on the bar.

"Hey now, let's not forget I saved you too. Why is it always harder to remember the good parts?"

He dropped his hand, revealing an alluring expression. His camel sport jacket and casual white T-shirt complemented his tanned skin and the little bit of scruff bordering his jawline.

I was doing everything I could to normalize the rhythm of my heartbeat, but damn, he was making it hard. This man carried himself in a way that made him instantly five times more attractive than any other man in this bar.

"It's Grey. Grey Prescott."

*Grey.*

My god. Even the name suited him.

"Okay, Grey, what can I get you?"

"Your name," he smoothly responded.

"Ha! Good try," I mocked. "If you don't tell me what you want, I'm serving the next person."

"Just as feisty as I remember. My favorite."

"Do you see this bar?" I lifted my hands and looked around to emphasize my comment. "It's packed, and my dad wouldn't be very happy if he knew I was standing here wasting my time when I could be making him money…" The confidence in my tone surprised me.

"So now you think I'm wasting your time, huh?"

"You really know how to push a girl's button, don't you?"

Flustered and not wanting to give him a chance to respond, I moved toward the guy next to him, clearly a part of his group based on his overdressed appearance. "Hey, what can I get you to drink?"

He was quick to respond. "I'll take six Sex on the Beach shots."

I glanced down at my inventory, scanning the bottles before landing on the peach schnapps. "Sex on the Beach. *My favorite,*" I said, shooting a cheeky look in Grey's direction.

"What a coincidence. Me too," the guy said, chuckling at my comment.

Grey's friend wasn't my type with his blond hair and blue eyes, but that wasn't the point. I could feel his intrusive copper eyes watching my every move, and while I hated to admit it, I loved knowing he was looking.

"Six Sex on the Beach shots coming right up."

While I poured the vodka, cranberry juice, orange juice, and peach schnapps, I did my best to avert my eyes in every direction except Grey's, but I failed.

*Twice.*

The first time I snuck a glance, his back was turned as he chatted with his friends. But I got greedy and as I threw the cocktail shaker above my head, using both hands to mix together the contents inside, I was drawn back in his direction, and this time, I wasn't so lucky. He was staring right at me. Our eyes locked and my stomach immediately dropped. I felt anxious, excited, and like I might throw up at any moment from the rush of his gaze.

His jaw tensed.

Pulling my stare away, I poured the shots. "Here you go," I said, smiling as I slid the tab toward the blond-haired friend.

"I got it, Will," a voice boomed as Grey casually grabbed the flimsy bill before I could let go.

Our hands met, and sparks of energy infiltrated my belly. Our hands lingered, his on top of mine.

I couldn't put my finger on it, it sounded silly even thinking it, but there was something there. Something between us that made it feel like we hadn't just met for the first time only a couple of hours ago.

"Thanks, man," Will said, snapping me back to reality as I stole my hand back.

"Anytime."

As I tried to focus on anyone but this man, I fidgeted with the glasses that sat underneath the bar before moving to another customer.

"Hey, Steven! Let me guess. A Bud Light and a shot of Jameson?" I smiled. Steven was one of Dad's friends and at the bar almost every night.

"You got it," he shot back.

Grabbing the Bud Light, I desperately tried to eavesdrop on the conversation happening at the end of the bar.

"Grey, I can't believe you're finally back. What's it been? Like ten years?" One of the guy's voices projected over the music as he slapped him on the back.

Grey's voice was lower than his friend's as he responded, "Almost eleven."

"Damn, man. Well, we're glad to have you this summer. Let's make it a good one," his friend said before I heard a large clunk.

A handful of "Cheers!" followed as the group of six dudes clinked their glasses together. I snuck a glance as they all threw back their shots, all of them except Grey. Instead, he placed his shot glass on the bar, his eyes catching mine yet again.

Adrenaline raced through my body, but I snapped my head away and made my way toward the center of the bar where Sam stood.

"We haven't had a Memorial Day weekend like this one in a long time." Her voice was loud as she tried her best to be heard over the thumping of the music.

"I know, this is insane," I responded. "I haven't seen Mom or Dad since I got here."

"They're around, but it's hard to see anyone else when your attention is focused on one person."

I whipped my head in her direction, and the shit-eating grin plastered on her face gave her away.

"I was simply helping a customer," I said nonchalantly.

"Uh huh. If only all our customers could look like him, right?" she asked, motioning in his direction.

I wanted to look, but out of my periphery, I spotted his outline moving toward us. I spun in the other direction, hoping Sam would help me out with this one.

"Oh no, this one's all you." She giggled.

And just like that, I found myself again staring at Grey Prescott, all six feet of him.

"So, what are the chances I can get a rum and ginger now that you're done trying to prove a point?"

"That's dramatic. But yes, I'd be happy to help. Light or dark rum?"

"Is that even a question?"

"Well, yes. That's why I asked it."

"Dark." His voice matched the word that left his mouth. "Spiced, to be exact."

"We've got Sailor Jerry's," I stated.

"Even better," he said, emphasizing each word.

Throwing together his drink, I put in a little extra effort than normal, simply because I could.

"Here you go, Grey. And for future reference, a rum and ginger with spiced rum is also known as a Dark & Stormy," I stated, matter of fact.

"Is that so, Miss...?"

"Ms. Morgan," I answered. "MJ, actually."

*Shit.*

He was good. Pulling my name out of me without even trying.

"Nice to meet you, Ms. Morgan." He grabbed his drink, and then just before he turned toward his group of friends, he winked as he said, "I mean, MJ."

The letters eagerly rolled off his tongue and he casually licked his lips.

Once his back shifted to me, I released a heavy sigh and my entire body relaxed against the bar.

"Since when did you start giving summer fuckboys the time of day?" Sam's voice startled me.

*Since they showed up looking like Grey Prescott*, I thought, but decided to keep that to myself and instead chuckled at her comment.

"I haven't. I was just hoping for a big tip. You know those out-of-towners give the best tips."

She pursed her lips. "I'm sure they do."

"Stop! I didn't mean it like that," I giggled, tossing my bar towel in her direction. "You're being ridiculous."

"Probably," she said. "Speaking of ridiculous and summer boys, the one I've been talking to invited me to a holiday kickoff party tomorrow and I'm absolutely not showing up alone, so I'll pick you up at nine? And before you say no, remember just a couple days ago when you told me you wanted to have a fun summer?"

With my arms crossed in front of my chest, I exhaled in her direction.

"In fact, I believe you even said you wanted to let loose and live a little... So, here I am, being a good friend and presenting you with an opportunity," she said, emphasizing her comment by using her hands to push an imaginary platter toward me.

Shaking my head back and forth, I said, "I knew I shouldn't have said that out loud. I had a feeling you'd keep that in your back pocket until you needed some leverage. I just didn't expect you to use it so soon."

"Nine, it is." Her grin took over her entire face.

"Please tell me this isn't the same guy from last summer..."

"This isn't the same guy from last summer..." she repeated.

"Sam!" I shouted.

"I'm sorry, MJ. I can't help it. I love a little summer fling, and it's helpful when you don't have to find a new one every summer," she chirped. "Looks like you might have one of your own this year."

"Ha," I huffed. "I'm going to go with no, but thanks for the thought."

Although, thinking about even the slightest fling with Grey sent my mind spiraling.

"Why not?" she asked, and her serious tone made me do a double-take.

"What do you mean why not?"

My hand rested on my hip as I leaned against the bar.

"I mean... why not? Why can't you have a summer fling? Were you not standing right here during our previous conversation?" She cocked her head to the side. "Want my advice?"

"I have a good feeling I know where this is headed, but shoot."

"Go with the flow this summer. Let yourself have a good time. Hell, you might even start to enjoy yourself," she said, poking fun at me.

Her words echoed through my ears. Maybe a summer fling wouldn't be the worst thing? Especially if said fling resembled a tall, dark, and handsome Grey Prescott.

"Hey, girls." My dad's voice caught me completely off guard and immediately made me feel weird as I was daydreaming about summer hookups.

"Hey, Dad! This crowd is wild."

"I know. I'm grateful, but I definitely wasn't prepared. Glad you're here! Although, Sam did a great job holding down the fort."

"Thanks. It got a little dicey, but I survived. Happy to have some good back up," Sam responded as she gently bumped her hip into mine.

"No worries, I'm happy to help," I said.

"She sure is."

I shot a glance in her direction. If only looks could kill.

"I think the crowd might finally be dying down. I'm planning to close the bar at eleven. Let me know if either of you needs anything," Dad told us.

"Sounds good," we said in sync. "Love you big!" I shouted after him.

"Love you bigger," he said as he made his way through the crowd.

By the time I got home it was past midnight. I took my makeup off, put on my pajamas, and crawled into bed, completely exhausted. Rather than pass out like my body demanded though, my brain wouldn't quit.

Tonight, my thoughts were different than normal. Tonight, while I replayed my shift, my memory kept landing on him.

Grey Prescott.

We didn't have any other communication, but I'd quietly kept my eye on him for the rest of the night until he and his drunk friends left.

I kept racking my brain for something to explain my infatuation. I'd seen boys like him before. The well-dressed, flirty type who thought could get any girl they wanted based on the thickness of their wallet.

But he was different. He intrigued me.

"Liv, you would've simply died. This boy was everything you and I imagined a boy from the city would be, and for some reason he showed interest in me, or at least I think he did." I sighed, daydreaming about what it would be like if she were here to chat with. "I miss you every single day. I thought it would get easier, and in a sense, it has, but it's nights like these I feel like a giddy teenager, wishing I had my best friend to talk to, that I miss you the most."

I realized I'd been talking out loud, which I only found myself doing when I was desperately craving a conversation with her. When I was alone in the peace and quiet, I talked aloud to her simply because I knew she was listening.

"I miss you further than the moon, Liv. And I love you deeper than the ocean."

And with that, my brain finally shut down.

## Chapter Eleven

I blinked my eyes open only to slam them shut the second I caught sight of the bright light streaming in through the open curtains.

"Ugh, already?"

I'd set my alarm for my run, but here I was again, dreading the actual waking up part. I rolled over, throwing my hand to my nightstand, scouring the table for my phone. I forced myself out of bed, got dressed, and walked out the door before I could talk myself out of it.

Today's run was quieter than normal. Probably because the entire town was sleeping off their hangovers and had no intention of moving until it was time to start partying again. Honestly though, it was nice, and the quiet gave me extra time to be with my thoughts.

The summer sun was already a scorcher, and the heat radiating off the sand forced sweat beads down my back, making it an easy decision to cut my run a little short. My feet pounded the pavement as I neared my apartment building. Unlocking my door, I heard my phone vibrating on the counter. Apparently I'd forgotten it on my run, and the fact that I didn't even realize I ran without music should tell you how loud my thoughts had been.

Sam:

Don't forget, you're coming with me tonight. You better not try and get out of it. You know I can't show up to this party by myself.

Me:

Calm down, I'm coming with you. But what are you wearing?

Sam:

Anthony bought me a new black dress for tonight :)

Me:

Well, shit. Now I'm absolutely going to have to go buy something.

Sam:

You're welcome for giving you the perfect excuse to go shopping.

Me:

Ugh. I'll see you at 9.

Sam:

ILY!

Me:

Love you too.

The words I always ended my conversations with.

*I love you* was something I found myself saying all the time. It took me a while to get to that point with Sam, but once I did, I never missed a chance to say it. You've got to be heavy on the *I love you*s, because life was just too damn unpredictable. I learned my lesson the hard way that you could never tell your people you loved them too much, because you never knew when it might be your last chance.

I set my phone down and headed for my bedroom.

By lunch, I'd already showered, attempted to write—unsuccessfully—and decided to head down to the shops to find something appropriate to wear tonight. I tried to picture an outfit but couldn't, so the optimism was slim.

Wave Break was the first store I tried. The store's boho beachy vibe appeared effortless, but every outfit I tried on looked like I was wearing lingerie, which definitely wasn't the look I was going for. Next was Salt & Air.

"Hey, MJ!" a familiar voice shouted from behind the counter.

"Hey, Hayley. How are you?"

"I'm good." She smiled. "Just trying to stock the store. I heard we're supposed to have quite the crowd this weekend."

"I can confirm that is the case. The Wharf was wild last night. Probably the biggest crowd I've ever seen," I said.

"More people means more business, so I guess we can't complain," she admitted. "I haven't seen you in here for a while. Anything specific I can help you with?"

Hayley and I graduated the same year and had stayed acquaintances. She opened this cute little boutique after her dad passed away and left her with an inheritance.

"Sam is making me go to a party tonight and I have *nothing* to wear. I need a dress, or something a little different than my typical jeans and T-shirt ensemble."

"I've got the perfect thing." She disappeared behind the back wall, and then returned with a cream-colored chiffon dress. She placed it in a dressing room and said, "Let me know if you need anything else."

"You're the best, thank you," I replied before stepping behind the light blue velvet curtain.

I examined the dress. It was embroidered with a floral pattern—royal blue, golden yellow, and pale purplish-pink flowers covered the entire dress. The long sleeves were sheer, which I loved. It was cut lower than I was used to and pulled together in the center with a golden circle, along with two cutouts under each boob.

I was nervous, to say the least.

I slipped out of my shorts and tank top, pulling the dress over my head.

I maneuvered each boob around until I was somewhat satisfied with their placement. I continued to adjust while stepping over to see my reflection. I tilted my head to each side, glancing at myself, shocked by the fact that I didn't completely hate it.

In fact, I sort of loved it. All the colors reminded me of Liv.

The cutouts hit in just the right spots, accentuating my waist and flowing out from there.

"Just checking on you. What do you think?" Hayley's voice popped up right outside the dressing room.

"I'm not sure, can I get your opinion?" I asked, pushing the curtain to the side.

"Damn." Her eyes trailed up and down. "You should definitely be wearing things like this more often."

"Really?" I asked, hesitantly running my hands up and down the dress.

"Yes, really. You look hot."

I smiled as I re-examined myself, pleased with what I saw. My reflection sent a sudden jolt of excitement through me.

"I'll take it," I said.

Normal parties in our town consisted of kegs and swimsuits. No one was showing up in a dress like this, but I wasn't going to a normal party.

"Thanks, Hayley," I said, pushing the store door open. "I hope you have a good Memorial Day weekend!"

"You too. Have fun at your party!"

My parents' house was only a few blocks from Salt & Air, so I decided to trek that way and check on them. They still lived in the same house I was born in. In fact, my room was still the exact same as when I lived there, down to the heinous zebra print comforter that I just *had* to have.

The streets leading home were plucked straight out of a movie set. Trees draped over the top, so much so that it was hard to see the sky between all the branches. Almost every house was a perfectly painted pastel color, adorned with quaint wraparound wooden porches.

Stopping in front of the only white house on the street, I made my way up the sidewalk and to the front porch. When my parents bought this house, it was neon green, and while Dad wanted to go with a light blue, Mom insisted on a more neutral color. However, it wasn't the white paint that made our house stand out, it was the ungodly amount of lilac-colored hydrangeas that easily stood five feet tall and towered over the front porch.

Those hydrangeas weren't just pretty to look at; their meaning extended far beyond their beauty. They were Liv's favorite, and after she died, Mom surprised me and planted ten lilac hydrangea bushes. She said planting the bushes would ensure that Liv would always be around us.

I couldn't see Mom, but I could hear her voice coming from around the house. Walking to the back porch, I was greeted by Mom, Dad, and the Mitchells. "Hi! What are you humans doing?"

"Oh, you know, just enjoying one of John's famous mojitos to kick off the long weekend," Dad said, holding up his glass that was dripping with sweat. "Want one?"

"No, thank you. I was just stopping by to make sure you don't need any help tonight. With Sam and I both off—"

"We've got it covered," he said, cutting me off mid-sentence. "Go have fun. Sam told us she's taking you to a party. That'll be good for you."

"Do you have something to wear?" Mom chimed in.

"Mom, I'm twenty-eight years old. I can figure out my own outfits," I joked, although I was dying to tell her about my new dress. "But since you asked... I did stop by Salt & Air on my way over and picked up a new dress."

I pulled the bag from behind my back.

"A dress?" she chirped.

"Leave her alone, Kelli," Dad piped in with a smile.

"A dress," I said, holding the piece of material on display for everyone to see.

"Okay, MJ, I love," Jess said. "All those colors. It reminds me of Liv."

My heart fluttered. "Me too. That's exactly what I thought when I bought it."

"It's beautiful, and I bet it looks even more beautiful on." Mom stood, coming face-to-face with me before drawing me into a hug. "I'm glad you decided to go. Have the best time, my girl."

"Thanks, Mom."

"Don't do anything we wouldn't do..." Dad's chuckle echoed through the screened-in porch.

"Hell, MJ, guess that means you're free to do whatever you want. Andrew and I have pretty much covered everything you can possibly do in this town. Looks like the world is your oyster," John said.

"You do all realize that I have in fact been to a party before, right?"

Everyone grinned at me.

"Oh my god, you humans are ridiculous. If you don't need anything else, then I'm headed home to get ready. Goodbye," I joked, waving to them. "I love you all."

"We love you," they said in unison.

If Liv's and my parents were close before the accident, they became inseparable after.

Selfishly, I loved it.

It made me feel closer to Liv, and it gave all of them the comfort they needed while also allowing them to grieve together. But most importantly, it solidified that they'd never leave this town.

I'd already lost Liv; I couldn't lose them too.

# Chapter Twelve

I was spritzing a little extra hairspray here and there when I heard my phone ding. I went with a low messy bun and paired it with a set of gold hoops. I left my makeup simple and natural. The dress was already more than I was used to.



It was most definitely not three minutes when my phone dinged again.



Dashing for the stairs, I snagged my tan sandals and gold clutch. Anthony's black BMW came to a screeching halt in front of my apartment building, sending a sense of unease through my body.

Even after eleven years, cars still made my skin crawl. However, tonight, it looked like I didn't have any other choice.

"Okay, damn. Where have you been hiding?" Sam hollered as she rolled down the passenger-side window.

"Oh my god, stop. It's just a dress." Concealing my embarrassment, I clung to my sandals and climbed in the back seat. "Hey, Anthony. How are you?"

"Hey, MJ. I'm good. Stoked for this party, it's going to be absolutely wild. You girls better be ready." His eyes gleamed onto Sam before returning to me. "How have you been?"

"You know, living the life."

"Oh, really?" The ambiguity in his voice was deafening.

"Ha," Sam rebutted.

I giggled. "Okay, rude. But I've been good. Just the same old same." I paused, knowing my next sentence would surely go straight to Sam's head. "Excited for a night out. Glad Sam forced me to come." I threw my hand over the back of the passenger seat, jokingly smacking Sam's shoulder.

"Mhm. You're welcome. You can thank me later."

The tiny inkling of doubt about this dress had vanished as soon as I saw Anthony and Sam. Anthony was wearing a white linen collared shirt and khaki pants, paired with a black blazer. Sam was wearing way more than a simple black dress. I'd never seen her in anything so trendy.

I let out a deep breath as I relaxed against the leather seat, but it only lasted until Anthony laid his foot on the gas pedal. Gravity pulling me backward, and I reached for anything to hold on to, finally landing on the side of my seat and squeezing so hard my knuckles turned white. I would wager there was probably more than one fingernail imprint on the leather.

"Is this at the same house you went to last year?" I asked, trying to make conversation.

"Nah, my other buddy decided to have it. His house is way more dope than last year's," Anthony responded.

Thinking back to what Sam had told me about last year's party, I couldn't imagine a "more dope" house. It had a massive backyard, and said backyard backed onto the ocean. There'd been a DJ, dancers in cages, and a man shucking oysters, for fuck's sake. How could anything top that?

"Nice. I can't wait to see it," I replied.

I sat quietly for the remainder of the drive, watching their interactions. Sam was smitten; I could tell by the way she leaned toward him, hugging onto his right arm that he'd casually laid in her lap.

She was a grown-ass woman and could make her own decisions, but I wanted her to remember that it was easy to get caught up in the shiny, glamorous things that surrounded these men.

We'd always just be the *summer girls.*

"We're here."

"Holy shit," Sam said.

I'd been fidgeting with my hands, but her comment made me look up. In front of us, at the bottom of a steep driveway, stood the most beautiful house I'd ever seen.

My mouth dropped open.

The sight itself was un-fucking-believable. The property spanned at least three acres across the beach. The grounds were strung with more lights than I could count, and each one highlighted something more picturesque than the one before it.

The vast house was finished with traditional shake siding, giving it the ultimate beach cottage look but on a much larger scale. The substantial pillars that decorated the double-story wraparound porch were spectacular. I'd never seen a house this big, and I'd lived here my entire life. To be fair, the house was tucked away, so even if you passed by the driveway, you'd never suspect what lay just past it.

Anthony pulled up to the circle drive.

"Good evening, sir. I can take it from here," the valet said as he simultaneously opened mine and Sam's doors.

"Thanks, man," Anthony chirped back.

So... I guess we have valets at parties now.

"This is wild, Sam."

"No, this is *absurd*."

I stepped out of the car and instantly noticed the landscape. The abundance of manicured bushes and flowers decorated the perimeter, at least as far as I could see. There were hydrangea bushes that overtook the lower portion of the porch, and of course they were perfect, just like the house. They looked like they'd just been pruned for the cover of a magazine. Hydrangeas were a popular choice on the northeast coast, but these hydrangeas were the familiar lilac color that I'd grown to love so much.

A tiny smile crawled across my face.

I'd already fallen in love with the house and I'd barely seen any of it.

"This way, ladies," Anthony said, motioning toward the front door.

He opened one of the massive white doors and we were immediately welcomed by loud music and people chattering.

"Thank god I bought this dress today," I said, looking down and admiring my purchase, feeling more confident by the second.

"Huh?" Sam asked, clearly mesmerized by what lay in front of us.

"Oh, nothing. I was talking to myself."

The entryway was a spectacle in itself. The double doors led to towering ceilings and one enormous gold light fixture that hung at least thirty feet above our heads. The light-washed wooden floors and white walls made the space feel even bigger than it was, which seemed impossible.

The walls, or at least the ones that were in sight, were decorated with art that I was sure cost more than my entire salary, and each of the pieces was accessorized with golden wall sconces.

Crown molding effortlessly outlined the doorways, floorboards, and ceilings. Honestly, it was art in itself. The chunky wood was painted to match the walls but added the most breathtaking detail. I couldn't stop admiring it.

I began taking in the people that had gathered for the party. You could tell with one glance that these weren't locals. Their outfits were designer, their makeup and hair clearly professionally done, and the aura that floated through the air was different, but dare

I say... exciting? For the first time, I didn't mind that I wasn't surrounded by locals. Instead, I was getting to experience how the one-percent lived.

Honestly, it was a bit of an escape.

The outfit, the house, the party, the entire night was a chance for me to flee reality for a few hours, and at this point, I wasn't going to turn that down. I was very much embracing a Liv mentality, and that made me proud.

"I'm going to grab a drink, do you want something?" I offered, looking back at Sam.

"No, I think Anthony went to grab me one. I should've had him get you something too. My bad."

"No worries. I'm excited to scope out the rest of this house anyway. I'll be back."

Making my way through the crowd, I admired what I presumed was the living room, the colossal space decorated like it had been staged for a *Southern Living* photoshoot. Enormous white couches, enhanced with navy pillows that were flawlessly placed, added an air of coziness. Sliding glass doors made up back wall of the room and gave way to an unreal view of the pool. Even more unreal was the view of the ocean just beyond the edge of the property.

Set up halfway inside and halfway outside was one of three bars that I'd already spotted. This was unlike any makeshift bar I'd ever seen, staffed with three bartenders and every type of alcohol you could imagine.

"Any chance I could get a dirty martini?"

The cute bartender smiled in my direction. "Absolutely. Gin or vodka?"

"Vodka, please."

"Regular or blue cheese olives?"

"Oh! Blue cheese, please."

"My kind of girl," he said, winking.

Maybe I should wear dresses more often.

"One last question, how dirty?"

I smirked. "Extra."

"No surprise there," came from a familiar voice beside me.

My stomach plummeted and my face heated. I looked to my left, and I couldn't help the slight grin that took over my mouth.

Grey Prescott, perched casually against the bar. His navy sport coat lay nicely on his broad shoulders as he placed his right elbow on top of the bar, resting his other hand under his chin. A hungry expression flashed across his face as our eyes met, making the muscles in his jaw tighten.

Returning my gaze to the bartender preparing my martini, I responded, "I should've known you'd be here. This party screams entitled rich guy."

"It's hard not to attend a party hosted at your own house, now isn't it?"

My mouth dropped slightly, but I quickly pulled myself together.

"Makes sense," I said, pursing my lips and nodding.

His fingertips swirled around the lip of his glass that sat on the bar. "Which part? That I'm an entitled rich guy or that this is my party?"

"Honestly? Both," I said. "I should've known you were responsible for a party as over the top as this one, simply based on how you came barreling into town yesterday."

"Okay, that's not fair," he said, very matter of factly.

"Oh? And how so? Please explain to me, Mr. Prescott, how your abruptness into town gave me no choice but to assume that you're just like all these other New York City transplants? Here one second and gone the next." I sneered impishly.

"Well, Ms. Morgan," he said, emphasizing my last name. "To tell you the truth, you caught me at a bad time. I was dealing with my dad and some of his work shit, and honestly, I wasn't paying attention. And for that, I'm very sorry, but you did show up to my party, which I'll take as you giving me a second chance."

"I've never been big on second chances."

"Well, that's a shame. I wouldn't be here if it weren't for second chances."

I found his comment odd but brushed it aside as the bartender chimed in, "An extra dirty martini for you, miss."

"It's Miller, and thank you." Giving him my biggest smile, I slid over a five-dollar bill.

"You don't have to tip, you know. I always take care of my staff," Grey said.

"Oh, I'm sure you do. But he's cute, and he makes a great martini," I said, taking a sip for show. "Mmm."

His eyes darkened, a smoldering expression dancing across his face and making my insides flutter. "Miller, Miller, Miller…" he started. "You can't go around flirting with everyone but me." He swiped his thumb over his lip as he looked me up and down, motioning toward my dress. "Especially looking like that."

All the heat from my belly rushed into my cheeks. Instinctively, I dipped away from his gaze, grabbing my martini from the bar while I decided what to say next. The idea of a fun summer was at the forefront of my brain, and I couldn't ignore the way this was presenting itself at just the right time.

I confidently relaxed my body back in his direction, making sure to meet his eyes before letting the words slip from my mouth. "Who says I'm not flirting with you?"

Using my teeth to pluck an olive off the toothpick, I watched as Grey seemed to be at a loss for words.

His hand, the one that gleamed with that fancy watch, moved to his chin, rubbing the dark scruff that covered the base of his jawline. He clicked his tongue. "Well, isn't this going to be interesting."

"I sure hope so," I taunted before moving toward the living room. "See you later, Grey Prescott."

"If I'm lucky, Miller Morgan," he declared. "By the way, tell Sam I said hi."

His comment stopped me in my tracks. "Wait, how do you know I'm with her?" I asked.

"This town isn't very big, or did you forget?" He paused. "And my guy Anthony is head over heels. She's all he's talked about since last summer. He went on and on about how no other women compare to the women in Montauk, so much so that I felt compelled to make the trip to see for myself."

"That seems a little dramatic."

"Not as far as I can see," he mumbled under his breath.

Despite the obvious compliment, I continued. "Well, I appreciate the enthusiasm, and I'm really glad to hear that Anthony may be a better guy than I initially made him out to be. Sam deserves that."

"You might learn something about trusting those stereotypes of yours, like not to have them at all because most of the time they're wrong." His body was now casually resting against the wall, exposing his chest beneath the unbuttoned linen shirt he wore underneath his jacket.

I couldn't help but let my eyes wander for a moment, until I forced my martini glass to my lips. Taking a sip, I started to choke, the sting of the alcohol piercing the back of my throat like a hundred tiny knives.

"I'll keep that in mind," I stifled out.

*Focus, Miller.*

It took me a few minutes to spot Sam among the sea of people, but once I finally did, a sense of relief washed over me.

"You didn't tell me that Grey Prescott was the host of this outrageous party!" I shouted over the loud music.

"Huh? What are you talking about?" She looked at me, confused.

"Grey Prescott. The good-looking guy from the bar last night. This is his house."

"Well, I mean, honestly, that tracks. He's hot and he lives in a stunning house. May I ask what you're doing here then?"

It was my turn to be confused. "As opposed to being at home in my bed?"

"No, MJ. As opposed to being in Grey Prescott's bed. Remember, you're a grown woman and you have the right—no, you have a *duty* to go have some fun. Seriously. Go jump his bones."

"Oh my god. You're getting a little ahead of yourself over there. You got me out of my apartment, you got me into a dress, and you got me to a Montauk summer party. I'd say we are way ahead of schedule on this fun summer of ours," I informed her.

It was clear from the slight sway in her stance that unlike me, she'd enjoyed a few pre-party cocktails and now tipsy Sam was dying to break free. Thankfully, based on the comment from Grey, I felt more comfortable with Anthony being in charge of her tonight.

Confirming my suspicion of tipsy Sam, she changed the subject. "Take a shot with me," Sam insisted.

"I'm too old for that shit."

"C'mon! If you're too old, then I definitely am. Please? You just admitted you never come to parties like this, so you might as well enjoy it."

"Have a little fun, MJ." Anthony's voice hit me, triggering a memory and revealing a sliver.

Liv always used to tell me to "have a little fun." She was always the fun one in our duo, and she knew if she told me to, I would. She had a way of making everyone feel like it was time to participate, and even more so, making them feel like they *wanted* to participate.

I hesitated, flashes of those memories flooding back.

Grief was a funny thing.

One minute you were enjoying yourself, completely oblivious to the darkness that still hid in the shadows of your mind, and the next you found yourself drowning in a sea of memories. Although, with this particular memory, I couldn't help but smile, because if Liv could see me now, she probably wouldn't believe it. We always dreamed of partying in these houses, the ones that sat unoccupied for most of the year and then brimmed with life during the summer months. This was the exact kind of party we always wondered about—the ultra-exclusive ones you only heard about through the gossip that rolled through town. Now I was here, standing in the middle of one, and I had to cheers to that.

"I'm in."

"Wait, really?" Sam sounded unsure.

"Don't make me wait too long or I might change my mind."

"Anthony, two lemon drop shots, stat!"

"You've got it, babe."

Knowing that Anthony had been talking about her before he even made it back to town this summer gave way to a warmth in the depths of my belly. Although, that could've been the extra dirty martini too.

Either way, I liked it.

"I know I'm kind of drunk, but I think I'm into him. Like, really into him," Sam said.

"I'm here for it."

"You are? Okay, I'm not that drunk. Yesterday you were telling me off for hooking up with him again this summer and now you're here for it?" she asked as she stared at me, waiting for an answer.

"I know, I know, but let's just say he's growing on me," I responded. "Oh, and some insider information about him has been shared, and I'm happy to confirm he's earning my approval."

"Okay, now you have to fill me in. I need to know everything. I—"

"Two lemon drop shots." Anthony returned faster than I expected, and he wasn't alone. "This is my man, Grey."

The interruption caused Sam and I to both misplace our thought processes.

The name left his mouth, but Grey and I had already made eye contact. Something about the way he looked at me made me feel vulnerable. I looked down, double-checking that nothing on my body was exposed.

"Grey, this is—"

"MJ," he interrupted. "We met last night. And then again at the bar just now." His tense gaze never faltered from mine until he spoke again. "You must be Sam. Anthony hasn't stopped talking about you. It's a pleasure to finally meet you," he said, extending his hand.

Sam's face lit up, taking his hand in hers. "You too."

"Cheers to an unforgettable summer," Anthony said, grinning as he held up his glass, making eyes with Sam.

While I knew his toast was referring to him and Sam, I couldn't help but feel hopeful. Maybe this summer *would* be unforgettable, for all of us.

At least, I'd begun to let myself hope so.

# Chapter Thirteen

The tangy alcohol burned as it slid down my throat, immediately igniting a warmth in my body. The air around me buzzed and I found myself gravitating toward the dance floor.

"Sam, let's dance."

"You know I can't turn down an invitation like that," she said.

I tore her hand away from Anthony's but not before she placed quite the kiss on his lips, Grey and I awkwardly standing by. I tried not to make eye contact with him; the moment felt too intimate.

"She's mine now," I said, smiling as I pulled Sam in the direction of the sliding glass doors that had been left open for the night. Making our way toward the music, I stole a glance at the bar just in time for the cute bartender to send me a wink.

"Okay, he's cute," Sam teased.

"I thought so too, but—"

"But he's not Grey Prescott."

"That's not what I was going to say."

"Is it not?"

"I was going to say that I'm focused on enjoying dirty martinis and dancing the night away."

"Fair enough."

"But also, he's not Grey Prescott," I admitted.

We both burst into laughter as we stepped outside.

The night air was warm, but not unbearably so. The makeshift dance floor was located on a massive concrete slab that surrounded the pool. The music was thumping so loud, you could feel the crowd radiating from a few feet away. I wanted to be close to the DJ, but I couldn't seem to find him at first. Then I spotted a floating stage in the pool and realized that was, in fact, the DJ.

How in the hell was that even possible?

I weaved in and out of people until I found the perfect spot smack dab in the center. Just in time too, as the first notes of "Feels Like Summer" by Samuel Jack filled the space around us. I felt invincible.

There couldn't be a more perfect song for this exact moment.

I would've sworn Liv was here, dancing right next to me, experiencing this moment, this entire night. And in that instant, everything felt right. It had been years since the accident, and not a single day went by that I didn't find myself missing her, but I was proud of myself. Proud of how far I'd come.

Time had continued on, but somehow missing her still felt consistently present.

I didn't think I'd ever fully heal from losing her, and sometimes that was a hard pill to swallow. But being here and fully enjoying myself felt like something to be proud of. Something to share with her.

Sam grabbed both of my hands as we moved our bodies to the beat of the music and I tossed my head back, mouthing the lyrics.

When the song came to an end and the crowd seemed to disperse a little, I turned to Sam. "I'm going to grab a water, you want one?" I asked. "And I'm kind of in the mood to flirt."

Sam shook her head. "I like this MJ. She's a good time, a real good time."

I swayed to the bar, grinning ear to ear.

"Another dirty martini?" The bartender paused to flash me a smirk. "Extra dirty?"

"Actually, can I just grab a water?"

"Of course," he responded, reaching for a glass. "So, what brings you to *this* kind of party?"

"What? Don't I fit in?" I teased, knowing exactly what he meant by *this kind of party*.

"Oh, no. You fit in better than most. It was your use of the word *please* that really gave you away." He chuckled.

"Ouch." I laughed. "My friend is dating one of these guys and dragged me along so she wouldn't be alone. Although, I have to admit, I could get used to these kinds of drinks."

I leaned over the bar, resting both of my elbows on the top and holding my chin in my hands, making it clear that I was at least trying to flirt.

"Are you from around here?" I asked.

"No. I moved here a couple weeks ago from California. Just looking for something new."

"I wondered. I haven't seen you around before."

"Yeah, I'm still trying to get used to the small town feel of things. Like the whole everyone knowing everyone else thing."

"You'll get used to it, and then you'll never leave." My thoughts trailed off. "I will say, it's not a bad place to move to. I've lived here my whole life, and there is something really special about this town."

"Now it all makes sense," he joked. "But yes, I have to agree with you. There is definitely something special about this town."

He slid a tall glass of ice in my direction before filling it with water. "Well, I better get back to work before I get fired from my first job." His eyes darted from me to someone behind me. "But I'm happy to be your bartender all night," he said.

I picked up my water and swiveled back toward Sam, but not before his eyes caught mine. Grey's intense glare sent my heart racing as though I'd been caught doing something wrong. The rush of adrenaline was intoxicating.

He casually took a sip of his drink, the dark substance hitting his lips.

A Dark and Stormy.

He lowered his glass as his tongue traced his lips, catching any remnants of his drink before he effortlessly tipped it in my direction and shot me a wink.

Doing my best to appear unbothered, which was proving rather difficult, I raised my glass, smiled, and turned away. Pleased with myself and my ability to keep my composure, I quickly spotted Sam leaning against one of the cocktail tables that was set up around the perimeter of the pool.

"Holy shit, you were gone long enough. I thought maybe you decided to take Mr. Bartender into the bathroom for a little quickie."

"Funny," I scoffed. "No quickie, but I did enjoy flirting with him."

"That's a good excuse. I'll forgive you."

Before I could say anything else, I noticed she was holding two more shots. "Absolutely not, Sam."

"But, like, are you sure? Because I got Slippery Nipples, and everyone knows those are your favorite."

"Are you hand-delivering me a Bubba's breakfast sandwich in the morning?"

"If that's what it takes."

"Damn you. Fine."

"Don't act like you're not having fun," she said, handing me the shot glass full of light brown liquor. "I'm seeing a different MJ tonight. One that I think I could get used to."

"Oh my god, you're being so dramatic."

"Your flirting with the bartender was fun, but those stolen glances that you and Mr. Prescott having been sharing from across the room could make anyone hot and bothered."

I laughed, revisiting that moment, wishing I could feel that rush again. I didn't know how to explain it, but the way he looked at me made me feel desirable, like I was the only girl in the entire room. We barely knew anything about one another, but somehow, he felt familiar.

"You saw that?"

"I'm pretty sure everyone at the party saw that," she said.

The drinks were starting to go to my head as the words I spoke came a little easier and with less of a filter. "I mean, I'm not sure what it's about, but I can't say I'm not into it. He's hot, and my god, the way he looks at me has me tempted to see what else he can do."

I threw my hand over my mouth, shocked I'd spoken so many of my inner thoughts out loud.

"I don't blame you one single bit. That man is undeniably sexy and undoubtedly mysterious."

We both started giggling before she tugged my hand from the table and pulled me back toward the music. My body seemed to move more freely now, and I wasn't complaining. My dress spun perfectly with the rhythm of the music, and I found myself lost in a world of lyrics and dirty martinis. Did it get better than this?

Sam swirled me back to reality, and I noticed Anthony dancing up behind her. I let her go, finding myself back in my own world.

It was clear from the number of party people that'd made their way to the dance floor that the party was revving up, and just like us, everyone was gravitating toward the music. Obviously feeling the momentum, the DJ started a killer mix that faded into "Feel So Close" by Calvin Harris.

The music pumped through my chest and made me feel like Calvin Harris himself was playing a set right in front of me. As soon as the beat dropped, the crowd went wild. The movement drew the crowd closer, bodies filling in one after the other, but not in an annoying way, more of a cohesive way that made you want to keep dancing.

My hands flitted around my body, as if someone else had taken control. I felt free. For a second, I pictured myself as seventeen again, dancing in Caleb Davis's living room with Liv. We were so young, so carefree, and so innocently unaware of what lay ahead of us. The realization paused my happy thoughts, but only for a brief moment.

The presence of another person quickly pulled me back, his hot breath walking across my neck. "You probably shouldn't be dancing like that. Someone might think you're flirting with them and want them to join you." His voice was somehow smoother in a whisper tone, if that was even possible.

"That wouldn't be the worst thing in the world, would it?"

The words left my mouth, and immediately his body tensed behind mine. He lifted his hand and just barely ran his fingers up the sleeve of my dress. I paused, thinking to myself that if this dress didn't have sleeves, I might have simply melted from his touch on my bare skin.

For a second, I leaned my head back into his chest, getting caught up in the euphoria of it all. The outside air had dropped to cooler than it was before, but the air around the both of us was only getting hotter. Our bodies synced without any effort, smoothly swaying to the beat of the music.

"Depends on who that someone might be." His breath crawled down my neck this time, the smell of rum filling the air between his mouth and my nose. "Because if it's anyone but me, I can't think of anything worse."

"Good thing that someone is you then." I rotated my body, the want in his voice setting my skin on fire as our faces were only a few inches apart. He studied me as if I were his next meal, dark and hungry, and when he inched even closer, our lips nearly grazed one another.

All of this newfound confidence had me needing to catch a breath.

"I'm going to run to the bar, need anything?" I asked.

Grey's low but audible huff only fueled the desire in my belly.

"Yeah, I do." His pause was accompanied by a lopsided smirk. "I'm gonna need you to stop leaving me hanging like this."

"Don't forget, you were the one that said this was going to be interesting, remember?"

Peeling my body from his, I headed to the bar but veered in search of a bathroom because now that I'd stopped dancing, my bladder was screaming at me. Except, in a house this size, I had no idea where to start.

I found a promising hallway next to the bar and took my chances. The first door I opened was some sort of library. Floor-to-ceiling bookshelves covered three of the four walls. There was an overstuffed leather chair that resided just behind a dark wooden cigar table. The room was impeccable, but the urge to pee was stronger. I pulled the door closed and moved down the hallway.

The next door I opened was an abnormally large hall closet, although I shouldn't be surprised given that everything in this house appeared to be abnormally large. At the end of the hall, I stopped at a set of double doors, hoping there'd be a bedroom and preferably a bathroom behind them.

"Thank god," I said to myself.

The first pee after you started drinking had a sense of urgency unlike any other.

Stepping into the pristinely designed bedroom, I quickly admired it before spotting the bathroom and making a dash for it. I maneuvered my dress up as I sat, immediately feeling relief. Sitting on the toilet, I glanced around the room but immediately realized this wasn't just any bedroom. It was definitely the primary one.

The double sinks propped on opposite sides of the room were separate but connected by a center vanity that sat lower than the other two. They were modern but classic. The floating bases were natural wood–colored with black hardware and marble countertops. Two rounded black mirrors sat centered above the sinks, each one enhanced with a wall sconce that provided subtle golden light.

I moved toward the sink to wash my hands and was confused when I spotted the shower—or should I say bathtub? Or was it both? There was an enormous black bathtub sitting behind floor-to-ceiling glass shower doors. Both the bathtub and shower were confined to one, but it was the most breathtaking space I'd ever seen.

At least ten people could've showered at the same time, which I wasn't sure was necessary, but regardless, it was beautiful.

Tipsy MJ really struggled to stay focused.

I faced the sink once again, washing my hands, drying them, and making my way back toward the loud party. As I reached the doors, I grabbed for the handle, but as I pulled it open, someone else was pushing.

Then it all registered. This was Grey's house. Which meant this was Grey's bedroom.

# Chapter Fourteen

Grey watched me as he stepped closer, his cologne wafting through my nose as I inhaled deeply. The musky scent of citrus and masculine leather infiltrated my senses.

"I didn't expect it to be this easy to get you to my bedroom," he teased.

My heart was racing so fast I could feel it echoing through my ears. I didn't know if it was the drinks, the urge to rip his clothes off, or both, but either way, I was struggling with what to do next. My thoughts were fuzzy around him, but he didn't need to know that.

"You're ridiculous. I just needed to use the restroom, and this was the first one I found."

"Uh huh. Whatever you need to tell yourself," he said.

We were so close now I could feel his breath on my face.

"You do know that not every girl you come into contact with wants to sleep with you," I suggested.

Though, I couldn't decide which girl I was. Because at this exact moment, I was leaning toward the girl who *most definitely* wanted to sleep with him.

"You're right, but you're not every girl…" He trailed off. "That's been made abundantly clear by the fact that despite my best efforts, you've consumed my thoughts for the past twenty-four hours."

While I, too, had been struggling to think about anything that wasn't in the shape of a dark and mysterious six-foot man ever since our first encounter in the middle of the street, he was too smooth, and there was no doubt in my mind that he'd said that exact thing a million times before.

"Does that line usually work for you?" I taunted.

Before he could say anything, I stepped to the side and beelined for the door.

Just when I thought I was in the clear, he gently gripped my left arm, pulling me toward him. He held my hand against his chest, his heartbeat drumming against my palm. The steadiness made me feel closer to him, as if his heartbeat was doing its best to calm the racing of my own heart.

The look in his darkened eyes was different than before.

His mouth rested a mere inch from my ear, and the seduction in his voice as he said, "I don't use lines, but if I did, that wouldn't be the one I'd use on you, trust me," made my body quiver.

A rush of want flooded through me, and in that split second, I wanted to kiss Grey Prescott so fucking bad, but I couldn't muster up enough conviction. Instead, I deflected.

"What line would you use then?" I said, half curious, half trying to give myself time to decide what to do next.

"There isn't a single pick-up line that would accurately describe what I want to do to you."

I swallowed at the ruggedness of his tone.

I assumed that our flirting was just that—flirting. And while I'd allowed my thoughts to wander to places that I probably wouldn't admit out loud, I never imagined in a million years that he'd toyed around with similar thoughts.

"I've run through all the different ways I'd have my way with you ever since I saw you behind that bar last night. That red lipstick. Those tight little jeans. That white top attempting to hide what was underneath," he said, pausing to take in my reaction.

I didn't know if he expected me to respond, but there was no chance I was going to be able to form any words.

"And this," he said, barely grazing my leg as his free hand brushed up my dress. "You show up to my party. At my house. Looking like this."

The heat of his fingertips ignited like fire. If I wasn't trying to ignore the desire growing throughout my body, I would've thrown my head back in pleasure. His mouth nuzzled close to my neck, not quite touching it but close enough.

Chills flooded my entire body, and the tiny hairs on my skin sprung up, electrified.

"Careful." My breathing appeared calm, at least for the moment, as I did my best to hold my own. "I'm not wearing any panties."

Grey's eyes flew to mine, his jaw clenched as he tightened his grip on my left thigh. "Don't tempt me, Miller Morgan."

I reveled in both his touch and his words, imagining what it would be like to feel his fingertips on every inch of my body. I swallowed hard at the thought.

"Or what," I said as I started to spin out from under his grasp.

I didn't get far before he nudged me back against the door, pinning my hands to his chest. He wrapped his fingers around the base of my neck, his eyes staring straight into mine, those gold flecks seemingly more prominent in his low-lit bedroom.

The want crawled up my throat.

*Fuck it. I'm supposed to be living a little, right?*

I pushed my lips into his and my entire world erupted.

He wasted no time returning the favor. I moved my hands from his chest and grabbed both sides of his sport coat, pulling him as close as I could. Our kiss was intoxicating, and I couldn't get enough.

A soft whimper left the back of my throat and his grip tightened around my neck. The thirst growing between us was obvious, and within seconds, his tongue was crashing through the barrier of my lips. Our mouths eagerly clung to one another, desperate for the taste.

But then, right on cue, my intrusive thoughts came barreling in, one right after the other, pulling me straight out of this dreamy moment and into a massive wave of doubt. What was I doing here? This wasn't me. I didn't do random hookups like this.

I pulled away.

"Well, aren't you full of surprises," he said, swiping his finger across his lower lip.

I stood silently, trying my best to regroup.

"You okay?" he asked, but before I could say anything, a knock rattled behind my head. He stepped back, allowing me to move from the doorway before opening the door.

I found myself wanting to reach for my lips, missing the presence of his. While his back was turned, I stole a touch.

"Hey, man. Sorry, I need a bathroom."

"Seems like a common theme tonight," he responded. "Be my guest." He motioned toward the bathroom.

Bewildered by the feelings that were running rampant, I took once last glance at the delicious man in front of me, hoping to sneak a peek without him noticing, but his eyes were already on me. No words left either of our mouths, but they didn't have to. What just happened between us was more than either of us were prepared for, that much was clear.

"I'm sorry," I muttered. "I have to go."

There was something inexplicable yet natural that gravitated us toward one another, but I couldn't figure out what it was. I was conflicted in more ways than one. Denying the pull I felt, I made my way back to the commotion of the party.

The bar was crowded, but I stopped anyway in an attempt to get another water. The pleasure fog began to lift, and slowly the reality of Grey Prescott washed over me.

It came all too naturally for him. He was a smooth talker, he was gorgeous, and he had a shit ton of money. With a trifecta like that, he didn't have to try to get women, that I was sure of.

I was attempting to lean into this whole live a little thing, but my ability to do so was dwindling. I wanted to be a fun, carefree girl, one who had random hookups, but it was hard. Although, thanks to that moment of short-lived, I'd at least have that moment between us in my memory for the rest of eternity.

Between the lasting tingle on my lips and my incessant thoughts, a sense of tiredness overwhelmed me. I decided it was best to call it quits.

I searched the party for Sam and Anthony but couldn't find either one of them. In fairness to Sam, I'd been a little MIA, and honestly, I wasn't sure for how long. When I was drinking, time either seemed to stand still or move at a ridiculously fast pace.

And after that kiss, it had done both.

From the look of it, the party was dying down—some people lounging by the pool, others walking toward the door. I pulled my phone from the gold clutch around my wrist and was shocked to see the time—half past midnight—and two missed calls and a text from Sam.

Shit.

Sam:

> Not sure what the hell happened to you! I'm guessing that you had a swift exit from the dance floor and made your way home. I'll call you tomorrow. Love you.

I never wanted anyone to worry about where I was, ever. I quickly typed a message back.

Me:

> So sorry, long story. Chat tomorrow. Love you.

Now I was pressed with figuring out how in the hell I was going to get home. My apartment was only about two miles away, so walking seemed like a good option, but I knew ordering an Uber was the smarter one. The loud music from inside was making it hard to think, so I waded through the remaining partygoers and out the front door.

As I stepped outside, the cool ocean air felt refreshing and a bit sobering. I hadn't realized just how flushed I was until now, and the breeze flowing through my dress was everything. I took a seat in a rocking chair at the front of the wraparound porch. The white wooden chair gave a stunning view of the lilac hydrangeas that I'd admired so much upon arriving here tonight.

From this spot, a three-car garage came into view. A black silhouette was leaning up against the side of the garage, which piqued my interest. The rocking chair creaked as I stood, and as I walked over, I was surprised to see the cute bartender smoking a cigarette.

"Funny seeing you here," I said.

His body perked up. "Just catching a few minutes to myself before I head out."

"Oh! I didn't mean to interrupt," I said.

"Nah, you're good. It's Miller, right?" he asked, sucking in a large breath of cigarette.

"Yeah," I responded. "You're already leaving? The party isn't even over yet."

"Says the girl standing out in a dark driveway all by herself." He chuckled before adding, "They cut a few of us because the party is slowing down. Granted, I've never been part of a seven-bartender staff, but then again, I've never been to a party like this."

"Ha. Then it's a first for both of us. Although, these kinds of parties are pretty frequent during the summer months. Things really slow down after Labor Day though, so enjoy the chaos and the extra-large tips while you can."

"You're not kidding about that. The guy who owns this house handed me five hundred dollars in cash and told me I made some of the best dirty martinis he'd ever had. And you want the kicker? I'm pretty sure I didn't make him a single dirty martini the entire night, but who was I to disappoint the man?" he said, pleased with himself.

The butterflies in my stomach rumbled against their cage that hung on my insides.

"Oh. Well, I guess if he's going to throw these kinds of parties, the least he can do is take care of the people he hires, right? And I can't say I disagree with him; those were some damn good martinis."

"Thank you. I take pride in my skills. And trust me, you're not going to find me complaining about any tips," he said, stepping away from the garage and into the light.

Now that I was able to see him in a less hazy light, I wasn't sure he qualified as a man. In fact, looking closer at him, he was far too young for me, maybe twenty-one at most. He was cute, but cute was the only way to describe him, and after the recent encounter I'd had with Grey Prescott, it was crystal clear that I wasn't after cute.

He interrupted my thoughts. "The better question is, why are you out here? You're too pretty to be out here all alone."

Now his flirty comments made me silently giggle.

"Well, aren't you sweet, but I'm not alone. I'm talking to you. And I'm getting ready to order an Uber."

"Wait, do you need a ride?" he asked. "I'm about to head back to drop off one of the catering vans at Floyds." He pointed in the direction of the white van parked a few steps away. "I'm happy to give you a lift back to town. I don't know where you live, but considering the size of the town, I can't imagine it's too far."

Floyds was a quick walk from my apartment, and while he was still technically a stranger, there was something comforting about riding with him versus an Uber driver, especially considering my brutal anxiety of cars. Floyds had been around for years, and Floyd himself was a regular at The Wharf, so I felt confident in his choice of employees.

"Really?" I asked. "That would be perfect."

He smiled, pushing the key he held in his hand until we heard the doors of the van unlock.

"Don't mention it. I'm Adam, by the way."

"Nice to meet you, Adam."

Relief washed over me, knowing that I'd secured a ride home and would be crawling into my bed in a matter of minutes. I walked to the passenger door, but before I could grab the handle, someone else beat me to it.

"So, your parents taught you not to give your name to strangers, but they didn't teach you not to get in a car with one?" The deep voice on the back of my neck was one that I'd never forget after tonight.

"Sir," Adam sputtered.

"Call me Grey," he interrupted.

"Grey, I was just giving Miller a ride home so she didn't have to wait for an Uber." His fingers fumbled with the keys.

My eyes were glued to Grey, watching the tiny muscles in his structured jaw tense once again. "I appreciate it, Adam, but I'll make sure she gets home. Thanks, man," he insisted.

"Sure thing. Thanks again, Mr. Prescott. I mean, Grey."

With that, Adam slid into the driver's seat and drove up the driveway in record time.

"You weren't actually just going to get into a car with a complete stranger simply because you wanted to leave my party that badly, were you?"

"As a matter of fact, I was. Floyd is a regular at the bar and a friend of my dad's, so I knew I had nothing to worry about," I mocked. "I'm just ready to be home. I've played Cinderella long enough."

"You could've just asked me for a ride before you decided to bolt from the party."

"A ride," I started. "From you?"

"Yes, from me. At this point, I don't see anyone else out here capable of giving you one," he said.

"Grey," I started. "You've been drinking. I already go out of my way to avoid cars, so there is no way in hell I'm getting into a car with someone after they've been drinking."

"First off, I'd never drink and drive. Ever. Secondly, I've only had a few sips of my Dark & Stormy over a four-hour period." His voice emphasized the name of the cocktail. "Regardless, I wouldn't be the one driving you."

"Okay, well in that case, I'm just as capable of ordering an Uber as you are," I blustered, a little miffed.

"MJ, I'm not ordering an Uber. My driver will take you."

"Your driver?" I asked.

Right on cue, a black SUV crept down the driveway.

"Oh." I folded my arms in defeat. "And by the way, I didn't bolt. I just needed some fresh air and decided it was probably time for me to go home after all that." My hand uncontrollably reached for my lips.

He cocked his head. "I disagree. In fact, I don't think you could've chosen a worse time to leave. However"—he threw his hands up in defeat—"if a ride is what you wanted, a ride is what I would've given you."

"Easy for you to say," I chirped.

"What do you mean?"

"This is just a regular Friday night for you. Not for me. I don't normally go to parties like this, in houses like that." I pointed to the porch. "And I never kiss guys like you. I'm just a girl who grew up in a vacation town and never got to vacation."

A coy smile displayed itself on that handsome face of his. "But yet, here you are... attending a party like this, in a house like that." He tenderly brushed his bottom lip. "And kissing a guy like me."

"Yeah, I know. Tell me about it. All I was trying to do was embrace the chaos a little, mix things up a bit. Not continue to live the same repetitive life that I have ever since..." My words were coming so fast I almost didn't stop in time. "I was just trying to live a little, you know?" I paused. "What am I talking about, of course you do. Look at you."

"Actually, I don't know it as well as it may seem. My days might look different than yours, but they're just as monotonous. Trust me."

The silence hung heavily in the air.

"Maybe we both need a lesson on letting loose." He chuckled, but his words illuminated a sliver.

What would Liv tell me to do at this exact moment?

The urge at the bottom of my belly told me everything I needed to know.

"Ms. Morgan." Grey reached for the rear passenger door. Guiding me into the back seat, he placed his hand on the small of my back, his fingertips like tiny sparks. "A ride home."

Our eyes locked as he went to shut the car door, but before he could, I shoved my hand in the way. "Come with me?" I asked.

His eyes darkened and he traced his tongue along his bottom lip.

"And the surprises just keep on coming."

Grey didn't seem like a summer fling kind of guy. He struck me as more of a one-night stand kind of guy, but either way, I was determined to embrace the chaos.

# Chapter Fifteen

"Where to, Mr. Prescott?" his driver asked from the front seat.

I didn't know how long we'd been sitting there in silence, but it must've been longer than I'd realized.

"MJ?" Grey asked.

"Oh. Um, I'm in the apartment building just across the street from The Wharf."

"Yes, ma'am."

The "ma'am" felt a little much, but who was I to argue.

"What does the J stand for?" Grey's seemingly interested comment caught me off guard. He appeared to be playing the part of a guy who gave a fuck about what my initials stood for, but at least this conversation was taking my mind off the fact that I was in a car.

"Jean. It's Miller Jean," I said, playing into it. "After my grandmother, but I've always just been MJ. My best friend started calling me that after we decided Miller was too much of a last name, and it just sort of stuck."

"MJ..." He paused. "I like it." His hand shifted, landing on his upper thigh. "So, MJ, why is it that you asked me to come with you?" The silence was loud, but his voice quickly filled the void. "Not that I'm complaining, trust me. But the way I remember it, you were the one who so abruptly stopped us earlier."

His comment was so straightforward, something I wasn't used to with him. We'd shared stolen glances, comments with hidden meanings, and even a kiss filled with so much tension I thought I might explode, but we had yet to talk about any of it.

While I tried to decide what I was going to say, I focused on the closeness of our bodies. His left leg was barely touching my right and feeling him that close again sent my thoughts wandering to places they shouldn't.

Oof. MJ. Focus.

"Do you want me to be honest?" My head shifted to look at him as my heartbeat shimmied in my throat, thankful for the darkness of the back seat and the security blanket it provided.

"You've been honest since the moment I met you, why would you stop now?"

I'd decided back at Grey's house that I needed to quit talking about getting out of my rut and start actually getting out of it. Things wouldn't change unless I changed them, and while in the big scheme of things that seemed daunting, having a little fling with Grey seemed like a doable start. And dare I say fun. Everything was temporary with him. He was here for a few months, gone for the rest.

"I decided to say fuck it and have myself a little summer fun, let loose, and I thought I'd start with you."

His gaze traveled to me, but I couldn't make out his expression. I'd hoped my comment wasn't too much, even though he'd told me to be honest.

But now, the silence was deafening.

Then, just when I was sure I'd made this awkward, I sensed his weight shift ncxt to me.

His presence crept closer as he leaned into the space between my jaw and collarbone, his head almost touching me. The scruff on his face tickled my cheek, instantly transmitting electricity to every inch of my body, and his mouth moved a mere breath from my ear. "I'll be the most fun you've ever had," he whispered.

Without hesitation, my hand jumped from my leg to his in an instant, my fingertips clenching his thigh while goosebumps erupted in anticipation.

The driver cleared his throat. "Mr. Prescott, we've arrived," he said before stepping out of the SUV.

Within seconds, the door was opening and Grey was making his way out of the car too, but not before taking my hand and pulling me out with him. "Thanks, Daniel."

"Of course, sir. Would you like me to wait down here for you?"

"No, he won't need a ride home tonight," I jumped in.

Grey's eyes flashed to mine, a devilish grin aimed in my direction. "I guess I'll be staying the night. I'll see you in the morning."

He tipped his hat and chuckled. "Have fun."

We made our way up the stairs, hand in hand, Grey following closely behind me. I fumbled for my keys, unlocking my door and eagerly tossing my stuff onto the counter. I didn't want to wait any longer.

For a split second, I thought about what this would look like in the morning, but I quickly pushed the thought aside. I was on a high, and I was going to ride this one out for as long as I could because I wanted Grey Prescott, and I wanted him now.

As he stood in the doorway of my apartment, I couldn't help but admire him. He was tall, strong, and so damn charismatic. His lush brown hair tousled just perfectly. The white collared shirt that lay underneath his jacket was unbuttoned enough for me to get a taste, but not enough for me to feel satisfied

I could've stared at him all night, except that wouldn't have been any fun, and I was desperate for fun.

"That dress needs to come off... immediately," he demanded.

And clearly so was he.

He stripped off his jacket, the light linen material of his shirt revealing the muscles in his arms. By this point, I really just needed to touch him, so I obliged his request.

I slowly maneuvered my arms as elegantly as possible, but before I was able to get myself free, Grey had removed the distance between us and was standing in front of me.

In one fell swoop, he'd turned me around and pulled my back against his chest, his breath hot on the nape of my neck. "Let me."

His fingertips edged up and down my arms, igniting little fires everywhere they went, until my dress fell to the floor.

My body relaxed. Completely. I tossed my head back into his chest.

His lips just barely connected with my skin, leaving little kisses all down my neck and onto my shoulder, and the tiniest gasp escaped my mouth.

"My turn," I said, twirling back to face him.

It wasn't until I saw the look on his face that I remembered I'd skipped the bra and panties tonight. The way his expression heightened as he drank up my naked body, like he was trying to hold himself back, made me feel sexy. Empowered even. I wanted to blame the martinis for this ridiculous amount of confidence, but that would be a lie. It wasn't the martinis that made me feel this way; it was him.

Slowly my fingers went to work. Each button revealed a little more than the one before it. And with every button, I lost a little more self-control. The desire in my belly was running rampant and the eye contact itself was enough to have me start begging. He tossed the white shirt on the back of my barstool behind us, the dim light in my apartment shadowing most of his upper body, but my god, the part that was visible was mouthwatering. Subconsciously, I nibbled on my lower lip.

As he edged closer to me, the rest of his body was highlighted in the moonlight that shone through the window. My eyes were immediately drawn to his chest and the prominent scar that perforated his flawless skin. I was intrigued, but I was more interested in trying to figure out how to get his hands on me as fast as possible.

I unbuttoned his khaki pants, inching toward his zipper without ever breaking our gaze, fully aware he was growing harder with each second.

"Are you having any fun yet?" I teased.

He raised an eyebrow, stopping my hands from unzipping his pants the rest of the way. "My fun hasn't even begun. Once I start, you're never going to want me to stop. That, I'll make sure of."

"Is that so? And where is it that you're going to start?"

Without hesitation, he said, "First, I'll let myself get lost in that body of yours. My eyes are begging to admire every inch of you with no distractions." His voice was steady and methodical, so much so that my heartbeat slowly began to mimic the rhythm of his voice.

As he closed the little bit of space that separated us, he went on. "Then, I'll touch you. Giving my fingertips—"

The word *fingertips* left his mouth, and simultaneously I felt his touch on my collarbone. I released a deep breath.

"—permission to explore everywhere."

We were breaths apart at this point, his soft mouth pressed into my ear. Chills covered my entire body by the sheer presence of this man so close to my naked body.

"I'll take my hands on a tour of you, starting here..." His left hand danced around my boob before firmly grasping it. The eagerness sent my body into pure ecstasy, and I shuttered my eyes closed as a soft moan left the back of my throat.

"Then I'll slowly make my way somewhere else..." He trailed off, but only for a second before he picked up where he left off. "Somewhere more deserving." His hot breath went missing, forcing me to open my eyes before he dragged his tongue across his perfectly plump lips.

I knew what he was referring to, but I wanted to *feel* it. This man was doing his damn best to work me up, and I was here for it. This was top-notch foreplay.

"Uh huh. Where?" I panted.

His right hand stayed put at his side while his left began making its way down my body. Tracing the outline of my body, he moved slowly. I arched my back, hoping to find more contact, because the fire that flickered from his fingertips was addicting.

"Am I getting closer?" he asked. But just when I thought he was going to give me exactly what I wanted, he paused and took a small step backward. My body did its best not to lose contact with his hands, but I stopped myself before I lost my balance, hastily putting myself back together before he noticed.

"Not even a little." I smirked.

If he was going to play the game, then so was I.

Strolling toward the kitchen, I stopped just short of the wicker barstool that sat underneath the kitchen island. Grey's shirt effortlessly hung on the back, and I shrugged it over my naked body and sauntered to the kitchen.

When I turned around, I was more than pleased with what I saw—his mouth slightly ajar, his gaze following my every movement. Moving toward the wine bottle that was perched on my counter, I pulled a glass from the cabinet.

"Would you like a glass, Mr. Prescott?"

A slight sense of astonishment decorated his face, but it wasn't long before it washed away and was replaced with that all too familiar grimace of his. The same one I'd quickly found myself yearning for.

"I'd love one, Ms. Morgan," he said as he moved into the kitchen, leaning against the pantry door right next to me.

His bare upper body was within my reach, but I refrained from following through with my inner dialogue. I grabbed another wineglass out of the cabinet, along with a corkscrew. I managed to gracefully open the bottle and poured the cherry-colored liquid into both glasses.

Turning in his direction, I handed him one glass and took the other into my hand. "Here you go," I said as I tipped the glass in his direction.

We both knew the end goal here. What in the hell were we waiting for?

I sipped a little wine from my glass, in every attempt to not be the one that was going to give in first. I pulled it away from my mouth a little too soon, feeling wine trickle down the side of my mouth. I attempted to wipe it before he could notice, but I was too late.

# Chapter Sixteen

I n a blur of movement, his glass was on the counter and so was mine. Before I knew it, his tongue was cleaning up the remnants of wine that'd fallen from my mouth. His mouth was so close to mine, flushing my desire to the surface.

Swiftly, he picked me up and placed me on the counter. The cold granite on my ass ripped my breath from my chest, forcing a gasp from my mouth.

"I'm not waiting any fucking longer to have my way with you," he panted, his thirsty eyes moving up and down my body.

"Please," I begged, my mouth salivating with the thought. I wrapped my legs around his lower half and used them to force him closer to me. His body fell into the empty space so perfectly, enough so that I could feel him everywhere. All of him.

His hands brushed both of my thighs as he rested them on top of the counter. His eyes flashed in my direction and within seconds, he was smashing his mouth against my lips, his tongue searching for mine, hungry and desperate.

I loved feeling like he wanted me, like he might combust if he didn't get more, so I was surprised when he pulled away. I desperately clung to his mouth until the very last second, enjoying the lingering taste of him as I ran my fingertips across my bottom lip.

"Please what?" he demanded.

A smirk danced across my face. "Please make me wish this wasn't temporary."

The tension in his jaw made me feel like I'd said something he didn't like, but he quickly stole me away from my thoughts as he started kissing my neck. My head fell backward as I let the pleasure devour my entire body.

My body scooted closer to the edge of the counter, desperate for him to move faster.

His mouth moved to mine once again, but this time it wasn't his mouth that took my breath away, it was his fingers as they pushed inside me. I instinctively reached out for him, grasping for anything that would keep me stable, landing on a handful of his delicious brown hair.

"Grey," I panted, gripping his hair tighter. "That feels so good. Please." I gasped for air. "Don't stop."

My praise must've fed fuel to his fire because he deepened his position inside of me, the movement of his fingers supplying me with an abundance of pleasure.

"I wouldn't dream of it." His cockiness sent a buzz right through me. "How am I doing so far?" he asked, his words tickling my mouth as he spoke.

If his fingers felt this good, it wasn't hard to imagine how the rest of him would feel. The thought itself had my body trembling.

I slowly peeled myself off the counter. The absence of his grip left me breathless, and the tiny whimper that escaped his mouth even more so. "You could do better…" I muttered as I casually slinked out of his shirt and dropped it to the floor.

This was thrilling, and we'd only just begun.

It wasn't long until I felt his presence close behind me. "Is that so?" He grabbed my arm as he pressed his body into mine. I was surprised, not by the sudden sound of his voice but by just how much of him I was feeling. He was aroused—that much I knew—and now I was going to get exactly what I wanted.

*Him.*

"You might want to be careful what you wish for," he continued, the warmth of his breath sending a match to the already ignited fire in the pits of my belly.

Without turning to face him, I responded, "I know exactly what I'm wishing for, and I'm getting a little impatient."

His grip on me strengthened and I felt my words hit their mark as his arousal grew against my back.

He spun me around and thrusted me against the closest wall. The greediness had me practically dripping with desire. Using my hands, I searched for the button on his pants, remembering I'd already started unzipping them earlier, making my job easier. He quickly ripped something out of his back pocket and threw it on the bed behind us. I slinked my way down, tugging at his khaki pants and boxer briefs too.

The pure sight of him standing there above me had me wondering how I'd even gotten myself here in the first place, but damn was I glad I did.

Maneuvering himself the rest of the way out of his pants, he demanded, "Come here. I want to be able to look you in the eyes when I make you come."

I bit my lip, inhaling. "That's fucking hot."

Our mouths crashed together with more intensity than before. Grey placed one hand around the length of my neck, devouring me with each stroke of his tongue, and I nibbled at his lip.

His breathless voice was hot as he whispered, "Give me what I want."

"And what is it that you want?"

"You."

As he trailed kisses over my collarbone, I inhaled deeply, attempting to breathe those last few words out into existence. "Yes. You can have me. Please fucking have me."

His fingers found their way inside again just as the words left my mouth.

I didn't know if it was all the buildup or the fact that we undoubtedly had chemistry, but either way, this moment was euphoric. So much so I went searching for something to help steady me. One hand landed on the bathroom door frame on my left and the other gripped his wrist as his hand still clung to my neck.

With every movement of his fingers came a bigger bolt of pleasure. I was teetering on the verge of an out of body experience, but I wasn't ready for this moment to be over yet.

"You feel fucking incredible."

The words sprung across my cheek as his lips hovered on the side of my mouth. A tiny, audible moan left the back of my throat and floated between us.

"Just in the past twenty-four hours I've imagined a hundred times what this would feel like, but not even my imagination could've dreamed up something this good," he panted, sweat beads forming on his brow. Releasing me from his possession, his gaze trailed up and down my body. "This is too good to let you finish already."

The absence of him was enough to have my body craving more.

"Over there," I said, motioning to the bed.

I stripped myself off the wall and pushed his body toward the bed. My palm landed on that permanent mark that I'd spotted earlier and his firm chest underneath it. A sinister grin sprawled across his face as he walked backward with my guidance.

"You can take control of me anytime you want," he muttered, taking a seat on the end of my bed.

"Be careful what you wish for," I mimicked.

"I know exactly what I'm wishing for, and I'm getting a little impatient." He winked playfully.

I dropped to my knees right in front of him, pressing his chest back until he was resting on his elbows before I placed my hands on top of his legs.

"God damn," he breathed.

I never took my eyes off of him, even after taking him in my mouth. I watched as he slipped into pure ecstasy from feeling my mouth around him. He wrapped his hand in my hair, gently guiding me up and down.

Subtle moans and soft whimpers left his mouth each time. "MJ. Holy shit."

The comment made me grin. I held all the power, and he knew it.

"Come here," he said, pulling me on top of him. "While I do enjoy that pretty little mouth of yours..." His fingers trailed my bottom lip. "I'd rather us both enjoy ourselves."

I reached for the condom that he'd tossed on the bed and tore it open.

"Let me," he said, taking the latex material from my hands as he rolled out from under me. He pushed me on my back and hovered above me, just far enough that I couldn't physically feel him.

With his right hand, he slipped the condom on, never breaking our stare. As I watched him, my fingers traced his sculpted body. The muscles in his arms were prominent as he held his weight above mine. The look in his eyes said he was ready whenever I was.

I subtly nodded and breathed, "Yes."

The consent floated in the air, but only for a millisecond before he spread my legs just wide enough for him to push himself inside. The size of him forced a gasp out of my mouth. I sucked in the air around us, allowing my body to ground itself amid the abundance of pleasure that was coursing through my veins. Eventually, my grip landed on the soft material of my bed sheets, clenching them with as much force as I could.

He pulled out too quickly. My body went with him, the desperation obvious. He then guided himself back in and a wave of shivers crashed through me. My mouth was slightly ajar as my breathing deepened. The barely audible "Fuck" tied to my breath floated between us as my lips rested against his cheek.

Our mouths were playing a game of foreplay themselves, struggling to find each other as we moved in tiny sporadic movements from the desire mounting below. With every thrust, he buried himself deeper.

Gazing up at him as he moved rhythmically back and forth, he looked close to the finish. I, however, wasn't. But per most one-night stands, that wasn't completely abnormal. And to be fair, he'd already far exceeded my expectations. Simply watching him as he neared the edge proved pleasurable in itself.

Just when I thought he was going to finish, the movement stopped.

His eyes met mine. "You think I'm just going let you watch?"

"Sort of?" I admitted.

Something ignited within his eyes, a desire of some sort. "One day you'll learn not to underestimate me."

Smoothly, his hand walked down my body, stopping right near the direct point of my pleasure. He used his fingers differently this time, more *efficiently.*

A needy moan slipped through my mouth. "Right there. Please don't stop."

With a rugged breath, he suggested, "Here?"

He emphasized his words while continuing to move his fingers in a circular motion, my body begging him not to stop. The movement was better than anything I'd ever managed to do to myself.

"Fuck, Grey," I said, my words staggered.

"Say it again."

"Say what?"

"My name," he rumbled. "Say it again because it sounds even better coming from your lips when I'm inside of you."

His copper eyes shifted, appearing darker than before. He moved his fingers with a little more intention this time, all while never losing his rhythm inside of me. I was seconds away from coming completely undone.

"Please, Grey... don't stop."

"Fucking hell, MJ. I'm going to come."

The words left his mouth and anticipation filled my belly. I was close, he was close, we were *close*.

I tightened my legs around his lower half as the pleasure surged through me. Grey plunged in once more as he neared the end. Despite his own pleasure building, he never stopped massaging my neediest areas. I was brimming with fullness, and my back arched as I reached the peak.

"Mm," he moaned, sinking into me, our bodies merged into one.

A whimper left my mouth as I dug my fingernails into his broad shoulders.

Our heavy breaths crowded the room around us. Grey rolled to his back and propped me onto his chest. I obliged, feeling the effects of what had just transpired in his increased heartbeat.

"Well, damn. That was more than I anticipated."

"I told you to be careful what you wished for," he teased.

"I'd wish for that over and over again."

# Chapter Seventeen

We lay in silence, but nothing about what we were doing was silent.

Our bodies spoke to each other, humming in harmony, breaths echoing through the air as our chests heaved in sync. I found myself tracing the divots on Grey's chest, exploring the parts of his body that I'd missed. My eyes diverted to the tattoo that lay just above his heart, a set of roman numerals.

I wanted to know more about it. Hell, I wanted to know more about him, but I didn't feel like I had the right to ask. After all, we didn't know anything about each other, and as much as I hated to admit it, I assumed that after tonight I probably wouldn't be seeing much of Grey Prescott. At least not like this. In all of his naked glory.

That realization made me both sad and relieved, which was confusing, I knew, but this whole night had been confusing. The idea of not experiencing this again, *him* again, left me uneasy, but on the other hand, that meant things wouldn't get complicated.

"Have you lived here your whole life?"

More personal questions?

"Um…" I stuttered. "Yeah, born and raised here. I always thought I would leave, but I guess I just never got around to it."

"It's always easier said than done to leave something you've known your whole life."

"Isn't that the truth. Sometimes I still think about leaving, but the longer I'm here, the further away it feels," I said, choosing to be honest.

"It's always going to feel far away until you do it, you know? If you want to leave, you should. Because no matter what, you can always come back. Home will never not be home."

I lifted my head and rested it on his chest, snagging a better view of him. His hand was tucked behind his head and he looked relaxed—his eyes pointed at me, his lips just barely parted, and his breathing perfectly content.

"Home will never not be home. I like that," I said. "I didn't know you were such a wealth of wisdom, Grey Prescott."

"There's a lot you don't know about me." A sense of hesitation resided in his voice before he spoke again. "Stick around and you might find out more."

"Is that an invitation?" I teased, even though his comment made me nervous. Afraid of the silence, I kept talking. "Speaking of, how come I've never seen you in Montauk before?"

"Who says you haven't?" he responded.

He interlocked our fingers together and raised them in the air as he examined how they mingled with one another.

"Trust me, I would've remembered you."

His broad smile revealed each one of his perfect teeth. "It's my first time back to town in years. Life hasn't always played nice, and unlike you, it was easier for me to leave and harder for me to come back. But I wanted this summer to be different, so I finally got back here. And it seems I made the right decision."

He was speaking in riddles, but as hard as I tried to decipher what it was he was saying, I couldn't figure it out.

"But Montauk is exactly how I remember it," he went on. "It's just as perfect as it was all those years ago. Being back here makes me wish I wouldn't have waited so long."

As I listened to the words that left his mouth, the vulnerability of it all was a little uncomfortable. Thankfully, the sudden urge to pee gave me an excuse to catch my breath.

"Sorry, I have to go to the bathroom." I maneuvered out of the bed, taking the bedsheet with me. "But Grey?"

"Yeah?"

"Don't dwell on the past. It has a way of bringing down your present."

He laughed, a low wholesome laugh. "Well, well, well. Look who the insightful one is now."

I pranced into my bathroom and closed the door behind me, the weight of my body falling heavy against it. I released a deep breath before pushing myself off the door and making my way to the toilet, my thoughts running wild.

I wasn't sure how I wanted to proceed next. I'd already told his driver he was staying the night, so casually expecting him to leave probably wasn't in the cards. And it wasn't that I wanted him to leave. It was that I'd enjoyed this way more than I expected, which meant allowing him to stay only gave me more time with him. Pretty sure the definition of letting loose didn't include anything beyond fucking.

"See, this is why I need you Liv," I whispered to myself. "I can't do this whole carefree thing. I'm always too worried about what comes next, always anticipating the other shoe dropping. And I already know what comes next with Grey... He goes back to New York. Ugh, why aren't you here to teach me how to be more like you? I hate that you're gone."

My whispers paused when I heard an unfamiliar ringtone. His voice was muffled through the door, but there was sense of urgency in it. The call was short, maybe a minute long, and then it was silent again.

"MJ?" Grey shouted before knocking on the door.

I yelled back, "Yeah, I'll be out in one sec."

"I have to go. I'm really sorry, but I just got a call and—"

"Oh, okay. No worries," I butted in, doing my best to mask the disappointment that hovered beneath the surface. I was thankful for the door separating us because my facial expressions weren't easy for me to disguise.

"I'll see you around?" he asked, sounding a little unsure of himself.

"Yeah. Sure. I'll see you around."

I'd finished going to the bathroom just as his phone rang but found myself still standing there with my sheet chaotically wrapped around my naked body, glaring at my reflection.

Slowly pushing the door open, I peered around my apartment. And just like that, he was gone.

I walked to my closet and threw on an oversized T-shirt and some black boy short undies before stumbling back to my freshly fucked-in bed. The blankets were rumpled and some of the pillows had made their way to the floor. I put it back together, very half assed, partially because I didn't want to think about it, but more so because I just wanted to close my eyes.

I tried, like *really* tried.

But every time I attempted to sleep, my mind wouldn't allow it. Instead, when I closed my eyes, I was met with flashes of him. *Everywhere.*

His lips. His body. His mouth.

A few times I reached up and touched my lips, just to make sure he wasn't still there.

The thought of never seeing him again, or at least never seeing him like I did tonight, left an idling pit in my stomach. Initially, he was going to be my outlet for a little fun, and while he'd absolutely been that, I'd started to pick up on pieces that might prove I'd been wrong about him. But the reality of the situation mocked me. This was a one-night stand, and it made me feel silly to think of it as anything else. Anything more.

He didn't, because if he had, if there was something more, he wouldn't have left.

Sometime between the Grey Prescott hallucinations and me telling myself to knock it off, I drifted to sleep.

"Mmm. Grey," I whispered, feeling his fingers trace my inner thigh.

"MJ, open your damn door." Sam's voice sounded distant, but the obnoxious pounding on the door did not. I blinked my eyes open, realizing I'd been dreaming and *wasn't* in fact having sex with Grey Prescott again.

Mental note: This was what I got for attempting to have a fun summer. The wild one-night stand was something I'd prepared for, but the trench of persistent thoughts about it was not.

"Holy shit, I'm coming," I yelled in the direction of the knocking as I stumbled out of bed and rubbed my temples.

Swinging the door open, a gust of Bubba's breakfast took over my sense, greasy and satisfying. Exactly what this hangover needed.

"Oh my god, you are the best human," I said, grabbing the grease-stained bag of food out of her hands.

"You're hurting that bad?" she asked, walking into my apartment and sitting down on one of the barstools. "I figured you came home and went straight to bed. I half assumed you would've been on your morning run when I got here."

"Ha. Not happening." I laughed. "Today will consist of vegging out on the couch and catching up on some of the trashy TV I missed earlier this week. Plus, it's rainy, so basically the weather is begging me to be lazy."

"Fair enough. So, how'd the rest of your night go? I tried to find you before we left."

"It was... eventful, to say the least."

"Eventful as in Mr. Prescott eventful? Or eventful as in cute bartender eventful?"

I walked over to the counter and grabbed a paper towel before ripping the warm bag open. "This sandwich is heaven on earth. I don't know what I did to deserve a friend like you, but I'm so grateful," I told her.

"You're so damn dramatic. And you're also trying to change the subject. But based on the two wineglasses sitting on the counter behind you, you've got some explaining to do." Her smile gave way to her excitement as she sat on the barstool with her arms crossed, patiently awaiting the metaphorical tea.

"Shit," I muttered, turning to see the half-drunk glasses of wine. Memories of what took place right here, in this exact spot, had chills invading my body. "Well, considering the bartender turned out to be far too young for me, it's safe to say it was not eventful in terms of the cute bartender."

"And what about Grey?" She was virtually falling out of her seat waiting for my response.

"What about him?" I took a bite of my sandwich, hoping if my mouth was full, I might buy myself some more time to decide what details I wanted to disclose.

"C'mon, MJ. Spill."

"Hmm. Where do I start? I went to the bathroom last night and accidentally found myself in his bedroom. Before I could get out of there, he came in. We found ourselves in quite the predicament and ended up making out, but then we got interrupted by a drunk dude needing to pee." I paused, proud of myself for sounding calm despite the elevating beat in my chest that would suggest otherwise.

"What. You're lying…"

"I'm not." I smirked. "And that was only the beginning."

Sam's mouth was slightly open before this conversation, and now it was practically touching the counter. "Please tell me that is his wineglass sitting on your counter?"

"That is his wineglass sitting on my counter." I scrunched my face, trying not to show how much I was relishing the fact that I'd slept with him.

"Oh my hell," she said. "The girl who didn't even want to go to the party last night ended up bagging the hot-ass host of said party. Don't say I never did anything for you."

"If I remember correctly, you had your own priorities last night."

Sam blushed. "Anthony is pretty great. In fact, he was the one who reminded me of the Bubba's breakfast delivery that we needed to make this morning."

"He's already a winner in my book then. Is he waiting for you?"

"No, he dropped me off and said he was going to run a few errands, but I told him I was headed to The Wharf after this anyway."

"Well, isn't that sweet," I responded. "You got a fuck and a breakfast."

"I'm assuming by that comment that Grey didn't offer as much?"

"Hardly. He didn't even stay the night. Which is fine, honestly, it was probably for the best." My thoughts trailed back to last night. "After we had sex, we started talking, and he seemed so genuine."

"Okay, wait, I'm lost," she said. "You had sex, and then he wanted to get to know you, and then he left, but you're glad he did?" she questioned. "I mean, I understand in most cases people get to know each other before they sleep together, but does the sequence of events really matter?"

"No, obviously not. It's just that I didn't anticipate him to be that kind of guy, so then I didn't know what to do next. I went into it thinking we met each other at a party, we could hook up and just see each other around town here and there. So his gentleman-like tactics really threw me for a loop and I ultimately came to the conclusion it was probably best he leave."

"My god, your thought process is absurd. And I say that in the nicest way possible."

"Sure you do," I mocked. "Okay, but in fairness to me, he was the one who got a phone call and left in a hurry. It wasn't like I just hid in the bathroom until he left."

"That does make it little bit better, because I definitely wouldn't have put that past you," she joked. "Anthony did say Grey has some shit he's been dealing with, so maybe that's why he left in such a hurry."

"I mean, maybe. Or maybe after we both got what we wanted, it just made sense," I replied, doing my best to sound uninterested. "Anyway, I'm working at seven tonight. Dad wanted me in a bit early because of how crazy Thursday and Friday were. He told me they did a record night last night, which is kind of surprising considering the amount of people at Grey's party."

"No shit. This weekend already feels way busier than the last couple of years combined," she said. "Speaking of, I should probably head out. Chris closed the bar last night and we all know what that's going to look like."

Our giggles filled my small apartment.

"I'll see you tonight." I moved toward my front door just behind Sam. "Thanks again for breakfast. You're saving lives left and right."

"See you tonight. Love you."

"Bye. Love you."

I closed the door and made my way back to my breakfast sandwich, grabbing my phone from the counter first. I let myself mindlessly scroll through social media. I was bound to do whatever I could to keep from thinking about last night's events.

Although, without even realizing it, I pulled up Google and typed in *New York*. Random facts about the city and population popped up, which I wasn't looking for, but in all honesty, I wasn't sure what it was that I *was* looking for.

The uneasiness washed over me and I exited out of my search and pulled up social media.

Shades of red, white, and blue appeared on my screen. Pictures of Memorial Day weekend flooded my feed, and a sudden sadness washed over me. Holiday weekends were everyone's favorite in town, and as much as I loved these weekends, there would always be a sadness that lingered.

*Liv.*

Not a single day went by that I didn't think about her. While every day brought its own memories, holiday weekends served the most. The good, the bad, and the downright awful.

Years had filled the gap since that specific Labor Day night, and while things had definitely gotten easier, I still found myself struggling through some of the hard moments. After the accident, I spent a few years in weekly therapy until I thought I'd had an appropriate amount of time to grieve the loss of my best friend. And yet, as I stood here in my kitchen, all these years later, I didn't think there would ever be enough time for me to grieve her.

I found myself missing her in moments like these, when I had something to tell her or something to talk to her about. Times when I wished I could just pick up my phone and hear her voice on the other end. Times when I wanted nothing more than to go sit on the beach with her, toes dangling in the water as we gushed about the previous night's hookups and checklists for the summer. Those were the moments that felt the hardest.

If I was honest, I was afraid no one would be able to fill the hole she left behind, and honestly, that scared the shit out of me. The simple thought of it could send me spiraling. Determined to avoid that, I took another bite of my delicious breakfast sandwich, curled up on my couch, and lost myself in shitty reality TV.

# Chapter Eighteen

Nearly a week had passed since that night with Grey, and I was doing my best to push it aside, but I'd be lying if I said I didn't think about it at least once a day. I hadn't heard a single thing from him, and it seemed like I wasn't going to.

Moseying to my room, the open computer screen caught my eye. I desperately wanted to write, I *needed* to write, but I still wasn't exactly sure what I wanted to write about. There were some ramblings of different ideas here and there, but nothing that stuck. And that frustrated the hell out of me.

When I was younger, I used to write all kinds of short stories. I could put something together in a week. You want a rom-com? How about a fanfic starring your favorite band member? Or even better, what about an emotional story of loss and love? Great, because I could've given you any of those at any given moment.

And now I spent hours staring at this stupid-ass screen with a bunch of nonsense typed up and all I wanted to do was scream. It was no coincidence that my writing had suffered after the accident. Hell, it'd taken me years to even warm up to the idea of writing at all, let alone think it was a good idea to try writing a full-blown novel.

My fingers touched the cold metal, slamming it shut. "Fucking useless," I mumbled.

I clicked on a summer playlist on Spotify and laid my phone on the bathroom counter, hoping the music would lighten the mood that I'd found myself in. I dropped out of the matching sweatsuit I'd been wearing.

My music jam session worked, and I was feeling a bit lighter after my steaming hot shower. And thankfully so, because I was headed to The Wharf for my shift and didn't need Sam, or anyone else for that matter, suspecting a single thing.

I opted for a royal-blue sundress. A surprising choice in comparison to my usual jeans ensemble, but it was supposed to be hot as hell and the bar didn't tend to have the best air circulation. It most certainly wasn't because I wanted to look the part in case a tall and dark someone happened to grace us with his presence.

Wallet, check. Keys, check. Phone, check.

I grabbed my stuff and headed out. My mood had already shifted a bit, but it lifted even more so after I made my way onto Reef Road and the town's energy surged around me.

"MJ, just let it go," I muttered repeatedly to myself as I made my way across the street.

The patio was aglow from twinkling lights and music floated through the air, drowning out the conversations. There wasn't a single open seat, and inside wasn't much different.

Dad bombarded me as soon as he saw me come through the front door. "Shit. MJ, I'm glad you're here. Sam is getting slammed behind the bar. This crowd is nuts. I haven't seen anything like for years, but I love it." His smile stretched from ear to ear.

This place meant so much to Dad, to our entire family, so seeing The Wharf brimming with people spilling onto the patio made my heart so full.

"Ah! Me too." I smiled back.

"By the way, I love the dress. It looks very nice," he said, winking in my direction before disappearing behind the door that led to the kitchen.

I was feeling extra grateful to all the people here, and also a little grateful that Dad noticed the more than normal effort I'd put into my outfit choice. His comment gave me the affirmation that I needed.

I wiggled my way through the bustling crowd of people engulfing the bar, sneaking glances every now and then just to see if I could catch a glimpse of anyone familiar. No such luck. Finally, I made it to the bar, flipped up the countertop, and stepped through before taking up residence on the opposite side of Sam.

"Shit. This is wild. You should've called me, I could've come in sooner."

"No worries." She slung three shot glasses out of the dishwasher and poured what I suspected was a Washington Apple into each glass, peering over her shoulder. "Based on your texts earlier, I figured you needed a good couch rot before coming to this madhouse."

"I appreciate you for that. The couch rot was top notch. But it's probably good that I have to work because if I sat there any longer, I might have become one with the couch." We both giggled simultaneously. "Anything eventful happen yet?"

"If this is you casually trying to ask if there have been any handsome city boys in tonight, then no. Nothing eventful on that front. However, Chris over there is about to have himself an eventual night by the looks of it."

I followed the direction of her finger and ended on Chris and some girl I'd never seen before aggressively making out against the wall of the bar. "Lovely. I'm sure Dad is going to be thrilled to see one of his employees sucking face while on the clock."

"Let the man live," Sam said. "He's desperate for some female attention, and it looks like he found it in the form of a blonde from the city."

I took a few orders, doing my best to multitask. "Hey now, didn't you find yourself a flashy summer hookup from the city as well?" I pressed.

Sam was at the far end of the bar, taking care of her own customers. "Speaking of flashy summer hookups..." The words left her mouth, and my stomach immediately sank while my heartbeat rapidly increased.

I thought she'd spotted Grey, hence the wild body reaction, but instead, I looked up and saw Anthony strolling to the bar. A wave of disappointment pounded against my insides, returning my stomach to its rightful location and my heartbeat to a normal pace.

"Hey, girls!"

"Hey, Anthony," I responded.

"Hi." Sam bounced over to where he stood, her face immediately lighting up. I'd never seen Sam so head over heels for a guy. She wasn't usually one to get attached, but who was I to judge.

I had a one-night stand and now I was showing up to work in sun-dresses and scanning the room for any sign of the guy.

"Hey, MJ, have you seen Grey?" Anthony's face was as casual as could be.

"Uhm, me?" I paused. "No. I haven't seen him since the night of his party." Which wasn't a lie. Although, it'd technically been the early hours of the following morning when I'd last laid eyes on him.

"Weird. He left his own party that night and no one's really talked to him since, except for a few random text messages in the group chat," he said.

"He probably left with a girl," I blurted out.

Anthony shook his head. "I doubt it. Grey doesn't waste his time on random hookups. He won't go after a girl unless he's really into them, and I can count on one hand how many times that's happened in the ten years I've known him. It probably had something to do with his family, but it was sort of odd that he left his own party..."

My cheeks felt red hot from Anthony's comment. Sam kicked me behind the bar before clearing her throat and pulling me back into the conversation.

"Oh. Yeah. He left with me to give me a ride back to my apartment. But he got a phone call shortly after we got there. Seemed like something important," I said.

Anthony's face brightened. "Ah, makes sense. The phone call, I mean."

"It does?"

"Yeah. I'm sure it was some family *emergency*," he said, emphasizing the word with air quotes.

The confirmation that it was probably family-related and not girl-related had the butterflies in my belly drying off their wings.

I went back to taking orders. Some rum and Cokes, vodka sodas, a handful of beers, and a few rounds of shots later and the night was moving faster than expected.

"Dude, look!" Will shouted, motioning to the TV that hung above the crowd in the corner of the bar. He was part of Anthony's group, most of whom were still lingering, which was fine by me because their tips were better than anyone else I'd served.

"What?" Anthony and a few other guys responded, turning to see what he was gawking at.

Intrigued, I looked too.

# Chapter Nineteen

Those copper-colored eyes were just as penetrating through a TV screen.

Standing tall and confident in the most dashing blue suit was Grey. His generally effortlessly styled hair was now done with much more effort and product in it. His casual, routinely unbuttoned linen shirt was replaced with a stiffly pressed white-collared one and accompanied by a burgundy tie. His stance was somewhat protective as he stepped into the spot next to the most beautiful older woman I'd ever seen.

She wore a cherry red pantsuit that paired exquisitely with her black heels and matching red lipstick. Her arms interlocked with an older man who stood front and center on a patriotically decorated makeshift stage. The man resembled Grey a smidge, but in a colder, much harsher sense of the word. His face held little emotion, and his eyes were decorated with dark circles that no amount of makeup could cover.

I was still trying to piece together exactly what I was seeing when a banner flashed across the bottom of the screen. *Breaking News:*

*Stanley Prescott Announces Campaign for Re-Election as Mayor of New York City.*

I took my gaze away from the TV, but the other prying eyes did not. Except Sam, of course, whose eyes were locked on me.

"Don't say a word. I don't want to hear anything you have to say right now," I said, shaking my finger back and forth. "And before you ask, no, I had absolutely zero idea about any of this."

She threw her hands up in surrender, her mouth hanging open in awe as she returned her stare back to the TV.

Shocked was a good way to describe my current state. I smiled at the fact that this, for the most part, confirmed Anthony's suspicion of a family emergency.

Then, peering at the TV from under my eyelashes, I immediately felt anxious. The realization I'd allowed myself to let him decide my mood for an entire week stared back at me.

I'd learned, especially after losing Liv, that once you let someone in, even just a tiny bit, you gave them a string of your emotions, a way for them to have a little tug on how you felt or what you thought. And god forbid that person ever left you, whether of their own free will or tragically. Because if that happened, you ultimately lost one of your strings forever. And as someone who had experienced that, it was really hard to ever feel whole again.

I'd done too well for too long, protecting myself and my emotions, never allowing anyone too far in, so this idea that Grey had already infiltrated tiny fragments of my mind scared the living hell out of me.

"Well, I guess the secret's out now…" Anthony's deep voice trailed off in my direction.

"Secret?" I responded.

"Grey never wants anyone to know who his father is. He says it makes people treat him differently and he feels like he's never able to make his own path because he's always following in the footsteps of his father. That's why he was so excited to come to Montauk this summer, because very few people know who he is. To most, he was just another guy from New York City."

"I mean, it makes sense, but is being the son of the mayor really all that bad? I feel like those footsteps might lead to opportunities that others would kill for a chance at," I stated.

"You haven't met Stanley Prescott," he ranted, allowing a tiny smirk to slip past the cracks of his lips.

Dad's voice came from behind me. "MJ, I love you, but I don't pay you to stand around and watch TV."

"Very funny, Dad."

"What has your attention anyway? I've never known you to watch the news." He chuckled as he took another load of dirty dishes from the server's station to the back.

Still partially trying to catch a few glimpses of the TV here and there, I went back to pouring shots and opening beers. It was in that moment that I realized just how different our lives were—Grey's and mine.

"Can I get a Dirty Shirley? I feel like I've been waiting for forever," a high-pitched voice shouted at me. The Jack Johnson currently playing through the speakers made it a little difficult to hear what she was saying, but I could tell she was annoyed. I recognized her. She was the girl Chris had been making out with earlier in the night.

"Yeah, of course. Dirty Shirley, coming right up."

The blonde didn't respond as I did my best to be quick with her request. Confrontation is my worst nightmare, and she looked like she could've medaled in it.

"Here you go." I smiled in an attempt to please her.

She scooped the drink from the table and returned to a group of girls who somehow all resembled each other. Hair, tan, boobs. Hell, even their faces looked like they'd been deliberately modified to mimic one another.

Once everyone at the bar appeared satisfied, I made my way to Sam. "I was wrong about the girl Chris was kissing. She is, in fact, awful."

Sam laughed. "I'm usually not wrong when it comes to reading people."

"Oh, is that so?" I suggested. "If you're such a good people reader, then what were your thoughts about Grey when you first met him?"

"Surprised you even care what my thoughts are," she said as she wiped down the bar.

"I mean, I don't really. Just more so interested in what you have to say."

"He seems nice. A bit intriguing. But I definitely feel like he's got some sad, damaged thing going on, or maybe he was just trying to hide the fact that his father is the mayor of New York City."

She pointed to the TV; his family still plastered all over the screen. "Either way, he'll do just fine for a summer fling."

"Ha. I'm not sure what we did the other night categorizes us as a summer fling, but glad to at least have the professional's opinion, just in case," I teased.

*Summer fling.*

At first, I wasn't sure I was interested in one. I figured a one-night stand would be enough fun for me to get my fill and continue on with my mundane life. But would having Grey Prescott to play with for the summer really be such a bad thing? Granted, the amount of real estate he was already claiming in my brain might signify trouble later on down the road.

Holy shit. Whiplash. I was so conflicted.

"Liv?" I murmured under my breath.

Although, as I stood here staring at this pristinely put-together man on the local news, I was realizing that I may not have to worry about any type of summer fling at all. Hell, I may never see him again. As far as I knew, he could be spending the remainder of his summer in New York City with no intention of stepping foot in this town again, at least not for the foreseeable future.

The bar stayed fairly busy the rest of the night but started to die down around ten.

"I'm going to go take the empties to the trash and grab some refills," I said in Sam's direction as I held up the empty liquor bottles. "Why don't you head home, you've been here a lot longer than me."

"You sure?"

I nodded, regripping the black plastic bags.

"Oh my god, you're the best. Anthony is going to be thrilled. He was hoping to catch a late movie down at the beach."

"Then what the hell are you still doing here? Go."

"Okay, okay. Bye." Sam hugged me and was out the door.

"Love you."

"Love you," she hollered back.

There were still a few stragglers left, but being that one of them was Steven, my dad's friend, and the other was Steven's buddy, I was confident the place was in good hands while I took the trash out.

"Steven, I'm taking the trash out. I'll be back shortly. Do you mind watching the bar?"

"You got it!"

"I'm still here, MJ." My dad's voice startled me as he walked in from the patio. "Don't you go leaving this place under the supervision of someone like him." Dad chuckled as he smacked Steven on the arm.

The two massive black trash bags clanked together as their weight seemed to grow. "I'll be back."

I pushed the back door open with my butt and stepped outside, and the music and commotion from inside disappeared. I was met by a warm salty breeze and the peaceful nighttime sounds that accompanied this little town. The roar of the waves in the distance. The chirp of the crickets singing their song. The sway of the trees as their leaves brushed together.

I set the heavy trash bags on the ground.

Sometimes it was little moments like this that brought me back to everything good about this place. That showed me there were slivers of Liv in every corner. But it was also moments like this that made it hard for me to ever imagine myself leaving.

This exact spot, for example. Liv and I had our first big fight. We both stormed off, swearing we'd never talk to each other again. But within two hours, we'd found ourselves back here, ready to apologize. I smiled, thinking about just how ridiculous that sounded now. If you asked me what that fight was about, I wouldn't even be able to tell you.

Or the little bit of woods that resided directly behind The Wharf. She and I used to spend hours playing hide-and-seek, building forts—if you could even call them that—and lying on the ground, staring up at the sky, talking about what our futures would look like. Neither one of us would've ever predicted this.

A single tear built up in the inner corner of my eye, telling me I'd had enough time out here in the quiet. It was peaceful in spurts, but hang around too long and I was a blubbering mess.

I trudged toward the metal dumpster that sat in the back parking lot of the bar and sat one of the bags down before attempting to push the heavy lid up and open. I was trying to avoid having to put both bags down, which was a mistake, because now one of the bags was sliced open, allowing nasty restaurant remnants to seep out onto my white Converse.

"Shit." I groaned.

"Need a hand?"

I jumped at the voice, looking around for the culprit, my eyes landing on *him*. He stood there with one hand in his pocket and the other tugging at his chest.

"My god. You scared the living hell out of me."

"Sorry. I've been sitting in my car, trying to figure out how I was going to explain myself to you, and then I saw you come outside and knew this was my moment," he said.

"You don't need to explain yourself, Grey. I saw you on TV earlier."

"Dammit," he said. "That wasn't how I wanted you to find out. I was hoping we'd have a chance to get know each other a little more before I dropped the whole 'my father is the mayor of New York City' thing."

"It's kind of hard to get to know each other when one party disappears." The bite in my voice surprised me.

"I know, I'm sorry. I should've never left you the way I did that night. I owe you an apology."

"Grey, it's okay, you don't owe me anything." Together we maneuvered the bags into the dumpster with limited spillage.

"Yes, I do. Please just let me make it up to you." His raised eyebrow and crooked smirk were enough to have me begging but I resisted.

"I have plans."

"When?" he inquired.

"Tomorrow. All day." I was lying and I didn't even know why.

The excitement of him being here after thinking maybe I wouldn't see him again was impairing my judgement. And selfishly, I wanted to see if he was going to work for it.

He cocked his head to the side. "You're lying."

I folded my arms across my body. "So what if I am?"

"Please. Just a couple of hours. There's something I want to show you." His voice was a little desperate, making the flutters in my belly react in full force.

"You can't show me anything I haven't seen before. I've seen every single inch of this town."

His lips slipped into the tiniest smirk. "Want to bet?"

Puzzled, I responded, "A bet?"

"I'm willing to bet that I can show you something in this little town of yours that you've never seen before."

"And if you win?"

"If I win"—something sort of seductive rolled across his face as he shifted his body from one foot to the other—"I get to finish what I started the other night."

The bluntness of what he wanted was hot as fuck. But also, what was it that we didn't finish? Because I was pretty sure I finished.

I couldn't help but smile. "And if I win?"

"I'll let you decide that one. You can tell me tomorrow when I pick you up."

Fortunately for me, I knew he wasn't going to win. I'd spent my entire life in this town. I could walk the streets with my eyes closed and still know exactly where I was at any moment. The skeleton of this town mimicked my own. I'd explored every crevice, every hidden path, and every secret beach within Montauk's city limits.

So, what was my prize going to be? The unknown excited me.

"Fine." I dropped my arms to my side, turning toward the bar. "Pick me up at noon."

I swore I could hear the smile in his voice when he said, "Wear a swimsuit."

With my back turned, I threw a thumbs-up in the air and walked away.

Chucking my keys on the counter, I looked at the clock on my microwave. It was just after eleven, which meant I'd have a chance to get plenty of sleep, so I was forcing myself to set my alarm for a morning run. The fresh air and quiet time alone with my thoughts would be necessary before my little hoorah with Grey.

As I got ready for bed, I slipped out of my work clothes and into my favorite oversized T-shirt, washed my face, and brushed my teeth, all while replaying my encounter with Grey over and over again.

Should I have said something different? Should I not have agreed to go with him tomorrow? What was his end goal? And what in the hell was I doing?

"Liv, help!" I begged. "One minute I want to have fun, let loose, and fuck Grey Prescott. The next I'm trying to push him away and never see him again. It's giving serious whiplash vibes." I laughed out loud at my comment. Liv used to always say I struggled with commitment, and clearly, she wasn't wrong.

The problem with Grey was that I just couldn't say no to him.

And while the idea of him was fun, the idea of him leaving at the end of the summer scared the shit out of me. I rarely let people in, and in the off chance I did, it wasn't usually temporary.

My thoughts unraveled as I crawled into bed and turned out the lights. I lay there, staring up at my swirling ceiling fan, and wondered to myself as the breeze whipped my hair whisps around, tickling my cheek... What was it about Grey Prescott that made me want to be around him so much? Why was he so damn intriguing?

# Chapter Twenty

*B*eep, *beep, beep.*

Ugh, I swore I'd just fallen asleep.

Dragging my body to a sitting position, my feet dangling just above the floor, I wiped the sleep from my eyes and threw my messy blonde hair into a low ponytail.

I went straight for the closet, knowing damn well if I didn't, I'd get distracted and find too many excuses not to go. Because if we were being honest, all I wanted to do was curl up in bed with a cup of coffee.

It was still early when I got out of the door and the humidity was already trying to start a fight. So much for thinking a body shower would suffice after this run. I'd be needing a head-to-toe refresh.

I made my way down the stairs and onto Reef Road.

Town was quiet, but that wasn't a shock. I heard people still partying in the wee hours of the morning when I got up to pee. You could say people were definitely more of night owls versus early birds, especially during the summer season.

The water splashed onto my ankles as I listened to the pounding of my tennis shoes against the compacted sand. The runner's high was hitting today. My feet glided gracefully with the waves, and before I knew it, I'd already run two miles.

Running early in the morning meant the beach was basically a ghost town, minus a few other runners and some of the local surfers who hit the waves at the ass crack of dawn. The two miles back home seemed to last a little longer than the previous two, and my mind wandered its way back to the past.

The last summer that Liv and I spent together was the one right before senior year. We spent our days tanning at the beach and our nights hopping from one party to the next. We were the new seniors; we could do what we wanted.

There was one night in particular when we were out at a party and we both felt on top of the world. We had our whole lives in front of us. We walked home that night, hand in hand and a little drunk, gushing about all the things we couldn't wait to do that summer. And looking back, we did almost every single one of them.

We wanted to skinny dip in the ocean? We did. Twice.

We wanted to fall asleep under the stars in the woods behind The Wharf? We did. Well, we did until four in the morning when there were some suspicious noises and we decided to take our sleepover back inside.

But most importantly, we didn't want to have any regrets. We both wanted to make the summer before our senior year unforgettable.

And it was.

Just not in the way we'd ever imagined.

"Earth to MJ!" Chief Williams's voice barreled through my inner dialogue.

"Hey, Chief."

"Good morning, darlin'," he chirped. "And what did I tell you about that? Call me Michael."

"You know I can't do that." I smiled, stopping in front of him as he rested on the bench outside of our local coffee shop.

He shook his head. "I've long since retired from the fire station, young lady, which means I'm no longer 'chief.' You know that."

"You'll always be a chief in my eyes."

"You're sweet as sugar, aren't you," he said. "Sorry I missed our last meet-up. My grandson came into town and asked me to get lunch."

"No worries. Actually, I ended up writing a few words."

"Is that so? I take it the story is slowly coming to you then?" he asked, his eyebrows raised.

"A big emphasis on slowly. But like you told me, any words are better than none."

"Exactly."

I placed my hands on my hips, still trying to regulate my breaths. "And while I don't really have any idea where the story is going, I know eventually it will come to me, or at least that's what I'm hoping happens."

The bell on the coffee shop door chimed and a voice followed. "Here you go, grandfather."

Lifting my head to the left, my heart sank. Or rather, it dropped out of my body.

*Grandfather?* No fucking way.

"MJ?" Grey looked as confused as I felt.

"*Grey?*" I returned. "Did you just say grandfather?"

"Yes," he answered, handing Chief Williams his coffee. "Black with two sugars, just how you like it."

"Thanks, Grey," he said, grabbing the coffee from his hands. "I see you two have already met. Although, that doesn't surprise me in a town this size. MJ, this is my grandson. The one who lives in New York City that I'm always talking about," he commented. "Grey, this is MJ. MJ and I have known each other for quite some time now. Life brought us together in a less than desirable way, but we decided to make the best of it."

Grey's gaze remained on me, appearing to scope out my entire body before landing on my eyes. "I see."

"Your grandfather is a great man," I responded. "I'm lucky to get to spend my Thursdays with him."

"That you are. I'm jealous."

My eyes wavered, moving from Chief Williams to Grey. Looking at them now, the resemblance was definitely there.

"MJ, you should join us. Grey and I were just going to grab some breakfast."

"I would, but I was hoping to get in a few words before I—" I broke off, not wanting to reveal my plans with his *grandson*, not when my brain was still swimming with the revelation. "Before I... go out later."

"Out? With who? Where?" Chief Williams questioned, ever the snoop. "Anything you want to share?"

I chuckled. "Just going out with someone who stumbled in from the city. The guy thinks he knows our town better than me, but don't worry, Chief, I'll be sure to set him straight."

"That's my girl." He stood from the bench and embraced me in a hug. "Next Thursday?"

"Sorry, I'm so gross from my run," I offered, wrapping my arms around him. "But yes, we're on for Thursday." I stepped away from our embrace and looked toward his grandson. "Nice to see you again, Grey."

"You too, MJ." A smile creeped up the side of his mouth before he let a quick wink slip. "Maybe I'll see you around."

A million little chills rolled down my spine. "Bye, you two. Have a good breakfast," I said.

The fact that Grey was Chief Williams's grandson definitely counted for something, right?

Liv always believed in signs. She constantly talked about how everything in the universe happened for a reason. She was a firm believer in that. I, on the other hand, struggled with the concept, especially after the accident. Nothing about what happened to us could've had a reason, but sometimes I would try to find one, simply because I was desperate for anything to cling to.

I would look for a sign. A reason. Anything.

This. This was a sign.

All morning, I'd been second-guessing my decision to hang out with Grey this afternoon, but after that encounter, I knew Liv was sending me a sign.

And for the first time, I was going to listen.

# Chapter Twenty-One

"Last Night" by Morgan Wallen was blasting through my phone speakers as I hustled through my shower. Grey was going to be here at noon, and while that was a long way off, I knew I was going to need all the time I could get to mentally prepare.

Thankfully, I'd already planned out my outfit in my head while I was in the shower.

My navy bikini was slung over the towel hook in my bathroom. The top was a simple spaghetti strap that tied in the center with a bow. The bottoms were high-waisted and slightly cheeky. Looking in the reflection, I fiddled with the straps, turning to look at my backside.

"Shit," I said as I looked down, noticing I needed to shave.

Leaving my swimsuit on, I quickly hopped back into the shower. It was a real bitch being a woman sometimes.

Drying myself off for the second time, I rifled through my dress-er drawers until I came across my favorite pair of Levi shorts. They were light-washed with a frayed hem and a few strategically tattered rips. I yanked them over my swimsuit before pulling my oversized linen button-up off the hanger.

Perusing my makeup bag, Liv's voice frolicked through my head. *The prettiest girls aren't the ones with a lot of makeup, but rather the girls who know how to use the littlest makeup in the most flattering way.*

I applied a tinted sunscreen, some blush, a little mascara, and a light lip gloss. Finishing, I tapped my phone to check the time. Perfect—now to grab a quick breakfast, a cup of coffee, and maybe even stare at my computer screen in an attempt to get some words out.

When I heard a knock at the door, I jumped and checked the clock, wondering how he could already be here, but my eyes landed on my word count.

"Holy shit, that's a lot of words," I said.

I didn't remember the last time I wrote that much in one sitting. Sitting a little straighter in my chair, a smile appeared.

"Coming," I shouted.

I clutched my mesh beach bag that was resting on the barstool and slipped into my navy waterproof Birkenstocks. Another knock came just before I opened the door.

"Impatient much?" I asked.

His scent came bursting through the doorway, a mix of citrus and masculine leather. With his smell came an immediate effect on the rest of my body. A shiver started at my nose and shimmied its way to my toes. His right arm rested on the side of the door frame just above his head, making his strong stature all the more evident.

"Just a little." He smirked. "Did you bring a swimsuit?"

My shirt was closed by only one button, so I pulled it open wide enough for him to see the swimsuit underneath. His eyes flashed to my chest before looking back up at me with a raised eyebrow. "Mhm. That answers that question."

"Uh huh," I stated. "Now, where are we going?" I asked, pulling the door shut and locking it.

"That would ruin the surprise, now wouldn't it?"

"I told you, there is no surprise. I've literally seen every inch of this town."

"We'll see," he said, stepping to the side and signaling for me to go ahead of him. "It's the light blue Bronco parked right up front."

Blue Bronco? How many cars did this man have? Taking the last stair, I peered through the building doorway, expecting a brand-new souped-up Bronco, but instead, what I saw was the most perfect car I'd ever laid my eyes on.

There, parked in front of me, was a 1976 Ford Bronco in mint condition. The light blue paint was similar to that of the sky and paired perfectly with the brown leather interior and white removable top. The top was strapped with two surfboards, one yellow and one pink.

While I hadn't particularly been a fan of cars for a while now, I could always appreciate one, especially one as perfect as this. Dad and I used to share a love of cars, old ones in particular, but after the accident, my love for them was never the same.

I pulled my sunglasses to the bridge of my nose and peered out from just above them. "Damn."

"She's perfect, isn't she?" His voice was close behind me. I turned, expecting his eyes to be on the car, but instead they were locked on me. I froze.

He was talking about the car... wasn't he? Because for some reason, the way his eyes were eating me up made me unsure.

"The car, I mean. It's perfect," he stuttered, fiddling with the keys that rested in his hand.

"More than," I responded. "What is it, a seventy-six?

His eyes widened. "Shit. You're good. I wouldn't have picked you for a car girl."

"I wouldn't have picked you for a guy who drove anything that wasn't foreign." I grinned as I moved toward the passenger seat.

"Ouch." His voice was overflowing with sarcasm as he hopped in.

I sat in the passenger seat, pushing my sunglasses up my face and pulling my bag close to my chest. My body had already been on a rollercoaster of emotions since Grey showed up on my doorstep, but now instead of enjoying the ride, I was a little queasy. It never got easier. My heartbeat got louder and my cheeks got hotter. The rush of warmth flushed my face, and I took a deep breath.

"You ready?"

"Ready as I'll ever be," I responded, trying to focus on the road ahead of us.

His key slipped into the ignition and the engine purred underneath my feet, vibrating through my seat. The sound around me seemed to dull the chaos inside of me a little, but it still took me a few minutes to realize we weren't moving. I looked over, his big brown eyes stared back.

"MJ, what's wrong? You look like you're going to be sick. Are you okay?"

Out of nowhere, I heard the words unexpectedly spilling from my mouth. "I was in an accident when I was younger... A car accident."

"MJ..." His body abruptly shifted toward me, his empathetic eyes brimming with sympathy. "I'm so sorry," he said, his hand reaching for mine. "Sorry, I shouldn't have—" He started to yank his hand back, but I clung on so he couldn't.

Acknowledging my gesture, he squeezed tighter. "I didn't notice when we rode together the other night. If I had, I would've never planned to drive us."

The memory of us in the back of that black SUV reappeared in my head, bringing a smile along with it. "The anxiety around cars is always present, but sometimes it's just more blatant than others. Other things were on my mind that night, not to mention I was a little tipsy. But it's okay, I'll be fine," I said, wrapping my other hand around his arm that rested in my lap.

"Glad to hear that I was able to provide that distraction for you." He beamed. "But I'm happy to walk, if you want. It's not too far from here, and I could totally go for some fresh air."

"No. No, that's okay." Shaking my head, I kept going. "There's no way I'm turning down a chance to ride in this car."

Reluctantly releasing our hands, I fastened my seat belt.

Catching his movements in my periphery, I watched as he tugged at his chest. In the exact same place he had on the first day we met.

He slowly started backing out but stopped. "If at any point the anxiety becomes too much, just tell me. I'll pull over wherever we are and we can walk from there."

His sincerity was so pure, I could've melted right there in my seat.

"Okay," I responded with a smile.

He took his right hand and placed it on my leg, immediately giving me goosebumps.

"MJ, I'm serious."

"I will, I promise."

He pulled his hand from my leg and casually returned it to the steering wheel. A breath escaped my lips as if he'd pulled it with him.

I tried to focus my thoughts as he pulled the Bronco out of the parking spot. There were others that understood my struggle with cars. My parents, of course, and Sam, but none of them ever mentioned it. They never brought it up, per my request. But now I was wondering if that'd been a mistake, because getting to express those anxieties out loud, to allow someone else to get a glimpse of what I harbored inside—and to have those feelings acknowledged—was more therapeutic than I'd ever imagined.

Although, if you'd told me a couple of weeks ago that I'd be sharing this with Grey, I'd have laughed in your face. But maybe he wasn't as easy to read as I initially thought. While I'd seen quite a bit of him—or rather most of him—he was still managing to keep me on my toes. The mysterious, handsome city boy who knew his way around the bedroom was also emotional, aware, and not afraid of big scary feelings. This all felt a little risky, borderline treacherous.

And then before I could overthink it, I said, "Thank you."

He glanced over with a slightly confused look on his face. "For what?"

"For listening. And for understanding," I said, letting out a breath. "I don't normally just come out and share that with people, especially people I have only known for a short amount of time."

"It seems there is a lot you don't share, MJ." His eyes were on the road, but he kept talking. "I'm always here to listen. Sometimes the noise inside our heads is so loud that in order to quiet it, we have to let it out."

"Anxiety takes up residence in your head too?"

"What gave it away?"

"No one could speak so clearly about it without having experienced it themselves," I responded.

Now I was curious—what demons did he fight with, what struggles did he endure, what anxieties engulfed his mind? Because I couldn't imagine someone like him struggling.

But that was the thing about anxiety. It didn't discriminate. It didn't care about your social status or what kind of family you had. It didn't care about your house, your car, or the unlimited possibilities that awaited you. It didn't matter who you were.

Keeping my eye on the road ahead, I spoke again, desperate to know more. "What finally made you come back to town this summer?"

"It's a long story."

I waited, assuming he'd say more, but he didn't. "Well good thing I've got the whole day," I said, seeing his smile grow.

"Does that mean you're mine for the entire day?"

The way he said *mine* sent me quivering in my seat, so much so that I needed to readjust myself to make it less obvious.

"It means I don't have any other plans, so I have plenty of time to hear your long story."

A smug look spread across his face, admitting defeat. "Fine. I used to come here every summer, but then I had some health issues and things got a little muddy throughout my teenage years." His strong hands gripped the steering wheel. "All of a sudden, I blinked and multiple years had passed. More things happened that made things even messier, and while I attempted to deal with them, it made more sense to do it in New York than here. Time passed, and it was easier to forget this place, and the chaotic life I live made it easier to stay away, so I did."

I wasn't sure what I expected him to say, but that wasn't it. The tension in his grip visibly loosened on the steering wheel and he dropped his left hand to his lap. His answer was still extremely vague, but in a way, it seemed as though he'd been wanting to share even that with someone for a while now.

Surprising myself, I reached for his hand, lacing our fingers together. He looked down, then back to the road, then to me. Smiling. I wanted him to know that like him, I was listening.

"Time has a funny way of moving so quickly that in one blink you can basically be living a different life. You can't dwell on it or you'll just continue to lose more of it. You're here. You came back. That's all that matters," I said. "What was it that brought you back here? Was it your grandfather?"

"Partially. My grandfather and I stayed in touch; I made sure of it. But there were other reasons for me to come back. Reasons that at the time, when I was younger, seemed hard and uncomfortable. For the last couple of years, every summer creeped up and then was over before I could commit. But then this summer was different." He paused. "This summer... something drew me back. I can't explain it, and I know that sounds ridiculous, but everything inside of me told me I had to." His entire body relaxed against the back of the leather seat.

"It doesn't sound ridiculous. Trust me," I insisted. "How does it feel? To be back here, I mean. Are you glad you came?"

"It feels exactly how I remember, only better."

A smile inched across my face. "And what about all the stuff that you were avoiding? It wasn't as bad as you thought, was it?"

His relaxed body tensed up again, like I'd struck a nerve.

"To be honest, I haven't dealt with it, and I wasn't even sure I was going to when I first got here. But each day I'm here, I feel myself inching closer to facing the hard shit, the shit that I've avoided for too long."

While I wanted to know what he was talking about, I didn't want to press. Not yet, at least. Everyone had to open up on their own terms, and while things were flowing particularly easily between the two of us, it didn't feel like the right time.

"You should." I nodded my head.

"I will," he agreed.

Getting antsy and ready to be out of the car, I asked, "Are we there yet?"

"Patience."

"Oh." I smirked. "You mean like the same kind of patience you had earlier at my door?" I said, reaching for my beach bag and grabbing my sunscreen.

"Exactly like that." He chuckled, his mood lightening. "Oh, and MJ..."

"Yeah?" I looked up at him.

"We're here."

# Chapter Twenty-Two

The salty air frolicking around me confirmed we were near the water, which meant wherever we were, there was no doubt in my mind that I'd been here before.

His voice was filled with so much certainty, I almost felt bad as I lifted my head from the inside of my beach bag and— I gasped.

My eyes darted in every direction, doing their best to land on something familiar, something I'd seen before. But each time they reached another spot, there was no familiarity to be found. Only something more beautiful than what they'd seen last.

What lay in front of me could not possibly be a part of my little town. There was no way in hell that something this beautiful had been kept hidden from me—and all the other locals for that matter. There were no secrets in this town, especially not ones that looked like this.

"Holy hell," I uttered.

He could barely contain himself. "Unbelievable, isn't it?"

"You could say that."

Straight ahead lay the whitest sand I'd ever seen. The water was incredibly blue, almost to the point that I thought I might be looking at a photograph. It was so clear I could see straight to the bottom, but that wasn't even the best part.

Because across the cove stood a waterfall.

We stepped out of the car, making our way to the drop-off. It wasn't much, maybe a foot or two above the water. I put my feet right up on the edge, letting the adrenaline course through me. The view was indescribable, and I was fixated.

Grey cleared his throat, bringing my gaze off the view in front of me and onto the one next to me. He wore a short-sleeved linen shirt with a pair of navy-and-white-striped seersucker swim trunks. Swim trunks that I normally would've found annoyingly short, but for some reason I didn't mind on him.

"Surprised?" He lifted an eyebrow.

"Only a little," I teased, pinching my fingers to demonstrate. "But, really, where are we?"

"Just a little southeast of Montauk Point, but the overgrown vegetation makes the turn-off almost invisible to anyone passing by. I used to come to this spot and draw…" I could tell he had more to share, but he stopped before starting again somewhere else. "I used to come to this spot almost daily after things got really shitty. I'd come here and just *be*… for hours."

"Okay, if I'm being honest, it's one of the most beautiful things I've ever seen. It's so serene, almost magical, and yet so simple. Just some rocks, water, and sand," I responded. "How did you even find this place?"

"My grandfather was the first one who brought me here when I was five or six. He'd been coming here with my grandmother for years—it's where they fell in love. After that, it became a beloved place. A calm place. Anytime my parents were looking for me, my grandfather was always the one to come get me because he knew I'd be here. He promised me it would be our secret, and still to this day, it has been." Grey's lips turned up slightly, leaving the smallest smile across his face.

"I can see why you'd want to keep it a secret. It's like having your own little slice of heaven right here in Montauk. I would've loved to have a place like this after the accident. A quiet place where no one could find me."

"Well, now you do. There's only one stipulation…"

My focus went to him.

"It has to stay a secret." The word *secret* slipped through his lips in a way that made me feel eager to keep it, simply because he was asking.

"I can do that," I agreed. "But only if you answer one question."

He pressed his lips together, but not before his tongue swiped quickly across them as he stared right at me. "Let's hear it."

"Why bring me here? Why share your favorite spot with me after keeping it a secret from everyone else for so long?"

I half expected a quick-witted smart-ass response, so his longer than normal silence surprised me.

"Honestly, MJ, I don't really know." His soft demeanor was charming. "I can't explain most things I do when I'm around you. You quite literally came running into my life, and ever since then, I find myself gravitating toward you every chance I get. After leaving you the other night, I couldn't shake the feeling that I might've permanently messed up whatever this is between us, and that bothered me. Drove me fucking insane actually. And on my way back to town last night, I knew I wanted to show you something, some*place* important to me. And you're the first person I've ever met that I knew would appreciate it as much as I did. As I do," he finished, never letting his eyes leave mine.

"Oh." I bit my bottom lip.

He shook his head. "Sorry. I'm sure that's not what you expected."

"Please don't be sorry." I grasped his arm. "It wasn't what I expected, you're right about that, but you've been exceeding my expectations since the moment I met you. And I feel it too—that weird tug, the one that always seems to know when you're near. It's been there since the day you almost ran me over." I sent a smile his way and winked. "Even when I try to pretend like it isn't because I'm afraid what it might mean, it still tugs."

Grey pulled me to his chest, our bodies so close together I could feel his heartbeat pulsing against mine. His fingers traced my jawline before pushing a strand of my hair behind my ear. He inched his lips a mere breath from mine and whispered, "I told you this was going to be interesting."

The last word left his mouth as he pushed our lips together. His tongue crashed through my lips and found mine. This kiss wasn't like any of our previous ones. This kiss was softer, sweeter, more intentional.

In sync, our lips pulled away, our bodies still close.

"Now it's my turn to ask a question," he said.

"Go ahead."

"Are you going to admit it now?"

My eyebrow perked up and I taunted, "I'm not sure what you're talking about," even though I absolutely did.

His jaw neared my ear, sending a warm vibration over my body when he spoke. "Oh, but I think you do."

A tiny giggle slipped from my mouth. I edged my lips near his again, our skin barely touching. "You won," I whispered.

Grey pulled back and a silent whimper left my mouth. "I'd already won before we even got here…" Perplexed, I titled my head a little to the right, and he continued. "I was spending the day with you regardless of the outcome."

His response brought a hotness to my cheeks and my hands instinctively moved, wrapping themselves around the back of his neck. I went in for another kiss, but just as I closed in, he swooped me into his arms, cradling my weight under my knees and around my waist.

"Either way, I was getting you wet today."

My head flung up from his shoulder in an attempt to see the look on his face. There he was, grinning from ear to ear, looking like he was about to indulge on his favorite snack.

"Excuse me?" I asked playfully.

In an instant, he lunged us both off the edge and into the blue water.

"Grey!" I squealed.

The cool water devoured us, and as I surfaced, I pushed my hair out of my face and wiped my eyes, grateful I'd gone with the waterproof mascara this morning.

"You're a shit." I giggled.

"I got you wet, didn't I?"

"Very funny."

"Oh, you didn't…" He paused, combing his fingers through his thick brown hair that somehow came out of the water *still* looking styled. "You didn't think that I was referring to something else, did you?"

The way his voice dropped sent my belly scrambling. Flashes of him and me together resurfaced, and I found myself biting my lip to keep my composure.

"Of course not. That was just a one-time thing."

My words were meant to ruffle Grey's feathers, but the way his mouth dipped open and his eyes darkened had me second-guessing.

Turning, I casually swam to the little beach below the edge where we'd been standing. I removed one salt-soaked item of clothing at a time as I stepped out of the water. As I found a spot on the beach, I unbuttoned my jean shorts and peeled them off my body, leaving only my navy bikini.

Grey was wading toward me in the water and I moved to face him, combing my fingers through my hair, hoping to look a little less like a wet rat. Peering up, I noticed he'd already taken his shirt off. His body glistened from the sun and water droplets trailed down his rigid abdomen.

*Damn.*

Dragging my gaze up his body before finally landing on his eyes, I watched as he did the same, his tongue tracing his lips in the process. Normally, my intrusive thoughts would've made me feel vulnerable in a moment like this, but something about the way he looked at me made me feel sexy as I stood there in nothing but my swimsuit.

"Just a one-time thing, huh?" he said, putting weight on the word *just*. He walked past me and moved toward the rocks. He winked and mumbled under his breath as he walked by, "Keep telling yourself that, MJ."

Grey Prescott was a man full of surprises. When I'd first met him, he appeared to be just another well-dressed city boy who came to town for the summer with no intentions other than to hook up with strangers and party with his friends.

Now I wasn't so sure that was the case. And while part of me was excited at the idea that he had similar feelings to the ones I'd been feeling, it also terrified me. At least before, when I thought this was just a random summer hookup, there weren't any feelings involved. No messiness, no bullshit, and most importantly, no chance of losing someone.

I'd been there before, and ever since then, I'd been trying to avoid it at all costs. If I never allowed myself to feel that deeply, then I would never give someone else the chance to hurt me that deeply either.

# Chapter Twenty-Three

Perched on the hot sand, the peace that overcame me had me feeling like I'd been here before, with him.

"Do you want your bag?" Grey's voice reeled me back, echoing from above where he'd parked the car.

"Yes, please," I shouted back, thankful he'd pulled me from my thoughts.

"Here you go." He reappeared, sliding on his square Ray-Bans.

"Thank you," I said, grabbing my bag.

"Now, let's get back to this discussion about that one-time thing you were talking about. Can you give me your definition of the term?"

Throwing my towel down on the sand, I shot him a look. "A definition? I think it's pretty self-explanatory. I'm not sure there's much else to talk about. We'd been drinking. We hooked up. You left. That was the end of it."

I was halfway kidding, more interested in his response versus actually meaning what I said.

"First of all, I'm sorry for leaving, I really am. I was summoned back to the city on behalf of my incredibly narcissistic father, and

I wanted to ignore the call, but I knew I needed to be there for my mom. But—"

"You—" I started to speak, interrupting him, but he held his finger to my mouth, shushing me.

"Let me finish," he demanded. "Secondly, I'd barely had anything to drink. I rarely drink, and when I do, it's in moderation. Lastly, that was not the end of anything. Unless that's what you want."

"I don't know *what* I want," I admitted, flustered. "I mean, it's obvious I want you, but I'm not sure what that even looks like." This kind of honesty was risky, but releasing it outweighed the risks.

"We both know how this goes." I was too afraid to look in his direction. "You stroll into town for the summer. Host your fancy parties and say all the right things, just enough to hook me, and then come Labor Day, you're gone." I breathed, trying to ignore the pang in my stomach.

My god. I was fucking mortified for what he was going to say next.

His response came quick. "MJ, you have no idea how this goes, because honestly, neither do I. But given I've never had this type of unexplainable connection with anyone else before, that alone tells me I won't be able to just leave."

His confession had me screaming to look at him, but I resisted. Afraid that if I saw his face, I wouldn't be able to say what I was about to.

"It's easy to say things like that when you're in the moment. It's easy to get caught up in the lust of it all. This town is magical, especially during the summer months. It has a way of making you feel invincible, making you feel like nothing else exists out there in the world." I breathed, feeling like I'd been holding that in since the first time I saw him.

I broke my own rule and looked in Grey's direction. I expected him to still be looking up at the water, and my breath was pulled straight out of my chest when I found him staring right at me.

"I don't know who broke your heart, but I really fucking hate that they did." The serious, empathic nature of his words almost took me down.

Part of me wanted to be angry at him, because he didn't know what he was talking about. Liv had broken my heart, but it wasn't her choice. But then the other part of me felt like I could finally take a deep breath. Like somehow, he'd been able to dig through the bullshit and knew what I was really trying to say.

"Either way, I'm going to do whatever it takes to spend as much time with you as possible this summer, Miller. See where this thing goes. Yeah, I might take you to some fancy parties, and I'll sure as shit attempt to say all the right things, even though you have a way of making that difficult sometimes." He grinned at me. "But more than anything, I'm going to do my best to show you that not everyone leaves."

His body inched closer to mine until I could feel him touching me. He wrapped his arm around my shoulder, pulling me into his chest.

"Sometimes you don't have a choice," I whispered.

"What do you mean?"

"Leaving. Sometimes you don't have a choice."

"Right now, all I know is leaving you would be my last choice."

He pressed a kiss into my temple, the sweetness sending me into a daze.

We both sat in silence for a few minutes, drinking in the scenic view that was painted in front of us. The clouds were showing off today, looking like they'd been plucked straight from a cotton candy machine.

I shimmied as the late afternoon breeze blew through.

"Here," he said, grabbing his shirt from behind us.

As I went to wrap it around me, Grey pushed his hand in the way. "What's that?" he asked, moving the white shirt to get a better look at the dainty tattoo that decorated the left side of my rib cage. His pointer finger traced the permanent ink just beneath my armpit.

"It's a lilac hydrangea."

It was tiny—only about two inches long—and extremely detailed yet simple. The stem was a single black line with three tiny green leaves near the top. The single bloom was shaded in a lilac purple, the individual petals stark against my skin.

The tattoo had turned out perfectly and was something I'd been so happy with, but sometimes, now that so many years had passed, I often forgot it was there.

"I like it." His tone was curious, but not enough to ask any more questions.

It got me wondering about his tattoo, the group of roman numerals inked just about his heart. "What does yours mean?"

"It's a date I never want to forget."

There was more to that story, but similar to other times, Grey chose to only share a piece of the puzzle. But I was okay with that, because a fragment was better than nothing.

The car ride had been quiet so far, only blurry snippets of small weather cottages and people peddling on pastel bikes whooshed passed us.

I was still processing the comment Grey made back at the beach. I believed him when he said leaving me would be his last choice, but I wasn't sure why. The time we'd spent together had been incredible, but it had been brief.

What made him so sure that this—whatever *this* was—was a good idea? Because as much as I liked the idea too, the hesitation was still there.

"Let me make you dinner at my house this week?" he offered.

"Oh, I would, but I have plans," I lied.

"You have plans this whole week?" Suspicion colored his tone and he peered in my direction as the Bronco rolled to a stop at the light.

I racked my brain for an excuse while fiddling with the seat belt. "I told my dad I would help him dewinterize his boat." Confident in my answer, I smiled at him.

I was hoping the light would turn green before he had the chance to answer, but it didn't.

"Miller Morgan, you're full of shit." He lightly chuckled, the deep sound drifting between us.

"I'm not!" A grin hid just behind my lips, threatening to expose my attempt at keeping a straight face.

"You may think that I don't know a thing about boats based on the simple fact that I spent most of my life in New York City, but what you don't know is that during my younger years, I spent a lot of time at the marina, here in Montauk. And I know for a fact that dewinterizing a boat can be done in a single afternoon."

Shit.

I said I had some imaginary deadline to meet for the hypothetical book I'm writing. But then again, that would've intrigued him, and he would've no doubt asked more questions, leading to answers I didn't want to provide.

"In that case, how does Thursday sound?" I said, smiling as a sign of defeat.

He peeked at me over the top of his black sunglasses, a smug look decorating his face before he drew his eyes back to the road.

Nervous about his lack of response, I went on. "I have to work the next three days, and based on how packed we've been so far this summer, I have to pick and choose my days off."

Pulling the Bronco back into the same spot he'd parked this morning, the car went silent as the keys came out of the ignition. I was seconds away from opening the passenger door and sprinting to my door when his voice startled me. "Thursday. It's a date."

Secretly excited about his response and also attempting to ignore the sense of thrill that inhabited the base of my stomach, I looked at the floorboard, grabbing my bag before leaning up and reaching for the door handle. Instead, I came up short.

The door was already opening and Grey's hand was extended out, waiting for me.

"Bye," I said, attempting to pull my hand away from his and move toward the stairs, but finding myself stuck.

Grey pulled me into him, his broad chest consuming me as his arms tangled around my lower half. He rested his head on top of mine, hugging me tighter. The embrace caught me off guard, which was odd considering we'd been far more intimate than a simple hug, but this felt more vulnerable somehow.

We pulled away just a little, staring at one another. The gold specks in his dark brown eyes seemed to glisten.

"See you Thursday," I said.

"See you Thursday," he agreed, his lips pressing into my forehead, forcing my eyes shut as I relished the feeling.

As much as I didn't want to let go, I did.

"MJ..."

I stopped just before I got to the first step, rotating until I saw him standing next to the driver's side of his light-blue Bronco.

"I'm not going anywhere."

My jaw unclenched and a rush of relief ran through me, paving the way for the big smile that spread across my face.

I didn't say anything. Instead, I returned to the stairs, making my way to the top.

Unlocking my door and stepping inside, I dropped my bag in the entryway. My smile was still plastered in the same spot as I fell against my closed door. Energy radiated throughout my entire body, leaving me giddy as I flailed my arms around.

I couldn't wait for Thursday.

# Chapter Twenty-Four

G rey and I texted practically every day, but nothing held a candle to physically being with him. Although some of his text messages did come awfully close.



Oh my god. *Play it cool, MJ.*

I'm always up for a good challenge. And thank you.



For what?



For giving me the visual I desperately needed to be able to get through this meeting.



Glad I could be of assistance, Mr. Prescott, see you tomorrow.



Can't wait, Ms. Morgan.

Looking forward to dinner tomorrow gave me the energy boost I needed to step into the restaurant. A whiff of cleaning products overcame me, which was the ultimate sign that you worked at a bar.

"Hey, MJ." Dad's voice echoed from behind the bar.

"Hey, Dad. How's it going?"

"The lunch crowd has been pretty slow today, but that's to be expected. You got any plans this weekend with your days off?"

For a second, I considered mentioning my plans with Grey, but then I realized that would only lead to more questions, so instead

I redirected the conversation. "No, not really. I'm going to try and work on getting some words out. Heavy on the *try*."

"You'll get there. All good things take time." He paused. "Don't give up."

"Thanks, Dad. I'm trying my best."

"That's all you can do. And remember, your mom and I are here to support you however we can. Dreams don't happen overnight. Take this place, for example," he said, extending his hands around him. "I always wanted to own my own restaurant. It took me longer than I thought it would to get here, but nonetheless, here I am. Or rather, here *we* are."

"Did you ever think it wouldn't happen?" I asked.

"On more than one occasion. I used to obsess over feeling behind, as if my dream was going to disappear if I didn't achieve it by a certain time. But that's the best part about dreams: they don't have expiration dates."

"They may not have expiration dates, but can they be less realistic over time?"

"Of course they can. But I know what you're getting at, and your dream of living in New York and becoming an author is just as realistic today as it was on the first day you dreamt it up," he said.

Feeling pessimistic, I asked, "Do you really believe that?"

Dad's eyes softened. "I absolutely believe that. Don't give up on yourself, MJ. You're capable of more than you think, and deep down, I know you'll get there someday. And when you do, we'll be standing right next to you."

"That'll be one of the best days of my life," I admitted.

"For all of us," he said.

"I love you so big, Dad."

"I love you bigger, sweet girl."

I smiled, grateful to have parents like mine, but then it faded. I understood what Dad was saying, but my dreams seemed further and further out of reach the longer I waited, and part of me always felt like leaving this town meant leaving Liv. I just wasn't ready to do that. I didn't know if I ever would be.

Dad's voice barked up from behind the bar again, pulling me from my wandering thoughts. "Oh! By the way, I told Sam not to worry about coming in tonight. I figured it being a weeknight you could handle the crowd. Plus, it might be nice for you to work solo and cash in on all the tips. That way when you *do* decide to move to New York you can't say I never helped."

"You're the best."

He laughed. "I try. I'm going to check on the few tables that are enjoying an early dinner before the late crowd disturbs their peace. Let me know if you need anything."

"Will do!" I said, taking that as my cue to get the bar prepped and ready for the night. I started with the rubber mats that were hanging over the deck outside, drying from last night. Pulling them off, I slugged them back behind the bar just as the bell on the front door jingled.

"I'll be right with you," I called out.

Throwing the mats down, I popped up, expecting a customer waiting for a table, but instead I was met by an older woman holding a bushel of lilac hydrangeas.

Two *dozen* lilac hydrangeas, to be specific.

"I have a delivery for Miller Morgan." The lady smiled.

My stomach dropped in excitement, like I was waiting at the top of a rollercoaster.

"That's me," I responded, raising my hand in the air like I had a question for the teacher.

She heaved the vase on top of the bar, the glass clanking against the countertop. "Well, aren't you a lucky girl."

I returned her comment with a smile and a "Looks like I am. Thank you!"

She turned back toward the door, and while I was eager to see who they were from—even though I had a pretty good idea—I played it cool, waiting for her to leave before plucking the paper card from the middle of the flowers.

*Strawberry Field Flowers* was stamped in the center of the card, along with an address. A local floral shop that had been around since before I was born. I flipped the card to the back.

*Just a little reminder that I'm not going anywhere — G*

I quickly turned the card back over, reeling with excitement. I held the card to my chest and grinned before sliding it into the back pocket of my jeans. The flowers were gorgeous. They were so full they almost looked fake, but the smell radiating off of them proved otherwise. Wrapping my hands around the cold glass of the vase, I lifted them off the counter and placed them next to the register.

I thought about putting them in the back, but part of me wanted them to be seen. Not that anyone would have a single clue where they came from or whose they were, but I'd know, and that made me feel special.

Slowly, one customer at a time, the early evening turned to night and the crowd picked up.

"What can I get you?" I tossed two vinyl coasters down in front of a younger couple who just walked in.

"I'll take a Coors Light. What do you want, babe?" The guy turned to the girl who sat to his right.

"Uhm, I'll take a vodka soda with a splash of lime." She smiled.

I'd never seen them before, but our town did provide the perfect scenery for a romantic getaway. "Of course. Coming right up."

Snatching a bottle of Coors Light from the minifridge, I popped the top off just as a group of familiar faces walked through the front door. Moving toward the bar was a group of guys I'd known for years, ones I'd grown up with. Most of whom had graduated, moved out of this town and on with their lives. However, they still resurfaced every summer, to shoot the shit with each other and visit their families.

Leading the pack was Caleb Davis. The last boy Liv had her eyes on. The last boy she flirted with the night of the accident. Caleb Davis was still just as attractive as he'd been back in high school, with his slick black hair and dark skin. Caleb and I were nothing but acquaintances. After Liv passed, I sort of kept my head down and to myself for the remainder of senior year, so any greetings I got back then were simply from a place of empathy for me having just lost my best friend.

However, in a town as tight-knit as ours, these reunions made it seem like we'd been a lot closer.

"MJ!" he shouted as he led the group to the center of the bar.

Handing the two drinks over to the couple, I casually tossed my hand in the air. "Hey, Caleb."

"Eight dollars," I told them, laughing at the astonishment on the guy's face. "That's what you get when you drink in a small town."

"I'll take it. Keep the change," he responded, handing over a ten-dollar bill.

"Thanks. Enjoy Montauk."

Throwing the cash into the register, I swiveled to face the crowd, landing first on Caleb and all of his friends.

"What's up, guys?" I said, slinging a bar towel over my shoulder.

"Long time, no see." Caleb's voice was deeper than I remembered. "We'll start with—"

"Let me guess, six Jameson shots and six Jack and Cokes?" I smirked.

A grin spread across his face. "Damn, you're good."

"Or you all just order the same thing every time you're back in town." I returned his grin with a sarcastic smirk and went to work on the order.

The Wharf was fairly busy but nothing I couldn't handle. Once most everyone had already been helped, I stayed near the guys as I made their drinks. "How have you all been?"

A few of them popped off quick comments, but Caleb was the only one to give me his full attention. He always made sure to check in with me when he was back in town.

"Things have been good with me. Busy as hell at work, but I guess that's what happens when you're trying to move up in a city where everyone is trying to do the same. Can't complain though. Glad to be home for the next couple of weeks to celebrate the Fourth. How are things here?"

"They're good. Same as usual. Not much has changed since last summer. You know how it goes." I slid over the shot glasses full of dark liquor.

"Yeah." He chuckled. "I do. Have you given any more thought to joining us in the city?"

A shot of doubt flickered across my face.

"Okay, okay, I had to ask just once." He laughed, handing out the drinks to the guys. "But I'm serious. If you ever decide you want to move, I'm just a phone call away. I'd be happy to give you advice on neighborhoods or any other info you might need."

"I appreciate it. I'll keep that in mind."

This time, the mention of moving to New York didn't completely terrify me. In fact, it seemed a bit intriguing. Where would I live? What would my apartment look like?

"Can we get some service over here? We've been waiting for fucking ever."

I stopped daydreaming and looked over at the commotion. A group of about five people stood a few feet away, the leader of them a tall bald man. Caleb turned in the direction of the group, and the rest of the guys followed suit.

"It's okay, I got them," I said.

"Can you give me a second, please. I'm helping these customers and then I'll be right over," I firmly responded. I'd worked here long enough to have seen my fair share of assholes.

Sliding the drinks toward Caleb and his friends, I said, "Cheers, guys! Let me know if you need anything else."

"Cheers!" erupted from the group as they clanked their glasses together.

"It's about damn time. If you all were smart, you'd staff this bar with more than one bartender."

Doing my best to avoid confrontation, because it was obvious this group had already been drinking, I ignored the comment. "Sorry about your wait, what can I get started for you?"

"How about some drinks on the house? It's the least you could do after the shitty service we've had since stepping inside this place."

"Like I said before, I'm sorry about the wait, but as you can clearly see, it's just me tonight. I'm doing my best to get to everyone. I'm happy to take your order now, what can I get you all?" I repeated.

Perks of knowing the owner was that I didn't have to put up with shit from anyone, especially people who were just straight-up dicks.

"We'll take five whiskeys on the rocks. And make them strong," he grumbled.

I got to work, pouring the liquor a little heavier than normal because I didn't want to deal with them any longer than I already had.

"Here you go." I slid the drinks across the bar. "And if you or any of your friends yell at me like that again I'll have to ask you to leave."

I may not enjoy confrontation, but I also wasn't going to be treated like that. I didn't wait around for a response. I moved on to the next customer, but not before one of the women from the group muttered, "What a bitch."

They burst into laughter, but I knew they weren't worth my time.

The next hour passed quicker than expected due to a burst of post–dinner rush customers.

Caleb and his friends left the bar around ten, as did most of the crowd. There were a couple of local stragglers left, but it was everyone I was used to closing down the bar with.

"Hey guys, I'm going to go take the trash out. I'll be back, and we'll be closing down in the next twenty minutes or so."

One of them said, "Sounds good, darling. I'll take my check when you get back," and the rest followed with nods.

"Perfect." I pulled the two black trash bags behind me, both of them barely hovering over the ground because of their weight. Using my body to push the back door open, I made my way toward the dumpster. Again, I found myself attempting to get the lid flipped open and failing.

After the third try, I grunted, "This is useless." The bags were going to have to sit by the dumpster until Dad could come and help me.

"Well, well, well, look who it is," a scratchy voice mumbled from the darkness.

"Hello?"

A sinister laugh strummed from the woman's mouth. "If it isn't the local bitch bartender who told you she was going to kick you out of the bar."

I still couldn't see their faces as they hid under the cover of the shadows, but I recognized their voices. The bald-headed man and his rude sidekick.

My heartbeat rumbled awake, my senses on high alert. It was one thing to be firm in the safety of the bar, but it was another when confronted in a dark parking lot with no one else around.

"You owe my friend an apology," the woman chirped as they both stumbled into the light, clearly intoxicated. "If it weren't for people like us, this shithole wouldn't even survive."

"Look, I don't want any trouble," I responded.

"You sure acted like you wanted trouble when you were on your high horse in there, threatening to kick me out," the man barked.

They were both obviously pissed off. Mixed with the fact that they were drunk, it was a less-than-ideal combination. Not to mention, there were two of them and only one of me. My pulse tripled, the blood rushing to my face, making me feel queasy.

I turned, pretending to be calm as I moved back toward the door.

"I'm not done talking to you, bitch." The man's tone got more aggressive as their footsteps clunked closer.

My heart rate spiked, pounding so heavily I could feel it in my head.

*Get to the door, MJ, just get to the damn door.*

Nearly to the handle, I reached out, attempting to pull it open. Within seconds, another hand charged in and slammed it shut. "I said I wasn't done talking to you. Did you not hear me?"

The air around me filled with the scent of whiskey and I could hear the woman's cackle not too far away. I honestly didn't know what I was going to do next, and that in itself scared the living shit out of me.

"Hey, everything okay over here?"

The burly, insufferable man startled at the sound. His body shifted just enough so that I could see who was standing in the distance.

*Grey.*

# Chapter Twenty-Five

"Grey, please! Help me!" I panicked. My words were quick and smushed together, but I was desperate for him to intervene.

In a blur, he was there.

He ripped the man away from me by the collar of his shirt and bodily threw him in the opposite direction. "Get the fuck away from her," he yelled, his voice laced with anger. The man stumbled and fell to his knees and his accomplice quickly ran to his rescue.

Grey snapped his eyes in my direction, his hands rubbing up and down my arms. "Are you okay? What happened? Who is that?"

I couldn't respond. Instead, I wrapped my arms around his neck and pulled him closer, my head falling onto his chest. The familiar scent of him sent a sense of safety to my brain.

"Yeah," I breathed. "I'm fine. He didn't touch me. They're just some drunk, pissed-off customers that were in the bar earlier."

"I would've killed him if he laid a single finger on you."

I used the rhythm of his steady heartbeat against my ear to calm down. The sense of security at having him here made me feel weightless, like I was floating.

Grey's presence almost made me forget that the two drunk asses were still here. Looking over, I watched as the man peeled himself off the ground.

I stepped away from Grey, using his protection as an excuse to speak up for myself. I grabbed his hand before I spoke. "You two are real pieces of shit, you know that."

The man spit back, "And you're still a bitch."

Grey took a subtle step in front of me. "Don't you dare talk to her like that. You're just begging for another taste of that pavement, aren't you?"

The man stood, presumably calculating his next move.

"And don't think about ever stepping foot back in this bar," Grey went on. "You're damn lucky you didn't touch her, because if you had, you wouldn't have been able to drag your sorry ass off the ground, I can promise you that."

The man chuckled as he and the woman turned to leave.

"You heard them. Get your ass off my property before I call the cops."

I swiveled toward my dad, who stood under the light at the back door, and sent a soft smile his way.

"This bar is a piece of shit anyway," the woman screamed.

"And the bartenders fucking suck," the man added.

Grey's hand clenched in mine. He took another step forward, clearly with every intention of saying or possibly doing something more, before I pulled him back.

"They're not worth it. Let it go," I whispered.

The two culprits stumbled down the street and into the darkness.

"You okay, sweetheart?" Dad's tone was littered with concern as he moved closer to the two of us. "What happened?"

"I'm fine, Dad." I let out a deep breath. "Those two were in the bar earlier and tried to cause a scene. I guess they didn't like it when I politely told them to ease off." I rubbed a hand down my arm, the night air suddenly cool. "Anyway, I'm just grateful Grey was here," I said, my eyes gleaming up to his.

"What in the actual hell. Did you recognize them?" Dad asked.

"No. They were loud and rowdy. I figured they were probably on vacation by the way they came in thinking they were better than us. They were less than pleasant to deal with, but I didn't peg them as the dark alley kind of people. Just goes to show that you never know."

"I don't understand the audacity of some people," he said, shaking his head. "I'm sorry. I should've been there earlier to help, but a few shipments got delivered and I was restocking in the back."

"Don't be sorry. It's not your fault."

"I'm just glad—" Dad looked at Grey, clearly having forgotten his name.

"Grey. Grey Prescott, sir." He pulled his hand free from mine and threw it out to meet my dad's in a firm shake.

"Grey. It's nice to meet you. I'm grateful you were here to help my daughter." A full smile spread across his face, making me nervous for what he was going to say next. "You wouldn't happen to be the same *G* who sent the hydrangeas for my daughter, would you?"

"Dad!" I gasped.

"Ha. Yes, sir. That would be me." Grey's genuineness toward my dad sent sparks of happiness all around me, like a Fourth of July firework.

Dad looked at me first, smiling. "What? The flowers stick out like a sore thumb. I wanted to know where they came from." He chuckled before facing Grey. "But based on the mile-wide smile that's plastered on my daughter's face, I'll let this one slide."

I was so caught up in their exchange I didn't realize they were both staring at me, and that smile dad mentioned was still very much plastered across my face.

"MJ, why don't you head home? I'll finish closing up. I love you big."

"I love you bigger. Thanks, Dad."

"It was nice to meet you, Grey. I hope I'll see you around."

"You too, sir. Next time I send your daughter flowers, I'll be sure to send them to her house." He chuckled, reaching to shake Dad's hand again.

"Good man," Dad said, shaking his hand and walking back into the bar.

"Thank you." My eyes met his. "You don't know how glad I am that you were here. That you're here now. I don't want to know what he would've done had you not stopped—"

"Don't finish that sentence," he said, one hand in his pocket, the other just barely grazing his chest.

My face scrunched in confusion.

"Don't finish that sentence because I don't even want to think about what could've happened. The thought makes me fucking furious," he finished, his fingers still putting pressure on the left side of his chest.

"Grey." I grabbed his shirt and pulled him toward me. "I'm okay. A little shaken up, but fine…" I tugged him even closer, our lips dancing with one another. "Because of you."

Deleting the little space left between us, I pushed our lips together. A kiss so vulnerable, my knees went weak. His hands reached for either side of my face while my hands wrapped around his waist. Our lips pressed together, our tongues syncing in perfect rhythm.

"Damn, I've missed you." He smirked. "Can I walk you home?"

I bit the inside of my cheek. "I'd like that."

Turning away from The Wharf, I grabbed Grey's arm, and a sense of never wanting to let go wandered through my brain as he walked me home.

Walking out of my bathroom after opting for a somewhat cute matching set, I scanned the room for Grey, finding him in the corner of my room near my desk. Noticing the familiar Word document on my screen that was a compiled jumble of all my inner thoughts that I hoped to one day turn into a story, I immediately felt like I could vomit.

"What's this?" he asked when I approached.

"Oh. That's just a mess of words that I wrote."

"MJ, this is good. Like, really good."

"How much did you read?" My heart sank, realizing that a character in my so-called story eerily resembled him. If I wasn't already mortified, now I wanted to crawl into a hole and never come out.

"Enough to know that you have serious talent." He rested his lower half on the edge of my desk, folding his arms across his broad chest. "The way you pick each word and connect it with the next is addicting. I didn't know you were a writer."

"I guess you could say that. Although, I'm more of an *aspiring* writer."

More serious this time, he spoke again. "Do you write?"

My face shifted into a puzzled gaze as I stared at him. "What do you mean?"

"I mean, do you write?" He lowered his hands, placing them on my desk behind him.

I hesitated. "Yes—"

"Then you're a writer. Not an aspiring writer... an actual writer. It's as simple as that. Don't sell yourself short, MJ. You write, and from the little I read, you're damn good at it."

Listening to the words coming out of his mouth, I believed what he was saying. How did he make it sound so simple, so matter of fact, when I'd spent years trying to decide if I had what it took to call myself a writer.

Grey stepped closer, sliding his arms through mine and landing on the small of my back. One hand stayed put while he placed the other under my chin, lifting it until our eyes met. His alluring expression was one I didn't want to look away from.

"Got it?" he demanded, his fingertips dropping to my exposed collarbone.

His confidence in me sent my body into a frenzy.

"Got it," I whispered.

"Good." He barely stepped back, holding up his pointer finger. "But I do have one question."

"Shoot."

"How do you track your progress when your goal is to write a whole-ass book?" he asked, and his interest in my work made me swoon.

"Simple. A word count. It can get overwhelming if you try to dissect it more than that. So, you just take it one word at a time."

"Oh yeah, I'm sure it's as simple as that," he joked, pulling me into him again.

He softly kissed my lips, then trailed down the length of my neck, the scruff on his jaw tickling my skin. A few giggles slipped from my mouth as he slowly worked his way back up to my lips, planting one last kiss.

I instinctively pulled him into a hug, squeezing him tighter. "I've never felt safer than when I heard your voice in that parking lot."

"I'm just really glad you're okay," he replied, sounding grateful.

Even though I could've stayed in his arms for the rest of forever, we released each other at the same time.

"Now that I know you're home safe, I'm going to head out. But we're still on for tomorrow, right?"

He stepped toward the door and so did I.

I reached for him, grabbing his hand in mine. "Stay?" I sighed. "Because I've missed you too."

His gentle eyes brightened as they looked me over once more.

"And I'd rather not be alone tonight," I added.

His soft grin eased the anxiousness in the pit of stomach that was still hanging around from earlier. "If it were up to me, you'd never have to be alone again."

Feeling content with asking him to stay, I walked out of my bedroom and toward the kitchen.

"Want some hot tea?" I asked, banging around the cabinet in search of a mug.

"No, I'm good. But do you want me to find us something to watch?"

"Say less." I giggled. "I hate trying to decide on a movie, so you better surprise me with something good."

"No pressure or anything." Grey slumped onto my couch.

Peering over the counter into the living room, I smiled as I watched him casually sitting there. His light-wash jeans, cuffed at the bottom, lay perched on my ottoman. His upper half was covered with a tan-colored Henley, two of the three buttons undone. He was resting his right hand over his head while his left hand messed with the remote.

I never saw myself here, with him, enjoying a casual movie night, but here we were.

"*Blue Crush*, seriously?" I asked, strolling into the living room.

Grey moved his hand, making a perfect spot for me to plop into. "What? Not a fan?" he asked.

"No, I actually love this movie. I just never would've guessed this as your pick," I said, holding my warm mug with both hands.

"This movie is one of the most underrated movies of the early two thousands."

Our laughter filled the little space there was between us. I nuzzled myself right up next to him, finding that I fit perfectly in the space he'd left for me.

Somewhere during the private surfing lessons, I started to doze. Our bodies melted into one another, the sound of the movie playing in the background. His body was behind mine, my head resting on his arm. Neither of us spoke, but we didn't have to, because our silence said everything.

# Chapter Twenty-Six

Opening my eyes, I quickly realized that I'd spent the night on the couch, one of my arms still dangling off the edge. I reached out, hoping to land on a familiar frame next to me, but came up empty-handed.

I perked up, hoping to see Grey somewhere. I scanned the room, but disappointment smacked me in the face when I found an empty apartment staring back at me. Throwing my feet to the side of the couch, I stood, sleepily walking into my bedroom.

A yellow sticky note stuck perfectly to the center of my computer screen caught my eye across the room. A coy smile snuck out.

In Grey's surprisingly legible handwriting, it read,

Peeling the note from my computer screen, giddiness took over my body and I started uncontrollably flailing my arms and legs like a schoolgirl.

"Liv, you would absolutely lose your mind if you could see me now. I somehow managed to snag the most attractive—and maybe kindest?—man alive. He's protective, supportive, and knows his way around the bedroom. A true gentleman in my eyes, and I have no doubt he would be in yours too." I let out a gulp of excitement. "I would do anything to have you here with me, I miss you so fucking much."

Sometimes I swore she was in the room, listening to me, and other times I spoke aloud as a way of coping with the harsh reality that she wasn't.

Grief really was such a bitch. I was supposed to share these moments with her. We were supposed to be a part of each other's lives forever. To celebrate each other's highs and be there during the lows. Sometimes, I hated myself for being the one who survived. It felt wrong. It felt unfair. Why did I get to experience the rest of my life when Liv lost hers?

At times I found myself imagining what life might look like if she hadn't died and we'd instead found ourselves living out our dreams in New York City. Me, a successful writer, spending my days falling in love with fictional characters; Liv a modern-day David Childs, spending her days buried in sketches of the next New York skyscraper. Both of us, spending our nights together, going to chic bars and indulging in overpriced cocktails.

It seemed silly now, unrealistic even. A life like that felt so far away, distant, almost as if it was a story I'd written before. One I could recite every line to but that would never be known.

The way grief manipulated its way back into your brain during the least opportune times was something I'd never get used to. Grief didn't care if you were having a good day, it didn't care if you were standing in line at the grocery store or sitting in the park having a picnic. It snuck up on you when you least expected it and did its best to pull you back under.

My phone pinged, bringing the grief spiral to a halt. In a way, I figured that was Liv's way of making sure the grief didn't get too far in.

A text from Sam illuminated my screen.

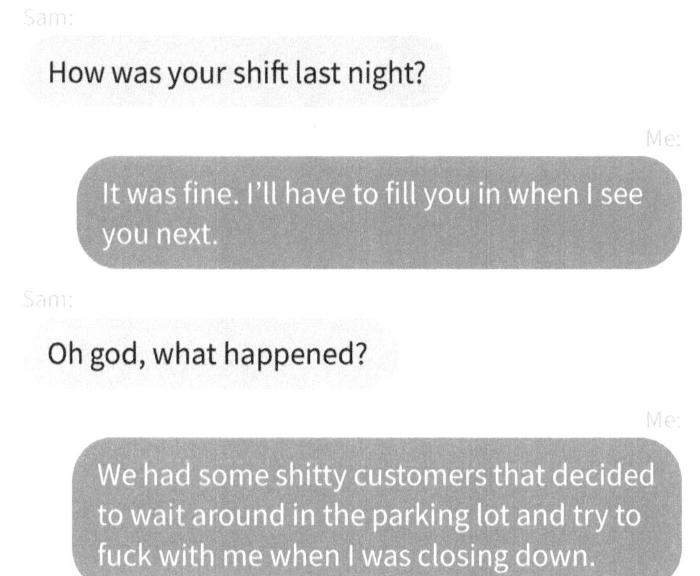

Sam:

What the fuck! What is wrong with people? Are you okay?

Me:

I ask myself that question on a daily basis. But yes, I'm fine.

Sam:

What are you doing tonight? Want to get an ungodly amount of junk food and lie on your couch?

Me:

Can't. I have plans. I'm having dinner with Grey.

Sam:

MJ! WHAT!

Me:

I know, I know. Let's get lunch this weekend and I'll fill you in. I promise.

Sam:

Fine. Let's chat later and we'll figure out a day that works. I love you.

Me:

I love you too.

Setting my phone down, I moseyed to the fridge, only to decide a smoothie from down the street sounded better than anything I could make.

Plus, some fresh air would probably do me good.

Berry Good Smoothies was a staple in Montauk and had been around since before I started high school. The owners were sisters, Ashley and Niki, and they were the sweetest. They'd brought their tiny space to life in more ways than one.

The walls were splashed with a lime green paint that almost blinded you, especially in the mornings when the sun peered through the windows. Palm leaves, surfboards, and other exotic plants lined the interior, leaving little clearance to get to the counter, but I didn't mind. It made it feel neighborly, cozy.

"Hey, Ashley, can I get one Green Goddess and two of your PB&J smoothies?" I asked, reaching into my bag to retrieve my wallet.

"Coming right up! How's your mom and dad? I feel like I haven't seen them for a bit."

"They're good. In fact, I'm headed their way after I get these smoothies." I wanted to check in with Dad after last night, make sure there wasn't any more trouble after I left, and he never said no to PB&J. "Things have been crazy at The Wharf lately, they don't have time for much else."

"It's been crazy around here too! But I have to admit, there's really nothing better than the buzz of this town during the summer," Ashley said.

My grin grew. "I couldn't agree more."

The blender hummed alive, smoothing out all the ingredients into a delicious breakfast that I couldn't wait for. Note to self: hot tea doesn't suffice for dinner. Not that food was on my mind last night. I much preferred devouring the sight of Grey Prescott's body tangled in mine. I'd choose that over dinner any night—

"MJ." Ashley's voice anchored me back to the present.

I grabbed the three smoothies, smiling at her. "Thank you, have the best day."

"You too, sweet girl. Tell your parents I said hi."

Mom and Dad's house was only a couple of blocks from Berry Good, and thankfully so, because the morning sun was already uncomfortably hot. The sensation of tiny sweat beads rolling down my back confirmed it.

I strolled around the corner, and to no surprise, I spotted Mom tending to her garden out front. "Hey, Mom."

"Hi, sweetheart," she responded, dropping her shears to the ground and taking her gloves off, one finger at a time. "Please say one of those is for me."

I handed over the cold beverage, along with a straw. "I come bearing gifts."

She took a long slurp of her smoothie before opening her mouth to talk. "The best way to start my morning. Your dad is out back fiddling with something on the house. It might be a good idea for you to go find him, maybe take his mind off whatever it is he thinks needs fixing." She laughed. "Your dad and a ten-foot ladder should never be placed in the same sentence."

"Oh jeez." I laughed with her. "I'm on it."

I thought I'd gotten away with no mention of last night as I aimed my body toward the back of the house, but I was wrong.

"Don't think we aren't going to chat about your night last night. The scumbags from the bar. Grey Prescott. All of it."

With my back still facing away from her and my foot paused mid-step, I tossed my hand in the air. "I hear ya."

Hearing Grey's name leave my mom's mouth made the dormant butterflies in my belly flutter to life.

"Dad?" I yelled. No response. "Dad!" I yelled louder this time.

"Back here."

Luckily, he was only a few rungs up the ladder when I spotted him around the back. "Here you go. I brought breakfast."

"What a heaven send you are."

"My god. Do you and Mom not feed yourselves? You're ravenous."

"We both woke up raring to go. Or I should say, your mom woke up before me and was already out in her garden by the time I rolled out of bed, so I figured I should get to work too." He smiled.

My parents were two peas in pod. They shared the kind of love that people wrote about in books. The fierce and loyal kind that everyone hoped to feel at some point in their lives.

"Well, I just wanted to come and check in after last night, make sure those shitheads didn't cause any more trouble. But more importantly, I wanted to see if we were still on for our annual Fourth of August cookout? You guys haven't mentioned it yet, and it's not that far away."

"Of course we are. We can figure out the details later, but I'll plan on grilling steaks. Jess and John said they'd take care of the sides."

We'd done this annual dinner for a few years now. Summer holidays were always a little tough for me, for all of us, really, so instead of a Fourth of July cookout, we did a "Fourth of August" one. The craziness of the holiday was gone, but we still got to enjoy all the best things about it.

"Mmm. My favorite. Just let me know what you want me to bring."

"Maybe that boy from last night?" Mom's voice got clearer as she stepped closer, a massive smirk painted on her face.

"Mom!" I squealed, taking a big gulp of my smoothie in an attempt to mask my smile.

"Speaking of, I liked him. When are you going to see him again?" Dad asked, entirely too interested in my dating life.

But with that comment came a rush at the realization that I was going to see him in a few short hours.

Playfully slapping my dad's arm, I screeched, "Stop!"

"What? I saw you smirking behind the bar after those hydrangeas got delivered."

Mom piped in. "He got you flowers and you haven't even told me about him yet."

"Mom, he got me flowers literally *yesterday*. Why do you think I came over here first thing this morning? Give me a chance," I whined, defending myself.

"Okay, fair enough. I'll let this one slide. But I want to know everything."

"And I promise to tell you everything. However, I do need to get back home. I plan to do some writing before he picks me up for dinner." I winked.

She gasped, her eyes widening. "Miller Jean Morgan, I cannot believe you. A new boy and possibly a new book?"

"You're getting a little ahead of yourself, Mom. But I am happy to report that I've written more in the last couple of weeks than I have since I started writing again. Not saying there is any correlation between the two, just thought you'd both want to know." I took another slurp of my smoothie.

"I'm proud of you." Dad smiled. "I never doubted you for a second."

"Me neither. Now go. Go write that story that we're all waiting for," Mom insisted.

"I love you big. Talk soon." Pushing my palm to my lips, I sent a kiss in their direction.

"Love you bigger," they said in unison.

The morning faded to afternoon and with it came a slight breeze, making it much more enjoyable than this morning. I decided to take my writing to the beach for a little change of scenery.

But instead of my usual overcrowded spot, I went somewhere new.

Luckily, I remembered how to find my way back to Grey's secret hideaway fairly easily. Pushing my way through a number of overgrown but luscious bushes, I finally heard what I was after—the tranquil sound of rushing water, confirmation that the serene waterfall was waiting for me on the other side.

Finally stepping through the last bit of vegetation, I laid eyes on the spot Grey had taken me to. Instead of finding my way down the rocks and onto the sandy beach, I perched myself on the top of the dainty drop-off, slinging my feet over the side.

I dropped my bag on my way, some of the contents spilling out next to me.

Grabbing my laptop, I cracked it open and began writing. My process more or less looked like mindlessly scrolling on my phone for a while, returning to my computer and typing a few words, finding the perfect song to match the vibe, and then repeating the above steps for a few hours. Although vicious, this routine was the only way I managed to get any words out of my head and onto the screen in front of me.

Slow and steady.

My computer screen stared at me, the cursor blinking obnoxiously, waiting for me to do something productive. Despite the fact that I'd written more words in the past month than I had in a while, something still wasn't quite there. The words were jumbled and randomly strung together. And while the story might be buried somewhere in all those letters, right now it was lost, and someone needed to tell it where to go.

I slammed my fingers down on the keyboard in frustration.

"Liv, what the fuck am I doing here?" My head flung back, forcing me to stare up at the clouds snailing their way through the sky. "I keep trying to write, but every time I do, I get stuck." I threw my hands to my face, letting the weight of my head fall into my palms. "I keep finding myself going back to the same point in the story. The beginning of the end. I can't figure out how to write it because it hurts too much, so I write around it. I fill in the darkness with lightness and fluff. But the problem is, eventually I have to write it. Even more than that, I *need* to write it if I'm ever going to bring this story to life, and I think for the first time ever, our story is the one I want to write."

My phone pinged next to me. For a brief moment, I imagined the text being from Liv. Like she heard me talking to her.

The thought faded and my perception focused.

Grey:

Word count update?

Me:

Don't you know you're not supposed to interrupt the writer when they're writing?

Grey:

Miller. Don't change the subject. I'm holding you accountable, what's the word count?

Me:

Okay, okay. Let's just say it could be more. But now you're distracting me. My goal is 1,000 words by the time you come pick me up.

Grey:

Hit your goal and I'll make tonight worth your while…

The desire in the lower half of my body roared to life from a single text. This was bad, but I didn't care. I was inspired.



In need of some musical inspiration, I snagged my headphones from my bag. Pressing shuffle, I looked away, waiting for the first song to load.

And then, there it was, my sliver.

*Liv.*

Just across the cove, there was a single hydrangea bush swaying in the breeze. It wasn't the familiar lilac color I loved so much, but it didn't need to be for me to know that Liv was right here with me. A smile blossomed, straining my cheeks.

Then, almost like magic, the music caught my attention as "This Love" by Taylor Swift picked up. The tune floated into my ears, uncovering the story that'd been lost among all those words. This time, the lyrics represented something entirely different. This time, a depiction of an epic love story between two best friends that, while ending tragically, deserved to be heard.

In just under two hours, I clocked almost 3,000 words, and for the first time *ever*, my story began to take shape.

245

# Chapter Twenty-Seven

"All right, this has to be it, my god," I said, talking to myself as I examined the light blue sundress with subtle white flowers in my floor-length mirror. I was going for effortless but cute, and thankfully this dress was both of those things.

I flung my hands in a fanning motion. I'd tried on damn near fifteen outfits and at this point, I was sweating. I leaned closer to my reflection, swiping my fingers in the corners of my mouth, removing any residual lipstick that crowded the edge of my lips. My tousled blonde curls fell perfectly down my back, and the sudden burst of confidence had me anticipating the night ahead even more.

"MJ?" Grey's voice trailed down the hallway and into my bedroom, startling me. My heart stuttered at first before kickstarting itself into high gear.

"Be right there," I shouted. Grabbing my chunky white Converse, I plopped down on my disheveled bed and quickly pulled them on before making my way toward Grey.

Expecting him to be waiting for me in the entryway, I moved in that direction, only to be startled again by a loud sound that came from the kitchen.

"Shit," Grey said, clearly flustered.

"What are you doing over there? Looking for all of my secrets?" I joked, trying to get a glimpse of whatever it was.

All six foot and some odd inches of him standing there, in my kitchen, was a sight I never knew I was missing. His broad shoulders put a strain on the thin material of his light blue button-up, hinting at the strength of his back muscles. His chinos were suctioned to every inch of his lower half, and I couldn't resist nibbling my lower lip.

My eyes trailed up his body just as he twisted to look at me, a defeated expression on his face. Confused, I opened my mouth to speak, but he cut me off before I could say anything.

"For you," he said, pulling a bushel of lilac hydrangeas from the counter behind him. "I was trying to get them into a vase for you but failed. Miserably." A tiny smirk developed in the corner of his mouth.

Beaming, I said, "You didn't have to—"

"I know I didn't have to, but I wanted to." He paused. "We forgot to bring your flowers home from the bar last night, so I wanted you to have some for your house too."

My god. This man had turned me into a ball of mush.

"Thank you," I responded, knowing I wasn't well enough to form an actual sentence.

"Anything for you," he said, his voice dragging with him as he strolled closer.

He raised his hand up, inches from my collarbone, and I felt the sudden urge to feel his fingertips on my skin.

A subtle gasp slipped through my lips. The breath between us was buzzing.

But just as quickly as it was there, it was gone. I opened my eyes to find him looking right back at me. Except this time, his expression wasn't one of defeat. Instead, his smoldering gaze was laced with seduction as the tiny muscles in his jaw tightened.

"Ready to go?" he asked, canvassing my body.

I raised my eyebrow and smirked, sarcastically responding, "Like what you see?"

He nibbled his lower lip. "Even more than I remember."

Outwardly, I was doing my best to stay calm, cool, and collected, because inside, my body was completely unhinged.

Pushing a stray piece of blonde hair behind my ear, I attempted to change the subject, afraid that I might do or say something irrational if I didn't. You know, something like "Fuck dinner, take right me here, Grey. I'm begging you."

Thankfully, I got ahead of my rogue thoughts.

"Should we head out?"

His silence lingered. With one hand in his pocket and the other massaging his jaw, his deep voice filtered through the air. "We probably should."

The words were enough to send every single one of my nerves firing off.

I forced myself to move toward the door, and he followed closely behind.

Coming down the stairs, I expected to see that beautiful light-blue bronco perched in a parking spot, but after a quick scan, I came up empty. Uncertainty spread across my face as I looked at Grey.

"You were hoping for the Bronco, weren't you?" A devilish grin mounted his face.

"Maybe just a little," I said, scrunching my face. "No, but really, if we're not driving, how are we getting to your house?"

His grin returned. "Can you trust me?"

"Grey…"

"Can you?"

Glancing down the small picturesque street, then back up at him, standing there so patiently, I nodded. "I can."

"My girl," he said, grabbing my hand and pulling me in the direction of the water. When I didn't budge, he continued. "Are you coming or am I going to have to carry you?"

Blushing at the thought of this man carrying me across the busiest street in town, I responded, "I'm coming."

His hand stayed laced in mine, neither one of us willing to let go. The quiet chatter of the townspeople enjoying their dinner, the salty breeze floating by, and the bugs beginning their nighttime symphony making it easy to get lost in the moment.

I looked toward the sunset, the sun almost hidden beneath the water, only a glimpse remaining, and smiled. I knew if Liv could see me now, she'd be proud of how far I'd come. How much

I'd stepped out of my comfort zone recently. How much I was enjoying myself.

"I know you don't love being in cars, so"—Grey peered over at me—"I figured we'd take another form of transportation."

I tilted my head to the side, bemused, and watched as his eyes shifted to the water before quickly following his line of sight.

A low gasp left the back of my throat and my hand flung to my mouth. There, only a few feet from where we were standing, tied up to a tiny dock, was a vintage Chris-Craft.

The outside was flawlessly painted in a nautical navy blue, with gold block letters centered across the back, spelling out *A Second Wave*. The interior was made of the same pristine wood that'd clearly been well preserved. Even the seats were wooden, but they were covered with navy-and-white-striped cushions. The captain's chair matched perfectly in a pearly, cream color. This boat was something similar to what you'd see while scrolling Pinterest.

"Is this yours?" I said, my mouth hanging open.

"It is," he said, running his hands through his hair. "I bought it a few years ago, hoping that it would push me to come back here, and it's sat dry-docked until just recently."

My eyes still dancing over every detail of his boat, I said, "It's perfect. Growing up in a town like this, you learn to appreciate and understand boats, especially ones that look like this."

"I thought you might like it."

"I love it."

Hand in hand, we made our way onto the dock as it wobbled underneath our weight, creaking every so often.

Grey stepped over the side of the boat, gracefully planting himself inside.

I firmly gripped the side, attempting a somewhat nimble movement while Grey's back was turned, knowing I wasn't going to look half as graceful as he did. Unfortunately, the plan didn't work, and the slack in the rope allowed the boat to slowly drift from the dock all while I still had one foot planted on it. "Shit."

Hearing the panic in my voice, Grey instantly spun around. "Here. Grab my hand."

I reached for him, trying to control the weight of my body, but was unsuccessful. Just as the remainder of my body left the dock, so did our balance. He fell onto the seat behind him, my body landing on top of his, my legs on either side of his torso.

"Well, if I knew it was going to be that easy to get you on top of me, I would've showed you my boat sooner," he said, his tongue slowly trailing his upper lip.

I slapped his chest. "Hilarious."

The position made it almost impossible not to stare at him, and as I did, I couldn't help but feel something for this man. Being around him was easy, talking to him was easy, everything with him was just *easy*.

"Sorry," I muttered, still straddling him.

I started to push myself off of him, but not before he caught my face in his hands. "For what?"

"I was lost in my own thoughts."

"Is that such a bad thing?" he asked.

His question shook me, because normally, I would've said yes. I'd spent so much of my time lost in my own thoughts—the dark ones, the sad ones. But now that he mentioned it, my thoughts when I was around him were neither of the above. When I was with Grey, my thoughts were clear, fresh, hopeful.

"Actually, no…" I breathed. "It's not."

"I'd love to be able to see inside that pretty little head of yours," he said, my face still pushed against his palms. "Maybe one day I will. You know, when you publish your book."

"Maybe one day," I said, smiling despite myself. I again attempted to remove myself from his lap, because my self-control was wavering with each passing second.

"MJ?" He pulled me even closer. "I want you to know that I think you're incredible. You're unlike anyone I've ever met. If I would've known that you were here, I never would've waited this long to come back."

His words were sweet as they left his mouth and filtered through the air. A response wasn't coming to me at the moment, but the urge to kiss him definitely was. Before thinking too much into it, I pressed my mouth hard against his.

His hands lowered from my face, and he gripped my hips as he pressed his body against mine. The slightest moan edged its way from the back of my throat but was quickly silenced by Grey's mouth consuming mine.

Eventually, our kisses softened, almost as if our bodies were satisfied, at least for the moment. Or maybe we both realized this town was too small to have spontaneous boat sex two minutes from the main drag.

"I'm starving," I offered, leaning back, my arms still slung around his nape.

His eyes darted down to where my legs still clung to either side of his thighs. "Me too."

Giggling, I said, "Grey, I'm serious."

"Okay, okay, fine. It's only a ten-minute ride to my house. Make yourself comfortable." He motioned toward the empty seats at the back of the boat. Grey untied the boat, walking back to the captain's chair, stopping only to lean down and plant a kiss on my forehead.

Smiling, I stared out to the ocean. I was grateful that we were traveling via boat instead of car. While my anxiety around cars was subdued whenever I was with Grey, the sea always brought me some much-needed solace.

The rumble of the engine coming to life and the last few rays of sun on my face convinced my eyes to shut. Moments like this made it hard for me to believe that all the hurt I'd endured could exist in the same world as all of this joy.

As we idled out from the dock, I imagined what Liv would say if she saw me sitting here—in this boat, with this man, smiling. *Truly* smiling. I'd like to think she'd be happy for me. That she'd be cheering me on. It was wild to think that ever since her death all those years ago, I could count on one hand the number of times that I'd known this sense of contentment.

As Grey pushed the throttle down, I felt lighter than I had in a while, almost like I was floating while the air breezed through my curls. I'd kept Liv's death so close to me for so long, I never imagined feeling the need to share it.

I sort of assumed that I'd always be sad. Maybe not fully sad, but at least partly. Like little fragments of my being would harbor sadness no matter how much time had passed and no matter how much happiness radiated around me.

I didn't know how long we'd been cruising or how much longer we had to go, but I made the spontaneous decision to let him in on my grief.

"My best friend died."

# Chapter Twenty-Eight

Grey cut the throttle and his strong posture immediately softened as he began moving toward me.

"Miller." My name left his lips like a warm hug, embracing me as soon as they hit my ears.

"It's okay, it was a long time ago," I responded. "I'm not even sure why I just blurted that out. Oh god, I'm sorry," I said, a wave of uncertainty coursing through me.

"Don't ever say you're sorry for sharing something with me. Ever," he said, wrapping me in a hug. "I can't even begin to imagine what that must've been like." His strength surrounded me, both physically and mentally.

He was *safe.*

"I was seventeen when it happened." My tear ducts swelled, threatening to spill over. "Remember when I told you I'd been in a car accident?"

He nodded, pulling me closer, if that were even possible. My back rested against his chest, both of his arms draped over my shoulders, giving me something to anchor myself to. "That was the accident I was talking about. It was Labor Day weekend before our senior year of high school. We were on our way home from a party that'd gotten busted by the cops," I said, pausing to ground myself.

Grey squeezed a little tighter. "It's okay, I'm right here."

Taking a deep breath, I continued. "A driver crossed over into our lane and hit us head on. Our car hit the guardrail and flipped, and the driver fled the scene and was never caught. We were left upside down until the firefighters and paramedics arrived. I made it out alive, and she didn't. She died on the way to the hospital." The last word left my mouth as the first tear fell down my cheek. It was as if the words had transported me right back to that night, eleven years ago. My body shuttered. "I never even got to say goodbye." The tears were full-blown waterworks now.

"Jesus, MJ. I'm so fucking sorry." He rested his chin on top of my head and I let myself lean into his blanket of strength. "That's horrific. Heartbreakingly so."

"It was unbearable. The pain, I mean. It was the dark, messy, debilitating, unsure how you're going to get out of bed kind of pain. The absolute worst kind," I admitted.

"I know I can't make it any better or take away any of your hurt—because trust me, if I could, I would—but for what it's worth, I can promise to be here for you when you want to talk about it, or even when you don't."

"That means a lot, thank you," I said, my voice shaky.

A silence drifted between us as the waves rippled around the boat, making us teeter back and forth slightly. I didn't know if it was the serenity of the open ocean, Grey's arms sheltering me, or the simple fact that for the first time—possibly ever—I'd said all of that out loud, but in a flicker of a moment, I felt a tiny piece of me become whole again.

"Thank you," he said from behind me. Confused, I cranked my neck to the right to get a better view of his face.

"For what?"

"For telling me all that," he said. "That couldn't have been easy. And based on what I've picked up on since being around you, you don't tend to overshare, especially with things like this."

"You're not wrong," I admitted. Returning my gaze to the water, watching the little ripples move closer, I smiled, processing what he'd just said.

"I know I'm not." He beamed back confidently. "But I also knew you'd been holding something in that you weren't ready to share with me. I didn't know if you'd ever feel comfortable enough to share, but I hoped you would. And now that you have, I just want you to know that I meant what I said before. The most painful pieces are often the hardest ones to share." A heavy breath released from his chest, but he still seemed tense.

A sense of comfort rolled through me, and just as I began to settle into it, Grey's breath quickened.

"Maybe one day, I'll be as brave as you and share a piece of my hurt too."

The words fell from his mouth in a moment of vulnerability, and this large, formidable, protective man revealed a new layer about himself.

Selfishly, I wanted to know more, but more than that, I wanted to comfort him. And the fact that he'd given me a glimpse of him that not many people had seen was enough for me right now.

"I'll be here, ready to listen whenever that day comes," I replied, snuggling up to him.

"I know you will," he said, dragging his right hand underneath my chin and pulling it upward. "There's no doubt in my mind." His breath was hot against my mouth, but it didn't last long before the space evaporated.

Each kiss we shared was better than the last. This one was sweet, soft even, and felt more intimate than the rest.

"I should probably get back to driving this boat," he said, pulling away.

"Do you have to?"

"No. I absolutely do not. I can stay right here with you for the rest of the night."

Right on cue, my stomach rumbled off some sort of argument to his last statement.

"On the other hand..." He chuckled. "I think I should get us home and get you some dinner."

"My stomach thanks you." I giggled.

He made his way back to the captain's chair and the boat picked up speed within seconds. The sun was now completely behind the horizon, leaving us little light except for the reflection of the stars on the water.

Grey effortlessly docked the boat. While he secured it, I managed to maneuver myself off surprisingly well. I stood, waiting for him to finish.

"Ready?" he asked, pulling my hand into his and guiding me in the direction of his house. His *perfect* house.

The house was exactly how I remembered it. Floor-to-ceiling windows and sliding glass doors made up the entire back facade. Grey pushed through a wooden gate that separated his property and the beach.

The pool was lit up just as much as the rest of the estate, the water appearing blue from the lights that lay below the surface. Sliding one of the glass doors open, Grey stepped aside, ushering me in first.

Last time I was here, this room was filled to the brim with partygoers and loud music. At the time, that was exactly what I wanted, but I had to admit the silence we were met with now was nice.

"It's even prettier than I remember," I said, gazing up at the ceiling in awe.

"I'd have to agree."

My eyes met his, a coy wink flying in my direction as he looked me up and down.

The rush of heat to my cheeks was unavoidable, and also quickly becoming a common theme when I was around this man.

"Kitchen is this way," he said, motioning to the other side of the house. The one opposite of his bedroom, because yes, I still remembered exactly where that was.

He started to walk in that direction and I trailed behind him, still taking in every tiny detail of his house.

There was no way he decorated by himself.

Grey switched on a light, illuminating the kitchen in front of us. Another immaculately designed space, maybe even my favorite one.

"Holy shit. This kitchen is bigger than my apartment. It's gorgeous."

"The kitchen is one of my favorite places to be, so I wanted something very specific." He walked to the sink and started washing his hands. "Over there"—he pointed—"behind that door, you'll find some wine. Pick out any bottle you want, and I'll get us something to snack on while I prepare dinner."

"You're making dinner?" I asked before grabbing the door handle.

Grey looked around the room. "It isn't going to cook itself," he joked.

"I mean, obviously, but I just assumed you had someone who did that for you."

"MJ..." he started, drying his hands on the black towel that previously hung over the sink, embroidered with a gold *P*. "Despite your previous assumptions of me, I can, in fact, cook my own meals. I even prefer it." His face was etched with sarcasm. "Wait, you thought I asked you to dinner at my own house and was going to let someone else make it?"

"Kind of? But I'm pleasantly surprised."

"Well then aren't you in for a treat." The word *treat* left his mouth and I could have sworn he was alluding to something else. Or maybe I just hoped he was.

The doorknob was cold on my palm as I twisted it. The smell of mahogany wafted across my face and into my nose. "Holy shit. When you said you had some wine, I assumed there was going to be a few bottles on the other side of this door, not an entire cellar."

"One day maybe you'll quit assuming things about me. Although, I do revel in constantly surprising you."

"I do like surprises, especially ones in the form of wine cellars," I joked. "Speaking of surprises, after this, I'd love to go wander around the library of yours that I stumbled upon during the party."

"You're welcome to wander around anything you want."

Stepping through the door, I was transported to my own private cellar. All four walls were equipped with floor-to-ceiling wine racks, and it looked like each wall held 150 to 200 bottles. That wasn't even counting the unopened cases that rested on the floor, lining the perimeter of the room.

"Any bottle?" I bellowed from inside the cellar.

"Any bottle. Whatever your little heart desires."

"Say less," I muttered to myself. I grabbed a bottle that was calling my name and walked back into the kitchen. "How about this one?" I asked, holding up a bottle of cabernet with a fancy label and a name I couldn't pronounce.

"The perfect choice. Wineglasses are over there"—he pointed to a cabinet—"and opener is in the drawer next to the fridge."

Grateful the wine opener was electric because my manual opening skills were subpar, I poured Grey a glass and then one for myself.

"Here you go!"

"Cheers," he said, relieving me of one of the glasses. "To this."

"To this." I smiled.

The dark cherry notes soaking into my lips, immediately hitting me with an oaky but sweet taste that almost melted in my mouth. "Yum." I licked my lips so I wouldn't waste a single drop.

"Are we sure we have to eat dinner?" His smug smile shocked my senses awake, tempting me to give in.

"I'm sure. No one performs well on an empty stomach." I grinned. My words sounded even better out loud than they did in my head.

"Hell, MJ. With a mouth like that, I may not give you a choice." Grey's eyes fired in my direction, darkening by the second. He threw the dish towel over his shoulder while simultaneously shaking his head at me.

Feeling pleased, I plopped myself on the counter, right next to where he'd been preparing the food.

"For you." Grey slid over a wooden cutting board that was filled with a variety of cheeses, crackers, and salami.

"I could get used to this."

I'd already come to learn that with him, words just slipped out before I had a chance to think them through.

"What exactly is it that you could get used to?"

Nervously, I pulled the wineglass to my lips, taking a large gulp. The silence was heavy as I scoured my brain. And of course, after unwillingly blurting out my previous comment, it was as if my brain conveniently decided to stop functioning.

"Because I was thinking the same thing," Grey said, completely unfazed, before returning to wrap the bright green asparagus in bacon.

I grinned, hiding behind the ruby-red liquid that sloshed around my glass.

Watching him work around the kitchen was a brand-new turn-on. The man had rolled up his sleeves, revealing his toned forearms, before getting down to business. He cut, diced, and chopped, only pausing every so often to take a sip of wine.

"Let me guess, you wanted to be a chef, but your father told you that chefs don't make any money…" I joked as I plucked a piece of cheese from the charcuterie board.

"An architect, actually. Although, now that you mention it, I do really enjoy cooking. I'm sure that would've pissed him off just the same."

A heat wave flooded my face. "Wait, Grey, I didn't mean that. I was totally just being an asshole. I shouldn't—"

"MJ. It's fine." He chuckled, pausing before he continued. "I mean, you're essentially spot on. My father did tell me that if I pursued a career as an architect and not a politician, he would disown me."

He tried to sound unbothered, but his hyperfixation on slicing the bread in front of him made it obvious that wasn't the case.

"Ugh, that's brutal," I responded. "I can't even wrap my brain around that. My dad's over here giving me a job and telling me to follow my dreams. I guess that really puts things into perspective, doesn't it," I thought out loud. "Shit, I'm sorry. I didn't mean it like that. It's just that my parents have always been my biggest cheerleaders, and I don't think I would've survived the accident if not for them."

"You don't have to apologize for having good parents, MJ," he teased. "Some of us just didn't get so lucky in that department, and that's okay. My father was threatened by me the second I entered this world. Especially since he was no longer the center of attention. Our relationship never had a chance. Thankfully my mom is a saint and more than makes up for my narcissistic father."

"It still sucks, but I'm glad you have your mom. Moms really are superhuman." I took a swig of my wine. "Wait, so did you go into politics?"

His comment made me realize I didn't even know what he did for a living.

"I did, or rather, I am. Politics are so fucked. It's really all about how much money you have, what family you're a part of, and who you know. Technically, I've been in *politics* since before I could walk. But I only recently made it my full-time gig. Before that, I attempted to make a name for myself *without* my father. I acquired a few properties, some personal projects, but quickly realized that the entire city of New York is under my father's regime. Ultimately leaving me no choice but to give into his antics. *For now.*"

"Jesus. That's such a different world than the one I live in. It's hard for me to even wrap my head around all of it. That pressure sounds like a lot. I mean, shit, I get stressed when I don't meet my made-up deadlines. I couldn't imagine my dad being a mayor of a whole-ass city, especially one as big as New York, holding such unrealistic expectations."

"You sort of just get used to it. Or at least I like to pretend to. My entire life has revolved around politics ever since I can remember, so it's just something that's always been a part of our family. At Christmas, it's there. On birthdays, it's there. It doesn't matter the day, it's just always there with us. Sounds weird saying it out loud, but I promise, you just learn to ignore it, or I should say that I have learned to ignore it."

"I guess..." My voice trailed off. I wasn't exactly sure what I wanted to say next. On one hand, I sort of understood where he was coming from, or at least how it felt to want to make your parents proud. On the other hand, I'd seen firsthand how quickly a life could be taken and how important it was to live a life worth living. "Have you ever gotten to do anything that you wanted?"

"I have, here and there. I opened a little coffee shop that I absolutely adore. My own little oasis. That one really pissed him off. And I have a few other ideas floating around but they'll take time, and I have to be patient if I'm ever going to really be able to tell him to fuck off."

"By the looks of it, you'd be just fine without him," I insisted.

"Remember, everything isn't always as it appears. Although, more than anything, everything is just too damn complicated at the moment, but I'm working on it. In fact, that library you stumbled upon is the inspiration behind one of my biggest ventures."

"Oh. Now I'm intrigued. But I do get what you're saying, the part that everything isn't always how it seems. Just don't forget you have the right to be happy too. Are you?" I asked. "Happy, I mean."

He abruptly stopped mashing the potatoes he'd been preparing and looked at me, his expression perplexed. I hadn't assumed my question would be a tough one.

"It has it perks, some of which make me happy." He trailed off as his attention moved around the beautiful space around us. "Take this house, for example. I designed it myself. I never would've had an opportunity like that if it weren't for my father."

"You designed it?"

"The entire thing. Drew the sketches myself."

The intricate details of this house were incredible before, but now... now that I knew he'd designed it, it looked different. More beautiful than before.

"Grey, this place is incredible."

"That might be the best compliment I've ever gotten." He smirked. "Taste this and tell me my cooking is just as incredible as my design skills," he said, handing over a wooden spoon full of mashed potatoes, steam still rising from them.

The spoon hit my lips and a gush of flavor immediately overtook my tastebuds. My head started nodding aggressively before I could even swallow the deliciousness. "Yes. The answer is yes."

"My girl."

# Chapter Twenty-Nine

"Could you still get used to this?" Grey asked as he seductively pulled the fork from his mouth, finishing his last bite.

The meal he'd prepared was delightful, and it had me convinced this man was a Jack of all trades.

"You could say that," I responded, taking a sip of the cabernet that paired seamlessly with dinner, nudging my plate toward the center of the table.

Grey had insisted on eating dinner outside, and after seeing his space, I wasn't complaining. Tucked away, a few steps down from the rest of the house, was the outdoor space of my dreams.

There was a firepit strategically placed in the center of a towering brick wall. Mounted just above it was a TV, and there was a cream-colored couch that mimicked a cloud and looked like it should've been placed in a living room, not outside. To the left of the couch sat a wooden table made for four, and above our heads were twinkling lights that lit the area just the right amount.

"Did you save room for dessert?"

Without any warning, my right eyebrow shifted upward and I blurted out, "Does dessert involve you?"

"MJ, what did I say about that mouth of yours…"

I grinned, doing my best to tame the fire that was bellowing inside of me.

"I'm sorry, I couldn't help myself," I started, giggling. "You brought me here, gave me wine, and fed me dinner."

Soft music floated around us and the tension in the air sent a million chills down my spine. I could only assume this was one of those pinch-me moments.

Like the ones they always told you to take a mental picture of, the ones where you found yourself feeling the authentic happiness that only appeared every so often and made you believe in magic. When the world around you felt hopeful and all of your worries and fears seemed to dwindle, becoming insignificant compared to the weight of your happiness.

For me, this kind of happiness had become a distant memory, something I hadn't allowed myself to even think about. But with Grey, I sensed it here and there, little glimmers that begun to slip through the cracks and dance around us. But now, at this very moment, it was everywhere. All around us.

"Grey?"

My eyes met his as he scooted closer to me, his large arms wrapping around my lower half. "Yeah?"

"I'm happy," I said, a smile blossoming.

He smiled too, revealing his perfectly straight, white teeth. "MJ?"

I turned my neck to meet his gaze. "Uh huh?"

"Remember when you asked me if I was happy earlier?

I nodded.

"I can confidently say, with you in my arms and the ocean waves behind us, I've never felt happier. I never want to let go of this moment."

A warmth filled my insides as I nuzzled into his chest.

"And MJ?" He paused, waiting for me to look at him again. "I'll do everything in my power to keep that smile on your face, because it's something everyone deserves to see."

My body moved to straddle him, and as soon as I could feel him under me, I pressed our mouths together.

Grey's hand found my neck, our kiss deepening as he pulled me closer.

Ripping his mouth from mine, his voice tickled my ear when he whispered, "Are you going to let me fuck you right here?"

I could feel the want, not just in his voice, but underneath me too, making the self-control I was clinging to almost invisible. "I'll let you fuck me wherever you want to."

"I was hoping you'd say that." The muscle in his jaw tightened. "I've been waiting all night to see that dress on the floor."

Slinking up my arms, his fingertips twirled around the dainty blue straps. His warm lips trailed behind, leaving little kisses everywhere. My straps slowly fell down as the rest of my dress slid upward, Grey's hands grabbing at my waist. The wetness between my legs was growing and my desire for him even more so.

"Grey…" His name trickled from my lips.

"Want to go inside?" he asked.

"Does it look like I want go inside?"

"Well..." He snickered as his gaze dropped to my hardened nipples.

I giggled. "Dammit... no. I don't want to go inside. Now quit making me wait."

Enthusiasm strode across his face as he teased, "Wait for what?"

"For you to fuck me." I let my fingers find the waistband of his pants.

I didn't know what it was about him, but when we were together, I was able to be myself. It was empowering, almost intoxicating. I never would have been that upfront with a man before, but then again, never had I been with a man like Grey Prescott.

"I'll take that as permission." He lowered his voice, somehow sounding more authoritative than before. "Stand up. Over there, by the fire."

Writhing inside from the tension between us and wanting—no, *needing* to be touched by him, I obliged. I dashed toward the large brick fireplace, my back to Grey, the seconds dragging on as I waited for him to come closer.

The sound of his zipper sent a spark of endorphins flying. I was losing both my composure and my patience as I slowly edged backward.

"Easy there." His hot breath radiated onto my neck and my head unconsciously tilted back, landing in the space between his chin and his chest. The softest moan tracked its way up my throat and slipped from my lips.

"Please, Grey, I'm begging you."

His hand reached over and up to my neck, all while his tongue traced the invisible line from my collarbone to my earlobe, sent my senses into overdrive. Gently turning my body to face his, I saw he was now shirtless and his pants were unzipped. If that wasn't enough to send me into a frenzy, Grey dropping to his knees surely was.

His fingers tangled themselves in what little fabric was left on my body. "Black lace… I should've known." His dark eyes met mine while his hands painstakingly dragged the material to the floor.

He returned his attention to my body, leaving an abundance of kisses on my inner thigh, pausing only to say, "I can't wait to feel you around me."

The words plunged me over the edge.

"Then don't," I urged, somewhat aggressively.

Licking his lips, he stood, pulling a condom from his back pocket and ripping it open with his teeth. "Trust me, I'm not going to. I've waited long enough."

Hunger flooded his expression as his pants dropped to the ground while he gripped himself, rolling the condom down. In an instant, our mouths crashed together, the sting of cold bricks pressed against my back. Grey had one hand resting on the brick next to my head, the other digging into my hips and he guided himself inside of me. A sense of euphoria came over me, darting from my fingertips as I dug them into his back.

A hungry moan left the back of his mouth. "Give me your leg," Grey mumbled against me.

"I'll do anything you want me to do," I said, desperation filling my voice as I lifted my left leg.

"You feel fucking incredible," he panted. "Holy shit, MJ." His hand gripped my inner thigh even tighter, sure to leave a bruise, only turning me on even more.

"You're going to make me scream," I gasped.

His eyes flashed as his hand covered my mouth. "Your screams are for me only," he whispered into my ear.

Both our breaths eased closer to the brink, picking up the pace with each second that passed.

"Grey—"

"MJ, I'm going to come." His voice was shaky as he thrust deeper.

"Let me see you finish," I said, opening my eyes.

This man hitting the peak of pleasure, all because of me, was something I needed to witness.

He threw his head back and thrust into me again, somehow managing to go even deeper. His back arched and his grip tightened on my leg. "Fuck." His breath heaved. "MJ." The words blurred together with a low growl, telling me he'd finished.

His body went heavy, but it only lasted for a second before he dropped to his knees.

"What are you—"

But before I could finish, his mouth consumed me, his tongue working in circles that ignited little pleasure fires all through me.

Tearing himself away, those copper eyes hungrily stared up at me. "One day you're going to learn... I'm not going to let you just watch." Within seconds, his mouth was back on me, but this time with the help of his hands.

My god, this man was a magician when it came to women's pleasure.

"Grey, holy shit."

"You turn." The words echoed through my ears just as my body reached its climax and everything around me blurred. Grey made it to his feet just as I finished, allowing my body to find support on his.

"I really could get used to this."

Grinning, Grey reached for my hand as we hazily stumbled back to the couch. He pulled on his khaki trousers, and I reached for his button-up.

There was just something about wearing his shirt after fucking him that felt right.

"I think I'm already used to this," I replied as I buttoned it up.

I stood, grabbing our plates and walking back toward the house.

"You don't have to do that."

"You cooked; I clean."

"Or we can both clean. Because if you think I'm missing the opportunity to see you washing dishes in my kitchen, wearing only my shirt, then you've lost your mind."

Doing my best to balance the two empty plates, I swiveled my head, sending him a wink.

# Chapter Thirty

"Good morning," Grey said, his chest moving beneath me.

My eyes peeped open just enough to ask, "How long have you been awake?"

"Just for a little bit. I didn't want to wake you up; you looked too peaceful."

"I was. This bed is to die for," I said, stretching my arms over my head before propping myself onto my elbows.

Grey's naked body relaxed against his large wooden headboard, his arm propped behind his head. The fluffiest down comforter hid him from the waist down, leaving only his upper half exposed, and I was enjoying a front row seat to his exposed muscles.

The silence between us was serene. A salty breeze swam across my skin, piquing my interest, and I glanced around the room. The sliding glass doors that led to a breathtaking view of the ocean were cracked open.

My gaze shifted back to Grey. "What are you thinking about?"

"I was thinking how I could stay right here forever." His hand moved back and forth on his chest, near the roman numeral tattoo that permanently decorated his skin.

"Wouldn't that be perfect," I said, laying my head on his chest.

"I was also just thinking about everything, you know? How life can change so quickly. I mean, look at us. A few weeks ago I didn't even know you existed, and now I can't imagine not having you here with me. Sometimes it's so easy to get caught up in my career, especially with my father breathing down my neck all the damn time. But since being back here, I've had a chance to slow down and really think about what I want. Not what my father wants, not what anyone else wants, but what *I* want. And while I don't have it all figured out yet, one thing I keep coming back to is you. I want you."

"Grey, I..." I paused.

"It's okay, you don't have to respond." His voice was sincere as he placed his hand on top of mine.

Resituating myself, I put my finger to his mouth, looking him in the eyes. "But I want to. Because I want you too. I have since the moment I saw you, even though I didn't know it yet." I smiled. "You came into this town with something to prove, and I was ready to write you off because of it, but you've surprised me in the best way possible. You aren't the rich city boy with an entitled attitude—"

"Damn, MJ, that's what you thought of me?" A chuckle left his lips.

"Are you going to let me finish?" I harped, batting my eyelashes.

A smug smirk appeared on his face, along with a raised eyebrow. "Don't I always?"

"Touché."

*Focus*, MJ, my god.

"Anyway… in spite of my original assumption, I couldn't have been more wrong about you. You, Grey Prescott, are kind, compassionate, giving, and so much more than anything I could've dreamed up."

"Remember last night when I told you I couldn't be happier? I lied." He pulled me to his lips, kissing me softly. "This right here tops it."

I noticed the slight tension he'd been holding in his jaw unclenched as his hand once again tugged on that rigid scar on his chest. My finger traced the jagged skin and his body quivered in response.

"What happened?" I asked.

"It's a long story. One for another day."

His cold response made it clear it wasn't the time, so I gave him the courtesy of dropping the subject and relaxed back into him.

Between the warm salty air and Grey's constant breaths against my skin, I found myself dazed. His voice rattled under me, bringing me out of my stupor.

"Can I convince you to be my date to a Fourth of July party?"

"The Fourth isn't for a week and a half…"

The color drained from my face as that surfaced the reality of the ticking time bomb that was Grey and me, but I quickly swallowed, pushing the thoughts away and choosing to be present.

"I'm aware, but I didn't know how long it might take to convince you."

"I guess that depends on how convincing you can be…"

Wetting his lips, he repositioned us both. Me on my back, him hovering just above me. "Where should I start? Here?" he whispered, his fingertips finding my sternum as he trailed kisses downward. "Or what about here..."

Chills erupted as his lips hovered just above my belly button.

"Or better yet, how about here?" He coiled his fingers through the black lace that rested between him and pure ecstasy, his hungry eyes peering up to mine.

My body arched, impatient.

"Mhm, looks like I'm doing a pretty good job so far."

A subtle moan slipping through, I muttered, "Okay, okay, fine. I'll be your date."

"Thank you. That's all I needed you to say." He smirked, scaling his way back up my body and landing right next to me.

I had half a mind to yell at him for stopping, but I was also suddenly feeling inspired to write, and that wasn't something I could dismiss. The inspiration was calling, and I wanted to answer.

"I think I have to go." I skulked my way out of bed.

"You *think* you have to go?"

"Well, I don't have to, but I'm going to go," I said, the words still not really making any sense.

"I'm not following. Should I be?" he joked.

Collecting my scattered clothes, I tried to better explain. "Normally, I have to force myself to sit down and write, practically ripping each word from my head, but I'm feeling inspired right now. It's like there are words everywhere, ideas even. I don't want to lose them."

Fully dressed, I turned to face Grey.

He wore a smile so big, I could see his pearly white teeth. "Then what are you still doing standing there? Go, my little writer. Write."

"Eek!" I rotated toward the door then stopped and dashed back to the bed, planting a kiss on those plump lips of his.

"Daniel can give you a ride home. I'm not going to bother you because I don't want to mess with that creative mojo. So just let me know when you're done. You've got this."

# Chapter Thirty-One

It had been over a week and I'd barely come up for air.

The words had been pouring out of me like a fire hose, except they weren't a jumbled mess anymore. Instead, they were strategically placed and cohesive. Almost like the idea of writing an actual book wasn't as farfetched as it once seemed.

Even when I was younger, this type of inspiration didn't exist. All I could think about right now was this story and how it needed to be heard. I spent my days hunched over my computer, my nights plotting, and any spare minutes I had showering, eating, and checking in with everyone.

Everyone had been more than supportive to hear about my sudden drive to write.

Sam and Dad worked extra to cover my shifts, which thankfully meant I'd only missed two.

Chief Williams was more than okay with me canceling. And while our lunches were temporarily paused, his excitement for my writing was not. He sent me texts on a daily basis asking how it was going, among other things. I sensed his grandson might have shared a little insight too.

Speaking of his grandson, Grey had breakfast and coffee delivered to me daily—and by delivered, I mean Daniel, his driver, dropped it off at the same time every morning. A hazelnut latte, an almond croissant, and one single purple hydrangea.

Even though I expected it now, the sound of the doorbell brought a smile to my face.

"Good morning, MJ. Your breakfast."

"Thank you, Daniel."

"Mr. Prescott told me to tell you he'd be here at seven to pick you up."

Racking my brain for what tonight could possibly be, it finally registered.

*Holy shit, how is it already the Fourth of July?*

Caught up in my own thoughts, I'd failed to answer Daniel, who stood there waiting for an answer. "Tell him I can't wait."

"Very well. Keep up the good work."

A soft smile decorated my face. "Thank you."

Anticipation rushed through me as I bolted to my closet and pulled out my pre-planned outfit, thanks to Sam and her ungodly amount of clothes.

A mid-length red silk dress hung from my hands. It was perfect.

I still had no idea what kind of party we were going to or where it was at, but with this dress on my body and Grey on my arm, I didn't really care.

The day quickly slipped away as more and more words made their way into my story. The steam was wearing off a bit, but that was to be expected after the whirlwind of days I'd had. Not to mention, the female main character was finding herself at a crossroads, and I honestly wasn't sure which way she was headed.

I took it as my sign to call it a day and start getting ready for the party.

A short time later, my reflection stared back at me, my red lipstick and red silk dress about as patriotic as it got.

"Knock, knock."

"In here," I yelled.

Grey's footsteps rattled down the hallway and I grinned when I heard him say, "Holy shit."

"What?"

"No one's going to be looking at the fireworks tonight. That's for damn sure." Heat rose to my cheeks as the distance between us was eaten up by his strides. "Thank god you're mine."

I pressed his face between my hands, dropping a light kiss on his lips.

"That's all I get?" he asked.

"Do you see this lipstick? Do you really want that all over your face?"

"There is nothing I want more."

"Later." I winked.

"Promise?" he asked. "It's been too long since those pretty lips of yours have been anywhere on my body."

The thought itself provoked a wild shiver at the base of my spine.

"Promise," I whispered as I walked toward the door.

Per usual, Daniel was waiting for us at the bottom of my apartment stairs.

"Where are we going?" I asked, stepping into the car.

"Do you want to hear the good news or the bad news first?"

"Oh god."

Grey squeezed my hand as Daniel shifted the SUV into drive, sending me a look of comfort as we backed out.

"It's not that bad, I promise."

"Let's hear it."

Nothing could really be *that* bad when I was looking at Grey. Tonight, he'd opted for a blue suit, not navy, not quite royal, and it was accompanied by a red silk tie.

"Wait, your tie..."

He cocked his eyebrow. "What about it?"

Peering down at my dress, my fingers ran over the red silk, oddly similar to his tie.

"I have to give Sam some credit. I planned on buying you a dress, but when I went to ask her some questions, she told me you'd already asked to wear this one. So instead, I borrowed it one afternoon. I wanted everyone to know that you came to the party with *me*, so I had a tie made from the same material and color."

This man spared no detail.

Fire flooded my cheeks. "You know how to make a girl feel special, don't you?"

"One girl. I know how to make one girl feel special," he corrected.

My thumb rubbed the skin of his thumb as our hands interlocked. "Okay, sorry I interrupted. Let's hear the plan."

"The first part of our night is going to be spent at an over-the-top Fourth of July party that I promised my mom I'd make an appearance at. But…" His words hung in the air. "The second part of our night is going to make up for the first part. I can't tell you why yet though. You're going to have to trust me."

"I can do that."

I did trust him, but I couldn't ignore the nerves as I ran through the various scenarios of how the first part of our night would play out. His world still very much seemed ominous and overbearing, so to be at a party where I would be consumed by politicians and socialites made me jittery.

"We're here," Grey said, opening the car door and reaching for my hand.

"Thank you."

His voice was confident as he gripped me tighter. "Always."

Expecting another stunning beach house, I was surprised when the Montauk Yacht Club sat in front of us. The large property spanned miles down the beach and was no doubt a town landmark.

The main building was old, maintaining its original architecture and décor. Everything was made with traditional shake siding, similar to Grey's house, but instead of looking brand new, the siding was weathered. These buildings had seen their fair share of summers. The most prominent part of the yacht club was the pool overlooking the ocean, with its blue-and-white-striped umbrellas sprinkled everywhere.

It was clear the attraction didn't come from the actual buildings but rather the history behind them. The Montauk Yacht Club had been around since, well, forever. The traditions were rich and so were the members. The club was exclusive, and only the wealthy and most elite were given the opportunity to join.

"Oh," I blurted out.

"Have you been here before?" he asked as we climbed the stairs to the front door.

"Yeah, I have. Just not like this."

The Wharf had catered for the yacht club for years. I'd spent my fair share of evenings serving Montauk's wealthiest. And now here I was, on the other side.

"This will be quick, I promise. An hour, max," he confirmed, obviously picking up on my apprehension. "A few political big wigs host their annual Fourth of July party here. My father wanted to confirm their endorsements before the end of the summer, and this was a sure way to do it. You know, shake the right hands, say the right things, everyone gets drunk and goes home."

"Nope, can't say I do know what you're talking about, but I think I can handle an hour of shmoozing," I said, gripping onto his arm tighter.

His expression loosened before he shot a wink at me.

I smiled, even though I'd gotten stuck on a few of his words: *before the end of the summer*. I tried to suppress the nagging feeling of doubt and what felt like our invisible expiration date, but each time I almost forgot about it, it was mentioned again.

"Ready?" he asked.

"Let's get this over with."

Walking through two white wooden doors, a gust of ocean air whooshed past us, leaving remnants of salt on my lips. With the breeze came an abundance of conversation and the low rhythm of music in the background.

We were outside, but you would have never known it. The outdoor tent was lined with at least thirty cocktail tables, each housing a vase of pristinely placed red and white flowers, along with a tiny American flag.

Hundreds of people swam around us, all of them impeccably dressed.

Grey pointed out his mom as we headed in her direction, and she was just as beautiful in person as she was on TV.

"Hi, Mom," he said, leaning down to kiss each cheek.

"Hi, honey. Thanks for coming. I know your father will be thrilled."

"You know that's not why I came," he protested.

"I know it's not." She paused, glancing at me. "This must be your date?"

"Mom, this is Miller Morgan. Miller, this is my mom." His hand moved to the small of my back, sending a shot of confidence through me.

"Hi, Mrs. Prescott. It's so nice to meet you." I smiled.

Within seconds, she pulled me into a full-on hug. My expression must've been one of surprise because I swore I heard Grey chuckle.

"Please, call me Lisa. I've been dying for Grey to introduce us. You're all he talks about." She beamed, releasing me from her embrace.

"Mom!" he interjected, embarrassed.

"Sorry, Grey, but it's true," she said innocently. "You've never brought anyone around for me to meet, so I can't help but be excited."

"I've never been with anyone who mattered enough to introduce them to you," he said, his eyes locking with mine.

"That's fair," she said. Her relaxed posture suddenly jolted into something more serious, more practiced, as her eyes registered someone from across the room.

Grey must've noticed too because immediately, he directed his gaze to the same area.

I wanted to look, but I didn't need to because a booming voice came from behind me. "Grey. I'm so glad you decided to grace us with your presence."

Lisa took her place next to him, almost as if she was moving on autopilot.

"Hello, Father." Grey's disdain was heavy.

"Is this a date?" He haphazardly motioned to me, the word *date* sounding more like a formality than a question.

"This isn't *a* date; this is *my* date." His voice was stern as he cast a look of animosity toward his father. "You know what? No, this is my girlfriend, Miller Morgan."

Stunned, I almost couldn't move.

Grey nudged me, and I stuck my hand out. "Hi, Mr. Prescott. It's nice to meet you," I said, the words feeling stickier than they had with his mom.

"Uh huh." The words didn't even require him to open his mouth. "When are you going to be done playing house with your little local here and get serious about your career?"

Grey stepped toward his father until their faces were a mere inch apart. Grey quietly spewed venom as he said, "Don't you ever fucking talk about Miller like that again."

Stanley Prescott's face was blank, unbothered. "You're in public, Grey. Don't embarrass yourself."

"You've got to be fucking kidding me. I'm here. I showed up. And yet you still somehow find a way to degrade me, and even worse, her," he said, looking over at me. "I'm not sure why it makes you so angry to think that I might actually be happy, but it's pathetic."

"Look around, Grey. You're the one who has had everything handed to them on a silver platter, and yet you still can't figure out how to make something of yourself. Who's pathetic now?" His words were like knives as they pierced the air.

I lightly tugged on Grey's arm, pulling him back.

His father started moving away, slapping Grey's shoulder like he and his son had just been chatting about something as simple as sports. "I'd suggest you change your attitude before the Labor Day party, or I'll do it for you."

My eyes were on Stanley, but for the first time since the interaction began, I glanced at Lisa. Her eyes were filled with remorse, and the expression she was wearing was almost heartbreaking.

She followed behind her husband, stopping to give Grey a kiss on the cheek. "I love you."

"I love you too, Mom."

I smiled at her. Her hand gracefully landed on my arm and she murmured, "By the way, you look beautiful, Miller."

"Thank you," I muttered.

"Fuck this party, we're leaving," Grey said, angling us toward the exit.

Shockingly, no one seemed to notice the interaction that had just transpired between Grey and his father. Or maybe they did and they were just used to this type of thing.

Either way, I was happy to be getting the hell out of there.

We walked right past Daniel, Grey's steps heavy as they pounded the pavement.

"Are you okay?"

"I will be," he said. "He just makes me so damn angry. He's quite literally one of the most vile humans on the entire planet, and unfortunately, he's also my father."

"I know I probably shouldn't say anything, but... can't you just stop? Stop working for him or with him, whatever you're doing. Wouldn't that fix your problems?" I asked.

We kept walking, but this time, he took my hand in his. "I wish it were that easy. One day, maybe it will be, but I'm just not quite there yet."

He was speaking in riddles again, but I could tell that was intentional.

"So, how about the second part of our night?" I peeked over my shoulder, catching a grin crawling alongside his face at my attempt to lighten the mood. "Is that still happening?"

"You think I'm going to make you endure that shit"—he gestured behind us—"and then not follow through on my promise?" he asked. "You've got to know me better than that by now."

"I do, I—"

"We're here," he said.

As I looked in front of us, my mouth dropped open.

It was like something out of a movie. Lying on the beach was a blue-and-white-striped blanket with a wicker picnic basket, two glass flutes, and a bottle of champagne.

It was simple, and that made it perfect.

"Grey, it's..."

"The marina fireworks go off just out there, so we should have quite the view from here. Although, I'm not sure anything is going to beat the view I've had all night."

"There he is," I praised him, my eyes catching on his.

"Come here," he said, pressing his lips to my forehead. "I'm sorry for what my father said about you. Everything he does is with the intention to hurt others in order to make himself feel better. Nothing that came from his mouth was true. You have to believe that."

I did believe it, or at least I believed Grey, and that was all that mattered. But tonight had proved that Grey's world was vastly different than mine, and I wasn't sure how to process all of that.

My voice was subdued from nerves, but I knew I needed to ask. "But what about what you said? Did you really mean the whole girlfriend thing, or were you just saying that to piss him off?"

"I meant every single word I said. Especially that."

Just then, a loud boom echoed through the sky and countless flecks of color exploded in the darkness, lighting up the water and everything else in the vicinity.

The burst of color in the sky mimicked the burst of excitement in the depths of my belly and I couldn't help but smile. "This is my kind of Fourth of July."

He wrapped his arms around my shoulders from behind and engulfed me in a hug. I reached up to grip his forearms, enjoying his proximity.

"I wouldn't want to be anywhere else."

He grinned, his head dropping to the empty space between my chin and collarbone. His delicate kisses left little sparks everywhere they went.

One of his hands toyed with the dainty silk strap on my shoulder while the other snuck around my arm and up to my bare chest. His fingertips leisurely trailed down the front of my dress and when he dropped his hand to my thigh, my breath escaped me.

"Please keep going," I begged.

The movement started again, and this time, he gently pushed my silk dress out of his way. The warmth of his skin on mine made me shiver. Teasing me, he flirted with the little bit of material that stopped him from taking me over the edge.

"Tell me what you want," he growled.

"I want you to touch me." I inhaled. "Until I can't take it any longer."

The desperation in my voice must've made him confident. His fingers deftly moved my panties aside, removing the barrier between me and ecstasy.

My body ached for him, and I couldn't stop my back from arching. "Right here," I said, moving his hand to where I needed him most.

"We're greedy tonight, aren't we?" he whispered, his breath hot on my ear. "Right here?"

The words barely left his mouth before the friction of his fingers consumed me and I threw my head back into his chest.

"Right fucking there," I moaned.

His movements in all the right spots had me quivering so much my legs struggled to keep me balanced.

"Grey—"

Everything exploded all at once. Me and the fireworks above us, both erupting simultaneously.

"Oh my god," I breathed, my body falling heavy into his.

After a minute, Grey rotated me toward him before he spoke softly. "Happy Fourth of July, MJ."

"Happy Fourth of July," I said, kissing him on the mouth.

# Chapter Thirty-Two

My eyes popped open and I instinctively flung my arm to the other side of bed.

"Ow!" Grey exclaimed.

A big grin rolled across my face as I flipped over. "Just checking to make sure you're still here. You have a tendency to leave me lonely in the mornings."

"Of course I'm still here," he insisted. "I even stayed in bed despite wanting to go cook us some breakfast."

"How long have you been awake?" I asked. "I thought I was an early bird. Why is it that you always wake up before me?"

"I haven't been up that long. Just checking some emails, doing a few work things." He signaled to his phone. "Speaking of work things, I need to make a quick trip back to New York next week..."

I contemplated saying something, but due to the uneasiness that filtered through my brain at the mention of his *real* life, I opted to keep my mouth shut.

"I was hoping you'd come with me?"

Impulsively popping up from the bed, I grabbed his shirt off the floor and tugged it on. "I have to go to the bathroom."

A sigh of relief fell from my mouth as soon as I closed the door.

I glared at myself in the large oval mirror, whispering out loud, "MJ, what the fuck. Grey just asked you to go to New York with him, and instead of responding like a normal person, you acted like he asked you to help him murder someone. Get your shit together."

Resting my hands on either side of the matte black sink, my head fell and I closed my eyes, letting my mind run in circles. New York was supposed to be *our* place, mine and Liv's. It was supposed to be the start of our lives together, and then she died, and everything changed.

New York might've been my dream, but it was Grey's reality. Meaning whether I went with him or not, he was eventually going back. For good. Nausea engulfed me. Where would he and I stand after this summer? What would this look like in September? I shuddered at the thought of picturing anything without him in it. I dragged my head up, doing my best to wrangle these emotions.

I couldn't go to New York. I turned, taking a deep breath in hopes it would bring me the courage I needed to tell Grey I wasn't going with him. But just then, something caught my eye.

The familiar purple flowers that permanently decorated my rib cage poked out from the unbuttoned shirt I'd thrown on. I reached for the dainty ink, my body jumping from the coldness of my fingertips.

"Liv…" Her name fell from my lips, almost inaudibly.

"You okay in there?" Grey's voice filtered past the closed door.

Liv may be gone, but she was never far, and she sure as hell still knew how to push me out of my comfort zone. One thing I knew for sure was that girl was and always would be my driving force.

"Yeah, I'm good."

It was moments like this that made me believe Liv was 1000 percent here with me in one way or another.

I opened the door and saw Grey still in bed.

"Yes, I'd love to come with you."

Astonishment flooded his face as he rubbed his chest. "Really?"

"Yes, really," I said, leaning my weight on the thick white door frame.

Now that the initial shock had worn off, little pangs of excitement sprouted inside me.

Grey pulled himself from the bed, revealing that he'd only been wearing navy boxer briefs, a detail I'd forgotten from last night. That man was an image I wanted burned in my brain for the rest of eternity. His chocolate brown hair effortlessly flowed in all directions but somehow still looked good. His built body stood strong as he adjusted himself and swayed toward the bathroom, only stopping to plant a kiss on my forehead before stepping inside and closing the door behind him.

I made my way to a quaint light-washed wooden desk tucked perfectly into the corner of his room. Sprawled opened in the center of it lay a sleek back journal.

I knew I shouldn't, but Grey had seen my art, and now I wanted to see his. I began thumbing through it and was taken aback when I saw the pages were filled with the most beautiful sketches.

Buildings, bedrooms, restaurants, and everything in between. His dream of being an architect wasn't far-fetched at all; his drawings were spectacular. The lines were precise, the angles perfect, and the aesthetic absolutely stunning.

"Didn't your mom tell you not to put your hands on things that aren't yours?"

Startled and a little embarrassed, I turned. "Jesus, Grey, you scared the shit out of me."

"That's because you were doing something you weren't supposed to be doing," he said playfully, wrapping his arms around my waist.

"Grey, these are really good. Like *really* good. I don't understand how you didn't pursue architecture as a career."

The word architecture almost got stuck in my throat as Liv's voice echoed in my head. *One day I'm going to design the most beautiful skyscraper in New York City. It will stand out among the rest, with glass on the outside and dark rich wood on the inside. People will come from all over the world just to see it.*

She'd always dreamed of being an architect—something about the science behind the lines and the shapes, how intricate some buildings were and how the simplest designs could be the hardest to figure out.

"I wasn't kidding when I said my father basically scolded me anytime I mentioned I was interested in something besides politics." He sounded defeated as his hands slowly closed the journal, almost symbolically.

"From what I know about you, I can't imagine you're someone who lets people tell you what to do."

"I'm not," he confirmed. "Unless it's you."

"I'll keep that in my back pocket for another day." I winked, moving to collect my dress from the floor. "I have a lunch shift at The Wharf that I need to get ready for."

"What? I thought you had the next couple of days off?"

"I did, but then Sam texted me and asked if I would cover her today."

"Ugh, why are you such a good friend?" He threw himself backward onto the bed. "I wanted to spend the next four days with you, in bed, not leaving this house."

I slinked into my dress and fluffed my hair a bit, weighing my need for a shower versus just a little refresh before my shift.

"As tempting as that is—and trust me, after your performance last night, that is very tempting—I can't let Sam down. She always covers for me *and...*" I emphasized my last word. "Because I took her shift today, I'm sure she'd be happy to cover any of my shifts while we're in New York."

He sat up, a cheeky expression spread across his handsome face. "I'm planning on leaving Monday night and coming back Wednesday night. Think that'll work?"

I smiled. "I think we can make that work."

"Good." His voice was low as he made his way to me. We stared at one another in the mirror as he took the spot right behind me. "Because I wasn't going to take no for an answer." His hand grasped my chin, gently pulling me to him before claiming my mouth with his.

"Grey…" I giggled. "I have to go or I'm going to be late."

Stealing one more kiss, he murmured, "Fine. But at least let me give you a ride."

"Deal."

The thick black letters of the damn *Whalecum* door mat glared at me as I pushed the door open.

"Hey, Dad! Happy Friday."

"Well, hello there, MJ," he responded. "Looks like someone had a good time last night."

My cheery tone had even caught me off guard.

Feeling my cheeks run red, I scooted behind the counter and busied myself prepping the bar. "Speaking of last night…" I peered over my shoulder to see Dad inching closer to the bar until his elbows were resting on it and his palms were pressed into his face.

"Uh huh, I'm listening."

I was so giddy, I couldn't wait a second longer. "Grey asked me to go to New York with him for a couple of days. I told him yes, but if you don't think I should, or if you don't want me to change the schedule this late, I really don't have to go. I—"

"MJ," he cut in.

I took a breath. "Yeah?"

"Go."

My hands stopped what they were doing. "Really?"

"What do you mean, really?" he responded, walking behind the bar. "You should absolutely go. Do you see yourself right now?

You're beaming. I haven't seen you this excited…" He paused. "I haven't seen you this excited in a long time," he said, wrapping his arms around me. "I love you big, Miller Jean," he whispered as his grip tightened.

"I love you bigger."

He didn't have to say anything else; we both knew this was a big step. Something was happening that was a long time coming yet also looked a lot different than I would've ever thought.

Although, didn't it always look different than we imagined?

# Chapter Thirty-Three

I ended up working for Sam on both Saturday and Sunday in exchange for her covering my shifts while I was in New York. I agreed to tell her everything, sparing absolutely no detail, to bribe her into working for me.

Her response was a simple: "You make me proud, Miller."

Today had been spent trying to figure out what the hell I was going to pack. It was mid-July, and I had no idea what we'd be doing or where we'd be going. I was lost, and after a few social media searches, I was stressed.

The women were posh, their outfits plucked straight from the latest fashion week. And Grey had proved on more than one occasion that he was a man with style, something I very much enjoyed about him. However, now that same trait had me feeling a little anxious and unprepared for this trip.

My phone pinged on my nightstand.

Grey:

**I'll be there in 10.**

My stomach sank.

"Shit."

The open suitcase lying in front of me was loaded with a plethora of shit, none that I was sure even matched. Nonetheless, I zipped it up and hoped for the best. I was only going for forty-eight hours, this should suffice.

I heard a knock on the front door and yelled, "Come in!"

"You ready?" Grey asked, gliding through my bedroom door. "Oh, damn. You are ready. Look at you."

I was sporting what I hoped looked like a trendy, slicked-back bun that I had paired with loose-fitted tan trousers, a white tank top, and a pair of sneakers.

I blushed. "Stop. You're ridiculous."

"I can't argue with that, but I'm serious. You look beautiful."

I took a minute to admire him. In a pair of chocolate brown loafers, dark navy trousers that accentuated his... *everywhere*, and a cream-colored light sweater, Grey Prescott, per usual, looked delectable.

He was grinning at me, his hand subtly rubbing up and down where it always did right on his chest.

"Can I ask you something and you promise you won't take it the wrong way?"

"Of course, you can always ask me anything."

"Why is that you always rub your chest, right there?" I pressed at the spot on myself. "I've noticed you doing it a few times."

While I was still very much curious about his scar, I didn't want to bring it up, at least not directly. Not after he so clearly avoided the subject the other night. But that didn't mean I couldn't pry just a tiny bit.

Furrowing his brows, he glanced down, seeing his hand was still there. "I don't know. I've never even realized I was doing it."

His soft grip raised my chin, just enough so those copper-colored eyes could penetrate mine. "But if I had to guess, it's probably because the only time my heart ever differs in beat is when I'm around you."

I could've melted right there, but instead I pressed my mouth to his, tasting a wave of minty freshness as my tongue entangled with his.

"Now, I'm ready," I said, pulling back.

"Good." He winked. "Let me have your suitcase."

Pushing it in front of him, I froze as he carried it through my door. Despite the massive amount of excitement that swam through me, somewhere, deep inside, there was still anxiety too.

"Are you okay?" he asked when he noticed I was lagging behind. "Do you not want to go anymore?" Uncertainty dashed through his voice, his eyes showing disappointment.

"Grey, it's not that... I promise," I said. "New York City has always been a pipe dream of mine—well, actually of ours. My best friend and me. Before the accident, we were going to finish high school, graduate, and move to New York together. Go to NYU, where she'd study architecture and I'd study creative writing. And then the accident happened, and neither of us ever made it there."

Each time I released a piece of my story to Grey, I felt lighter. Almost as if when I shared these things with him, I no longer had to endure the painful memories by myself.

I could see his brain working through the new information.

"So that's why you darted to the bathroom when I asked you to come to New York with me, isn't it?"

"Mm-hmm."

"You could've just told me all of this then."

"I know, it just felt really hard in the moment. I'm not great at opening up about anything related to Liv."

Leaving the suitcase, Grey was by my side within two strides, embracing me in hug. "I can only imagine how hard it is, but I never want you to feel like you can't talk to me. Life is already hard enough, you can't keep all that shit bottled up. Trust me, it will eat you alive. And I'm really sorry you never got to experience New York the way the two of you had planned."

"It's okay. She'd want me to do this—better yet, she'd *make* me do this. And on top of that, she'd probably be yelling at me for not telling you sooner."

"She sounds like the girl you want as your best friend."

"She was."

"She may be gone, but I bet she'll always be right here," he said, his finger tapping just above my heart.

I couldn't help but smile before leaning in to kiss him.

"Wait. Hold on. Does that mean you've never been to New York City?"

"This does in fact mean that I've never been to New York City."

Winking, he tantalized me. "Well, then aren't you in for a treat."

He ushered me down the steps, following closely behind with my suitcase.

"Good evening, Miller. Good to see you again," Daniel said as he opened the car door for me.

"Hi, Daniel. You too."

I stepped into the back of the SUV and was immediately transported to that night a few weeks ago. A flame sparked inside of me as I recounted the events that took place in this back seat, feeling the heat rush to my head.

Grey's voice cut the memory short. "Comfortable?"

"Very."

He scooted closer to me, placing his hand on my left thigh. The warmth travelled through my pants and onto my skin.

"Ready, sir?" Daniel popped in from the front seat.

Grey looked at me. Realizing he was waiting for my response, I quickly nodded. "We are," he responded.

Only now did it hit me that we would be spending the next two and half hours in the car. With the anticipation of the trip, I'd completely forgotten about us having to actually get to the city, and now that reality was digging a pit at the bottom of my stomach.

My muscles tensed as I intuitively reached for Grey's hand on my leg. My abrupt move must've sent a warning signal to him because he immediately leaned in. "Everything all right?"

"Yeah. It just sort of slipped my mind that we'd be in the car for a while. My anxiety is definitely subdued when you're with me, but usually that's in five-mile spurts, not full-blown road trips." A nervous laugh slipped through my lips.

His low chuckle vibrated through the back seat.

"What's so funny?" I asked, thrown off by his lack of sympathy.

"We're not driving to Manhattan."

"Huh?"

"You thought after everything you've told me that I was going to make you sit in a car for more than two hours?"

"I mean, I just didn't think there was any other option..."

He took my face into his palms. "One thing you should know about me, MJ, is that I'm always going to find another option when it comes to your fears. I want to do everything in my power to take care of you. That I'm sure of."

"Grey—" I broke off and cleared the emotion from my throat. "Thank you."

"You don't have to thank me for wanting to take care of you. You deserve that much. You've experienced so much hurt in your life, the least I can do is never let you feel that kind of pain again."

His words were so genuine. I wanted to take them, bottle them up, and save them for a day when the emotions felt big and things felt hard.

I squeezed his hand as tight as possible before pushing my lips to his.

A sinister grin rolled across his face. "You don't have a fear of airplanes, right?"

"Airplanes?"

"Airplanes," he said, opening the car door.

Grey got out first before helping me do the same. The outside air was loud, intense, and whooshing around us.

I followed Grey as he led me to a smaller-than-normal airplane. There, at the bottom of a flight of stairs, was an older man in a black suit and a pilot's hat, waiting to greet us.

"Good evening, Mr. Prescott," he said, extending his hand to Grey.

"Hey, Jason. This is Miller Morgan."

"Nice to meet you, Ms. Morgan."

"Please. It's MJ."

"MJ," he said, nodding his head.

"And she's never been to New York City before," Grey offered.

"Is that so?" Jason asked.

I shifted closer to Grey and shook my head.

His sweet smile was so big, I couldn't help but smile back.

"Well, let's see what we can do about that," he responded before gesturing up the stairs. "After you two."

Grey's hands rested on my hips as he walked behind me. Gripping the metal rail, I took one last step before landing on the pristine, sand-colored carpet. The interior was obviously smaller than a typical plane, but it smelled of luxury.

The plane was equipped with four large captain seats up front, facing each other in rows of two. Toward the back, there was a set of four large leather seats, these a bit closer than the ones up front. On the left side, there was a leather couch—yes, an actual fucking *couch*—that extended all the way to the back.

"Oh my god," I whispered.

"Sit wherever your heart desires," Grey joked.

I immediately sat in one of the four seats up front, nervous that if I didn't choose quickly, this all might melt away like a dream.

Grey took the seat to my right, both of us facing the cockpit.

Unlike a commercial flight, there was no safety protocol, so we were ready for take-off within minutes. Jason's booming voice came over the speaker as he said, "Good evening, tonight you'll be flying with myself and my co-pilot Harry. From wheels up to wheels down, we're looking at about twenty-seven minutes, give or take. Sit back and enjoy the flight and the views. We'll be in New York City shortly."

"This is wild," I muttered under my breath.

"Wild in a bad way or wild in a good way?"

"Wild in a different way. This lifestyle is so... different. I'm not sure I know how to behave in a world where there are twenty-seven minutes flights," I admitted.

"By all means, please do not behave." Grey smirked.

Giggling, I smacked his shoulder. "Grey, I'm serious."

"Don't think about all that, just enjoy it. Enjoy the moment and be sure to keep your window shade up, you're not gonna want to miss the views."

I knew what he meant, but still. This all seemed a little too picturesque. His world was glamorous and flashy, and I wasn't sure I belonged.

I shushed my inner thoughts, staring at him. His thick brown hair was pressed up against the leather seat and his eyes were shut.

"*I* wasn't the view I was talking about," he said, peeking at me with only one eye. "That is." His hand lifted from mine and directed my attention to the tiny oval window next to me.

An audible gasp left my mouth. "Holy shit."

"I told you."

There wasn't a cloud in sight, giving the city full permission to look absolutely breathtaking. The number of lights below us was almost unbelievable. It was like I was staring at a real-life postcard of the New York City skyline from 30,000 feet. The tiny lights twinkled in sync, as if they were being controlled by a remote.

"I could stay up here forever." My forehead was so close to touching the window, I could feel the cold air radiating from it.

"You say that now, but the city is even more magical when you're experiencing it right in front of you, trust me."

I repositioned myself so my entire frame was facing him. "You haven't steered me wrong yet."

"And I have no intention of starting now," he said, planting a soft kiss on my temple.

In a matter of minutes, the plane was touching down.

"Hungry?"

"Incredibly so," I responded.

"Good. I have the perfect spot. It's only about a twenty-minute drive from here."

The warm air whipped across my face as I walked off the plane and stepped into another black SUV that was waiting for us. I gave myself a once-over and turned to look at Grey.

"Wait, I can't wear this out to dinner. You must let me change."

"You look perfect. Trust me."

Finding my seat, the anxiety flushed through me as I imagined myself walking into some fancy restaurant and feeling completely out of place.

"MJ, I'm serious. Don't stress." He squeezed my thigh. "Trust me, no other woman can hold a candle to you. You could be wearing a robe and you'd still outshine every single one of them."

A grin crawled across my face.

"And don't forget it." His voice was slightly demanding, and I kind of liked it.

He rolled the window down a little bit, letting in a whooshing wind that kept the rest of my unwanted thoughts at bay for now. The buildings, the lights, and the people all blurred into one chaotic beautiful mess as we drove past them.

Liv would've adored this place. She would've thrived in this madness. The sights, the sounds, the smells... She would've instantly morphed into this city, becoming one with it. The simple thought of her being here brought a smile to my face and a single tear to my eye.

The emotions were overwhelming, but somehow, they seemed manageable. Like I needed to feel all of them in order to fully grasp this experience for all that it was. The excitement, the sadness, the anger, the wonder, and even the sting of guilt.

I heard Grey's voice, once again saving me from my own thoughts as his fingers laced with mine. "I'm sure there is a lot to unpack here. Just know I'm always here to listen, and even more importantly, that plane can be fired up and ready to take us back to Montauk in ten minutes. You say the word and we're gone."

"I don't know how I stumbled upon someone as kind as you, but damn am I glad I did. I'm not sure I'll ever be able to let you go if you keep treating me like this," I said.

"Then my plan is working," he said, his eyes lighting up. Not from the city skyline, but from me.

And in that second, I realized I was falling for him. Completely and utterly falling.

"Mr. Prescott, we're here."

"Thank you."

Grey opened the door, stepping out before helping me to do the same. The calmness that lived in the car was gone, replaced instead with electrifying chaos.

"Times Square?" I asked. "I didn't picture you as the tourist type," I said. But then again, I didn't imagine we'd be taking a private plane to get here either.

"This way," he said, gripping my hand.

Every single inch of this city was beaming with life. There was chatter, car horns, and street music piercing the air. The buildings were all lined with lights and screens, so tall that I was convinced they touched the stars.

"Grey, this city is magical. It makes you feel *alive*."

He nodded. "It's difficult to understand until you're standing right in the middle of it. And now, I'm about to give you one of the best and most authentic New York City dining experiences you've ever had." His raised eyebrow and cheeky expression made me a little uncertain.

"Oh god. Now I'm worried."

"I haven't led you astray yet, have I?" he asked.

"No, no you haven't."

"I don't plan on starting tonight. Down here." He tugged on my hand, pulling me toward the steps and leading me into the... subway?

"What the hell? We're eating in the subway?"

Impatiently waiting for his answer, I took a breath to say something but got interrupted. The most magnificent smell wafted through my nose and into my stomach, sending my hunger pangs into a feeding frenzy.

"Pizza?"

"Only the best in the entire city. Maybe even in the entire continental US."

A few steps ahead of us sat the most quaint and impromptu restaurant, right there in the underground of the belly of Times Square. Painted the purest black with a white sign that read *See No Evil* in red block letters was the entrance. As we stepped inside, the smell only got more inviting. The black-and-white-checkered tile floors led way to the only about ten two-top tables and a row of six chairs that faced the kitchen.

The restaurant appeared almost full, with only a single table open and at least twenty people hovering outside.

"Grey, my man, what's up?"

"Dawson, hey! Did you get my text?"

"Sure did. I'll get you two right over here."

"Thanks, man."

"Anytime. Enjoy."

Good food, great sex, and a big heart.

This man was just begging me to fall in love with him.

# Chapter Thirty-Four

"Mhm," I mumbled, stretching my arms above my head before clutching the fluffy down comforter. If my eyes weren't open, I would've sworn I was wrapped up in the biggest, softest cloud in the sky. "I'm pretty sure I dreamed about the pizza from last night," I said as I turned to face Grey.

He was tangled up in the dark gray sheets of his king-sized bed, only revealing his right leg and his naked upper body, which was enough to have me wanting to scale him.

"All the events of last night, and *that's* what you dreamt about?" There was skepticism in his voice as his tongue lightly trailed his lower lip.

My god.

That man had magic laced in that tongue.

"Among other things." I winked playfully.

Grey's apartment took up the thirteenth floor of an old picturesque brick building on the Upper East Side. But despite the worn exterior, the inside was anything but. He'd done a complete remodel, transforming it into a modern but endlessly cozy apartment.

It boasted beautiful dark wooden floors, a fireplace that looked large enough to heat the entire city, vaulted ceilings that made the space feel even bigger than it already was, and a view of Central Park that many would kill for.

I couldn't help but picture this view in every season. The amber colored leaves falling. The softness and serenity of the first snow. The bursts of colors that signaled spring. The thought alone was magical.

"Thank god. I was afraid I didn't do a good enough job last night," he said, his eyebrow darting up. "I thought I might have to try again."

"Well, now that you mention it…" I trailed off, doing my best to hold back my giggle.

It didn't take long before he was rolling toward me, tickling me from every angle as we tumbled around on the bed, making a mess of the sheets, blankets, and ourselves. I didn't care though, because everything felt right.

Grey wrapped me in his arms and pulled me to his chest, my giggling tapering off as I found myself once again tracing that permanent mark.

I quickly went to retract my hand. "I'm sorry, I didn't—"

He trapped my hand under his, pressing his scar right against my palm.

"Remember when I mentioned that I had some health issues growing up?"

"Yeah, at the waterfall." I nodded my head.

"My health issues were actually pretty serious, and they were the main reason why I hadn't gone back to Montauk in so many years. Well, that and my own selfishness."

I snuggled in closer to him, meshing my fingers with his.

"Okay, I'm listening."

"When I was twenty, I—"

"Grey?" a familiar voice echoed through the bedroom door, but I couldn't put my finger on whose it was. The sound of footsteps ricocheted off the vaulted ceilings, coming closer.

"Shit." Grey catapulted from the bed and ransacked the room until he landed on his pants from last night. "Stay here, I'll be right back." He was more serious than I'd ever heard.

"Grey..." I began, but he'd already slipped through the door.

I was overcome with a wave of vulnerability as I stared down at my mostly naked body. Slinking myself out of bed, I grabbed some clothes from my suitcase and shuffled into the bathroom.

Everything was hot. I was flustered and I hated the rush of doubt that infiltrated my thoughts. Things with Grey were so damn good, but that was the scary part. Maybe it was all just a little *too* good.

Our expiration date was fast approaching with the end of summer looming, and here I was, waiting for the other shoe to drop.

Pulling on my black leggings and shrugging into my merlot-colored half-zip, I re-slicked my hair. After putting on my white socks and sneakers, I gave myself a quick little pep-talk, just enough to get me out of Grey's room and see who'd let themselves in.

"Grey, you need to take this seriously and quit fucking around. This is your career we're talking about. Being in politics isn't a regular forty-hour-a-week gig. You've got to be *on* twenty-four seven. That means you can't just go galivanting around Montauk pretending like you don't have any responsibilities. I've put my damn neck out there for you to get your foot in the door, and this is how you thank me? By spending the last month fucking around like a teenager? I need you in New York for at least the next week while the re-election efforts ramp up," he said.

"Okay, Father, I get it," Grey responded, sounding defeated. "Jesus, you don't have to be such an asshole about it."

*Father.*

I creeped around the corner, doing my best to go unnoticed. I silently shut the door behind me and pressed my back against it before letting a deep sigh empty from my chest.

The uneasiness was persistent after listening to Grey's father speak to him that way. It almost made me nauseous. I moved to the elevator, in search of an extra-large coffee.

Exiting his building, the bright summer sun scorched differently between the towers of the city, and thankfully, within no more than fifty steps, I stumbled across a quaint coffee shop.

The entrance was small but romantic, with an arched wooden door that stood out like a sore thumb among the typical glass ones lining the streets. The neon glowing sign overhead read *A Second Cup,* and a dainty coffee mug was perched next to it.

Inside, the scent of coffee beans tingled my nose. Looking around, it appeared that I'd been transported someplace else, someplace magical. It was painted almost entirely in a deep dark green. The cabinets, the walls, and even the ceiling. Everything was dark, except for the trees towering over the different-sized tables and chairs. Weaved baskets used as chandeliers dangled from the ceiling and dimly lit each table.

I no longer had to wonder why so many authors talked about writing in New York City. If I lived here, I would've written at least five books by now. The vibes were immaculate.

Taking my place in line, I continued to admire the tiny but perfect space around me. The barista's voice was the only thing that brought me back to reality.

"Hi there, what can I get started for you?"

"Hi! First off, this place is incredible. Secondly, I'll take a hazelnut latte with almond milk, please."

"Well, thank you. It is pretty great," she said, tapping the tablet screen in front of her. "Is that all?"

"Yes," I responded. "Actually no, I'm so sorry. It isn't." I couldn't go back empty-handed, but I had no clue what kind of coffee Grey liked. Panicking, I said, "Um. Can I just get a vanilla latte, please?"

"You got it."

On the walk back to Grey's apartment, I stressed that I'd ordered the wrong thing. Luckily, it was a short walk, because if it was even a minute longer, I probably would've turned around and got him something else.

Anxiety never slept.

Creaking the door open, I snuck inside, not wanting to interrupt him and his father if they were still arguing.

"—and then you bring back some charity case from Montauk? To what? Let her experience the city how we do? Show off all your shiny things just so you can sleep with her?"

My stomach sank as I listened in on a conversation I knew wasn't for my ears.

"Fuck off," Grey spit back. "She's not a charity case. She's a human being, and an incredible one at that. Maybe you could learn something from her," he scoffed. "She's not just another pawn in your game, and that's what pisses you off."

"Watch your mouth, son. Sometimes I think you forget just how much I've done for you. How many strings I've pulled to get you to where you are today. The calls I've made to make sure you were still standing right here. Don't you forget, without me, you wouldn't be here."

"You can pull me down all you want, you've done it my whole life, but don't bring Miller into it. Like I told you at the Fourth of July party, she's my girlfriend. That's not going to change, so you might as well leave her out of it and move the fuck on."

The silence was deafening, but despite the venom spewing from his father's lips, Grey had stood up for me. And in spite of the circumstances, my heart swelled.

"I'll be at the meeting next week. I know that's why you showed up here. So, if that's all, you can leave now." Spite filled Grey's voice.

"Very good. I'm happy to hear it. There will be a lot of important people there."

The sound of footsteps startled me as they moved closer, pausing just before they reached me. "Good to see you, son. Remember, this is your second chance. I'd suggest you use it wisely, because you won't get another one."

How did someone like Grey come from a man as vulgar as him?

I slipped into another room just as his father was pulling the front door open. When I was confident he was gone, I worked my way into the kitchen to find Grey standing with both hands gripping either side of his sink, staring out onto the city.

"I got this for you." My voice was soft and filled with uncertainty as I stood in the middle of his kitchen, two piping hot cups of coffee in hand.

He turned around until he was able to rest against the sink with his arms crossed. Still shirtless, his navy pants dipped low.

"An angel sent from above," he said, reaching for the coffee and putting it up to his nose. "And a vanilla latte." His mouth opened slightly, allowing the warm substance to flow to his lips. "I think I'll keep you."

It was odd, almost, how Grey managed to pop back into himself even after the shitty exchange with his father.

He may have appeared okay, but I could see the hurt hiding under the surface. I eased his cup from his hands and placed both our coffees on the counter before wrapping my arms around his middle.

I just wanted to squeeze him, as if I could squeeze all that hurt out. His once rapid heartbeat seemed to gradually settle the longer we were intertwined.

"That sounded brutal," I said.

"Oh, that? Yeah, as you've now witnessed on multiple occasions, that's just a typical conversation between my father and me," he breathed. "How much did you hear?"

I wanted so badly to thank him for standing up for me, but that would mean admitting I'd heard more of the conversation than I should have, and I didn't want to make him relive any of his father's malicious words.

"Not much. I snuck out shortly after you got out here and just got back." I kissed his cheek. "What was it you wanted to tell me before your father got here?"

I plopped myself onto the kitchen counter.

Grey's hands moved to his temples, rubbing them aggressively. "Can we talk about it later?" he asked. "I just want to be in the silence with you for a bit longer."

"Of course. Come here," I insisted.

His body sank into mine as I pulled his head to my chest.

"We can sit like this for as long as you want. I'm not going anywhere," I assured him as I ran my hands through his hair.

# Chapter Thirty-Five

"When did you get back?" Sam grilled me.

Our local coffee shop was cute, especially from where we were sitting in our window-seat booth, but it didn't hold a candle to the one in New York.

I pulled my coffee to my mouth and took a sip before acknowledging her question, not wanting to admit the truth.

"Um... last Wednesday," I told her honestly.

Her eyes slinked up from her coffee mug, the steam dancing around her. "Last *Wednesday*. As in almost a week ago? And you're just now agreeing to get coffee with me?"

"Yes... I'm sorry. I've been busy. But, Sam, it was incredible." A tiny smile freed itself from her mouth and I knew I'd been forgiven, which encouraged me to continue. "It was everything I could've ever imagined, and more. The sights, the sounds, the food, and the sex." I smirked.

"Miller Jean Morgan, you little slut." We both burst into laughter, drawing attention from nearby patrons. "Just kidding. I need all the details. Stat."

My face hurt from smiling after filling Sam in on the details, but I couldn't ignore the one and only negative part. "Well, you know, despite his father being a complete and utter prick."

"From what I've heard from Anthony, Stanley Prescott is nothing short of a narcissistic asshole," she responded.

"Yeah, you could say that," I said. "There's a lot of shit going on with that family, that's for sure. Honestly, it's the only thing that makes me hesitate about the whole situation."

"What do you mean?"

"Don't get me wrong, the trip was a dream. But that's just it... it didn't feel like real life. Grey lives in a whole different world than you and me. Private jets, personal drivers, and big fancy houses, for starters."

All of these thoughts had been swirling around my brain since I walked in on the conversation between Grey and his father. I didn't want to make Grey feel bad about his lifestyle, but I needed to talk to someone about it all.

"Not to mention the big elephant in the room: him living in New York City and me living here. I have no idea how we would make that work. And then I feel ridiculous for even worrying about that at all because I'm not even sure he's expecting this thing, whatever it is, to go past the summer."

"Oof." Sam huffed out. "First off, things are allowed to feel dreamy, that's the best part about being in a relationship, especially at the beginning. Things are new, fresh, and exciting. Secondly, it's also okay to feel scared, or a little hesitant as you put it, because this kind of shit is scary. New is scary. Unknowns are scary. And better yet, love is scary as hell. If it wasn't, it wouldn't be as epic as everyone says it is."

Sam always had good advice, but this was top of the line, even for her. "Damn… I was not expecting that."

"And another thing…" She faltered. "But you have to promise you won't get upset with me." I nodded, intrigued. "I don't think your fear is really coming from who Grey is. I think it comes from not wanting to lose him." Her head dropped but her mouth kept moving. "I think that after the loss you went through with Liv, the thought of letting someone else in, like really letting them in, feels incredibly terrifying, almost unbearable."

We sat in silence for a few moments, Sam letting me ruminate on her words. After a couple minutes, I finally said, "I think you're right."

She looked relieved she hadn't upset me. With sympathy I only ever allowed from her, she looked right in my eyes as she said, "And that's okay. But look at you and me."

I scrunched my face in confusion.

"I don't even think you realize it, but Grey isn't the first person you've let in since the accident. I am. It didn't happen overnight, and it definitely didn't always feel like it was going to happen at all. But, piece by piece, you let me in."

Sam wasn't the emotional type, but I swore I saw her bat away a tear.

"And you can do it again. I'm not saying it won't be hard, and I'm sure as shit not saying you won't ever get hurt again. What I am saying is that, as you know better than anyone, life is too damn precious to sit alone on the sidelines and watch it pass you by."

"Sam, I—" My voice cracked, trailing off.

"I can't tell you what's going to happen with Grey, or in your life outside of him, but what I can tell you is that you already have everything you need." She brought her palm up to tap the spot above her heart. "Your willingness to open up, the book that you so desperately need to write, and those dreams that you've put away so nicely in a box on a shelf in your mind. Everything is there, you just have to let yourself dig deep enough to find it," she said.

I toyed with the handle of my coffee mug, clearing my throat. "I guess I never really saw it that way, you know? You just sort of appeared in my life when I needed someone and have stuck around ever since. But looking now, I see the truth."

The realization of it all left me a bit stunned.

A single tear rolled down my cheek as I stood up to give her a hug. "I love you, Sam."

"I love you too, MJ."

"It's taken me years and a very blunt conversation"—I pulled away, smirking—"to see the importance of letting other people in. So, thank you."

"Always. You know I wouldn't have it any other way." She smiled, returning to her coffee. "When do you get to see him again?"

"Not sure exactly. He had some stuff he needed to do in the city, but he said he'd keep me posted on when he'd be back." I blushed.

"You're smitten, Miller Morgan, and I love it."

"I think I am."

The start of August was already here, and the first thing on my list on this crisp Saturday morning was a run. I was craving movement before my shift later. Bouncing down the steps, I took a moment to enjoy the slight breeze.

I placed my headphones on and cranked up the music, the familiar tune of "Play with Fire" by Sam Tinnesz drifting into my ears. I'd woken up to a good-morning text from Grey, which had happened every morning since I left the city and never failed to put me in a good mood.

We'd only been apart a week, but even that seemed too long. He was hoping to get back to Montauk soon, but things with his father kept popping up. I understood, but I was ready to see him again.

The sun was setting on summer, and the faintest voice in the back of my head wondered if the same was happening to Grey and me too. The thought itself sent my stomach sinking like a boat taking on gallons of water at once.

Clearly, I needed this run. And

I picked up my pace, the rhythm of my footsteps matching the rhythm of the song playing through my headphones. Running toward the beach, the sun pierced my skin, making me feel alive and shutting off all intrusive thoughts.

About halfway into my run, I begun to hear the echo of footsteps behind me. Normally, I wouldn't have thought anything of it, but it was 6:45 in the morning and most of the town was still asleep. Doing my best to be nonchalant, I slipped a glance at the runner.

"Surprised to see me?" Grey's voice trickled through the air. Stopping dead in my tracks, my jaw dropped as I registered that it was him, that he was really here. I bounded toward him, jumping into his arms. "I missed you too," he admitted.

"You didn't tell me you were coming!" I pulled away to get a better look at him. He was in a pair of black athletic shorts and a white T-shirt, which was probably the most casual I'd ever seen him.

"Well, then it wouldn't have been a surprise, would it?"

"This is true," I said.

"Mind if I finish your run with you?" he asked.

"Not at all," I said. "I didn't know you were a runner."

He laughed. "I'm not, but you are. So I figured I'd give it a try, especially if that meant seeing you run in those tight little shorts of yours."

Two months had gone by since we'd started hanging out and this man still knew exactly what to say to turn my cheeks cherry red.

"Are you sure that was only two miles? Definitely felt more like twenty." Grey panted as he bent over to catch his breath.

"You're dramatic." I giggled. "How long are you in town for?"

"I'm hoping to stay through the rest of the summer, so until after Labor Day weekend."

I so badly wanted to blurt out *and then what happens?* but the courage I needed was nowhere to be found.

Oblivious to my current spiral, Grey spoke again. "Speaking of Labor Day, it's a Prescott family tradition to have a massive party on the beach. I'm sure this year will be especially ridiculous with my father's campaign. But regardless, I'd like you to go with me."

Grey never got nervous, at least not around me, but I swore I could feel a sense of tension in his tone.

"Are you sure your father is going to want someone like me there?" I asked, shocked by my own vulnerability.

"Miller Morgan, haven't I made it abundantly clear that my father can dictate my career, but he sure as shit isn't going to dictate my relationships? Plus, he's probably just jealous because you catch the attention of everyone in the room without trying and he has to spend thousands of dollars to do so."

"You flatter me," I said. "And if that was your way of convincing me to go, it worked." My response lit up his face, something I'd never get used to. "On one condition." I raised my finger to him. "You come with me to dinner at my parents' tonight."

"Say no more. I'll be there." His mouth claimed mine, our tongues hungry for a taste of the other.

"Come in?" I asked, trying my best not to sound like I was begging.

"Don't tempt me." Brushing his lips with his thumb, he continued. "But there is something I've been meaning to do since the start of summer, and I think it's finally time."

"Oh. Okay. Do you need help with anything?"

His hand was doing it again, pressuring that same spot. "This is something that I need to do alone, at least right now, but I adore you for asking. How about I pick you up at seven and we'll go to your parents' together?"

"Sounds perfect," I said, leaning up on my tippy toes to plant another kiss right on his mouth.

"See you then."

## Chapter Thirty-Six

I already knew the answer to my question, but I figured I'd send a text to the group chat anyway. The anticipation of their responses was what I was really after anyway.

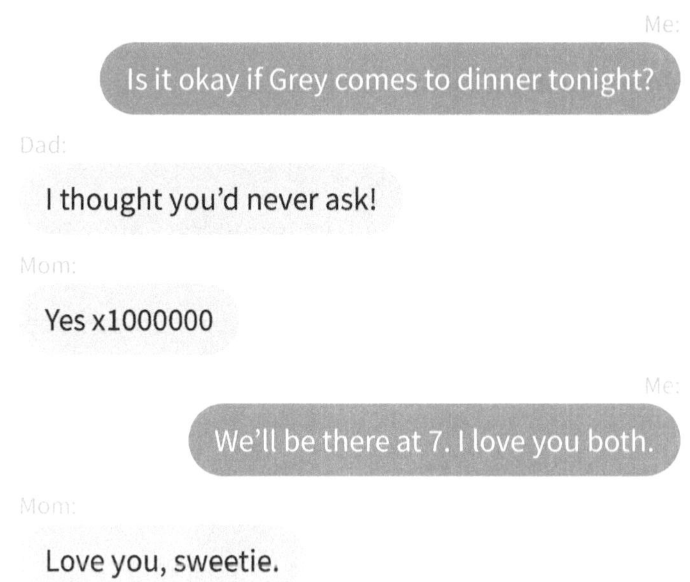


Pleased, I tossed my phone on the counter, vowing to spend the rest of my afternoon in the little corner of my bedroom, writing away. My fingers couldn't move fast enough for the thoughts flooding my mind.

Outside my window, the sun was slowly setting, the pink skies melting into the blue water, leaving me feeling hopeful for tonight's events.

I opted for a pair of white linen shorts and a black scoop-neck body suit. He was always punctual, so I knew Grey would be here any minute, and I snagged one final look at myself in the mirror.

Reaching for my black crossbody bag, I opened the door to Grey making his way up the steps to my apartment.

"Good evening, gorgeous."

"Hi," I said, feeling light, the ocean breeze floating around us.

There was something different about him. I couldn't quite put my finger on it, but he seemed... more content.

"Ready?"

"I am. The question is, are you?"

Placing a kiss on my forehead, he responded, "More than you know."

Making our way down the steps, I spotted my favorite baby-blue Bronco and smiled. Grey walked me to the passenger seat before opening the door and motioning me inside.

"Do you think I could drive?" I asked.

His head swiveled so quickly I thought it might fly right off. "Really?"

"Really."

"Be gentle on her," he joked as he tossed the keys in my direction.

Sliding into the driver's seat, anxiousness crawled up my throat. I wasn't sure what made me feel like I could do this, but I might have been wrong. I'd driven since the accident, but I could count on one hand how many times, and most definitely not by choice. And now, here I was *asking* to drive.

Grey slid his hand over my right leg. "You good?"

Taking a deep breath, I put the key into the ignition and the car rumbled alive. "I will be."

Little by little, things started feeling more comfortable. The drive was only about five minutes, but by the time we were pulling into my parents' house, I felt like I'd overcome something.

Grey hopped out of the passenger side and made his way to mine. Swinging the door open, he held out his hand before pulling me into a tight embrace. "I'm proud of you," he whispered, making the tiny hairs on my neck stand tall.

"I wouldn't have been able to do it without you by my side."

He responded with a gentle kiss on my forehead. "Then by your side is where I'll stay."

The smell of charcoal burning and a hint of citronella filled the air around us. As we moved toward the house, Grey stopped suddenly, pivoting back to the car. "Shit, I forgot something. One second."

He was gone and back in a flash, and now he had a bushel of hydrangeas—lilac, of course—and a bottle of wine. "For your parents," he stated.

"They'll love them."

Standing near the familiar door, I knocked once but pushed myself in before anyone could respond. "Mom... Dad... We're here!" I yelled.

"In here," Mom's voice echoed.

We maneuvered our way through the living room and into the kitchen, where Mom was washing something in the kitchen sink and Dad was uncorking a bottle of red. From the sound of it, John and Jess were here too.

"Hi everyone," I said, waving my hand in the air.

Grey immediately stepped up to my side. "Hi, Mr. and Mrs. Morgan, it's so good to finally meet you. Well, I guess I've already met you, sir." Grey sent a smile in Dad's direction. "And these are for you, Mrs. Morgan." Grey's voice was as confident and polite as ever.

"Oh, honey, it's Kelli. It's so nice to finally meet you, *and* you brought flowers. MJ, I think he might be a keeper." My mom was beaming as she engulfed him in a hug, throwing her gaze in my direction.

"Same goes for me. Just call me Andrew," my dad said, throwing his hand out.

"Andrew, it is," Grey responded.

"Why don't you go introduce Grey to John and Jess," Mom suggested. "Dad and I will meet you in there."

I turned, tugging him behind me and straight into the dining room. Stepping in, I admired the picture-perfect setup Mom had put together. A checkered tablecloth lay wrinkle-free on top of the long wooden table that'd been here since I was a kid.

She'd sat round jute placemats under classic white plates. On top of each plate was a folded linen napkin that matched the tablescape perfectly. Everything was cohesive, down to the candlesticks that were the same dark green as the little designs on the tablecloth. Mom loved hosting, she always had, and she'd take any excuse she could get to set a table for dinner.

"And this is John and Jess Mitchell, or who I like to call my bonus parents," I said, giving them my biggest grin.

I shifted my eyes to Grey, awaiting his response. But before he could speak, a loud crash grabbed our attention.

"Shoot!" Jess screeched, reaching for the tipped-over wineglass, which added a red puddle to the list of table decorations. She popped up from her seat and blurred past us. "So sorry, I'm going to go grab some paper towels."

Moving toward the spill, I attempted to help John scoop up the remainder of the wine without making more of a mess.

"I'll go grab some water too, see if we can't get that out of the tablecloth," Grey piped in from just behind me.

"Here, here," Dad said, tossing a bottle of club soda at me as he marched to the table. We both started drenching the stained areas. Mom would never say it out loud because she wouldn't want to make Jess feel bad, but this was one of her all-time favorite tablecloths. Dad and I both knew it, so we worked frantically to save it.

John jumped in too, wiping down everything that'd been splattered with the dark cherry shade.

"Kelli, I'm so sorry."

"Don't be. It's fine. A little red wine never hurt nobody," Mom joked.

"I brought more wine," Grey chimed in from behind the two women, sounding a bit less enthusiastic than I expected.

"He's definitely a keeper," Dad said, sending a wink my way. "Dinner should be ready in about ten minutes, so please, everyone, sit down and make yourselves comfortable. Grey, you're the only newbie here, how would you like your steak cooked?" Dad paused. "And yes, this is a test, because yes, there is only one right answer."

Grey softly laughed. "I'll take it medium rare, sir."

"No to the sir. But yes to the medium rare. You can stay." Dad's jokes were just that: dad jokes. He chuckled to himself as he stepped toward the porch that was located right off the dining room.

*Sit,* I mouthed to Grey while noticing Mom and Jess whispering in the corner, likely about Grey. I knew they worried about me and what my future looked like, and honestly, I'd had the same worries on more than one occasion.

Finally, everyone took a seat at the table. Grey and I on one side, Jess and John on the other, and Dad and Mom on either end.

"Andrew, this looks incredible." Grey's voice filled the room, but it sounded a touch unsteady. Reaching under the table, I rested my hand on his left thigh and gave him a little squeeze. His eyes caught mine, and without saying anything, I asked if he was okay. The almost non-existent nod he gave would have to suffice for now.

I chalked it up to nerves, but of course my intrusive thoughts started playing games with me, making me wonder if this dinner wasn't up to his standards. Or maybe he was realizing that I didn't fit into his world. Either way, the previous wave of excitement washed away and now a new wave of uncertainty wreaked havoc on my insides. Needless to say, I was dreading the next hour.

"Grey, what do you do?" My dad was seemingly unfazed by the lack of conversation in the room. Then again, reading the room had never been his strong suit.

"I'm currently trying to break into politics with the help of my father."

"Grey's father is Stanley Prescott. You know, the mayor of New York City. He just announced his campaign for re-election," I blurted out.

"Oh shit, I thought I recognized that last name. Speaking of politics, John, did you see that new…" Dad's voice faded into background noise as he and John continued on with their conversation, the one that had since turned into something completely irrelevant to Grey or me.

"Honey, do you two have plans for the rest of the summer?" Mom asked.

"Well, Grey asked me to be his date to his family's big Labor Day party, but other than that, I'll probably spend some more time writing. I think I might actually be getting somewhere with this story," I responded, happiness cartwheeling through my belly.

"You're writing again?" Jess asked.

"Yes. Well, I don't really think I ever stopped writing. But now, I feel like I'm writing toward something instead of just aimlessly, you know what I mean?"

"I couldn't be more elated to hear that," Jess said.

"Me neither. I'm proud of you, MJ," Mom added.

"We all are," Dad chimed in.

The small talk that continued throughout dinner was just that—small. Not that I needed some extravagant conversation, but I just assumed there would be a lot more questions or at least a little more interrogation. Who was Grey, where was he from, what was he interested in, general questions that would allow everyone to get to know him better.

"Thank you both for dinner, it was delicious," Grey said, hugging my mom and giving Dad a manly pat on the back. "I'm so glad to have finally met you both. Now I see where your daughter gets her witty personality and dashing good looks," he joked. "But in all seriousness, I'd like to spend a lot more time with your daughter, and I hope that means I'll be seeing you both too."

Mom's expression was one I could've taken a picture of. She adored him and she'd barely even had time to get to know him. Honestly, I couldn't blame her, because I felt the exact same way. "Good night, Grey, and thank you so much for the purple hydrangeas." Mom knew the meaning behind those flowers, so her extra emphasis on the color was to be expected.

And it was clear Dad felt the same. He didn't share the same enamored look that Mom did, but I could tell by how comfortable he'd been with Grey that he, too, approved of him.

"Bye, Mr. and Mrs. Mitchell. It was nice to meet you," Grey said, his voice floating through the entryway as he stepped outside.

"Bye, everyone. I love you all big," I said, blowing air kisses every which way.

Grey and I walked hand in hand to the driveway, and I paused when he walked me to the passenger side.

"Are you sure you're okay?"

"Yeah, of course," he said, smiling. "I've just got a lot on my mind right now. That's all."

I'd wanted tonight to be perfect. The people in that house were some of the most important people in my life and their opinion meant a lot to me. So, while Grey didn't necessarily do anything wrong, things didn't feel quite right either.

The drive was quieter than normal, but after getting back to my apartment, Grey started to filter back to himself.

*Thankfully.*

I almost pushed the topic multiple times, but my anxiety talked me out of it. I assumed that, per usual, it was something to do with his father, and while I wanted to be there for him, one could only talk about that man so much before everyone got exhausted. So instead, I brushed it away.

Everyone had off days, even Grey Prescott.

"Do you ever wonder why bad things happen to good people?" he pondered aloud, his strong body perched on my bed while I changed clothes.

I wanted to say "Yeah, only every single day," but then, before I could speak, I spotted the picture of Liv and me on my desk.

One thing I'd been telling myself for years whenever things felt hard or unfair was that Liv would never want me to feel sorry for myself. She truly believed everything happened for a reason, and I was desperate to cling to that.

At my lack of response, he started talking again. "Take you, for example. Why is it that you had to endure the loss of your best friend? Why is it that you had to process and grieve at such a young age? There are so many other people in this world who deserve a hurt like that, but not you."

I wanted to agree with him, but I wouldn't. For Liv.

"I hate to break it to you, but life's not fair. I could spend my whole life asking 'Why me?' but then I'd spend my whole life looking for an answer that doesn't exist. I could feel sorry for myself all day long, but that's only hurting me. Did it fucking hurt? Like hell. But did I make it through? Day by day, I did."

"Come here," he demanded.

I bounced onto the bed, my legs straddling his waist and his hands landing on my thighs.

"Sometimes I get so deep into my thoughts, I let them consume me. And the thought of you enduring so much pain is something I'm still trying to comprehend. I never want you to hurt like that again."

I wasn't sure why he'd been so consumed by these particular thoughts tonight, but then again, I was fairly familiar with anxiety and she didn't tend to give any reasons for her appearance.

"The thoughts will always be there, in my head too. I'd be lying if I said there weren't days that I question why such an awful thing happened to me, but I choose to believe that everything happens for a reason, even the hard stuff. Otherwise, I don't think I would make it out of bed most days."

I collapsed onto his chest, finding safety as he wrapped his arms around me.

"Everything does happen for a reason, that I'm sure of," he whispered.

# Chapter Thirty-Seven

We spent the next few weeks completely enamored with one another. Every moment we could be together, we were. Every second we were apart felt like an eternity.

With the summer heat dwindling and the ocean currents changing, Grey's political career was undoubtedly ramping up and he'd been making more frequent trips back to the city. With that came the doubt that now lived in the shadows of my brain as the end of summer approached.

It didn't help that Grey changed slightly with each one of these trips. He seemed to pull away, only a little, but enough, and that scared me more than anything.

When we were together, everything was good between us, really good. So I did my best to focus on that. We'd eventually have to talk about it, but I wanted to enjoy the last official party of the summer.

A knock sounded at my front door and I pushed away from my desk.

"Hi," I said, finding Sam at my front entrance.

"Damn, it's good to see you in the flesh. I was starting to think maybe Grey was taking you away from me for good. I feel like I haven't seen you in a month."

"That's because you haven't." I giggled. Our shifts hadn't lined up once in the last couple of weeks and my free time had all been spent with Grey.

"How are things? Never mind. The obnoxious grin on your face answers pretty much all of my questions," she teased.

"Yes. They're so good. Except that I'm supposed to be going to the Prescott family's Labor Day party tonight at Grey's house and I have nothing to wear."

"Shut up. You're going to that?" Sam screeched, an octave higher than normal. "That's literally the biggest political event of the year," she said enthusiastically.

"Stop. Please tell me you're going too?"

"No, I've never done well in political situations. But that's not the point. The point is that you are going as Grey Prescott's date."

"You're so dramatic sometimes."

"That might be true. But either way, I am so excited for you."

"I wish I shared that same excitement, but if I don't find a dress, I won't be going anywhere."

She raised her eyebrows while crossing her arms. "Who's dramatic now?"

"Ugh. It's just this part of Grey's world is daunting and, if I'm being honest, a little repulsive. Don't get me wrong, I can get behind a good party, but based on Grey's explanation, this isn't that kind of party. This is more of a political statement."

"But isn't that what Grey's trying to do? Make a political statement?"

"Technically speaking, yes. But is it really what Grey wants to do? Absolutely not, and that's the part I struggle with."

"Fair enough."

The doorbell rang, startling both of us.

"Expecting someone?" Sam asked.

"Not to my knowledge," I said, walking toward the noise.

Reaching for the handle, I swung open the door. "Daniel?"

"Good afternoon, Ms. Morgan. Mr. Prescott asked if I would deliver this to you before tonight," Daniel said, handing me a large black box that was decorated with a gold silk bow.

"Thank you."

"Of course. Have a good rest of your day, Ms. Morgan."

"You too, Daniel."

"You've got to be kidding me, right?" Sam's voice got louder as she got closer. "It's like you have your very own fairy god daddy." She tilted her head to the side as if she was unsure if that was the appropriate term for Grey.

I almost choked on my spit. "God daddy? Absolutely not."

"Just open the damn box," she snapped.

Placing the thing down on my couch, I untied the gold ribbon and tossed it to the side. The top slid off to reveal a single lilac hydrangea. Underneath lay a note decorated with Grey's handwriting.

MJ,

I know how you stress about these things.
I got this for you just in case.

P.S.: I got myself a little something but
wanted you to hold on to it until tonight.

-G

Setting the single stem and note on the couch cushion, I eagerly pulled out the black material that was folded to fit the box it came in. The dress dropped as I held it up to my body.

"Oh my god. A custom tie and now this." Sam gawked. "Go put it on."

Her reaction had me dying to see what the dress truly looked on. I excitedly shuffled to my bedroom in search of my full-length mirror, undressing and slipping into it in record time.

My mouth dropped open and immediately my hand shot up to cover it.

The black midi dress suctioned to my body in all the right places, accentuating my waist and fitting my hourglass body like a glove. The body of the dress was mesh, with a silky black underlay. The sleeves were my favorite part—also mesh but sans underlay with a dainty polka dot detail. The scoop neck revealed my collarbone and highlighted my chest in a tasteful way. This dress was classy but covertly sexy, and it was perfect for tonight.

Little bursts of excitement pulsed through me as I made my way back to the living room.

"Oh my god."

"You already said that." I giggled.

"I know, but it's even better now that it's on." Her eyes bopped up and down the dress. "Damn, that man did good."

"He did," I responded as my hands brushed down my sides, a smile sprawled across my entire face. "Okay, now I can be excited about tonight."

"As you should be." She let out a happy sigh. "You better start getting ready now," she said as she scooped up her purse and keys.

"I've got plenty of time." I waved her away.

"You better keep me posted. I love you," she said as she walked to the front door.

"I will, I will," I said. "I love you too."

The black box sat perched on my couch. Swooping it up, something lacy caught my eye. I pulled the material from the box, immediately blushing.

*This* was most definitely what he meant when he said he'd bought himself something too.

In my hands, I held a slinky black piece of lingerie. A flood of heat raced through me as I imagined Grey seeing me in it.

Laying the lingerie on the bed, I spotted something new. In bright red thread on the flimsy piece of fabric, near the part that would lie right over my hips, were two embroidered letters: *GP*.

I was *his*.

# Chapter Thirty-Eight

At seven o'clock on the dot, a knock came at my front door. "Come in, I'm just finishing up," I shouted from my bathroom.

I dabbed at the bright red lipstick, a nod to that tiny stitching detail that hid under my dress.

"It's even better than I imagined. You're absolutely stunning." Grey's voice was low, but the sincerity in it dropped my nervousness to a tolerable level.

"Really?" I asked.

He stepped closer to me, placing his strong arms on the small of my back. "Really. I still can't believe that I'm the lucky one who gets to have you on their arm tonight."

I planted a soft kiss on his lips before pulling back.

"You're lucky you've got that lipstick on."

Want fluttered through his words, making me grin as he grabbed my hand and led me to the door.

Daniel was waiting for us downstairs, and our drive to Grey's house was quieter than normal.

"Are you okay?" I asked.

"Yeah, of course. Why?" His thumb brushed my palm.

"I don't know. You just seem a little quiet. I wondered if maybe you were nervous about tonight? And whether you're sure about having me come as your date? I know your father isn't my biggest fan and—"

He moved so his entire frame was facing me. "MJ, I've never been more sure of anything than I am about having you by my side tonight."

I squeezed his hand tight, the only response I could muster. I believed him, I really did, but something wasn't sitting right with me. I could tell Grey felt the same, but I couldn't figure out what he was hiding.

"Sir, where would you like me to drop you off? There are a few unwanted cameramen at the front of the property, I could—"

"The front is fine, Daniel. Thank you."

Cameramen? I knew this party was a big deal, but that seemed a little excessive, even for the mayor of New York City.

"I want to show you off to anyone who wants to look." Grey tugged me into his side and planted a kiss on my temple. "Ready?"

My chest swelled as I took a deep breath in. "Ready as I'll ever be."

Grey stepped out of the car first, extending his hand to me. Deliberately slow, I made my way out of the back seat. My heartbeat picked up with each movement I made, mimicking the sound of the cameras clicking all around us.

I felt silly for feeling so anxious, but I'd never been a part of anything like this in my life. The closest I'd come was the junior prom when Olivia and I somehow snagged dates at the last minute and our moms obsessed over getting 1,000 photos.

Fortunately, Grey didn't even acknowledge the madness that surrounded us, and within a few seconds, we were walking through the front doors of his house. Though, if I'd known about the chaos that awaited us inside, I might have preferred never coming in. At least when we were outside Grey ignored the people vying for his attention.

His house was familiar in the sense that I'd been here before, but right now, it was almost unrecognizable. As we moved through the front entryway, it just didn't feel the same.

This was a party, but the feeling in the air wasn't one of anticipation and excitement like it was at the last party I attended here. Instead, it was stiff, almost suffocating.

The linens were stark white and pressed to a pulp. The all-white roses overwhelmed the entire house, large bouquets placed in every nook and cranny. The music was dull, something you'd find in an elevator in some quiet old building that doubled as a dentist's office. The guests were loud, but their voices were quiet. Their conversations appeared dim and lifeless as most of them stood with blank stares and fake smiles.

That is, until they spotted Grey.

All eyes were on him, which meant all eyes were on me too, and suddenly I was a fish out of water. It was obvious I didn't belong here.

I did my best to cling to Grey's previous comment about him never being more sure of his decision to bring me, hoping it would provide a sense of comfort.

Grey gripped my hand tighter, leaning toward my ear to whisper, "The only reason they're looking at me is because they can't take their eyes off of you."

A barely audible giggle fell from my mouth, only loud enough for the two of us to hear.

With his mouth still to my ear, he almost growled, "Good thing you're mine, and those little red initials prove it."

Chills sprinkled down my back and a shot of confidence flew to the surface. With all eyes on us, I smiled and wrapped my arm in Grey's. If I was going to be here, I might as well pretend to fit in.

I scanned the room, hoping I might spot someone I recognized. And I did. Just not who I'd hoped for. Instead, I landed on Stanley and Lisa Prescott. He was loud and boisterous; she was soft and quiet. She looked beautiful, elegant, but she was no doubt in her husband's shadow. I watched as she stood silently next to Stanley, smiling and nodding but never speaking.

Grey and I settled into a conversation with a couple who were around our age, which was a little breath of fresh air if you asked me. The husband, Scott, worked on Stanley's team and appeared fairly close to Grey. His wife, Ava, seemed genuine enough that I planned to stick by her side as long as I could.

"MJ, we're going to go grab some drinks," he said, kissing me on the cheek before walking away toward the bar with Scott.

"I have never seen Grey Prescott this smitten with a woman, and I have known him a very long time." Her voice was kind, and I really believed her intention was good, but the pressure of the comment had me stressed.

"Oh! You're the sweetest, but I'm sure there have been other women in Grey's life."

"Other women? Sure. But none that he would've ever dreamed of bringing to a party of this status. Especially on a night like tonight." She beamed back.

"A night like tonight?" I repeated.

"Yeah, you know, with him announcing he'll be joining his father's campaign. I mean, everyone knew it was coming. Stanley has been hinting at wanting his son to join him since before Grey could walk, but it'll finally be official."

The sinking feeling punched me right in the gut.

"Oh. Right," I quickly responded. The last thing I wanted to do was look clueless.

"One dirty martini. Extra dirty," said Grey, now back at my side. "Thanks."

I watched him mingle with his guests as the night continued on, and I realized that this was a side of him that I didn't know. One that was very different to the person I'd grown quite fond of. His conversations were about laws, policies, and a bunch of other stuff that flew over my head. And as much as he'd shared his distaste for politics with me, he was doing a pretty damn good job of convincing everyone else this was exactly where he was supposed to be.

While Grey conversed, I stood quietly next to him, nodding here and there, adding to the conversation when it seemed appropriate. Despite my best efforts, he knew something was up. He was constantly pulling me closer, sending me doting looks, and doing his best to wrap me into the conversation.

The heaviness lingered, a little more than I bargained for.

"Excuse me. I'm going to run to the restroom." I smiled at the couple we'd been standing with.

Grey whispered into my ear, "Use mine."

"Okay," I muttered.

I turned on my heels and shuffled to Grey's room, feeling grateful as I passed by a long line of women standing by the main bathroom.

Entering Grey's room, I quickly shut the door behind me, pressing my back against the door and letting a large sigh escape my body. The silence and familiarity of his room brought a solace that I desperately needed.

After using the restroom, I took a much-needed moment to catch my breath and sort through my thoughts. I stood in front of the mirror, wondering how I got here. I thought I would be able to handle this party, that I might even enjoy myself, but the longer I was here, the more that I realized I didn't know what the hell I was doing.

I was twenty-eight years old, working as a bartender at my dad's bar in the same small town I grew up in. I had no idea what I was going to do with my life. And honestly, that had never really bothered me until I stood in a room full of people who had their shit so much more together than I did. Everyone we talked to tonight was someone with a long list of achievements that far exceeded anything I'd ever done.

I'd always had big dreams, but they'd taken a back seat after losing Liv. Nothing really seemed that important anymore. Everything I'd ever known changed in an instant, and the only way to stay close to her was to stay here.

"Liv, what the fuck am I doing here? I don't belong in a place like this. I wanted this thing with Grey to be real, but I think I've always known it wasn't realistic. And seeing him in this kind of environment has only confirmed my fear. As much as he tells me he doesn't want a life in politics, he's a natural at playing the part."

It was moments like this when I would do absolutely anything to hear her voice on the other end of the conversation. But instead, I was greeted by silence, like always. I bowed my head, letting it fall between my shoulders, contemplating my next move.

"MJ?" Grey said, his voice drifting in from the bedroom.

Shit. I took too long. Now I really had to pull it together.

I swiped my pointer finger under my eye and fixed my hair before meeting Grey in his bedroom. I looked at him, seeing concern etched with desperation on his face.

"What's going on with you?" he asked.

I really wanted to say nothing was wrong. To put a smile on and go back out there like nothing was bothering me, but I couldn't. I wouldn't.

"I hear you're making a pretty big announcement tonight, huh?" The words came out harsher than I anticipated.

Stunned, he threw his head back, placing both of his hands behind his head. "MJ, I can explain. I—"

I cut him off. "Grey, what the fuck are we doing?" I threw my hands in the air. "Despite the fact that this summer has been incredible, we both knew this thing between us had an expiration date and this announcement of yours only confirms it. This could never work, we could never work, our worlds are just too different."

His face shifted, but I couldn't quite put my finger on the emotion. He took a seat on the edge of his bed. The same one we'd slept together in.

"MJ don't do this. Please. You don't understand," he said, ashamed. "I'm nothing without him."

Behind us, the bedroom door creaked open and a familiar, hate-filled voice said, "You're right. Without me, you are nothing."

*Stanley.*

"And if you don't get your ass out there and quit worrying about her," he said, his finger pointing right at me, "then you'll never amount to anything more than a pitiful little rich boy who hides in the shadow of his successful father. I've given you everything, even a second chance, and you can't even show me the decency to show up with a more respectable date than her."

His attention shifted to me. "MJ, is it?"

I couldn't respond even if I tried, but I didn't have time to anyway.

Grey lunged toward his father, ending up only a few inches from his face. "You can say whatever you want about me, everyone knows that always makes you feel better about yourself. But you keep MJ's name out of your fucking mouth. You got it?"

"Simmer down, Grey." Stanley arrogantly shook his head. "She'll never last in this world. She doesn't belong here. You and I both know that."

His chuckle was almost sinister as he slipped back toward the door.

The anger roaring through him was unlike anything I'd ever seen—his body tense, his eyes dark, and his jaw clenched.

Gazing back at us, Stanley kept antagonizing. "I suggest you chalk this one up to loss and get your ass back to the party. People are waiting for you, and if you keep them waiting too long, they'll get impatient."

Grey's movements were heated as he attempted to go after him, but I put myself in between him and the door. "Grey, he's not worth it. He's trying to provoke you. Let your actions speak louder than his words."

"He doesn't get to talk to you like that. No one does." He ran his hands through his hair. "I fucking hate him."

"Hey." I grabbed his arms. "His words don't define who I am. People who feel that small have to make everyone around them feel small too," I said, trying to crack a smile but lacking the energy to do so.

I believed what I was saying, but that didn't mean that Stanley's words didn't hurt.

"Grey." I shimmied closer to him as I took his head in my hands. "You've got to do what you've got to do. I get that. And it's important to me that I be there for you, no matter how much I wish this was going to end differently. You've been there for me this summer and I'm going to do the same," I said, holding out my hand, waiting for him to grab it.

"I don't want to lose you. I can't. You're just going to have to trust me on this one. I know it doesn't make sense right now, but it will. At least give me a chance to explain everything after the party. Please?"

I knew nothing he said would change my mind, but the building anxiety of losing him was too much to face at the moment.

"Okay." I nodded, and with our hands clasped we walked back to the party.

To no one's surprise, Stanley Prescott was standing on some makeshift stage at the front of the living room with a microphone in his hand. The light reflected off his obnoxious gold watch as he adjusted his suit, and his voice boomed through the house, leaving no one safe from the sound.

"I just want to thank all of you for being here tonight. The support I've received since announcing my re-election was more than I could've imagined. My wife and I are thrilled to continue supporting the city that we love most." A grimy grin spread across his face as he locked eyes with Grey. "But tonight, we have something even more special to celebrate..." His free hand motioned toward Grey and me. "Tonight, I get to officially welcome my son, Grey Prescott, to my campaign team. It's been a long time coming and a dream come true for the both of us. Grey, would you like to say a few words?"

He started to release my hand but hesitated. I squeezed it in response, in a sign of comfort and solidarity. I didn't want him to go, but he had to make that decision for himself, and regardless of what he decided, I wanted him to know I was there. His hand dropped from mine as he stepped forward, but not before turning back to look at me one more time.

As he moved away from me, the room spun in slow motion. Everything around me blurred except for him, crystal clear as he stepped onto the stage and took the mic. His anger had dissipated, or at least been masked.

His face went blank but only for a moment before his eyes locked on mine. Then, he smiled. "I couldn't be more excited to go on this journey with my father by joining his campaign team." Grey fired a death glare at his father. "Look, Stanley, it's everything you've ever wanted."

Stanley moved up to meet him, taking Grey's hand into his. The handshake looked like something you'd see between two business partners, not a father and son.

"A dream come true," Stanley confirmed.

Everyone cheered, whooped, and hollered, followed by a loud bang that sent red, white, and blue confetti floating through the air. The chaos of the crowd sent an understanding through me that would've brought me to my knees had I not forced myself to stay upright.

*She'll never last in this world. You and I both know that.*

It wasn't Stanley's words themselves that hurt, but rather the realization that he'd been right.

Looking around at all the people, all I could see was their fake smiles and hidden motives. Grey was good personified. He was kind and genuine. But unfortunately, he was stuck in a family that didn't want kind and genuine; they wanted selfish and money-hungry. And while I believed Grey was stronger than that, Stanley had dug his claws in so aggressively that Grey saw no way out.

I'd been waiting for the other shoe to drop, and standing here as the party continued around me, my world had stopped.

In order for Grey and me to be together, this would have to be my life, and that was something I didn't think I could accept. I may not have everything figured out, but one thing I was certain of was that I didn't want to end up like Grey's mom.

I wouldn't.

If I'd learned anything from Liv's death, it was that life was simply too short.

# Chapter Thirty-Nine

Taking one last look at Grey in his fitted black suit, my heart sank. The connection I had with him was something I didn't think I'd ever understand. It was undeniable, insatiable, and if I didn't know any better, I'd say magical. But as with anything in life, sometimes the hardest things didn't make any sense at all. The culmination of emotions left me breathless.

Grey's eyes met mine, and in that moment, we said more with our locked gaze than any words would've. I tried to smile but couldn't manage anything more than a small curl of my lips, tears brimming to the surface.

I needed to get the hell out of there.

I shimmied my way through the crowd, keeping my head down and doing my best to blend in until I found the door.

I gasped as the nighttime air coasted through me, the coolness sending a wave of comfort through my tense body. I realized I didn't have a way home, and on top of that, there were still a few determined cameramen waiting to catch a glimpse of something, anything.

Wiping away any remaining tears, I looped around the front porch and out of sight. I spotted a walkway hidden from the moon's blinding reflection.

I ducked behind a few bushes and found myself on a path that led straight to the beach. I wasn't sure what I was going to do from there, but at least I would be alone and away from all the people. I paused to rip my heels off, allowing the cool sand to take up the space between my toes.

The waves got louder, and so did the adrenaline pumping between my ears. It was so loud I thought I might drown in it. Treading through the sand, I marched to where the waves met the beach and froze. I couldn't move. I was afraid if I did, I was going to break into a million pieces.

If I was doing the right thing, why did it hurt this bad?

But I already knew the answer.

First, I lost Liv. And it was a pain that I quite honestly thought I would die from. A pain that tore me up and left me broken. A pain that kept me from allowing anyone in.

Until him.

Over the course of a single summer, I'd let him in. Fully. And now, just like Liv, I was losing him too. Except this time, I was the one choosing to walk away, and that somehow made it worse.

"Liv, I need you," I pleaded with the stars. "I just need you here with me."

"She's closer than you think," Grey said, his voice soft behind me.

Swallowing, I turned to look at him. There he was, standing five feet away. The sight of him alone almost brought me to my knees. His eyes, once so intense, looked lost as they met mine.

His lips tightly pulled down as he said, "MJ, please."

I didn't know how much longer I'd be able to keep it together, so I spoke quickly. "Grey, I'm sorry. I just don't think I can do this." I motioned toward the commotion of the party. "This world. Your world. It's all-consuming. It makes good people turn ugly, makes happy people angry, and I can't bear witness to that happening to you. You're too good and too kind. I want to remember you that way."

"It won't happen to me. I have a plan, MJ; I promise you that. I've been working my ass off to create something I'm proud of, and I just need a little more time. I'll do this campaign, and then I'll tell my father I'm done. I—"

"I wish it was that easy, but I can see now that it's not. Your father has his claws in so deep, I'm afraid you'll never get out. From where I'm standing, I can't even tell if you really want to."

He stepped toward me, almost too close. His hand reached for my cheek, but I stepped back, afraid that if I felt his touch, I might not have the self-control to leave.

"It doesn't matter what I say, does it? You've already made up your mind. You're going to leave, aren't you?"

The desperation in his voice broke me and a single tear trailed down my cheek.

"I have to," I breathed. "If I don't go now, I never will, and if we don't take this time to figure ourselves out, we'll never have a real chance. Because of you, I've come so far out of my comfort zone this summer that I'm desperate to keep going, to see what else I can do."

"But you said it yourself, you've always wanted to live in New York. Isn't that part of your dream?"

I smiled unevenly, but it wasn't enough to stop another tear from streaming down my face. "Yeah, it is. It really is. But I need to do it on my own terms."

"But then what if you never do it," he said, his voice teetering, his words rushed. Like he was grasping for anything that might make this make sense.

"Then I'll have myself to blame, but if I do it on your terms then I'm not really doing it for myself and it's no longer my dream," I said. "But what about your dream, Grey?"

"My dream will come with time."

"And so will mine," I added. "Your world and mine are very different, Grey Prescott. Maybe one day they'll intertwine, but not now. Not yet."

The outside air was dense as silence fell between us.

"MJ, there's something I have to tell you. I should've told you before, but I didn't know how. I needed time to process, and honestly I still do, but on the off-chance this is my last opportunity, I can't leave anything unsaid."

The seriousness in his voice was heavy, and my attention was his.

He stood there, staring blankly into the darkness, watching as the waves smashed against the shore, dissipating into nothing. The tension in his body was so apparent, I thought he might literally shatter.

Finally, his hand rose to his chest, forcefully palming the spot above his heart.

His voice was low, somber even, as he said, "You know that inexplicable pull that seemed to gravitate us toward one another? All those feelings that neither of us could justify? The ones that made us feel familiar to one another, even when we'd only just met..."

I looked at him, confusion flooding my face. "I don't understand. What does this have to do with—?"

"I didn't either, but now I do." He paused, wiping something from his forehead. "That night we had dinner at your parents' house... Remember after our run that morning, I said there was something I needed to do, something important? The real reason I'd come back to Montauk...?"

I nodded, not wanting my words to interrupt his thoughts.

"That day, after I left your apartment, I went to meet with the parents of my donor. Who at the time, I knew very little about." The words left his mouth in such a hurry that I almost missed them. He was speaking so fast I could barely keep up.

"I wanted to tell them thank you, that I was sorry it took me so long to come. To promise them that I'd do my best to honor their daughter. To tell them that not a single day goes by that I don't consider myself the luckiest person on the planet. To share the things that I've been able to do because of the selfless choices both they and their daughter made."

"Donor?" I questioned. "What do you mean donor?"

He rushed on, ignoring my question. "I was terrified of what they would say. Worried they would think I was selfish for taking so long to visit. But I couldn't have been more wrong about them. They were graceful, kind. They're just *good* people. They couldn't stop thanking me for coming. They told me their daughter would be proud that her heart was working for someone like me." The last words barely made it out before getting caught in his throat. "They talked about her in a way that made it feel like she'd been able to live on through me. For once in my life, they made me feel like I had a purpose."

"Grey, I still don't understand. Why didn't you just tell me all of this before?"

"Just wait. Please..." He paused to collect himself. "After I left them, I was on top of the world." He smiled, clearly reminiscing, but then his happy expression vanished. "But then we walked into your parents' house, and there they were. My donor's parents. I had no idea the name of my donor or anything about them, really. I'd chosen to stay in the dark, because selfishly that was easier."

"Wh-what?" I stuttered.

Everything muted.

I couldn't hear the waves pounding the shore. I couldn't hear the wind whipping through my hair. I couldn't even hear my own breath as it desperately tried to escape my mouth.

"I... I don't—" I cried out. "What do you mean?" Clamoring my hands harder into his chest, I wanted a better explanation than what he'd given me.

Grey grabbed my hands, guiding them to that spot right over his heart.

There it was, even in this uncharted moment. That familiar, constant rhythm of his heartbeat. The one that had tied me to reality and made me feel safe so many times. The same one that had reassured me that everything was going to be okay, just by existing.

He gripped my hands tighter, staring right at me as tears filled his eyes. "That day, I found out that my heart donor was eighteen-year-old Olivia Mitchell."

"No." I stepped back. "No, no!"

I violently shook my head as the air was ripped from my lungs. I couldn't breathe. I inhaled, hoping for something, anything, but all I could find was the weight of a thousand bricks slamming into my chest. Every fiber of my being was breaking, one by one. The weight was unbearable, forcing my legs to give out, bringing me to my knees.

I was hyperventilating, and it was fucking terrifying. A suffocating feeling that no one should ever have to endure.

"I... I can't breathe," I said, frantically grasping at my throat, cries slipping through each rapid breath.

"MJ, I'm right here. I'm not going anywhere. It's going to be okay," he said, even though his voice was just as unstable as mine.

*Liv*, I mouthed, no sound escaping as my body trembled.

In a split second, Grey was hovering over me, his body only a few inches from mine.

"I can't, Grey," I wept. "I can't do this. The parties, the lifestyle, and now this. It's all too fucking much."

Coercing my legs to stand, I forced myself to look at him. "Why now? Why come back after all this time?" I cried out, the sound of the waves roaring against the shoreline drowning out my voice.

My heartbeat pounded through my ears, the rhythm nauseating.

Grey approached me, stopping closer than I expected, so close I could see the devastation in his eyes. "It felt wrong for me to be here, living in a place where she should've been living. But something drew me back this summer."

Hesitantly, he placed his palms on my cheeks. Part of me wanted to pull away, but the other part knew his touch was keeping me upright.

"I know it sounds crazy, but I swear it was her. It was Olivia. She brought me back here to find you." The last sentence barely made it out of his mouth before he cracked, his breathing labored as he attempted to calm himself down.

A man of stature, a man who seemed so unbreakable, and yet, here he was, standing in front me, completely broken.

I found myself replaying pieces of our summer, reaching for anything that made sense.

"The health issues, not drinking very much... the scar," I whispered.

"MJ, I'm so sorry. I wish I had something else to say, something that might make this hurt less, but I don't. I'm so sorry."

My insides hurt, but even with all the pain, all I could think about was him. I wanted to scream at him as much as I wanted to hug him, but I couldn't do either.

My face still hung in his hands, but now our foreheads were pressed together, our wet faces staring at each other. Grey used his thumb to wipe away the tears, but they were coming too fast for him to keep up.

We both knew what was happening, and I think it killed us both just the same.

"I'm sorry," he pleaded, blinking the tears away.

"If you care about me, you'll let me go," I forced myself to say. The words splintered tiny cracks in my heart as I set them free, but there was too much here that needed processing. "You have to let me go."

Just as quickly as the words left my mouth, he dropped his hands.

"I'll let you go, only because it's not fair for me to hold on. But MJ..." His hand snuck into his pocket as he pulled something out. "Until we intertwine... A piece of me and a piece of Olivia. Because you'll never really lose either of us."

He opened his clenched hand, and in the middle of his palm lay a gold keychain with a tiny gold pendant.

"Grey," I said, hesitating to take it.

"I had this made the day after my surgery."

The metal was cold as he dropped it into my hands. My fingers instinctively traced the engraved lines that decorated one side.

"I always wanted to remember the sound of the heart that gave me a second chance. Now I know that heart was from someone who was loved by you, which makes it even more special."

The lines were Olivia's heartbeat.

Before I could respond, Grey started trailing back toward his house. He yelled over his shoulder, "I'll make sure Daniel is waiting to take you back to your apartment."

The abruptness of his departure stung, but we both knew that with the way everything had played out tonight, leaving was what came next.

His presence disappeared along with my breaths, but then I heard his voice again. "And MJ?" My heart jumped from my chest. "Promise me this isn't goodbye forever, just goodbye for now."

I sucked in my lower lip. "I promise."

Within seconds, the darkness consumed him. He was gone and I was left with only my thoughts. Everything in my brain was mushed together in a pile of hurt, sadness, grief, and heartbreak. A pile that, at the moment, seemed impossible to sift through.

I was completely numb, and I knew I couldn't be here any longer. I had to get away from all of it. I was afraid if I didn't, I'd never recover. I weaved my way back to the front of the house, adjusting my dress, putting my heels on, and wiping at my face in an attempt to appear less disheveled. As promised, Daniel was waiting for me.

"Ready to go home, Ms. Morgan?"

I took one last look at the beautiful house at the bottom of the hill before sliding into the back seat. "I'll never be ready for this goodbye, but it's time to go."

## Chapter Forty

"How are you?" Jess's voice was cautious as I sat curled up on my parents' screened-in porch. The earthy smell of rain permeated the air as light sounds of soft rock music trickled through the speaker.

Four weeks.

That's how much time had passed since I last saw Grey, and I'd spent my time since then finding comfort in either writing or with my parents and John and Jess.

"Here you go. Peanut butter and honey, your favorite," Mom said, returning from inside. She took the seat next to Jess, a steaming cup of tea in her hands.

"Thanks, Mom." I angled my body toward both of them. "I'm doing better. It still just hurts, you know? And I'm not really sure which part hurts the most. The part where Grey was Liv's heart recipient, the part where Grey's gone, or the part where now it feels like I've lost them both."

"I'm betting it's a little bit of everything," Mom said.

"I just have to keep reminding myself that Grey's life was driving a million miles per hour, and I was just getting used to being in a car again," I said.

"You're definitely right about that." Jess entered the chat. "He told John and me that he'd been spending the summer working to acquire a few different businesses, hoping to one day create his own story."

"Speaking of getting in the car again, what are you going to do next, MJ?"

Mom's question was so straightforward, it threw me off-kilter. Normally my parents were hesitant to ask me anything too specific, but not today. Today she got right to the point.

I stared at her, unsure what to say.

"I'm sorry, I didn't mean to come off as pushy. I'm just afraid if you sit around too long, you're going to lose the fire that sparked alive inside of you this summer."

"I agree with your mom," Jess chimed in. "You need to go after what you want, no matter how scary or uncertain that feels. We all know life's too short."

"What do you want?" Mom asked.

The question wasn't hard, and neither was the answer. I'd just never taken the time to say it out loud. Looking between Jess and my mom, the words poured out.

"I want to finish this damn book. I want to move to New York. I want to become an author. I want to chase my dreams."

They peered at one another before looking at me, considerable grins displayed on their faces.

"So what's stopping you? Wasn't that a big reason you ended things with Grey in the first place?"

"Yeah, but—"

"Yeah, but you didn't plan on him telling you that he'd received your best friend's heart, is that it?" Jess asked.

The bluntness. She and Mom were in rare form.

I nodded. "Right."

"But if anything, shouldn't that fuel your desire? You found a piece of Liv, or rather it found you. Yes, it was in the shape of a tall, dark, handsome man, but nonetheless, you can't deny that maybe it was her way of making sure you never gave up on your dreams."

"I guess I never saw it that way. But then again, Liv always did have a way with the theatrics, didn't she?" I teased.

"Yes, she did," they said in unison, chuckling.

It became abundantly clear that they'd decided this was going to be an intervention of sorts. Their words were calculated, and they had a response for everything I said. I could've been bothered by it, but looking at the two of them, I was just really damn grateful to have humans who cared about me that much.

Mom went on. "Remember when you told me that whenever you felt uncertain about what to do next, you asked Liv, and she had a way of pushing you to do it each time? If you're so unsure now, why don't you ask her?"

"I—" I went to respond, but then something indescribable happened. "Wait, Mom, what's that song playing?"

I grabbed the remote from the table, turning the music louder, and chills raced up my arms.

"Tears in Heaven" by Eric Clapton sifted through the air around us.

*A sliver.*

This was the one and only song that played at Liv's funeral, the one song that would always be hers.

"Looks like you don't even need to ask her," Jess said.

We all started laughing even as tears poured down our cheeks.

The song played, all three of us sitting in silence except for little sniffles here and there. As I contemplated the new perspective that Jess offered, with Eric Clapton as my soundtrack and Liv as my witness, something clicked.

For the longest time, I had allowed the sadness to consume me, ruminating on the fact that Liv was gone. That she'd been taken too soon. The sadness made me believe I wasn't worthy of happiness. That I didn't deserve it. It had forced me to think that I'd lost Liv forever, that without her, I was no one. But then Grey stumbled into town, bringing a piece of Liv with him. A piece that over the course of a summer allowed me to see I'd never really lost her at all. That regardless of where I was, she'd always be with me, and because of that, I was capable of anything.

"Jess, do you mind if I run by your house? There's something I want to get from Liv's room."

"Of course not. Take whatever you need."

I popped out of my chair and grabbed my stuff. "Thank you, you two. I love you both, big."

"And we love you," they said back.

Even after their move, John and Jess's house was only a short walk from my parents. I approached the pastel yellow door, to which Liv had given me a key a million years ago. John and Jess insisted I keep it, saying their home would always be my home too.

I took the steps two at a time, the old wooden floorboards creaking with each of my movements. Finding myself standing in front of a familiar door that wasn't so familiar anymore, I pushed into Liv's room.

I came here a lot after the accident, in the beginning. Being around her stuff and in her space gave me a sense of comfort. Frozen in the center of her room, I realized that I hadn't been back in years, and even with all the time that'd passed, everything had remained exactly the same. Almost as if it was being preserved.

Her white-framed bed was scrunched up into the corner of the room. Her ceiling was lined with fairy lights that she and I hung up when we were thirteen in an attempt to be like the "cool girls" in the movies. Her walls were covered, floor to ceiling, in band posters, magazine cutouts of famous actors that we were convinced we'd marry, and tiny polaroid images of her and me.

From the time we were ten up until our sophomore year of high school—when we started carrying cellphones instead of cameras—we took thousands of pictures with our polaroids, and the majority of them had made their way onto her wall.

I grazed my fingers over a few of the images, my touch seemingly pressing play on a memory from that exact moment in time. I landed on Liv's desk last. Her beautiful, white wooden desk that sat right under a window overlooking her mother's garden.

On top of her desk sat her sketchbook, the leather binding embossed with two golden letters.

*O.M.*

*Olivia Mitchell.*

Barely poking out from the top was yet another picture. Opening her journal, two bright young faces stared back at me. It was Liv and me from the last Christmas we had together, with the biggest smiles on our faces as we held up our heather gray New York sweatshirts. The anticipation that bubbled between us at the thought of living in the city was enough for you to think our parents bought us an apartment there, not some cotton sweatshirts.

Teetering toward her closet, I turned the handle and shifted to my knees. "Liv, please tell me you didn't throw it away," I said out loud, pushing boxes out of my way and throwing a few random blankets over my shoulder to clear the bottom of the closet. There, behind three shoe boxes, I spotted it.

Pulling the two-foot by two-foot, natural-colored bulletin board out into the daylight, I couldn't help but smile. At the top, in all different fonts, sizes, and colors, it read: *Liv & MJ's Dream Board.*

It was littered with *Sex and the City* scenes, the NYU campus, Liv's drawings of what our future apartment would look like, coffee shops, cute little restaurants, and right there in the center was another picture of the two of us. This one we'd specifically taken for the bulletin board. Liv and I sat crisscross on her bedroom floor, our thumbs pressed to our lips, our pinkies intertwined.

That night, we'd made a promise go to New York, no matter what.

This was my no matter what. No matter how hard it seemed. No matter how scary it felt. No matter how crazy sounded. I was doing it, because as I stared at that worn-out bulletin board, it hit me that Liv never got the chance to chase her dreams.

Her dreams would always be pictures pinned to a wooden board.

I, however, still had time to go after mine. To chase them fully with no regrets. I couldn't keep sitting around this town, letting my dreams collect dust in this closet. I had to keep my promise to Liv and to myself.

And that was what I was going to do.

I would go to New York, and I'd take Liv with me. Grabbing the bulletin board, I bounded down the stairs and out the front door, turning only to lock the door behind me.

The dewy grass and wet leaves left a crispness in the air. I took a deep breath before boosting into a full-blown power-walk. Rounding the corner, the bulletin board still in my hand, I spotted Dad's truck in the driveway.

As I got closer, I heard voices still echoing from the back porch and was grateful everyone was here. I busted through the screen door and found four wide eyes.

"I want to move to New York."

The silence between us was loud, but not loud enough to drown out the sound of my own heartbeat.

Dad took a long, drawn-out breath, and the anticipation of his response made me anxious.

"I never thought those words would leave your mouth," he said nonchalantly.

The breath I'd been holding audibly left my mouth as relief flooded through me. "Me neither, but I think I'm ready. I want to do this. Not just for me, but for Liv too."

They stepped toward me, embracing me in a massive group hug before each one of them took their turn giving me a squeeze.

"And before you ask me what my plan is... the answer is I don't know. I might've toyed with this idea for a little while now, but I never thought I would actually go through with it."

"MJ," Dad said.

"But I'll be fine. I can figure it out."

"MJ," Mom butted in.

"Yeah?"

Dad spoke again. "I was just going to ask you if you needed help with anything."

"Oh... I-I haven't really gotten that far. I just know that I'm going to go to New York, and I'm going to finish this book."

"Well, we are all here to help you in whatever way we can. Don't forget, this has always been your dream. It just took some time for you to understand that you're brave enough to go after it," Jess said confidently.

"I'm proud of you, Miller Jean," Mom said, the most genuine look on her face.

"We all are," John added.

My emotions bubbled to the top, spilling over into a plethora of tears. "Thank you. Seriously. I'm the luckiest girl in the world to have all of you in my corner, constantly supporting me." I smiled. "I love you all so much."

## Chapter Forty-One

The next two weeks were a blur of phone calls, emails, and me frantically questioning whether I was doing the right thing. Each time I experienced even a hint of doubt, I looked at the picture of Liv and me, the one where our pinkies were interlocked, and it was immediately replaced with anticipation.

"Damn, you condensed everything you own into these four suitcases?" Sam asked, walking into my now empty apartment.

"Well, I condensed the important stuff into four suitcases. All the other shit is stuffed into boxes and hiding in my parents' attic." I laughed.

"That makes more sense," she said. "How are you feeling?"

I canvassed the empty living room, landing on the luggage propped against the wall near the front door. "Excited, nervous, scared shitless... Pretty much every emotion, yeah."

"That means you're doing something right. Dreams don't happen without a little excitement and a whole hell of a lot of unknowns." Her tone wavered. "Don't worry—I *will* be coming to visit as soon as you get settled."

"I wouldn't expect anything less," I responded. "Sam, I just want to tell you that without you I probably wouldn't have survived the last ten years. You were a friend to me when I needed it most and you consistently showed up in whatever capacity I needed you."

"I'll always be here for you, MJ." She walked closer before wrapping her arms around me. "Just don't forget about me when you become the next *New York Times* Bestseller."

"I wouldn't dream of it." I pulled back for a second before bringing her into another hug.

"I better get going, I told your dad I would hold down the fort while he drops you off at the train station. I love you."

"I love you too."

As silence surrounded me standing in the doorway of my very first home away from home, the nostalgia washed over me.

The sun peered through the window, illuminating the space. "Here I go, Liv." I paused as the sun reflected off something and on to the wall. I moved my hand around until I landed on the dainty piece of gold metal that now permanently hung around my neck. The necklace I had made from the keychain Grey gave me that night on the beach.

A subtle reminder they were both still here with me.

"I'm sorry it took me this long to follow through on our promise, Liv, but better late than never, right?" I laughed softly, clinging to the necklace. "I think after all these years, it's become clear that I've wasted so much time staying put in this little town of ours. And what a lucky person I am, to have had that time to waste."

Selfish, really. Wasting time was a privilege not everyone had, and I was done taking advantage of it.

"I want to make the most of my time here. I want to do the things that scare me. The things that excite me. But most importantly, I want to do all the things we promised we'd do together. I know it won't be the same without you, but I've learned that just because I can't see you doesn't mean you're not standing right next to me. I love you, Liv. Deeper than the ocean."

The vibration in my pocket brought me back to reality. I swiped away a lingering tear and tapped the screen.

Dad:

> We're on the way. Be there in 5.

Me:

> Perfect! See you then.

I grabbed two suitcases and trekked down the apartment steps and onto Reef Road. Gazing around, I took a moment to appreciate the little town that lay before me. For so long, it had been exactly what I needed.

Montauk had been everything I'd ever known—the quaint little sights, the salty smells, and the joyful sounds were integrated into every fiber of my being. It was simply a part of who I was, and a part of me would always need it.

I couldn't help but feel sad and hopeful at once.

Mom and Dad pulled to a stop in front of me, Dad's hand resting on the rolled-down window ledge. "Good morning, my little New Yorker." His smile could've been seen for miles.

"Good morning." I beamed.

They stepped from the car and onto the curb.

"Is this everything?" Dad asked.

"No, I have two more suitcases upstairs."

"All right, I'll go grab them," he responded. "Why don't you go over there and give your mom a little extra love, I think she could use it." He winked.

"Mom." I squeezed her hand. "It's okay. I'm going to be fine."

"That's just it. I know you're going to be fine. You're going to be better than fine, and that's what makes this so bittersweet," she said, dabbing at the corner of each eye. "I've waited so many years for your sparkle to come back. Slowly but surely it has, but this time, it's even brighter than it was before. You're a beautiful woman, inside and out, and you're going to do amazing things. I can't wait to see the lives that you touch with your words. I'm so proud of you, Miller, and I want you to know that your dad and I are here for you no matter what. And always remember, you can find slivers anywhere. I love you so big."

"Dammit, Mom. I was doing my best not to cry, but how do you expect me not to when you say things like that?" I asked, leaning in to embrace her.

We both laughed while wiping away tears.

"My girls, come here," Dad said, lugging the suitcases down the stairs before tossing them into the bed of his truck.

The three of us took a few moments just to hug each other. I took a mental picture, because I knew this was something I never wanted to forget.

"Are you ready?" Dad asked, pulling away first.

"I'm not sure if *ready* is the correct term for how I'm currently feeling, but regardless, let's do it."

"Caleb is going to help you get settled, right?" Dad asked.

"Yes, he just texted to let me know he'd be waiting for me at my apartment."

"Perfect," Mom said.

I had taken Caleb up on his offer and he'd been a huge help. Within days, we secured an apartment for me. A task that proved to be much harder than I'd anticipated.

The train station was a quick ten-minute drive. I told my parents that I could've taken a cab, but they insisted on dropping me off. In fairness to them, I never did the whole college thing, so this was sort of an equivalent experience for them.

With my suitcases loaded, they walked me to the front of the train while I urged myself not to cry. Dad seemed to be trying to do the same. Mom, on the other hand, had no such luck. Her tears had been present since we stepped out of the truck.

Stopping just before the train doors, I inhaled a deep breath. "I want you both to know that I would've never survived the loss of Liv if it weren't for you. I would've never been able to pull myself out of the darkness and find my light again had I not had your unconditional love and support all of these years. I would be lying if I said I wasn't scared, but then again, I've been told that the scariest things sometimes turn into the most beautiful of things. I promise that no matter what happens in New York, I will always do my best to make you proud. I love you both so big."

"You've already made us proud, more than you know. And we love you even bigger." Dad's voice was steady until the very last word. He pulled me into one last hug, doing his best to mask his emotions.

"Boarding for New York City. Doors will close in two minutes," a man's voice boomed through the speakers overhead.

"I better get going," I said, pulling away.

"MJ," Mom said. "Just because you're leaving Montauk doesn't mean you're leaving Olivia. She'll always be everywhere you are."

I nodded, knowing that if I spoke, the words wouldn't make any sense. Stepping onto the train, I found my seat and peered out the window. As my parents made their way back to the truck, my mom stopped only once. She spun around, turning to blow me a kiss. I just had time to return it with a smile before the train picked up speed. Within seconds, we were out of the station and I was on my way to New York City.

My eyes traced the blurry landscape that floated by. I reached up, searching for the gold metal that dangled from my neck, landing on it quicker than normal. The indention that I'd become accustomed to pressed against my fingertips. Every time I felt the engraved heartbeat under my fingers, it was like I could hear the rhythm too. Rubbing the metal, I stared out the window, thinking about everything and nothing at once.

I wasn't the one who died that night, but a part of me did. For the longest time, I thought that part would find me again, but I now understood it was my job to find it myself.

"I'm doing it, Liv. I'm going to the big city to write silly little love stories," I muttered quietly.

# Chapter Forty-Two

*Three Months Later*
*January 2025*

Snow fell outside of my tiny studio window, and it was just as magical as I'd hoped it would be. While I'd grown to love the sounds of the city, the stillness this weather brought was sort of surreal, remarkable even. With the morning quieter than normal, I took some time to just be present and enjoy the hot coffee perched in my palms.

The holidays had come and gone. Mom and Dad came to visit for Thanksgiving and Christmas. It was obvious they were curious about Grey. They even tried to subtly ask about it a few times, but I never said much, and they never pushed any further.

This was harder than a normal breakup. He was everywhere, and no matter how hard I tried not to see him, I couldn't avoid it. Billboards, commercials, and even wrapped buses with Stanley's face were plastered all over the city, and ever-present right next to him was his undeniably handsome son. Or as most news outlets referred to him: the new up-and-comer.

Although, I didn't completely hate it. Despite how things ended between us, I knew I'd always hold out a sliver of hope that one day he'd decide to finally stand up to his father. Then, maybe one day, there would be space for him and me again.

What I struggled with most was that we both had feelings for each other, and we still didn't end up together. It seemed hating each other would've made this a lot easier.

On top of all of that, Grey still texted me every so often. Simple texts like "Just checking in" or "I hope you're doing well." Nothing life-altering but nothing I could ever bring myself to respond to either. My heart wouldn't let me because it knew I couldn't send back a simple response. I would've asked too many questions, brought up too many memories, and then I would've had to start the grieving process all over again. I knew I couldn't have handled that.

Until something changed in Grey's life, there wasn't space in it for me, so instead of dragging myself through unnecessary hurt, I decided to fall in love with something else.

*New York City.*

Over the last three months, my love affair with the city had blossomed. Every nook and cranny of this city crawled with details begging to be explored. The colorful graffiti on brick walls, the aroma of street food on every corner, the chaotic but harmonious melody of hundreds of thousands of strangers cohabiting... And the best part? With every new sight, there was always something there to remind me of Liv.

Specifically, the architecture.

This city homed some of the most spectacular-looking buildings. The library that was being built only a few blocks from my apartment was breathtaking, and I'd been admiring the building process from my window for months now.

From what I could see, one side of the building was made entirely of glass. It was modern, with a flat roof. The precise lines of each corner of the rectangular infrastructure were made with heavy beams of steel, giving it a clean and sharp look.

It was one of those things that made me feel like Liv was right here with me. I mean, a new library blocks from my apartment that stood to make a commotion with the design itself? It was like Liv was up there saying *Hold my beer, I've got this one.*

I chuckled aloud at the thought.

"Shit," I mumbled, looking down at my phone. I'd lost track of time and now I needed to hurry so I wasn't late for my shift.

I rifled through my closet, throwing on a pair of black ripped boyfriend jeans, a branded T-shirt, and a tan quilted jacket. Running my fingers through my day-old curls, I spritzed in some dry shampoo and called it good before grabbing my winter coat and darting out the door.

Thankfully, work was only a subway ride away and I was there in under ten minutes. Bursting through the door, the aroma of fresh coffee beans swam around me.

"Hi, Lauren. So sorry, the morning got away from me."

"Hey, MJ. No worries, you've got two minutes to spare."

Releasing the breath I'd been holding since stepping off the subway, I threw my bag and coat under the counter and tied my dark green apron around my hips.

"I'm finishing up cutting some fresh stems for the table, would you mind taking over the register?" Lauren asked, motioning to the customer approaching the counter.

"Hi! So sorry, welcome to A Second Cup, what can I get started for you?"

A sweet old lady stood across from me. "I'll just have a black coffee, please."

"One black coffee coming right up." I smiled.

That was the best part of this job: the people. Since starting as a barista here, almost everyone I'd come in contact with had been kind. But you couldn't blame them when this place transported you someplace magical each time you stepped foot inside.

After moving to the city, I knew if I was really going to write this damn book, I needed a flexible job. One that allowed me time to write while still earning an income. Over the last three months, I'd rediscovered my love of nighttime writing. There was just something satisfying about writing when the rest of the world was asleep.

Grabbing a to-go cup, I poured the scorching hot coffee into it and sat it back on the counter while I searched for a lid. "Lauren, have you seen—" Before I could finish, my eyes landed on a fresh stack of plastic lids. "Never mind, I found them."

I popped the lid on and handed it over to the lady across the counter. "Have the best day, and stay warm out there."

"Thank you!"

Turning to face Lauren, I asked, "Has it been slow this morning?"

"Extremely. Hence why I'm giving so much attention to these flowers."

"Need some help?" I asked. But just as I finished my question, our machine beeped, signaling we'd received an online order. "Are you kidding me? Who is requesting an order be delivered in this weather?"

"Someone who doesn't give two shits about us and just wants their coffee."

"Touché." We both laughed. "I'll take this one," I said, ripping the paper from the machine and scouring it for an address. "Thank god it's just a vanilla latte, and it's literally like fifty feet away."

I spun around to the coffee machine and started the routine process of making the drink.

"How's the book coming along?" Lauren asked.

"I'm so close, I can literally taste the ending, but every time I try to write, it doesn't make any sense."

"It will come to you. I remember when you first started working here and you were barely halfway done. Look at you now, already trying to figure out the ending."

"Maybe one day I'll finally get it right."

"And then will you tell me what it's about?"

I winked. "Maybe."

Reaching under the counter, I pulled out my jacket, slipping into it before tugging my purse over my shoulder. "I'll be back."

The snow was still falling, and while not silent, the streets were still much quieter than normal. I loved the chaos of the city, but moments like this made me understand why Montauk would always be a part of me, a special place that I would always return to.

Following the GPS on my phone, I rounded a corner and stopped in front of the building it led me to, my heart immediately plummeting to the bottom of my stomach as I recognized the facade. Pushing my way inside, I kept my eyes glued to the floor in front of me.

Frantically searching for the ticket, I ripped it from my coat pocket. The order was placed by an "MM." My heartbeat slowed a bit once my brain could comprehend that this order wasn't for him, for Grey. Waiting for the elevator, my breath was able to mostly return to normal, even though the possibility of running into him was still very much present.

The elevator dinged and the doors creeped open to reveal that it was—thankfully—vacant. I flung my body inside and aggressively pressed the button responsible for closing the doors. Once closed, I hit the number twenty-seven.

I'd only been to Grey's apartment once, and to say I hadn't been paying attention to my surroundings would be a slight understatement. I racked my brain trying to remember what floor he lived on, but I had no such luck. The elevator dinged again, signaling I'd reached my stop.

Slowly, I stepped out of the elevator. If anyone saw me, they would be convinced something was wrong with me. That, or they would think I was attempting to be in the next James Bond movie. Fortunately, luck was on my side and I didn't spot a single soul.

The apartment I was looking for was only a few steps from the elevator. I sat the coffee on the doormat, pressed the doorbell, and walked away.

"I don't recall asking for a contactless drop off," a man's voice called from behind me.

I froze.

That was a voice that I'd never get out of my head. But it couldn't be him. The ticket said *MM*, not *GP*. I must have been losing my damn mind. Convinced my head was playing games with me, I spun around.

There, in nothing but navy sweatpants and a glistening abdomen, was Grey. My entire body went numb. I wasn't sure why I was so affected by his presence right now considering his face was literally plastered throughout the entire city, haunting my daily runs. Although, in fairness to me, his outfits for press events consisted of a lot more clothing and a lot less bare skin.

"Grey," I muttered.

His big copper-colored eyes penetrated mine as he calmly said, "MJ. I was afraid you wouldn't come."

"Wait, what do you mean? How did you know I even worked there?

"I've known since the day you started. Hence why I used your initials and not mine for the delivery."

*MM. Miller Morgan*. Oh, he was good.

"And me moving to New York City, how'd you know that one?" I questioned.

"I didn't at first," he responded before disappearing briefly behind the door. "But I suspected when I went to your apartment in Montauk and found it empty."

I moved toward him, wanting to be closer while also keeping my distance.

His eyes shot to my chest and he immediately smirked. "I like your necklace."

The look on his face sent familiar flutters raging through my body. We'd been here before, and if I didn't leave, I knew where this was headed.

"Thank you," I said, stepping back, "but I better get back to work. I wouldn't want them to send out a search party for me," I nervously joked.

"They won't do that."

I cocked my head to the right. "Well, that's rude. I'm very much respected at my place of employment."

He crossed his arms, confidently standing in his doorway. "Oh, I know you are. But they won't do that because I told them you'd be gone for the rest of the day."

"Grey, what the fuck. You can't just go around telling people when I will or won't be at work."

"I mean, as the owner, I can do pretty much whatever I want in regards to my employees," he said, smirking. "Well, to an extent."

"Y-you own A Second Cup? That's the coffee shop you told me about? You're fucking kidding me. Aren't you trying to be a politician?"

"That's what I wanted everyone to think, but like I told you, I have other plans."

His words pulled the memory of that night on the beach back to the surface.

"The afternoon I spent with John and Jess changed things. They helped me see things from a different perspective. In a few short hours, they made me feel like I had a purpose. To live a life that Olivia would be proud of, a life that has meaning, a life that built on my dreams, not anyone else's. And while I'd already started planning my departure from politics, my conversation with them only confirmed my decision and lit a spark of determination inside of me. So—"

I held my hands up in protest, cutting him off. "Grey—"

"MJ, do you know what my dad said to me the day he called to tell me there was a donor?"

I shook my head.

"He said 'Don't say I never did anything for you, son. One day you'll be able to repay me.'"

Stunned, I couldn't help but acknowledge him. "What? You found out you were having a lifesaving surgery, and that's what your father said to you?"

Grey nodded. "See, the thing is, he didn't see it as his son getting a lifesaving procedure. He saw it as a way to use my health as a pawn in his game. And for a while, it worked. I let it work." He sighed. "But then I met the Mitchells. And it was in that moment that I knew I was going to do everything in my power to create something I was proud of, something *they* could be proud of, but I also knew I needed to be smart. So, quickly and quietly, I began acquiring different businesses that I found interesting, hoping I'd be successful enough on my own that I wouldn't need him anymore."

"And are you?" I asked, the words slipping out.

*"Breaking news, we're coming at you live from the office of Mayor Stanley Prescott."* The TV in the background sounded crystal clear all of a sudden. I pushed the door open, stepping to the side of Grey until all I could see was the screen.

"Well, this isn't exactly how I had this planned. A bit dramatic for me," he scoffed.

*"Stanley Prescott has an announcement regarding his son and everyone's golden boy, Grey Prescott."*

My head fell into my hands and the anxiety inflated like a bubble inside of my stomach. "I don't know why you shared all of that with me. All it did was get my hopes up that maybe, sometime soon, things could somehow be different between us," I cried out.

I quickly removed my foot from inside of the door and spun back toward the elevator.

"MJ, wait!" Grey's voice was louder than normal, tinted with unease.

"Keep walking, you're almost to the elevator, don't turn around," I whispered under my breath.

Pressing the button, the door dinged open immediately. I stepped inside and pounded the *L* button as fast as I could. The door creeped closed but not before I caught a glimpse of Grey staring at me, our eyes locking only for a millisecond but long enough that I saw the despair.

I could've sworn the elevator was caving in. Making it back down to the first floor, I rushed to the exit, desperately needing the frigid air to relieve the pressure inside my lungs. Shoving the door open, I gasped as the cold air stung my face. Being around him only reminded me of how much he meant to me, how much I missed being around him. Him having Liv's heart didn't lessen my feelings for him; it only made them stronger.

Remembering what Grey had said about my shift, I made the trek to the subway and back to my apartment instead.

I wanted to write. I *needed* to write. Seeing him brought up feelings that I only knew how to expel through writing.

# Chapter Forty-Three

The next several days blurred together. I barely moved from my computer except to eat, refill my coffee, pee, or snag an occasional few hours of sleep. When I had this kind of inspiration, I had to act on it. I wouldn't have been able to stop even if I tried, because the chaos of it all was rather addictive. I hated to say it, but I kind of liked it.

I'd written 40,000 words in the last week. All of a sudden, the ending of my story that I'd struggled to find was staring back at me on my computer screen. The words somehow meshed together in a way that made sense, even sounded good, and with only a few words left to go before I typed *The End*, I needed to take a break and really soak in this feeling.

I put on a pot of coffee and turned the TV on.

It was probably for the best that I did a quick little catch-up given how many days had passed since I'd connected with the outside world. I plopped the remote on the couch, a local news station illuminating the TV as I returned to the kitchen to wait for my coffee to brew. I planned on ignoring the fact that it was three in the afternoon and I was on cup number three. No one needed to know about the copious amounts of coffee I had consumed to write this book.

"*Good evening, New York City.*"

There it was again. That voice.

*Grey.*

I frantically searched for the remote so I could either change the channel or turn up the volume, and then I sat down and faced the screen.

"I want to thank you all for taking the news of me stepping away from my role in politics in stride. I can't tell you how much it means to me to have the city of New York supporting me on my new ventures."

My mouth dropped open. Did he just say he was stepping away? I sat forward on my couch, not wanting to miss a thing.

"While working with my father was something I've always pictured myself doing, I hope to get the chance to pursue another dream of mine now. One that I've held close to my heart for a long time. One that I wasn't sure would ever come to fruition. That is, until last summer, when I met someone who encouraged me to give my dream a chance. So, over the last eight months, I've had the privilege of working on something pretty incredible." I hung on to every single one of his words, desperately waiting for the next. "New York City, I'm excited to finally reveal our newest library, A Second Page, designed from the ground up by my new architecture firm, O.M. Architects."

A large piece of material that had been draped over the front of the building dropped, exposing the new sign.

Grey was aglow, an aura around him seeming to shine. "I'd like to invite you all to the grand opening, this Saturday afternoon. Library doors open at nine o'clock."

I fell back onto my couch, replaying his words over and over in my head. So, the news story at his apartment, the one I'd heard only the beginning of, wasn't another political announcement at all.

The nausea boiled at the base of my stomach. What was I supposed to do now? An email pinged on my computer, drawing my attention away, and I was thankful for the distraction even though I had no intention of checking it.

Because I was going to finish this damn book.

I reread my last few sentences, a sense of pride anchoring me to the here and now.

*One single heart had somehow brought me two of the most important people in my entire life. It was once hers, and now his. I loved her first, and now I'd love him forever.*

My fingers stroked the keyboard in an entirely unfamiliar pattern, typing out *The End*.

Two words on a screen. Two words I never thought I'd see. The tears propelled down my face and a smile leaped onto my face as I read them over and over again. It wasn't just the end that made me emotional. It was the realization that had come just before I typed those two words.

*...and now I'd love him forever.*

That was the truth.

Not just in my story, but in my life *too*.

My world was spinning. Holy shit. The doorbell rang.

"Coming!" I shouted. I was expecting a package today, but the delivery people should know to leave it at my doorstep.

Swinging the door open, I said, "Hi, do I need to sign—"

But the man on the other side of the door was not a delivery man. Well, I guess that wasn't entirely true, but he wasn't the delivery man I was expecting.

"Daniel?"

"Good afternoon, Ms. Morgan. I come bearing gifts, or rather an invitation from Mr. Prescott." I looked down and saw the most elegant-looking black envelope resting in his hands. "Here you go. Have a lovely rest of your day," he said, handing over the package. "I really hope you'll be able to make it," he whispered as though someone might hear him, even though my hallway was empty.

"Thank you, Daniel." I smiled and shut the door.

I tore into the invitation as quick as I could. The black envelope was decorated in beautiful gold calligraphy that read *Miller Jean Morgan*. If I wasn't so determined to see what was inside, I would've been able to enjoy the beauty of it a little more.

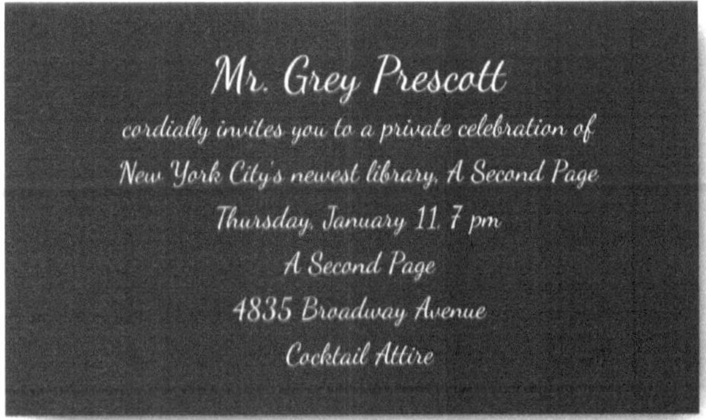

Scanning the invitation a second time, the date caught my attention. Thursday, January 11...? That was tonight. The man couldn't have given me a little more warning than four hours?

In reality though, it didn't matter. Between finishing my book and the realization that came with typing those final words, I'd already made up my mind. I was going.

And for the first time in my entire life, I knew what I was going to wear.

## Chapter Forty-Four

I had four hours to prepare for the event, and three of them were spent contemplating exactly what I was going to say to this man. I ran through every single possible scenario, including the most ridiculous and outrageous ones, because, well, that was how my brain worked and I wanted to be prepared for anything.

The last hour was spent getting ready. I curled my hair before loosely pinning it back into a messy low bun with a few chunky pieces left out to accentuate my face. I looked at the dress, imprinted with a floral pattern, and the familiarity made me smile. The same dress I wore to Grey's party the first night I experienced the feeling of his body on mine. I shuddered at the thought, the slightest hint of anticipation blooming inside of me.

I grabbed my gold clutch, a faux fur jacket, and confirmed I had my phone, wallet, and keys before heading out the door.

The night air was crisp and the streets were still showing signs of the last snowfall, making me second-guess my decision to wear heels.

"Screw it, I'm getting a cab," I called out.

"Ms. Morgan, that won't be necessary."

My hand shot to my chest. "Daniel! You scared the shit out of me."

"My apologies, Ms. Morgan."

"It's okay. But how did Grey know that I was going to accept the invitation?"

"He didn't, but he sent me anyway. Asked that I wait outside your building until at least eight o'clock. Dare I say I'm grateful I didn't have to stand out here that long," he admitted, opening the door to the back seat of the SUV.

"Dare I say I'm grateful that you're here," I said, smiling.

"Happy to be here."

The drive, while short, still gave my anxiety plenty of type to rev up.

"Enjoy your evening, Ms. Morgan," Daniel said, pulling me from my thoughts and back to reality. I glanced outside and noticed we'd already arrived.

"Thanks again, Daniel."

He smiled and tipped his black wool cap toward me.

The library was even more magnificent up close. The mixed metals and materials meshed together perfectly. The sign reading *A Second Page* could probably be seen from miles away. I climbed the steps quickly but carefully, eager to get inside and see every inch of his design.

The entry doors stood tall, at least twelve feet of solid wood, decorated with two black modern-looking door handles. Pulling on the right one, a gust of warm air blew past me from the inside.

"Good evening, ma'am, can I take your jacket?"

"Oh, yes. Thank you so much."

"You can make your way through there," he said, motioning his hand to another set of doors.

A woman in an all-black pantsuit and an important-looking earpiece waited for me. "Hi. Can I get your name?" she whispered.

"Miller Morgan."

"Ms. Morgan, I have you at one of the front tables. I'd suggest waiting until Mr. Prescott finishes speaking before making your way up there."

Peeking at my phone, the numbers reflecting back at me read 7:22. I was late.

"Perfect. Thank you."

Quietly stepping through the doors, I registered Grey's voice immediately. I stood in the back of the room, waiting until he was finished.

Looking up, my eyes latched onto Grey. His black suit was tailored precisely for his body, and the classic stark-white shirt and black bowtie made it a timeless look. Best of all was the lilac pocket square poking out of his front pocket. I couldn't help but smile. His hair, styled with what appeared to be a little more product than normal, looked longer than I remembered, but there were no complaints from me.

"I have a few more things to say before I promise to stop talking and let everyone enjoy the night." The crowd's laugh was synchronized, and even Grey let out a chuckle. Then, almost like a switch, his smile was gone and his tone turned serious.

"When I was twenty years old, I had a heart transplant. A life-saving one. At the time, I didn't know where the heart was coming from or who it belonged to. I just knew that I was getting it, which meant that I was getting a second chance. Years passed, and I continued on with my life. There was always a little voice in the back of my mind telling me that I owed it to the family to pay my condolences and say thank-you, but as time went on, I found it harder to do. Then, this past summer, something drew me back to Montauk, the place I once loved but struggled to return to because my donor's parents still lived there. I promised myself that I would meet them face-to-face and thank them for everything. And then, like life does, it threw a curveball my way," he said.

His smile returned as he paused to fidget with the pocket square that coincidently hovered over the famous spot on his chest, his eyes simultaneously scanning the room. I wanted them to land on mine, but they didn't.

"A curveball that appeared in the form of a beautiful but head-strong woman. This woman walked into my life and flung my world completely out of orbit. She and I spent the entire summer getting to know each other, and each day I grew more and more fond of who she was. She continued to amaze me with her determination and her love for others." His voice drifted, and this time, his gaze met mine almost immediately.

The fire in the pits of my belly roared alive. His hand tightened around the podium and his chiseled jaw tensed while both of us held our stare, neither wanting to be the first to look away.

"I know, I know. You're wondering how my romantic endeavors have anything to do with this story, but I'm getting there, I promise." The crowd softly chuckled again. "As our summer progressed, I finally dredged up enough courage to meet with my donor's parents, and it went better than I could've ever imagined. While heartbreaking, I felt a sense of connection that I will cling to for the rest of my life. My donor, Olivia Mitchell, died on her eighteenth birthday, when she and her best friend were hit by an oncoming driver." He fumbled on his words, pausing to check his emotions.

This time when his eyes met mine, they were filled with emotion.

"From what I've learned, Olivia Mitchell was an incredible young woman, one I wish I would've had the opportunity to meet. But then I guess in some weird, twisted way, I have. Here comes another one of those curveballs." He paused before continuing. "The woman I spent my entire summer falling in love with was Olivia Mitchell's best friend.

"I learned many things about Olivia, but by far the most kismet was that Olivia dreamed of being an architect too. Funny how things like that happen. And while she never got the chance to become one, I'm taking my second chance and becoming one for the both of us." The applause from the crowd was so loud I could feel it booming in my chest.

"With all of that being said, I'm thrilled to share with you my pride and joy, A Second Page Library. All donations the library receives tonight and every day moving forward will be given to a local transplant network. Along with that, I've asked members of the network to be here tonight to assist anyone who would like to register to be a donor. Thank you, and please enjoy the rest of your night."

The crowd cheered again, one by one moving to their feet as they applauded Grey.

I, on the other hand, was at a loss for words.

I watched Grey flow through the crowd, stopping every so often to talk to guests. He gave each one of them his undivided attention, smiling and laughing as though they were the first, but he never missed a chance to look over in my direction. I swore I smiled bigger with every glance.

I didn't want to approach him while he was speaking to his guests and I was secretly hoping to admire this place in all its beauty, so I snuck off.

Between the number of towering wooden bookshelves and the natural scent of all the books, I could've gotten lost in this place for hours. Somehow, amongst my exploring, I came across a bathroom and ducked in for a quick break.

"My god," I whispered. "Even the bathroom in this place is to die for."

The golden mirrors hanging over each sink were massive. Said sinks, matte black in color, convened on top of the counter. The stalls were completely clear until you stepped inside and shut the door, at which point they immediately clouded over.

Leaving the bathroom with every intention of heading back to the main space, I somehow took a detour and found myself lost in between the romance and fantasy sections. Not a bad place to be, if you asked me.

My fingers traced the spines of the freshly placed books, eager to touch each one as I envisioned the day I'd be able to do the same to my own book in a place like this.

"Like what you see?"

Grey's voice startled me back to reality, although this moment felt more like something out of a romance novel than reality. I spun on my heels and goddamn, he looked even more handsome up close.

"I sure do," I said, nibbling my lower lip.

He walked closer to me, leaving only the breath between us.

"Since the first day I met you, Miller Morgan, I quickly discovered that this heart beats for no one the way it beats for you." He guided my hand to his chest, resting it on top of that all too familiar rhythm. "And since that night on the beach, I've realized that without you in my life, my heart will never truly be whole. You'll always hold a piece of me with you, whether you know it or not. And honestly, I'm not sure how I'd survive that, but I know I need to try, out of respect for both you and Olivia," he said, squeezing my hand a little tighter as his smile spread.

"As I was speaking tonight though, there was a moment before I even saw you that I *knew* you were here. It was as if the missing piece had found its way back to me. And in that moment, it felt like for once in my life I'd done something worth being proud of, and I couldn't help but feel like I was the luckiest man in the world. Like every dream I'd ever dreamt was coming true all at once."

"Grey…" I paused, wanting to make sure I said everything perfectly, starting with my apology. "I'm sorry I didn't stay and listen that day at your apartment. I—"

"Please don't apologize. You couldn't have known what they were going to say."

"I know, but I just wish I would've given them a chance to finish, given you a chance to explain," I admitted.

With hopeful eyes and a genuine smile, he said, "But then we wouldn't have gotten this moment right here. And I have a feeling this moment is going to be one I want to remember forever."

"I couldn't agree more," I said, my expression giddy. "I want to say something, but it's a lot, so you have to promise you'll let me say it all before you respond."

"I promise," he said, peering down at mine.

"Olivia Mitchell was my best friend. When I lost her, I lost myself. The once lively young woman who had big dreams and aspirations was gone, just like that. For years, I just assumed that was my story, and I accepted that I'd never be her again. But then you roared through town, and everything changed," I said, the adrenaline flowing like magic through my veins.

"Suddenly I was laughing again. I was writing again. But more than anything, I was dreaming again. Over the course of just one summer, you helped guide me back to the woman I was before the accident. And then a funny thing happened when I found her. Even though she was just how I remembered, she wasn't me. That's the thing about grief, it irreversibly changes you. But I learned that it's not how you let the change bring you down, but rather how you let it raise you up that determines the trajectory of the rest of your life." I let out a deep breath, giving myself time to make sure this last part was perfect.

"And while I miss her every single day, and there isn't a moment that goes by that I don't wish she were here, I've realized that I'm one of the lucky ones. I tragically lost my best friend, but each day I'm with you is a day that I'm with her too. And how incredible is it that my love for Liv lives on through you." The words that I'd kept contained for so long were free, and just like that, so was I. The tears streamed down my cheeks. "Grey Prescott, I love you. I'm sorry it took me so long."

Grey placed my chin between his thumb and pointer finger. "Miller Morgan, I would've waited my entire life for you to come back to me, because now I get to spend my days loving you and my nights dreaming about you." His soft smile grew. "I think I knew I loved you from the second I laid eyes on you, and I don't want waste another second not kissing you."

Impatiently, he consumed my entire mouth in his. His tongue eagerly pushed past the entrance of my lips, and as soon as I tasted him, I realized how starved for him I'd been.

I dragged my mouth away, pulling a small moan of his with it. "O.M. Architects?"

"For her, *Olivia Mitchell*. It was the least I could do to make sure her dream lived on."

His confirmation had my heart swelling. I pushed my desperate mouth into his and within seconds, he'd pinned me up against one of the bookshelves and the air around us caught fire.

"Remember the last time you wore this dress?"

"Mmm," I acknowledged.

"And my hand ended up crawling up your thigh like this?" The heat from his palm was electrifying. "You see, MJ... the difference between this time and last time is that now, *you're mine.*"

"I'm yours. Completely and all-consumingly *yours*," I said, pulling him by his suit jacket until his soft lips were pressed together with mine again.

I drew away from his kisses. "As much as I'd love to continue making out with you in the stacks of this absolutely perfect library, I'd imagine there are people down there"—I motioned to the crowd of people below us—"who will be looking for you."

He threw his head back in disappointment. "Even though I'd prefer to stay right here, you're probably right." His tongue traced his bottom lip. "But at least I'll be returning with the most beautiful girl on my arm." He winked, releasing a shiver through me.

I grinned, smooshing a kiss to his cheek, the manicured stubble tickling me.

Moving toward the music and chatter, Grey grabbed my hand, latching it onto his arm. As we took the steps that led to the party, what seemed like the entire crowd slowly began turning their heads, giving us their full attention. It was like we were in a movie and everyone was waiting anxiously to press play.

In that moment, I was sure there was no better feeling. I turned to look at Grey, but he was already grinning back at me.

*I love you*, he mouthed.

"I love you too."

A single summer had changed the course of my entire life—all because I fell in love with the man who carried my best friend's heart.

# Epilogue

"I'm so nervous." My voice was shaky as I wobbled my weight back and forth.

"Don't be. You're going to do great. All these people are here for you. No one else but you," Grey said, pressing a kiss to my right temple.

"I think I just always assumed Olivia would be with me for something this monumental, you know?"

Grey stepped back, placing himself in my direct line of sight. "Oh, MJ, you're forgetting something..." He squeezed my hand. "She is always with you, right here," he said, pulling my hand to that comforting heartbeat of his, thumping against my palm.

A woman's voice stole my attention from him. "Hi, everyone. Welcome to A Second Page Library. We're so excited to introduce to you MJ Morgan, a brand-new author who has just released her debut novel, *Second Chances*."

I stepped from behind the dark red velvet curtain, making my presence known. This was the first time I'd seen the crowd, and the sheer number of people staring back at me was something I never could've expected. I paused, just long enough to take a mental screenshot of this moment and keep it with me forever.

"Thanks so much for having me. I'm so excited to be here." I beamed back at the librarian.

"Ms. Morgan—"

"Please, call me MJ."

"MJ, tell us a little bit about your journey, and how the story came about. If I'm remembering correctly, this book was loosely based on a true story, is that right?"

"That's correct. My story, actually." I sighed, feeling a soft smile emerging. "Like the main character in the book, I tragically lost my best friend. I remember the accident like it was yesterday. I remember it hurting so badly that I couldn't even cry. I remember thinking I'd never get out of the darkness that surrounded me. But if I've learned anything on this journey of mine, it's that most of the time, the prettiest rainbows come after the scariest storms." The cry that was lodged in my throat cleared itself as I gazed out into the crowd and saw hundreds of eyes staring back.

"I know this is an emotional story," she said, her eyes kind, "and if you don't feel comfortable doing so, please just say, but I know we'd all love to hear a little excerpt from *Second Chances*."

"Of course I wouldn't mind. I'm honored that anyone even wants to read it. But I'd love to start off by reading a part of the acknowledgements, if that's okay?" I responded.

"Absolutely!"

"To Olivia, my best friend, my soulmate, and my angel, you live in heaven now. That means I don't get to see you anymore. It means I don't get to hear your laugh. I don't get to see your smile. I don't get to hold you when you're sad. I don't get to celebrate with you when you're happy. I don't get to ask you for advice. I don't get to have you yell at me when I do something wrong. I don't get to tell you about the man that I've fallen in love with. You're gone, and I no longer get those pieces of you."

Feeling my emotions rising, I subconsciously reached for that all too familiar gold metal that dangled from my neck. My fingers landed on the lines of *their* heartbeat, the lines I'd memorized at this point.

"But instead of dwelling on all the things I don't get to do, I've decided to cherish all the things I *do* get. I get all the memories we shared together. I get to hold on to the way you played such a profound role in my life. I get to listen to the sound of your heartbeat. And I get to love you for as long as I live. Just because you're gone doesn't mean that you're not still here. I miss you, and I will always love you deeper than the ocean. Oh, and Liv? One more thing. You wouldn't believe it, but I'm doing it. I'm living in the big city writing silly love stories." My tears were on the verge of emerging, but I pressed on.

"To Grey, the man who completely shifted my perspective on life. The man who taught me that life is too short to be boring. The man who makes me smile and blush all in the same sentence. The man I wouldn't be standing here today without. I owe so much to you, and I hope you'll let me spend the rest of my life thanking you, even though that still won't be long enough. I lost Liv that day, but because of you, I'll always have a piece of her right next to me. I love you, Grey Prescott." I looked up from my book, and the first eyes that caught mine were his.

His lips moved silently. "I love you."

"To Chief Williams, thank you for saving my life and making me believe my story was good enough to be told. Without you, this story would've stayed locked away in my brain forever.

"To Sam, thank you for being the friend I needed when I didn't feel like I needed a friend at all. Our friendship is something I'll always cherish.

"And lastly, to my parents and my *second* parents, I would've died that day had you not carried me out of the hospital. Honestly, I think I would've died many days over without your love and support. We all lost someone that night, yet you four showed up for me every single day, even when Liv's death weighed heavy on all of us. For that, I love all of you, big.

A smirk spread from my lips, turning to the page that I'd previously bookmarked. "I'm sorry. I just know those acknowledgments were an important piece of my story, of this story." I motioned to the book.

"Don't be sorry. Your words are truly incredible. They're touching, real, and raw. Something I find admirable about your writing is the way you can evoke so many emotions from your readers. You're truly inspiring."

Her compliment made me blush, the heat filling my cheeks. I sat back in my chair, making myself comfortable before locating the spot on the page where I wanted to start. Clearing my throat,

I took one last gaze into the crowd, registering all the enthusiastic readers staring back at me with doting eyes.

Then, I started reading.

"'I used to think that the more people you got close to, the more chances you had of losing someone. That's why I've kept my distance from people ever since losing you. I've also recently discovered that being close to people who love you and care about you is worth the risk. No matter what the chances are that you might lose them. It's really as simple as that. Life without love is no life at all. So, love wildly, live bravely, and please never forget to chase your dreams. Life is too short, and most of us don't get a second chance.'"

# Acknowledgements

To my husband, Shane Charles, I wouldn't be the author I am today if it weren't for you. There will never be enough words to describe how grateful I am to have you as a partner in life. Without you, the constant doubt would've consumed me, and I never would've stood a chance at finishing this book. Thank you for loving me, but more importantly, thank you for consistently believing in me. I love you—*forever, forever.*

To my son, Augustine Charles, never stop chasing your dreams. One day you're going to light this world up with your passions, and I can't wait to sit front row and watch. I love you—*bigger than all the oceans.*

To my family, no matter how much shit you give me (looking at you, Zach), your support is what holds me up in the times that I desperately feel like I'm falling. To my sisters, Ashley and Nikita, you two not only support me but are there whenever I need something. To my brothers, Matthew and Zachary, you've always provided endless amounts of shit talking, but more than that, you've always supported me with just as much enthusiasm. Mom, you've always encouraged me to chase my dreams even when they were in the form of black hair and nose rings. You've allowed me to be me for as long as I can remember, and I'll never take that for granted. Dad, thank you for believing in me and my dreams. This book wouldn't be possible without you, and I'll never be able to say thank you enough. So, instead I'll keep chasing these dreams, keep writing these books, and always make you proud. I love you all more than you'll ever know.

To my friends, you all inspire me on a daily basis. Our phone calls, text messages, little conversations here and there—you're constantly providing me with inspiration in the form of real-life experiences. I wouldn't have half as many wild ideas if it weren't for all of you, so thank you. I love you, *big*.

To Maggie, everyone needs a human like you. You are smart. You are kind. You are the spark of energy that I so desperately needed in my life. You are someone I'm so grateful to know and someone that I'll cherish forever.

To my Instagram community, thank you. There isn't a day that goes by when I'm not grateful for each and every single one of you. Your excitement fuels my desire to write books. Your support pushes me when I need pushed. Your encouragement pulls me from the depths of writer's block. Without all of you, I could never have chased this dream of mine.

To My Editor, Annie (@anniereadsthings), I knew we were meant to work together after our very first phone call. Your passion for stories is unlike any other, and your ability to open up my creative mind is something I'll forever cherish. I'm so grateful to have worked with you and can't wait to work with you on many more books!

To My Editor, Brooke (@bookclubatbrookes), thank you. You've been with me for both of my books, and each time you're able to make me dig a little deeper. Your knowledge of the writing process is something I admire dearly. You're incredible at what you do and I'm so grateful to have you on my team!

To My Editor, Britt (@tropic.bookclub), thank you for making me look like I really have it together. Proofreading isn't for the faint of the heart and your ability to look at thousands of words and identify tiny mistakes is truly incredible. I'm forever grateful for you.

To My Book Designer, Sandra (@smaldo.designs), I'm so grateful to have found you. The cover for Diving In was everything, but the cover for The Breath Between Us was everything and more. You're not only ridiculously talented, but you're of the most gracious humans I've ever met. Your attention to detail is top notch and your openness to my ideas does not go unnoticed. Thank you for once again turning my dream into a reality.

# About the author

I'm an extra bubbly introvert who thrives in the chaos of storytelling. I write romance novels with BIG feelings and even BIGGER happy endings. I've been writing ever since I can remember. It's always been an outlet, one that allowed me to handle my own emotions while creating an escape for others too. Over time, the only thing that changed was that my diaries morphed into voice memos and sticky notes. I will say, I have to credit my success as a writer to my 2008 self who stayed up way too late writing fanfiction about Panic! At The Disco. There is truly nothing more authentic than a 14-year-old writer who fully believes she's going to marry a band member. When I'm not writing, I'm either chasing my tiny human in circles, frantically packing for a trip the night before, or figuring out how to create stories that will make people feel the same way they did at the Eras Tour. So, buckle up, Buttercup. And grab the tissues, because it's about to hurt so good.

STAY IN TOUCH:

authorbiancamiller.com| @biancamillerwrites

To learn more about becoming a donor,
please visit **www.organdonor.gov**